I0831876

HELL SKIN

A BOOK OF UNDERREALM

GARRETT ROBINSON

HELL SKIN

Garrett Robinson

The author greatly appreciates you taking the time to read this work. Please leave a review wherever you bought the book or on Goodreads.com.

Interior Design: Legacy Books, Inc.
Publisher: Legacy Books, Inc.
Editors: Karen Conlin, Cassie Dean
Cover Artist: Sutthiwat Dechakamphu

1. Fantasy - Epic 2. Fantasy - Dark 3. Fantasy - New Adult

First Edition

Published by Legacy Books

This book is for my family, the ones in my life who have helped me be the person I want to be, and who have kept me safe and sane enough to achieve that.

It is for the wild, untempered community I have found in this world, who love unreservedly and constantly strive to better themselves and each other.

And it is for everyone who has taken even a few steps in Underrealm. We have wandered farther than I thought we would, but I've enjoyed every league.

This ending is not the end, but it is one that's come at just the right time.

GET MORE

Legacy Books is home to the very best
that fantasy has to offer.

Join our email alerts list, and we'll send word whenever we release a new book. You'll receive exclusive updates and see behind the scenes as we create them.

And we'll send you a free ebook copy of Nightblade, the #1 Amazon Bestseller, as our way of saying "Thanks."

Interested? Visit this link:

Underrealm.net/Free

THE BOOKS OF UNDERREALM

THE NIGHTBLADE EPIC

NIGHTBLADE
MYSTIC
DARKFIRE
SHADEBORN
WEREMAGE
YERRIN

THE ACADEMY JOURNALS

THE ALCHEMIST'S TOUCH
THE MINDMAGE'S WRATH
THE FIREMAGE'S VENGEANCE

THE TALES OF THE WANDERER

BLOOD LUST
STONE HEART
HELL SKIN

THE TENTH KINGDOM

A CLOAK OF RED

RISE OF THE NECROMANCER

QUEST

THE CHRONICLES OF UNDERREALM
COLLECTION ONE

THE BOOKS OF UNDERREALM

CHRONOLOGICAL ORDER

NIGHTBLADE
MYSTIC
DARKFIRE
SHADEBORN
BLOOD LUST
THE ALCHEMIST'S TOUCH
WEREMAGE
THE MINDMAGE'S WRATH
STONE HEART
THE FIREMAGE'S VENGEANCE
HELL SKIN
YERRIN
QUEST
A CLOAK OF RED
THE CHRONICLES OF UNDERREALM

CONTENTS

CONTENTS

PREVIOUSLY IN THE TALES OF THE WANDERER

Sun of the family Valgun, a young woman from a noble house, snuck away from her family's caravan in the kingdom of Dorsea. Her kin were on a diplomatic mission to raise their station, and Sun disapproved of both them and their goal, though she had little hope of influencing either.

While exploring, she met Albern of the family Telfer, a renowned figure of some of her favorite legends—alongside a woman named Mag, known as the Uncut Lady or the Wanderer. At Sun's request, Albern began to tell her the tale of the adventures he and Mag had had in their youth.

The story began as an army swept down out of the Greatrock Mountains to attack the city of Northwood, Mag's home. The attackers were called Shades, and they were led by two people of note: Rogan, an immortal shadeborn and commander of the Shades' forces, and Kaita, a weremage. Kaita, in particular, had a personal reason to join in the attack—a longstanding grudge against Albern and Mag.

While Albern and Mag survived the destruction of Northwood, it came at a terrible cost. Kaita killed Mag's husband, Sten, before escaping Mag's wrath.

While Mag and Albern swore an oath of vengeance to slay the weremage, Rogan commanded Kaita to lead them north to Calentin, Albern's childhood homeland.

Albern and Mag followed Kaita to the small town of Lan Shui west of the Greatrocks. There, Kaita and the Shades had been conducting a magical ritual to lure vampires to attack the town, testing the method for possible use in the coming war across Underrealm. The vampires had the town surrounded, and no one was able to leave to summon help from other nearby settlements.

In Lan Shui, Mag and Albern met a blind old man named Dryleaf, who seemed surprisingly knowledgeable and well-informed for a denizen of such a small town. They also met the town's chief constable, Yue of the family Baolan, who initially viewed Albern and Mag with grave mistrust. But by working together, the three of them managed to defeat the vampires and free the town, as well as wipe out the cabal of Shades who had caused the problem in the first place.

Albern and Mag left to pursue Kaita, while Yue recovered from her injuries suffered in the battle. Dryleaf, however, accompanied Mag and Albern, for they desired his advice and counsel, and he wanted to return to the Birchwood Forest, where he said he wished to reunite with an old friend.

While Albern told Sun this tale, some of her parents'

caravan guards came looking for her. Albern helped her avoid them, and then asked her to help him with a small errand. He led her out into the woods, where he had previously built a little campsite, and resumed telling her the tale there. After the tale had finished, they were attacked by a vampire, just as in the stories—but this one was much younger, and much weaker, and they were able to defeat it, mortally wounding it and driving it back into the forest.

With the nighttime adventure seemingly at an end, Albern asked Sun if she wished to return to her parents. If she did not, he offered to let her accompany him in his journeys, traveling the land and ridding it of evil. After some deliberation, Sun agreed to go with him. They set their steps for the town of Lan Shui, and the next morning, Albern resumed his story.

The tale resumed with Albern, Dryleaf, and Mag reaching the city of Opara on the southern border of the kingdom of Calentin. In Lan Shui they had found information that this was where Kaita was heading. But in fact, it was only one more step in the long journey she was leading them on. As they had in Lan Shui, they found and wiped out a small cadre of Shade spies, but Kaita was not among them. Instead, they found out that she was proceeding to Kahuanga, the city where Albern had grown up as the noble child of a local lord, titled the Rangatira.

This came as devastating news to Albern. He was the Rangatira's son, but he had not returned home nor been in contact with his family since he left in his nineteenth year. With Albern being an ander man, his mother did not even know him as her son. They had parted on terrible terms, and he had no wish to see her again.

But with the news that Kaita had gone to Kahuanga, he knew he had to return home regardless. So he, Mag, and Dryleaf made their way to the region of Tokana where the city stood. They arrived to find that the local mountain trolls had become agitated, pushing aggressively farther and farther into human territories.

Immediately Mag and Albern suspected the Shades had a hand in the conflict. Just as in Lan Shui, they were secretly maneuvering other forces against each other so that they did not have to do the fighting themselves. Although Albern had grown up in the city, he had no idea what to do to stop the trolls; humans had not come into conflict with the creatures for untold centuries. It seemed their best hope was finding and killing Kaita and the Shades. With luck, that would end the trolls' motivation to attack the city.

Before long, however, they were captured by the Rangatira's forces, who mistook them for illegal hunters and brought them before her. To his shock, Albern discovered that the Rangatira was not in fact his mother, but his older sister, Ditra. Ditra had been the only member of his family who was kind to him as he grew up. His mother and his other sister, Romil, had died decades ago. Ditra was now as stern and hard-bitten as their mother had been, and Albern continued to hide his identity from her.

Upon hearing of their hunt for the weremage and the Shades, Ditra allowed them to continue searching the wilderness around her city. But in secret, she also assigned her lead ranger, Maia, to hunt for the weremage. Though Maia did not know it, Ditra had a personal stake in the weremage's fate.

After many more days spent hunting, Albern and Mag were almost killed by a troll. But Maia happened to be in the area, and he saved them at the last moment. Albern and Mag discovered that Ditra had assigned him to hunt for the weremage, and in the discussion, Maia mentioned her name. It was the first time Albern and Mag learned that the weremage's name was Kaita.

A flood of memories assaulted Albern. He remembered that Kaita had been a ranger and a guard in his mother's service, and that she had once been Ditra's lover. Now he understood that Ditra had been hampering his search for the weremage. Ditra did not believe that Kaita had turned to evil, and she wished to bring the weremage into custody safely.

Albern confronted Ditra with the truth, but she was livid at him for it. She imprisoned him, Mag, and Dryleaf, and then summoned Albern to her for a private conversation. In the course of their talk, she learned Albern's hidden shame: that he had known of the death of their elder sister, Romil, for decades, but still had not returned home. With Albern gone, and their mother blaming him for Romil's death, all her anger, bitterness, and resentment fell upon Ditra, ruining what was left of her childhood and turning her into the flinty woman she had become. Disgusted, Ditra sent Albern back to his cell with Mag and Dryleaf.

The next day, the trolls attacked the city. Dryleaf opened the jail door with a key he had purloined from one of the guards, and Albern and Mag ran to aid in the city's defense. When Ditra discovered what they had done, she did not throw them back in prison, but pressed them into her service while still keeping them at arm's length.

That changed when the Shades, led by Kaita, infiltrated Ditra's court and attacked her and her top lieutenants. Maia was killed in the fighting, and Ditra was injured. Only Albern and Mag's last-minute intervention kept Ditra from falling.

With Ditra's doubts at least mostly assuaged, she brought Albern, Mag, and Dryleaf into the fold. Together they coordinated the city's defense, fighting a desperate battle as the trolls attacked.

Amidst the fighting, Albern discovered that Kaita was indeed behind the trolls' aggression. She had taken troll form and seduced the pack's current leader, Dotag, guiding him to invade the humans' territory and kill as many as he could. Once Albern and Mag exposed the ruse, Dotag looked weak before his pack.

Another troll, Apok, challenged him for leadership and killed him, and then agreed to broker peace between trolls and humans once more.

Kaita, however, managed to escape. This time, Mag and Albern had no knowledge of where she might be going or how to pursue her. And so after a short time spent in rest in Tokana, when Albern had the chance to fully reconcile with his sister and her daughter, the three of them set off south again, heading for Opara and wandering, somewhat aimlessly, in search of Kaita.

As Albern was relating this part of the tale, he and Sun had reached the town of Lan Shui. There they met with Dawan, a medica of the High King. She had performed Albern's wending, helping him assume the body he desired, and she still checked on him often. She pronounced him to be in decent health, but also suggested he was getting too old to be going on any more adventures. Albern thanked her for the diagnosis and the advice, and then he took Sun outside of Lan Shui, where he had received word of a caravan being attacked.

Following the trail of the bandits, Albern and Sun discovered they had captured a store of magestones and were using them to conduct the same ritual that the Shades in Lan Shui had conducted long ago, drawing vampires from across the land to attack the town.

Sun thought this meant the Shades had returned, but Albern said these were not Shades, but only imitators.

Together, Albern and Sun managed to defeat the bandits and destroy their ritual, as well as the magestones they needed to conduct it. Together they set out again, but this time Albern asked Sun where she wanted to go. She asked if it would be possible to see Bertram, and Albern said that would be a grand idea—he had business to conduct in the city.

They set out upon the road northwest, with Bertram far beyond the horizon.

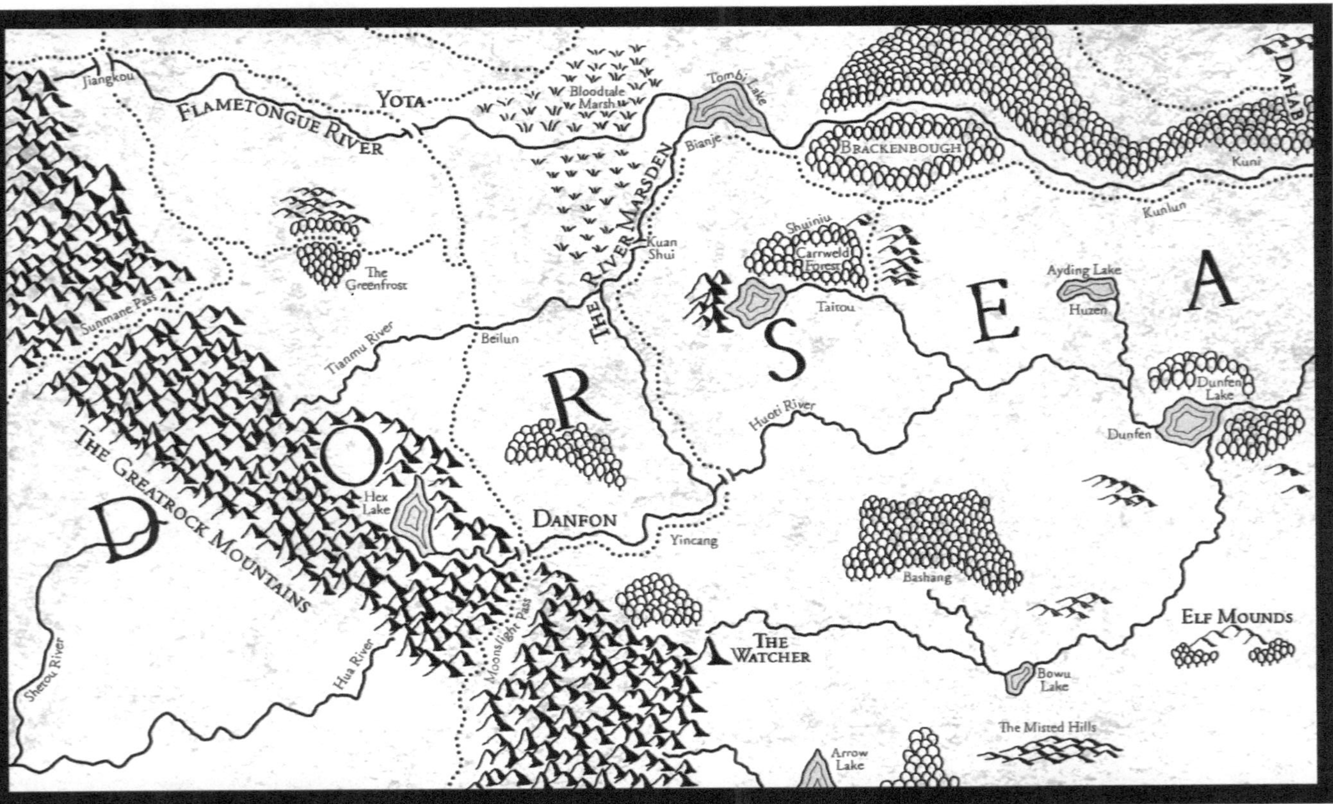
DOR SEA
Dahab
Jiangkou
Yota
Flametongue River
Bloodtale Marsh
Tombi Lake
Bianje
Brackenbough
Kuni
Kunlun
The River Marsden
Kuan Shui
Shuiniu
Carrweld Forest
The Greenfrost
Sunmane Pass
Ayding Lake
Huzen
Taitou
Tianmu River
Beilun
Dunfen Lake
Dunfen
Huoti River
The Greatrock Mountains
Hex Lake
Danfon
Yincang
Bashang
Elf Mounds
The Watcher
Moonslight Pass
Hua River
Sherou River
Bowu Lake
The Misted Hills
Arrow Lake

Hell Skin

A BOOK OF UNDERREALM

Garrett Robinson

ONE

Sun might have been forgiven for wishing the conversation would end. After all, no one had invited her to take part in it, and few things are worse than waiting on the edges of others' discussion, hearing what they have to say and yet having little to offer.

Her meal had gone some time ago, whisked away by a barman who gave her a wink and received a curled lip in return. Albern, however, still made deliberate and slow progress through his food, and the discussion he had begun with the woman at the next table did not aid his speed. Sun could not quite say why Albern had started speaking to her, except that it seemed to be a knack of his. He had a friendly and approachable manner, for all his appearance of a rough old man. Strangers found him easy to talk to, and he always seemed eager to speak to them as well. That was how Sun had met him, after all.

"And I say," Albern responded to the woman, "that the day we are all pleased with our kings is the day the world breaks. I have never known a time in which the commoner had only love for the noble, and I have lived a good deal longer than you have, if you will forgive my saying so."

"Why should I need to forgive a plain truth?" said the woman, chuckling. "And I do not wish for a *perfect* king. I only wish for a better one. This business on the Feldemarian border . . ."

Albern waved the stump of his right arm as if he had forgotten it was missing its hand. "Many lips have passed the news of those troubles to our ears. Who knows what is going on up there? But mayhap I will look into it before long, and then I will bring the truth back to you."

The woman reached out to clasp his left wrist. "A wanderer, are you? Then I accept your offer, and with gratitude. Only take care of yourself on the journey. The roads are not as safe as they were."

"When do you mean?" said Albern, grinning as he shook her hand. "The dream of eternally safe roads is another I have never seen come true. But we will be careful. Good day to you."

The woman gave a rueful laugh and, with a quick nod to Sun, rose to leave. The moment she had disappeared into the crowd of the common room, Sun leaned close.

"About time, old man. I thought you two would talk until sundown."

Albern shrugged. "I would not have minded it. Charming conversation is often in short supply."

Sun's brows rose. "I hope you do not mean to insult me."

"No, indeed. I have enjoyed our conversations more than any in a good long while. I imagine your impatience is what has had you bouncing in your seat for the last half hour? I wondered if you had to relieve yourself."

"In fact, I do. It is only that you kept seeming to be on the verge of finishing your talk."

Sun rose from her chair, though Albern was not quite done with his food. Sighing, he scooped the last few spoonfuls of stew into his mouth. "That is your trouble, Sun, or one of them. Always too eager for the end."

He led her through the common room and out the front door. With a kind word and a few copper slivers, Albern sent the stable girl to fetch their horse—their *horses,* Sun reminded herself. Albern had bought one for her. She could hardly believe that she owned a steed. All the horses she had called "hers" were, in fact, her parents' property.

Besides the horse, Albern had given her a new brown cloak—or new to Sun, at any rate, for Albern had clearly owned it for a while. But it was warmer than the blue one she had worn when they met, and it was also less conspicuous.

"If you need to relieve yourself, do it now," said Albern. "I mean to push our pace today."

"But you said we were an easy day's ride from Bertram," said Sun.

"Easy if we want to make the city by sundown," said Albern. "But I would rather get there ahead of the dark if we can. One of my friends in the city does not appreciate being woken at night—or being summoned, I should say, for he is usually already awake, and accompanied."

Sun scowled at him. "I suppose you mean to tell me that we will not have time for the story."

Albern chuckled. "Oh, were you anxious about that? Then be assured that I do not mean to gallop the whole way."

"That is all I needed to hear. I will return quickly."

She darted around to the outhouse in back of the inn. As with many places they had visited lately, it was only a wooden platform with a hole in it, but her nose did not curl quite so bitterly as it used to. She was growing somewhat used to conditions on the road, which of course were far less glamorous than the luxury in which she had been raised.

It made her wonder what her parents would think

if they could see her now. But that thought carried worry in its wake, and she shied away from it. Thoughts of her parents had pressed themselves more and more into her mind of late. Had they halted their procession, sending their guards to seek her across the land? Or would they have carried on, eager to begin the long process of raising their station to its former heights? Sun could not be sure, and it was useless to think too long upon it. Yet in the back of her mind was being scratched, as though by a scribe marking events in a tome of history, a map of where her parents would be each day.

They would reach Bertram before long. Not today, as Sun would. But not too far in the future, either.

Sun did not plan to be there when they came, however. And so she found it easier than expected to banish the last thoughts of her family as she rejoined Albern where he waited with their mounts. Sun patted her horse fondly on the neck as Albern handed her the reins.

"Have you thought of a name yet?" said Albern. "You know it is bad luck to ride a horse with no name."

"That was Mag's superstition," said Sun.

Albern smiled sadly. "I called it so at the time. Yet you already know my thoughts on many subjects have changed since then."

"My opinions have not been tempered by so many years as yours." Sun studied the horse in deep thought. She was a fine steed, though not fit for battle. She was too slight, and just a bit too skittish—trusting of Sun's judgement, but nervous at a sudden noise.

"I will name her Undvikar if it will reassure you. Though I will call her 'Vika' more often, for it comes more easily to the tongue."

Albern smiled, and she wondered if he knew the old tongue of Dulmun from which she had drawn the name. But he said only, "I hope you name her for yourself, and not for my assurance. But I think it is a fine name. Hello, Vika." He reached over and scratched the mare behind the ears, which she hesitantly permitted. "Now, let us be off."

They remained on foot and walked the horses at first, pressing into the busy traffic of the town's main street. Many wagons and carts were plodding their way through the shallow mud, heading east and west in roughly equal numbers. Those heading west were laden with goods, mostly foodstuffs to trade in Bertram. Those rolling east were mostly empty, or else held items from the city to sell in town. But though the crowd was thick, still there was room enough to weave through it, which Albern did with expert swiftness.

Navigating the press kept them silent until they left the town's western end. There the way opened before them, the carts having room to spread out. But before Sun and Albern mounted, she caught his gaze and spoke.

"I want to hear how Mag died."

Albern went still for a moment. Then, without answering, he climbed into his saddle. Sun did the same, but she kept her eye on him all the while. She half expected him to spur his mount, still without answering her. But at last he returned her gaze, peering at her from under his hood, which he had raised against the last chill of morning.

"This is the third time you have asked me to tell you that, and the first time you have said it so plainly."

Sun had expected him to deny her outright. His answer was not what she had asked for, but it was not a refusal, either. "You told me I may ask whatever I wish, though you are not obligated to tell me the story that I want."

Albern sighed and turned his eyes forwards again. When he spoke, his voice was sad and solemn, but strong. It was the tone of one speaking at the funeral of a dear friend: an acknowledgment of grief, but also a resolution to face the future without fear.

"They say the best tales never end, but that is a lie. All tales end. Yours, mine. Mag's. Yet while they still spin, in chorus they weave the tale of the world. And that tale shall never die, even if one day none of us remain to hear it."

He glanced at her again, but only for a moment. "It is as I said in the tavern, Sun. You are too eager to reach the end of the story. You would be wiser to enjoy yourself. Take your time. All things end, yes, but that does not mean we should charge recklessly towards that end, eager to meet it. And neither should we cower from it, afraid for it to find us.

"I have met many people who needed to learn that second lesson. Mag needed to learn the first."

TWO

WINTER HAD YET REFUSED TO RELEASE ITS FORBIDDING grip on the land of Dorsea when Mag, Dryleaf, Oku, and I rode down out of the Sunmane Pass. Of course, we had clothes to protect us against the weather, but there is a sort of cold that no cloak can entirely dispel, and it shrouded us. The peaks of the mountains at our backs remained snow-capped all year round. But now the snow covered everything from those peaks to the valleys and the wide-open land before us, shrouding it all in white. Even forests made little impression on the snowy blanket. Only the marks of towns and other settlements were plain to see, patches of brown that spouted the grey smoke of hearths into the sky.

You will remember that we had remained in Calentin for some time before continuing our pursuit of Kaita. The best information we had was that she had been heading southwest, and so that was where we went. We took the long road south through Calentin's eastern reaches, bearing my sister's writ, which let us pass unmolested through the lands of the other Rangatira.

In the city of Opara we rested for a few days, visiting our friend Victon and seeking what information we could. But there was precious little of it. All along our journey north, Kaita had been enticing us with a trail of clues, hidden just well enough to make us think we were terribly clever for discovering them. Now that she no longer wished to be followed, we were faced with tracking down a weremage in a wide-open world. That can be a nearly impossible task. We knew only of her connection to the Shades, and so it was information about them that we sought. All we had found so far was some vague rumor, gleaned from the Rangatira in Opara, of a plot that concerned northeastern Dorsea. And so that was where we had turned our steps.

The search was long and fruitless, and it weighed heavy on us. There is only so much time one can spend seeking one's quarry before one tires of the hunt. Sometimes we were desperate for any sign of Kaita. Other times we were apathetically numb and merely going through the motions of our journey.

No one had heard anything in any of the places we visited. There were no rumors of a rogue weremage. We could find no reliable information about the Shades.

It was now a week since we had come down out of the mountains, and we were drawing near to a small town by the name of Taitou. As we rode, Dryleaf often turned to face the south. He was blind, of course, but he had traveled these lands when he was younger. He knew the Birchwood was close, and he must have been thinking of Loren.

Loren would have been much on my mind as well, but I was preoccupied with Mag. She was my best friend, and we often jested and poked fun at each other. But ever since the Sunmane Pass, a dark mood had come over her. There had been an avalanche in those mountains, and though it posed no danger to us, Mag had been somber since.

I thought she might harbor worry for Dryleaf and me, imagining that she was dragging us along a more dangerous journey than she had at first foreseen. Or mayhap she only hoped, as I did, that the end of the road was near, and all her thought was bent upon it. But as we approached the walls of Taitou, I sought to cheer her up.

"What troubling thoughts leave you so grumpy?" I called out to her. "If you are not careful, your face will freeze in that frown—though I suppose that could only be an improvement."

She did not laugh. In fact, she barely glanced at

me. “No troubling thoughts,” she said. “Only a hope that the journey will soon be over. But mayhap that is a fool’s hope.”

“You should enjoy what you can of your wanderings,” I told her. “Look at the land we ride in. Is it not beautiful? Drink it in and let your cares go, while they are not pressing.”

“It has always been beautiful.” Mag tossed her head to the north. “I used to live two days’ ride from here, in the northern reaches of the Carrweld Forest. You can see its southern reaches there. Taitou was the closest settlement of any notable size—I once thought it was a great city.”

There are few things she could have said that would have been more surprising. In all our years together, Mag had seldom spoken about her past.

“I did not know that,” I answered after a moment.

“It was a small village.” Her words came slow, her voice careful. “A tiny village called Shuiniu. There I dwelled until . . . well, until I outgrew it, I suppose. One day I had to go out into the wider world, of which I knew nothing, and when I did, I had to pick a direction. South was straight into the forest. I knew of nothing interesting to the west or east. But I had heard tales of Feldemar, and it seemed a grand kingdom, and so that is where I went. And that led me to the Upangan Blades, and you. We met about a week after I left home.”

In a few moments, Mag had told me more of her

early life than in all the years of our youth. It was just like in Tokana, when she had told me of her love of the forests. And in that moment, as before, I did not know quite what to do. I suppose I was like you, desperate for her to give me more details and continue the story. But, if you will forgive me for saying so, I had the sense to rein in my questions—all but one.

"Do you want to visit?" I said.

Mag gave me a sharp look.

"We do not have to," I said hastily. "But we do not know where to go, and I think we can spare a day, or a few of them. Is there anyone there you wish to see?"

"No." Her answer came without hesitation. Her tone was not harsh, but neither did it leave any room for argument or doubt. And she did not explain further.

"Fair enough," I said, attempting nonchalance. But in truth, I was afraid I had sent her guard crashing back down, and I wished I had said nothing at all.

Two days after we rode out of the Sunmane Pass, a rider came out of the mountains behind us. She stopped at the last crest before the road descended into Dorsea's lowlands. The height was lofty enough to see a great distance, until it was easy to imagine one could view Danfon far to the southeast, though of course that was impossible.

She pulled her cloak a bit tighter around herself.

She had been searching for us, and her search had gone on for a long time. Disappointment in Calentin was close behind her, but now the trail was fresh again, and it led her into Dorsea.

With a grumble and a set in her shoulders, she nudged her horse forwards, down into the lands we had entered only days ago.

Dusk was still hours away when we reached the town of Taitou. At the western gate, guards inspected us with suspicion. This, of course, was routine to us now—from Constable Yue at the gates of Lan Shui to the Rangatira's soldiers who guarded Opara, we had practice dealing with servants of the King's law. We had a story already prepared and well rehearsed from long repetition.

But this time was different. In addition to four constables, two Mystics guarded the gate as well.

I knew many Mystics in my day. Some were good, like Jordel of the family Adair, about whom I have told you. A few were cruel. Most were somewhere in the middle. But for the most part, I rarely wished to get involved with Mystics if I could help it. If they were present in any situation, it was because things had gotten much worse than they should have. And with some exceptions, I knew them for a suspicious lot, willing to go to any length to solve a crime they were investigating. They were only too ready to eliminate anything—or anyone—they perceived as a threat to the High King's order.

So you can understand it was with some trepidation that we submitted ourselves to inspection by the redcloaks. More than their scrutiny, I feared that word of our coming might reach unwanted ears. The Shades had agents in many places, and I did not doubt that at least some of them had infiltrated the redcloaks. Yet there was nothing we could do, other than turn and ride from Taitou with all possible speed—and that would have been suspicious, to say the least. Then the Mystics would have sent out word to their order that three riders of our description had refused to submit to inspection, and that news would have reached Kaita in time.

So I fixed a smile on my face as I stood a few paces off from Foolhoof, my gelding. "Is there anything I can help you with, friend? If you tell me what you are looking for, mayhap I can tell you where to find it."

The Mystic, a stout man with dark hair and a heavy scar on his left cheek, frowned at me. It was his second time going through my things.

"If you were carrying what I am looking for, you would not tell me."

"Contraband, is it?" said Mag. "Or mayhap you seek a blue cloak?"

I winced. Dark take Mag. She almost seemed to enjoy taunting the King's law and those who served it.

Both Mystics gave her sharp looks. "An odd thing

to say," growled the second one, a strong-armed twixt with impressive scars on their bare arms. I wondered how they were not shivering with cold. "What makes you think of blue cloaks?"

"Come, my friends." Dryleaf was as polite as ever. "Do you imagine we are ignorant of the rumors about these Shades? Sky above, they attacked the Seat. It does no one any good to pretend at secrecy—not us, and not you, with your mission from the High King."

"Our mission is our own, and we will see to it," said the man. "But as for you three, what exactly do you know of the Shades?"

"Only what everyone knows," I said, shrugging. "They attacked the Seat, and then they vanished. All else is rumors."

The twixt glared hard. "What rumors, exactly?"

"Zhen! Lo!" said a new voice. "I hope you are not being rude to Taitou's newest guests."

Both Mystics yanked their hands from our saddles, smoothed their cloaks, and stood at attention, as another approached through the gate. As he came to a stop before us, the others saluted with fists over their hearts.

The first thing I noticed about the new arrival was his smile, for it seemed ever-present, and it flashed with well-kept white teeth. After that, I noticed that he was short—or a bit shorter than me, anyway—with several layers of fat beneath his clothing. He wore a red cloak, like most of those in his order, and the Mystic badge—three rods bound by a circle, with three-sectioned wings behind. But he also bore an arrow insignia on his tunic that told me he was a captain, the same as Jordel had been. My fingers played with a small bag at my belt holding one of Jordel's clasps, which I had taken from his body in token of memory. I was glad the Mystics had not wanted to search our every pocket and pouch.

As the captain came to a clipped halt, I found myself straightening as the Mystics had. It was the long-honed habit of drawing up before an officer about to inspect you. (Mag, if anything, slouched a bit more).

Dryleaf bowed his head as he heard the captain come to a halt. "Your fine warriors were doing only their duty, I am sure." He stepped forwards and offered his hand.

The Mystic captain stepped forwards and took his wrist gently to shake it. "They are dutiful, no doubt," he said. "Though they often inconvenience new arrivals more than turns out to be necessary. But what can one do? These are dangerous times. I am certain ones such as yourselves understand."

Mag cocked her head. "Ones such as ourselves?"

"Well, you understand me," said the captain. "Warriors."

Mag paused, appraising him for a moment. To cover the sudden silence, I stepped towards the captain and extended my hand as Dryleaf had done. "Of course we understand, Captain . . .?"

His eyes flashed as he took my wrist and shook. "You recognize the symbol. Few do. I am Captain Kun, of the family Zhou."

I managed to keep my expression neutral, but inside I winced. Recognizing a captain's arrow was nothing a simple traveler would be able to do. He suspected we were fighters, and I had just confirmed it.

But I said only, "I am Kanohari. And my friend here is Chao. Our elderly friend is Dryleaf." Mag and I were using false names, you will remember.

"I may be blind, but I say again that I think you overstate things," said Dryleaf, cheerfully snippy. "If I could see, I do not doubt I would find you almost of an age with me."

The joke was well rehearsed, and I chuckled. Dryleaf smiled. But Captain Zhou's eyes were on Mag. She was staring around as if in boredom, waiting for us to sort out the pleasantries. Kun saw it, and he pointed to her as he laughed.

"Do you see that? Her manner reassures me more than any words the three of you could speak." Still holding my right hand in his, he clapped his left hand over them both and turned to the Mystic behind him. "Look at her—Chao, they say. Not a care in the world. Not afraid of you two searching through her things. You would expect a little nervousness from an enemy warrior—pardon me; you *did* say you were warriors, did you not?"

"We did not," I said. "But I can answer you now

and tell you that we *were*. Both of us served as mercenaries in our youth."

Interest sparked in Kun's eyes. "Sellswords? How utterly fascinating. The High King needs soldiers now, with Underrealm threatened by war. Who knows when the armies of Dulmun will strike next? Or indeed, these Shades you were speaking about with such authority. I am certain Her Majesty would rather have you on her side than let the enemy snap you up."

This line of conversation seemed to be drawing into perilous territory. Mag's attention was fully back on the exchange, but I spoke before she could. "Our fighting days are long past us," I told him. "We are merely looking for a friend—another former mercenary who had gone to the coast to visit family. When we heard the Seat had been attacked, we grew concerned. We have journeyed long to seek her, for as you said, these are uncertain times. Fear not on our account. We are true citizens of Underrealm, and we would never lend our blades to vile traitors and rebels." I gave an easy smile. "But we are old citizens as well, and too weary of fighting to pledge ourselves to the High King's armies, even for coin."

Kun did not look disappointed, but only smiled broader and shook his head. "That is a pity. You seem as though you would be good to have in a fight. But I might have guessed that you had left your fighting days behind you, what with your companion. Meaning no offense, of course, Grandfather." He chuckled.

"Oh, that is quite all right, young man," said Dryleaf, matching the man's laugh. "Who could look at me and see a great champion?"

Oku padded forwards to sniff at Kun's boot, and the captain stooped to scratch his shoulder. "Well then," said Kun. "You are free to go on about your business, of course. But be careful. The Shades emerged from the Birchwood in strength, and seemingly from thin air. One wonders where they could be lurking now."

"One wonders indeed." I shook his hand once more and then helped Dryleaf into his saddle before gaining my own. "Thank you for your kindness. It is good to see that even in suspicious times, some have not forgotten the value of courtesy. Sky bless you."

"And may the moons shine upon your path," said Kun. He smiled as we left, and even gave a little wave just before we passed through the gate.

"That could have gone worse," remarked Mag as we passed into the streets of Taitou. "But I think that captain paid more attention to us than he appeared to."

"You are being paranoid," I said. "My only worry about him is that he might be too friendly for his own good. A trusting manner is welcome to travelers, but it might let more sinister folk slip through a net that should be tight."

"I hear your concern," said Dryleaf with a smile. "Yet it is better to find out one was too kind than to find that one has been too cruel and made others miserable for foolish reasons. I, for one, liked Captain Zhou immensely."

As we rode off, Kun watched us go. The constables at the gate, who had watched our exchange nervously, settled back into positions of rest. Zhen and Lo, the two Mystics posted there, remained standing at rigid attention.

"Well, Captain," said Zhen at last, "we shall continue our vigilance."

"Of course you will," said Kun, still smiling. "Nephew, follow these new arrivals."

Lo looked at Zhen in confusion. But Zhen's expression bent towards a frown. His face darkened, making the heavy scar on his left cheek stand out all the more.

"I prefer not to be referred to that way, *Captain.*"

Kun's smile widened. *My little sister-son,* he thought. *So eager to be seen as a man, when it seems only yesterday I had to help his mother dress him in the morning.*

"I am truly sorry," he said. "I keep forgetting. *Lieutenant* Zhen of the family Zhou—take another from your unit and follow them. Keep track of everything they do."

"But Captain," said Lo, "with the way you acted towards them . . . that is, do you think they are suspicious?"

"You think them above question because I was friendly?" said Kun, chuckling. "Of course I was polite. What possible benefit could result from rudeness? Even the darkest circumstances do not demand ill manners. But they are liars, all three of them. Retired warriors? Both of them have bloodstains on their boots and clothes—old stains, but not old enough. They are fighters, and they have fought recently. Within weeks. Follow them, and send any information directly to me."

"Are they Shades, Captain?" ventured Zhen.

"That is precisely what I mean to find out. The enemy surprised us once. I vow beneath the sky that they will not do so again if I can prevent it."

THREE

Now, you will recall that Mag said she used to live near Taitou. She did not explain further at that time. But later, I learned something of the place that she had called home before we met, and I shall tell you something of it now.

Shuiniu was a small village, as she had said. The people there mostly lived on their own merits. They farmed or hunted for sustenance, and they had a smith, a cobbler, and other crafters to see to the people's needs. They had some small trade with what they saw as "outsiders"; Taitou lay not far to the south, and the Dorsean city of Bianje stood on the border a few days to the northwest. Due west was the River Marsden, with many towns along its length. But Shuiniu was too small a place to receive great caravans from any larger settlement. Only small, modest traders came to visit the village, so that it was rare to meet more than a dozen outsiders in a year.

Mag apprenticed under a brewer in the town. The brewer's name was Duana, and she was as good a master to Mag as could have been hoped. Mag took to the craft with great zeal and exceptional skill. Under Duana, she learned the little tricks that would one day make her so renowned as a brewer. But she told me more than once that Duana's ale was much better, and I have often lamented that I never had the chance to taste it.

Now, at that time, there was a man in town named Ciaran. He was a Heddan, but he had moved to Dorsea in his youth. Being from so far away made him feel like an outsider, and deep in his heart was a desire for others to feel the same. He had a caustic manner and a cruel streak, and he was wont to create division between people where none had been before.

Naturally, he did not get on well with Mag, who tried to avoid him where she could. But her master owned the town's tavern as well as the brewery, and so it was impossible to avoid Ciaran entirely. Whenever she was around, he would barb and jab at her in subtle, veiled ways. I am sure you know what I mean—jibes which hide insults, but which he could always claim had been meant to be innocent.

I only heard of two times that Mag rose to the bait. The first was in the tavern, while Ciaran was downing a mug of her latest brew. He slurped at it and gave deep gasping breaths between each swig, a habit he knew she hated.

(That was a bugbear of Mag's, by the way. If I ever wished to annoy her, all I had to do was eat with my mouth open or smack my lips and tongue as I drank. Before long, she would pitch me into the nearest body of water she could find. I usually considered it worth it. I had to take my victories where I could, you understand.)

"This is fair stuff," said Ciaran, slamming his mug on the table a little too hard. "One day, someone might call you skilled at your craft, child."

Mag kept her gaze on the bar as she scrubbed it with a washcloth. "I thank you, of course."

"Then again," said Ciaran, "mayhap you have reached the pinnacle of your skill already. It can be that way. You reach a peak early on, and then you grow worse with time. If you find that to be the case, you must not be too disappointed."

Mag had very nearly scrubbed through the bar's varnish by this point. Her washcloth stopped, and a close observer would have seen her jaw muscles were like iron. She spoke before she could moderate either her words or her tone.

"Well, if I have already reached my peak, at least I

can say I have one skill. Mayhap in the future, you will be able to say the same, though I doubt it."

Ciaran's face grew as ugly as his heart. He was a large man, with arms thick and hairy, and a great barrel chest packed with muscle from his work at the anvil. He pushed back his chair with a jerk, the tavern filling with the screech of wood on wood. Most conversations around them hushed, unless the speakers were too drunk to notice the sudden tension in the air.

"I do not take kindly to insults," said Ciaran.

Mag looked quizzically at him. "No one does. That is why they are insults, you steer."

His face went beet red. "Enough. I would have accepted an apology if you had groveled. But not now. Come outside, and I will beat remorse out of you."

Mag's blood was up. Duana was nowhere to be seen. So she gave him a fierce smile. "I am no bard, and so I cannot describe how amusing such a threat is, coming from you."

Now the people around them were getting nervous, that curious tension that always surrounds a bar fight. They did not wish to see anyone get hurt—at least, not too badly—but there is still something thrilling about seeing two foes knock the stuffing out of each other. And never is that more true than when a grudge has long been fomenting.

"Outside," growled Ciaran. "Now." And he strode out the front door.

Mag lifted the hinged panel that locked off the bar

and began to follow him. But just then, Duana came out from the tavern's back room. She saw Mag heading off, and then she noticed that Ciaran was no longer in his chair.

"Where are you going?" she asked Mag sharply.

Mag glanced back at her. "One of our customers asked for my services."

"Mag!" said Duana. "Let it go. You have better ways to spend your time."

But customers were hurrying out after Ciaran, eager to see the fray. Mag gestured at them, and then at the emptying tables in the room. "Do I? There are no customers to serve. I will not be a moment."

She stepped through the front door. Ciaran waited in the street for her, hands clenched to fists at his side. He had rolled up his sleeves, revealing hairy forearms. His face was an ugly squint. Mag stepped up to him, and the contrast was striking: this smallish young woman before a hulking brute of a man. Some of the crowd's enthusiasm died.

"I shall give you one last chance to apologize," said Ciaran.

"And I will let you swing first," said Mag.

Then her face went dead. The light faded from her eyes. It was her battle-trance, and it chilled the villagers of Shuiniu to see it. Even Ciaran seemed stricken for a moment, and he hesitated.

But then he glanced around, seeing the villagers, knowing they were witnessing his doubt.

He swung for her face.

Mag grabbed his wrist and twisted. Her hand drove into his armpit like a knife. Ciaran cried out in pain as he doubled over.

Mag's fist pummeled his cheeks, his nose, his chin. She did not strike his barrel chest. Why bother, when thick muscle guarded him like armor? Only when he bent and twisted, trying to escape, did she hit his kidneys with punishing savagery. She knew where to strike to hurt him the most, all the places that can break someone no matter their size.

Ciaran cried out again and again, more plaintive each time. It was not long before he sounded more like a child than a hale and hearty smith.

She did not draw out his suffering. After beating him nearly into submission, she caught his wrist once more. Pinching the nerves, she sent him reeling off balance. With a sweep of her leg she tripped him. Even as he fell, she levered him over her shoulder. Screaming, he flew three paces to land in a heap among the crowd. He struck a few of the onlookers, but they did not seem to mind.

The crowd had murmured before the fight. When Ciaran had thrown his first punch, a few had cried out in excitement. But during the beating, everything had fallen to deathly silence. Now that silence reigned for a moment longer.

And then, all at once, the crowd burst into shouts and cheers. Some gathered around Ciaran's fallen form, trying to help him back to his feet. Others clustered around Mag, talking all at once.

Such was their excitement that not one of them noticed as her battle-trance fell away. For a moment, her eyes flickered with something like fear: the deep uncertainty of one who finds themself in a strange place, disoriented and alone.

None of the crowd saw it, but Duana, watching from the tavern's front porch, did. Her eyes filled with concern, even as Mag moved through the press to the door. Duana took hold of her arm.

"Mag," she said quietly. "Are you all right?"

A moment passed before Mag could force an uncaring smile. "Am *I* all right? Look at *him.*" She tossed her head at Ciaran, and then she gently pulled her arm from Duana's grasp to go inside.

It was the first time Mag ever fought another person. But of course, it was not the last.

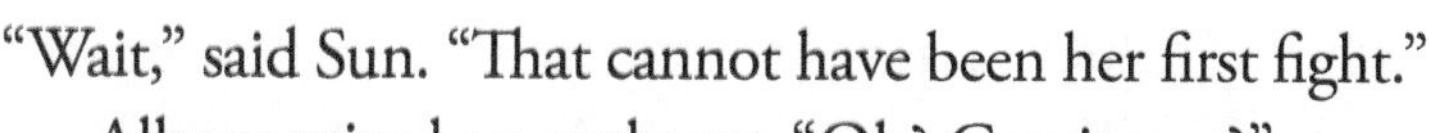

"Wait," said Sun. "That cannot have been her first fight."

Albern raised an eyebrow. "Oh? Can it not?"

"Of *course* not!" cried Sun. "Where did she learn how to do that? And . . . and her battle-trance. You told me you experienced something like it in Tokana. But you wondered what horrible fate could have befallen Mag that led her to discover it. You are telling me it happened by chance during some barroom brawl in a town no one has ever heard of?"

Albern shrugged, annoying her further. Not only did it seem he had no answer, but he seemed not to think an answer was terribly important. "She had no idea where it came from—the trance, or her skill at fighting."

Sun took a deep breath, and then another. "I am not asking about her, at that time," she said. "I am asking you, now. Do you know where her ability came from?"

That only earned her a grin. "You have sharp ears, and a sharper wit."

"That is no answer!"

Albern raised his arms as though pleading for mercy, but he kept smiling. "I have some ideas and some rather wild guesses. But they will sound outlandish if you do not know the story behind them. And that is the story I am telling you now."

Sun turned away from him and looked at the road ahead. The town was far behind them, and Bertram was nowhere in sight. They were in open country, with only the Bluewater off to the south to break up the landscape. There were no answers anywhere, and no relief.

"I hate waiting," she growled.

Albern laughed hard. "That is an understatement if ever there was one."

FOUR

It occurs to me that I have said little of Kaita.

She was in northeastern Dorsea at the time, as was our hope. In bird form, she could fly straight over landscapes through which we had to find roads to traverse. But such travel is exhausting to a weremage. A rider passes most of a journey's weariness to their mount, where Kaita felt the full burden of it in her own body. It wore her down more and more, as the days added up to weeks and weeks grew close to months.

But where we were wandering aimlessly, she knew where she wished to go. Thus she was far away from us when she reached an outpost of Shades southeast of the Dunfen lake. There they hid from prying eyes in the thick woods, which no one has ever cleared.

In raven form, Kaita ducked below the canopy of the trees. Flitting from branch to branch, she searched for signs leading to her kindred. Weariness and anxiety made her movements sharp and jerky, and she thrashed in her flight, moving like one enthralled by mindwyrd.

But at last she spotted a path, marked by trees carved with subtle signs that one could only see if they knew what to seek. After following the signs for a league, she at last spotted the fresh-hewn timbers of the Shades' buildings. The sight made her want to collapse from relief. Instead, she forced herself into one last desperate flight, covering the last few spans with a frenzied beating of her wings.

She landed in the center of the camp. Some Shades looked up curiously—and then all of them turned to her as her eyes began to glow, and her human form emerged from the raven's wings and black feathers.

Her close-fitting clothes were in the Shades' colors of blue and grey. But they were filthy with the grime of the road and threadbare from nights spent in dark dells and caves. Kaita knew it, and so she threw her hands up as the Shades drew their weapons and nocked arrows.

"I serve the master of death!" Her voice was half a croak, traces of the raven's call still lingering in her throat. "I am Kaita. There must be at least one here who knows that name."

For a moment, no one answered. Kaita feared they would shoot her down where she stood. Or they might take her prisoner, wasting priceless time in a cell until someone decided what to do with her.

But then, from the corner of her eye, she saw a wisp of a man straighten, sheathe his sword, and step forwards.

"Kaita?" His voice was as wonderstruck as the look in his eyes. "What in the dark below are you doing here?"

"Horata," she gasped, and her voice nearly broke on the word. She took a step towards him, doing it slowly so that her knees did not give out. "I might ask you the same. I thought you were in Feldemar."

"Reassigned," he said absentmindedly. He turned to the other Shades. "I know her! Lower your weapons. Someone go and get the commander."

The commander. Kaita's heart leaped. "Horata, who is in charge here?"

"Tagata," he said. Kaita's hopes fell. "She is a—"

"I know her well," said Kaita with a sigh. It would be a joy to see Tagata, but . . . . She put a hand on Horata's shoulder, more for support than out of affection. "I thought . . . I hoped Rogan might be here."

Horata looked upon her with pity. "I am sorry," he said. "We have not seen Rogan in weeks. Not since the assault on the Seat. I thought he was at the Watcher."

Kaita shook her head, stifling her anger to keep from snapping at him. It was hardly Horata's fault that he was wrong. "He is not. I went there first. They had not seen him since he *marched* to the Seat."

Horata frowned. "Where do you suppose he could be?"

"I do not *know.*" Now Kaita could not entirely keep the exasperation from her voice. "That is what I am here to find out."

Some of her exhaustion must have shown in her bearing, for Horata stepped closer. Putting an arm around her, he led her towards the central building of the compound. "Well, let us get you some food. Not to mention a place to sit down. You look as though you have taken a long road to get here."

"Longer than you know," said Kaita. And though she tried hard to keep an upright, regal bearing, she leaned heavily on him. It felt strange to be walking again after so many hours of powering along on wings. "Thank you, Horata."

Color came to his cheeks. "We are all children of the Lord. We owe each other at least so much."

Inside was a corridor that turned immediately right and left. Horata took her to the right, where soon they came into a mess hall. Some scattered Shades were sitting about the tables, but not many, for it was between the midday meal and supper. Once he had her seated, Horata ran to the kitchen and fetched her some bread and the remains of that day's soup.

Kaita had not realized how hungry she was until the food was before her. She tore into it like a woman starving, and when Horata fetched her some ale, she finished the first mug in but a moment. As she ate more and more, crumbs and ale sticking to her face, Horata's eyes grew wide.

"Dark below, Kaita," he murmured. "What has happened to you?"

"Nothing," said Kaita. "And much. I have been long pursued, many times cornered, and twice has defeat come crashing down at the moment of my victory. And now I seek Rogan, but for *dark's* sake"—she sent a fist crashing down on the table, tipping her mug—"I cannot find him anywhere."

Horata snatched up her fallen mug and replaced it with his full one. "Well, we can help, at least in one respect. Tagata will know exactly where Rogan is."

"Yes," said Kaita, her hands beginning to shake as she took up her bread and splashed it into her soup. "Almost at the end. Finally."

But how many times during this journey had she thought the same thing?

She shied away from the thought. Despair helped no one, least of all the one suffering from it.

Being so preoccupied with her food, Kaita did not notice when another Shade entered the dining hall and approached the table. Only when Horata looked up at the woman did Kaita realize she was there.

"What is it?" said Horata. "Where is the commander?"

The woman—a girl, honestly, barely older than the children—glanced fearfully at Kaita before she answered. "She has gone. Some errand of the Lord called her away, and no one knows exactly why. She took no one with her."

Kaita paused, her mouth partly open, still full of soup-soaked bread. "What do you—" She paused and swallowed so that her speech no longer slurred. "What do you mean, 'some errand'?"

"I do not know," said the girl, her face going pale. "No one seems to. She did not say when she would be back."

Kaita's hands stopped shaking. She went stone-still as she looked upon the girl, whose eyes filled with fear.

Tagata. The one person here who could tell her where Rogan was. And she had vanished just as Kaita had arrived.

"Dark below," muttered Horata. "That is ill fortune beyond belief. I am sorry, Kaita. But still, you are here now. You can rest. We can get you new clothes, and—you will forgive me," he chuckled. "But a bath might do you some good."

"Yes," said Kaita slowly. "Yes, it would. And I will enjoy sleeping in a bed rather than on the ground."

Horata rose and drew her up after him, leading her to the bath and fetching new clothes while she scrubbed the dirt from her skin. But all the while, one thought remained with her, persistent, tapping at the door of her mind and trying to persuade its way in.

Was it possible that Rogan did not *wish* for her to find him?

Was it possible . . . the thought did not bear dwelling on . . . but could it be that the Lord himself did not wish for her to have what she sought? That despite his promises, he did not intend to give her the strength she needed to defeat Mag?

In a rigid mind, the seed of doubt can take long to find purchase. But once it has taken root, it can never be entirely eradicated.

"It is time, my son."

Rogan's hand clenched to a fist, crumpling the missive he had been reading. It told him something he already knew: Kaita was searching for him, and she was running herself to death in the hunt.

But this was the first time his father had spoken of the matter since Kaita had failed in Tokana, weeks ago. When Father had told Rogan that Kaita would have to die if the Shades were to win the war.

He stood from the table in his small room.

"Why now, Father?" he said.

"Do you not trust in me?"

"Always," he said immediately. "Forgive my impertinence."

The Lord's laugh was gentle. "You are too quick to beg my forgiveness. Those who serve us feel the same way towards you that you do towards me—afraid of making the smallest misstep, even when they are only curious. You are always gentle with them. Remember to reserve that same kindness for yourself. To answer your question: it is time because I have seen that it is time. I have no greater understanding than you. I have only a better grasp of the sight."

Rogan shook his head. "Then I trust in you. Only . . ."

"Only you wish to delay the moment as long as possible." Rogan could feel the Lord's deep sigh in his bones, and he felt, too, the sadness that came with it. "I desire the same thing. Yet if we are to achieve our aims . . ."

"I know." Rogan's voice had faded to a whisper. "Very well. I will send word to Kaita and tell her where to find me."

"Thank you, my son."

His father left him, and Rogan felt empty, as he always did.

Soon he left his room. A short hallway brought him to the chamber where his advisors were in council. As he strode in, they were leaning over a map of Underrealm, discussing a new wave of raids into Feldemar. But the moment they noticed Rogan, the chamber fell silent. Everyone present looked at him, eyes shining with love, awaiting his command. Only Ikaia dared to smile, stepping forwards and gripping his wrist.

"Things are proceeding well, brother," she said. "Our brave warriors have done much to foment discord between Dorsea and Feldemar. And by all accounts, no one in either kingdom knows they are ours."

"Good," said Rogan. "And the affair in Danfon?"

"It only awaits your order." Ikaia answered without thinking. But as she caught the reason he asked, she straightened, and her eyes went wide. The air in the room seemed to thicken, and now they were all frozen, looking at him, hanging on his next words.

"The order is given," said Rogan. "Tell Wojin it is time to act."

He paused. Unspoken words hung on the air, and everyone could hear them. No one moved. Almost he stopped there. Almost he left his father's command unfulfilled.

But Rogan was a dutiful son.

"And send word to Kaita," he said. "Tell her where to find me. A long-overdue conversation must finally take place."

FIVE

The rider who followed us through the Sunmane Pass had lost our trail some time ago. Now she wandered from town to town, chasing every lead from barkeeps and constables. The growing spring had given fresh rainfall, and she could not keep it entirely out of her boots. She shook her feet every so often to keep the water from growing too cold with stillness.

Something had changed. When the rider passed others on the road, she met untrusting looks that soon darted away. Some suspicion might be understandable—she wore a hood and a mask, after all. But this was something more. Something must have happened in the area, but she had not had time to stop off and find out what.

Suddenly she spied a troop on foot, making its way west along the road. The rider sighed and set her shoulders as she recognized Dorsean uniforms.

Stay calm, she thought. *And say nothing if you can help it.*

But it did not seem that the sky had blessed her with fortune that day. As soon as the soldiers spotted the horse coming, they fanned out across the road to block its path. The rider pulled up in front of the troop, glaring at them from beneath a dark brown hood.

"Hail," said a soldier, wiping melted snow from her hair. "What is your business in these parts?"

"What business of yours is business of mine?" said the rider.

That seemed to stump the woman for a moment, and she glared at the rider while trying to work out an answer. "I serve the king," she said at last. "The true king. I keep his peace. Who do *you* serve?"

True king? An odd word for a soldier to use. But the rider put that thought from her mind. She could not answer it now, and it was thus only a distraction.

"I serve no one any longer," she said, voice muffled by the mask. "I am only looking for two friends in a strange land."

"A strange land?" said the soldier, eyes sharpening at once. "And what land is that?"

The rider cursed inwardly. "I only mean that I come from western Dorsea. I have never crossed the Greatrocks before."

The soldiers edged forwards, some of them reaching for their weapons. The woman who led them drew her sword halfway out.

"A quick reply, if not an honest one," she said. "I think we have a spy on our hands."

"I am no spy," growled the rider.

"Oh?" said the soldier in mock surprise. "I am sure a spy would never lie about such a thing. Search her belongings."

The rider gave a great sigh, her shoulders drooping as if in defeat. Two guards saw the movement and relaxed, straightening as they came forwards. Their hands neared the horse's reins.

With a great shout, the rider kicked at the horse's flanks. It sprang forwards as though stung, and the rider drove one booted foot into the face of each soldier. They fell back with cries and broken noses. The other soldiers scattered as the horse threatened to trample them. They shouted for her to halt, but their cries were impotent, for they had no steeds of their own. Quickly they faded into the distance.

Dark take it, thought the rider. *A fugitive, now. Another thing to blame the wanderers for, when I find them again.*

But what under the sky had happened in Dorsea, when the king's soldiers were accosting lone travelers on the road?

“The answer, of course,” said Albern, “is that there had been a coup in the Dorsean capital of Danfon.”

Sun stared at him in wonder. They had stopped for the midday meal, and a bite of dried meat hung in her almost-limp fingers, her mouth half-open.

“You were here in Dorsea when the war broke out?” she said.

Albern smiled at her. “You might have guessed that. I do not doubt you learned the dates of it in your tutoring.”

“I did not count the days of your story in my mind.”

“I will not dwell overlong on that tale,” said Albern with a sigh. “Others have told it elsewhere, and better than I could. I do not doubt that you have already learned something of it from your instructors in history. Suffice it to say that Wojin of the family Fei, uncle and chief councilor of the king, overthrew his liege and took the throne. His efforts went to waste in the end, thanks to the Nightblade—but of course, we did not know that at the time.”

Sun shook her head. “What was it like in the kingdom? They taught me it was a horrid, bloody affair, and I cannot imagine that you escaped the fighting.”

“No, we did not,” said Albern. “The war threw the whole kingdom into chaos. Indeed, it rocked the foundations of Underrealm itself. And word was not long in reaching us—nor was it long before we found ourselves drawn into the conflict."

After Taitou, we spent two eternal weeks in northeastern Dorsea, riding from town to village to hamlet and back again. But nowhere could we find anything to tell us where to go next. Our mood darkened. Winter, at last, began to give way to spring, which should have helped. But instead of good and gentle weather, the sky started to rain almost constantly. It drove into our faces and down the backs of our necks, no matter how we bundled up against it. And yet it was still too cold for the snow to melt away. It turned into a thick and horrible slush upon the ground, mixing into the dirt to turn it into a dark and sucking mud. Mag and I began to grow snappish with each other, and even with Dryleaf, though in his case we at least tried to restrain ourselves.

It was in the town of Huzen, not too far from the coast of the Great Bay, that we began to rethink our plan. We were in a tavern called the Spiced Fiddle, and Dryleaf had his boots off with his stockinged feet up near the fire. Any chance to rest near a hearth, safe from the freezing rain, now felt like a luxury.

The old man had sung earlier, and then he had given me a turn. I had performed my song about Jordel. Dryleaf and I had worked on it ever since I first shared it with him in Tokana, and I had been performing it in taverns for some weeks. Mag, bless her, did not poke fun at me over it, for she could sense how dear to my heart it was. Indeed, the first few times I had sung it in a tavern's common room, I had been unable to finish, and I soon fell weeping back into my chair. But enough repetition had allowed me to keep my tears from falling, though my heart was still heavy as I sat with my friends and discussed our options.

"Mayhap we have been taking the wrong approach," said Dryleaf. "We have avoided large cities thus far, for there are too many prying eyes. Yet at the same time, there are a great many listening ears, and also discerning minds to sift the truth from lies. Mayhap we would find better information in Danfon, or one of the cities on the coast. We might even take a small detour to the High King's Seat. I know some folk there who are able to gather news from all across the nine kingdoms."

Slowly Mag shook her head. "I am not sure that is wise," she said. "If Kaita, or the Shades, are indeed here in northeastern Dorsea, we would waste a great deal of time going all the way to the Seat. Do we not know anyone else who could help us? Someone closer?"

"I do not," said Dryleaf. "The only place I can think of would be Danfon, and that is farther away than the Seat."

"That would be no help, then," I said. "Mayhap we should not go seeking out cities after all. Three of the Shade encampments we found were quite removed from civilization. Mayhap we need to turn away from towns and hamlets and seek them in the wild."

"Oh?" said Mag, arching an eyebrow. "And where in the wild would you have us look? I am no ranger like you, of course, but I have heard the wilderness is rather large."

I glowered at her. "I am no ranger. What would you have us do, then? Dryleaf suggests the cities, and you say they are too far. I suggest unclaimed lands, and you say they are too large. Let us hear your proposal, then."

"Why not simply carry on?" said Mag. "We do not know but that our current course will bring us to our enemies."

"Yet we have no reason to think it will," I snapped. "It is only a vague hope that great fortune will befall us."

Mag frowned at me. "Just as it did in Lan Shui."

I threw my hands in the air. "Oh, certainly. One out of four times."

"Now, now," said Dryleaf. "She may have a point, boy. The wide world is too large for us to search completely. And cities—or smaller towns," he said hastily, nodding in Mag's direction, "have one great advantage: they are peopled. If the Shades cause trouble in the wilderness, and we come to the place a week later, the trees and beasts will offer us precious little information. But if the Shades' actions affect a settlement of any size, the news will linger long enough for us to find it. It will even spread."

I gritted my teeth. That was a good point, though

I was not quite ready to admit it. But I was saved from having to answer by a blast of horns outside the tavern.

I shot to my feet. Dryleaf sat up straight, clutching his walking stick. All around us, the tavern's patrons froze and looked anxiously towards the door. Then they began to move, some towards the outside, and some upstairs to their rooms. My mind gave a sickening wrench as I remembered the day Northwood fell.

"An attack?" I said, my voice gruff to hide my fear.

"It could be the Shades," said Dryleaf. "You two should go. I will be safe here."

"Get yourself to our room, at least," I said. He hastened to obey.

My bow rested against the wall, and I strung it quickly. As I did, Mag's battle-trance came over her. When I finished, she hefted her spear and shield.

"Outside," she intoned.

I followed her, slinging my belt quiver on and pulling an arrow from it. We burst through the door into the street, where we found Oku trotting nervously around. He gave a happy bark when he saw us and padded over to stand between us.

"Good boy," I said, patting his head. "Now, what in the sky is going on?"

A scene of chaos greeted us. Armed soldiers were killing each other in the streets. Thankfully, most of the fighting was a good distance away from the inn itself. I half-drew my arrow, but I stopped. There were no cloaks of blue in sight, nor any grey-clad fighters.

"I see no Shades," I said.

"Nor do I," said Mag in the toneless voice of her battle-trance. "It could be Dulmun."

"No, wait," I said. "Look at them, Mag. Every fighter wears the livery of Dorsea. The town's guards are fighting each other."

It was true. To a one, the soldiers before us wore the red and yellow of Dorsea. How did any of them know who to attack?

"Mayhap they are Shades in disguise?" said Mag in confusion. With no target for her spear, she had let the trance slip away.

"Mayhap," I said. A sick feeling was growing in my stomach. Something was wrong here, worse than it had been in Lan Shui or Tokana. "No way for us to tell. We should retrieve Dryleaf and flee."

Mag spun to me. "Flee?"

I pointed at the fighting. "How can we join the battle when we do not know who is on which side, much less which side is the right one? And what if the wrong side wins? Do you think we will be safe here in Huzen?"

"Very well," said Mag. "But where do we go?"

"We need not worry about the direction yet," I said. "This foe approaches from within, and so we must get ourselves without."

We ran back inside and fetched Dryleaf from the room. He took my arm and followed us down the stairs.

"What is it?" he said as we went. "Who is attacking?"

"We do not know," I said. "Dorsean soldiers are fighting each other in the streets. We have to leave the town."

His bushy brows drew together. "Dorsean soldiers . . .?" he said slowly.

"We have no more answers than that," I said. Mag threw open the inn's door, and we stepped out into the street. "And I would rather discover them from a place of safety, than in the midst of—"

"You! Halt!"

Two soldiers stood before us. The fighting had moved closer to the inn now. The guards who challenged us stood over a man's gutted body. He was wearing the same uniform as them. Now they raised their swords, approaching step by step.

"Go back inside. Now!"

Mag's spear came up, her voice toneless again. "That is not going to happen."

One of them, a bulky man with a scraggly beard, snarled at her. "We are servants of the true king, and you will obey our commands." He rolled his shoulder, the tip of his blade moving in a lazy circle. "Unless you are traitors, in league with the pretender?"

True king? Pretender? What was going on here?

The second guard had stepped to the side, and I was very aware of how close her sword was to Dryleaf. I nudged the old man behind me. Oku bristled and growled at the woman. But while I hesitated, trying to determine the right course of action, Mag had no such hesitation. She pounced on the bearded man. For a terrible moment, I feared she would kill him, but she only struck him down with the butt of her spear. He fell, stunned but not quite senseless, and Mag kicked his sword far out of reach.

The woman put up a better fight, managing to trade two blows with Mag. But then the spontoon's tip came around, and Mag slammed the flat of it into the woman's temple with a crushing blow. She fell to the mud of the street, poleaxed. Her limp body now lay in the pool of blood from the guard they had killed right before we arrived.

"What in the dark below is this?" I said.

"No time to find out," said Mag. "The horses."

All the stablehands had fled, so we fetched our mounts and rode hard for the west gate. Though we avoided the fighting where we could, sometimes we had to gallop straight through the battle. It was a horrible reminder of Northwood. I kept a tight hand on the reins of Dryleaf's horse. He clung to the saddle, bent over his mount's neck to make himself as small a target as possible. I wondered how terrifying this must be for him, hearing only clashing blades and death screams.

The western gate was closed. Four Dorsean guards stood before it, with halberds held forwards in warning. I thought I recognized them from when we had come into the town hours ago.

"Halt!" cried one who seemed braver than the rest. At least her hands were not shaking. "No one is leaving the town!"

"We only wish to escape the fighting!" I called back as we reined in our horses before them. "We are simple travelers. This battle has nothing to do with us."

"No one is leaving," she repeated, and her voice was grim. "By order of the mayor."

I sighed and looked at Mag. "Do you wish to . . ."

"I do not wish to, but I will," she said, and she dismounted.

The soldiers, bless them, stepped towards us, for they saw a clear threat in Mag's stance. But when they thrust their halberds at her, the space where she had stood was suddenly empty. She darted between their stabs and ducked beneath their slashes. Though they were well trained, Mag's grace made them look clumsy and foolish. Oku edged forwards, though he seemed reluctant to join her in the fight.

"Kip, Oku," I said. "She does not need us."

Oku sat.

Mag's spear lashed out three times, and one by one, the guards fell. She did not slash or pierce them but knocked them senseless with the butt or the flat of the blade.

Soon only the guard who had challenged us remained, and now her hands *did* shake. She took two steps back, and now she was up against the town wall.

"No one is permitted to leave!" she cried, voice trembling and eyes wide.

Mag's brow furrowed, as it might have at a growling puppy. Then she knocked the woman's halberd out of her grip and caught both her wrists in one hand. Pushing her up against the gate, she held the haft of the spontoon across her throat.

"Now then," said Mag. "Suppose you tell us what under the sky is going on."

The girl gritted her teeth and tried to free her hands, but she could no more move than she could have taken flight. I saw the moment the spark went out of her. Her shoulders sagged, and a held breath escaped her in a sigh.

"No one knows," said the woman. "Not for certain."

"Suppose you tell us what you suspect, or what you have heard," said Dryleaf. "That might be just as useful."

"And if I do not?" she said, glaring at Mag.

"I will not kill you," said Mag easily. "But I will have to give you the same headache I gave your companions, and we will leave the town regardless. I would rather not do that. We are no evil folk, but merely confused, and likely more so than you are."

"That hardly seems possible," snorted the woman.

She had stopped struggling against Mag's grip, and so Mag released her wrists and took a step back. But I saw that her foot stayed close to the halberd, ready to kick it away if the woman should reach for it.

The guard rolled her head and felt gingerly at her throat, where Mag's spear had pressed against it. "Thank you. In answer to your question . . . word has reached Huzen that King Jun is dead. May he be safe in the darkness. Wojin has taken the throne."

"Dead?" said Dryleaf. "How?"

The woman's face turned sour like old milk. "Wojin says the High King sent an assassin."

I could only stare at her. That was patently ridiculous. What possible reason could the High King have had for such an act?

"Who is this Wojin you speak of?" I asked the woman. "I do not know that name."

But it was Dryleaf who answered. "He is—or was—Jun's uncle." He cocked his head. "But he is not next in the line of succession. That would be His Excellency, Prince Senlin. What happened to him?"

"Wojin says that the High King's assassins killed him as well," said the guard, her eyes flashing. "But I do not believe it, and neither did my companions, and neither does the mayor. We are servants of the king, not Wojin and his hired thugs. It is Wojin's men who have attacked the town, for the mayor refuses to swear fealty to him. He thinks—and I agree—that Wojin staged a coup."

"With help from the Shades," said Mag, her eyes widening.

The guard turned to her, incredulous. "How do you know that?"

"We do not know it," I said. "Not for certain. But we are roughly as certain of it as you are that the High King did not have King Jun killed."

Mag grimaced at me. "It would seem, then," she said slowly, "that these are loyalists to Jun, the true king." She bowed her head to the woman. "I would never have attacked you if I had known. I beg your forgiveness—and theirs."

I held up a hand. "To be fair to ourselves, we *did* ask politely to leave, at first. And in that spirit, please apologize to your friends on our behalf, when they wake up with bruises."

"I shall consider doing so," said the guard. She eyed her halberd, but if she thought to seize it, it was only for a wistful moment. She motioned us forwards. "Go on, then, since I clearly cannot stop you."

In a moment, I had the gate up, while Mag kept a wary eye on the woman, just in case. Then we were through and out into the open countryside, while Huzen burned in battle behind us.

But as the guard went to rouse her comrades and rally them to the fight, two more figures slipped out the gate. They faded into the wilderness at once, following the tracks of our horses. One of them had a heavy scar on his left cheek.

SIX

We rode west until Huzen was out of sight, and then we rode a while longer, for safety. On a bank overlooking a small stream, we pitched our tents to camp overnight. Mag watered the horses while I took a hatchet and began cutting wood for a fire. I ended up cutting more than we needed. It felt good to slam my hatchet into the wood over and over again, taking out my frustration at our formless foe and rapidly worsening circumstance.

All the while, Dryleaf sat on a rock, his sightless eyes staring into nothing. "A civil war," he said after a time. "A civil war in Dorsea. Something I never thought to see."

"Nor did any of us, I am certain," said Mag. "Yet war threatens all of Underrealm."

"Conflict between two kingdoms is one thing," said Dryleaf. "Even the rebellion of a king against the High King—well, while it is hardly common, neither is it unheard of. But a king's soldiers killing each other in the streets . . . that is something else. In the turmoil of these times, I fear conflicts like these will cause the greatest harm: a nation turned on itself, kin against kin. Such a thing has hardly been seen since the days of Roth himself."

"I have no doubt the Shades are behind it," I said.

"Of course," said Mag with a shrug. "They have been behind every crisis we have seen on our long road."

Dryleaf sighed. "I am sure you are both right. It fairly stinks of their work. They have perfected the art of sending others to do their fighting for them."

"If only they would show their faces," said Mag. "I would give much to capture even one of them, to trace our way to Kaita."

"But now she will be heavily protected," said Dryleaf. "She must have rejoined her allies. Thus our way seems unclear. What are we to do?"

"Find Kaita," said Mag at once.

"Without getting ourselves killed," I added.

She smiled. "In a perfect world, yes."

"Mag."

"Dearest Albern."

"Mag."

"I am mostly joking."

"Mag."

Dryleaf wore a frown, and he began to stroke his beard. "Mayhap Kaita should not be our focus—our primary focus, I mean, for the time being."

I arched a brow. "Oh? What do you have in mind?"

"We could seek Loren," said Dryleaf. "Kaita has allies now—and even more than we thought if Dorsea now works with the Shades. Mayhap we should acquire some friends of our own."

Mag's levity vanished in an instant. A very curious expression came over her—uncertainty, anxiety, and . . . and something else I could not quite identify. I frowned as she shook her head.

"Loren and the others could be anywhere," she said at last. "Who knows how long it would take to find them? What strength might Kaita gather to herself in that time?"

I hesitated. That reasoning made sense. Yet I could not shake an uneasy feeling that there was more to it. Mag almost seemed to feel . . . guilty.

Dryleaf's expression had fallen, and he shook his head. "My dear, I think we must be honest with ourselves. We have lost too much time already. It has been two months since we saw Kaita last. If she wished to vanish forever, hiding in some far kingdom where we will never find her, she could have done that by now. If she wished to surround herself with allies, she could have done that as well. We can hardly worsen our situation by spending more time, especially if we spend it strengthening ourselves for the fight to come."

Mag had been resting her spear across her knees. Now she seized it, shot to her feet, and threw it into a tree five paces away. The spearhead stuck in the trunk, quivering, as Mag's hands balled to fists at her sides.

"Mag!" I said, frowning.

"What?" she growled.

"You may not like it, but you have to admit he is—"

"I *know* he is right, Albern." Suddenly her shoulders sagged. "Of course I know it. I have been thinking of little else for the last month. Sometimes I hardly know why we are even here in northeastern Dorsea. Chasing some half-baked notion from a Rangatira? We have nothing. Nothing at all. And even now, with civil war breaking out, there is no sign of the Shades. I am . . . I am tired."

Slowly, she paced over to her spear and pulled it out. Just as slowly, she returned and resumed her seat by the fire. I had sat up, tense for a moment, but now I began to relax again.

"I understand, Mag," I said quietly. "I am tired, too. And you, Dryleaf, may try to hide it, but I can see the weariness in your shoulders as well. So let us rest. Let us slow down, at least a little. We can stop our wandering, and see what we can learn about this civil war, if there is anything to learn."

"I cannot stop," said Mag. "I cannot. I have to find her. I would hate myself if I stopped trying. And you said you would stay with me."

"Of course I did," I said. "And I will. Always."

She looked away from me. "Then trust me. Searching for Loren now would be unwise. Sky above, she will not even kill in a fight. She would be little help in our hunt, and we would only endanger her if she joined it. It would be a waste of time, and we have wasted enough as it is."

I sighed. "All right, then, Mag. We will keep looking for Kaita. We . . . we can continue asking around about the Shades. They may have something to do with this civil war. If they do, they may be easier to find now."

Dryleaf had been listening to us silently, but now his head snapped up. Though his eyes were sightless, I could almost see a light in them.

"There may be another way," he said. "Loren is not the only ally we could seek. We could find others."

Mag arched an eyebrow. "And where do you mean to find them? I know few enough people in Dorsea. And if I do not want to spend a month searching fruitlessly for Loren, I certainly do not want to take the time for a tour of recruitment."

Dryleaf cracked a grin. "You will not recruit anyone. You will be recruited. That Mystic captain in Taitou. Kun, of the family Zhou. If anyone in the kingdom wishes to find and fight the Shades, it will be him. If we can ingratiate ourselves with him, we may learn something of our enemy's whereabouts."

I had to admit that this idea appealed to me. We had been listless and wandering in Dorsea for far too long. And Victon always used to say that even a bad plan, carried out swiftly and with certainty, is better than no plan at all. I could think of worse things than allying ourselves with servants of the High King, Mystics though they might be.

Mag, too, had a spark of excitement in her eyes. "It would certainly be better than our aimless wandering. But I do not know if that Kun fellow was as trusting as he appeared. I heard the smile in his voice, but I also heard a false tone in it, and something steely lying beneath."

"Yet he did offer to recruit us," I said. "And we can prove our worth to him. Only a fool would refuse to have the Uncut Lady on their side of a battle."

Mag scowled. "They will not know about that ridiculous title, because you will not tell them."

I widened my eyes. "Of course not. I would never."

"Albern."

"Dearest Mag."

Dryleaf shook his head, wearing a little smile. "I can hear the eagerness in your voices so plainly, I can almost picture your faces. And I think Kun will be more than grateful to have you."

A reluctant smile pulled at the corner of Mag's mouth. "Well, then. Let us try it. It *has* been a long time since we were sellswords."

"A long time indeed," I said. "Let us get some good rest tonight, then. Tomorrow, we ride to join the war for Underrealm's future."

SEVEN

"I CAN RELATE TO YOUR SITUATION," SAID SUN.

"Oh?" said Albern, cocking his head. "How is that?"

"Since meeting you, I have also found myself joining battles I did not expect," she explained. "Though of course, you and I fight no great battles of nations. We are monster hunters, I suppose . . . and whatever one would call it when we stopped those brigands near Lan Shui."

"Do not so quickly discount your actions—or, for that matter, my own," said Albern. "It is easier to see battles on a grand scale when looking through the lens of history. But a king's army is nothing but a collection of people. In ones and twos they join the fight, and in ones and twos they die—or they fight until they cannot anymore. You hear of them as part of a greater whole. But it takes wisdom to see that one is *always* part of a greater whole, whether you fight to save your loved ones, or you are hunting vampires in the woods."

That was a disturbing thought to Sun. After a moment's consideration, she thought she knew why. "But then, to what end? You say that you and I are rooting out evil, the way you and Mag did when you were younger. But if there is still evil today, is that not discouraging?"

Albern only smiled. "Good folk always seek a permanent end to evil. That is . . . well, I will not say it *cannot* be done, but it never *has* been done. But, after fighting for a time, of course someone is entitled to some well-earned peace. This, too, comes to us in ones and twos. A woman like Duana leaves the army in her autumn years, starting the trade she has long desired to practice. A couple like Mag and Sten meet, and fall in love, and build a life together."

Sun's voice grew hushed. "Yet evil found them in the end."

His expression dampened. "It did, at that. Because peace, like war, comes in ones and twos, and rarely to a whole nation, or the world. The world will never know peace. Not forever. But some people can. Doing good in your youth should, if fate is kind—which it sometimes is, despite appearances—let you enjoy a better world towards the end of your days. And that is no small thing to achieve."

Sun sighed, not entirely comforted. After all, Albern was close to the end of his days, and he did not live a peaceful life. But it seemed cruel to say so.

They had neared Bertram's southeast gate. Above them, the sky was now grey and hazy, the combined smoke from thousands of fires drifting up into the clean air. Here, the Bluewater and Blackwind rivers joined as they came leaping down out of the Greatrock Mountains to the east. Their mingled waters were called the Fangrong, and that great river ran to Dorsea's western coast.

Bertram had once been the capital of the kingdom, and it was easy to see the marks of that heritage in its bearing. The walls were among the tallest Sun had ever seen. Long, weighted banners by the gate bore a Dorsean longsword surrounded by a circle of stars, all yellow, on a red field. Over the walls, she could glimpse tall towers with the red tile roofs that were common across Dorsea, and balconies that surely gave a breathtaking view of the surrounding land.

Where the twin rivers met the eastern wall, they churned through two river gates. As the day cooled, the waters threw a slight mist into the air that gave everything a pleasantly dreamy quality. All of it made the approach to Bertram feel like riding up to a place from an Elf-tale, something half-hidden in clouds of vapor and magic, all of which might vanish if Sun turned her back on it.

But thoughts of her family would not leave her, and they spoiled the moment's enchantment.

Albern glanced at her from the corners of his eyes. "You seem nervous."

"Of course I am," said Sun. "Soon, we will be in Bertram. If my parents will discover me anywhere, it is likely to be here."

Albern seemed to think about that for a moment. He was silent so long that Sun finally looked over at him. His brow had furrowed, and his lips pursed, like a man trying to find words for a strange feeling.

"Out with it," she said. "What are you thinking?"

"I am trying to find a way to say what I mean without cruelty," he said slowly. "I understand your fear, Sun. And yet, I think you place too much stock in it."

Her brows rose. "Oh? Do you see my caution as foolishness?" She tried to keep her words light, but they held a bitter undertone.

"Not at all," said Albern. "But it is unhealthy to let fear rule our lives."

Sun wanted to tell him that she was not frightened, that she was only trying to be prudent. But as she thought on it, she realized that he was right. She was afraid. The thought of being dragged back into her old life—and the consequences she might face from her parents—was worse than she wished to contemplate.

She gritted her teeth. "I do not think the two of us can withstand my family's guards if they try to recover me."

"Yet we do not know if they will even find us," said Albern. "And we might ask others for assistance, if it should come to that. I have many friends in the city. And aside from that . . . well." His face broke into a broad grin, so pure that Sun felt her fear diminish. "I think you will greatly enjoy yourself here. Indeed, Sun, I think you will be reluctant to leave Bertram once we are done."

Sun snorted. "Of all you have said, I find that hardest to believe."

"Stories and belief."

They stopped talking as they reached the gate. It was open wide enough for several people to pass through abreast. But two guards with spears flanked the entrance, and they held up their hands in challenge.

"You there," said one. He was a squint-eyed man with bristling black hair and a beard to match. "Business in the city?"

"I have some friends to see," said Albern. "Nothing terribly exciting. I am afraid we are only simple travelers."

"Oh, we know you well enough, old man," spat the other guard, a thin woman with a jutting chin. "Rarely could your travels be called simple, and I suspect the same could be said for your aims in Bertram."

Albern leaned forwards in his saddle, eyes narrowing. "Ah, of course. Beilin, is it not? It is a long time since I saw you last."

Beilin spat. The gob of it hit the ground a few hands away from Albern's horse. "Some might say not long enough."

Sun stared flabbergasted at the guards. All her own concerns with Bertram fled her, and she could not hold her tongue. "I am a new traveler to Dorsea, but I am shocked to see such dearth of hospitality," she said hotly. "You claim to know this man, but I call that a lie. If you were aware of half the deeds he has done in his life—deeds that directly served this land and your laws, I might add–you would throw your gates wide before him and summon an honor guard to escort him through your streets."

Now it was the guards' turn to look shocked. But before they could reply, Albern lifted his hand. A sudden fit of giggling had taken him, and he could barely restrain it. His face had gone red, and his eyes watered as his chest jerked with silent laughter.

"Friends, please," he choked out. "There is no need for such posturing on my account. Beilin, you and your companion are welcome to search our things. We have nothing to hide from two upstanding servants of Dorsea's laws."

Sun stared at him. "But they—"

"They are only doing their best to protect their home," said Albern, still chuckling. "That is their duty.

You and I know our intentions in Bertram, and they are not dishonorable. Why, then, should we fear for anyone to question us?"

Sun, in fact, knew nothing of Albern's intentions here, but she was wise enough not to say so. The guards had subsided after their indignation towards Sun. Beilin turned and spat again.

"Get your dark-damned selves in," she said in a disgruntled tone. "But you had best not set one foot out of line, either of you. Rest assured that we will watch you while you are here."

"You always do," said Albern. "We thank you for your service. And send my regards to Captain Stockton, if he still serves the city. It has been long since he and I have spoken over cups, and I might take the opportunity while I am here."

The guards pointedly ignored him, having already moved on to the next in line who wished to enter the gate. Albern and Sun walked their horses through, and then they were in Bertram.

Sun found a smile leaping to her face at the noise of it, the smell, the bustle and the chaos all around. She had always been enamored of a city's frenzy. The press of people went about their lives, each of them caring only for their own affairs and not a whit for those around them. Yet there was an identity to a city. A shopkeeper might not know the tanner she passed in the street, but if an outsider insulted their home, they would unite in an instant against the offender. And as soon as the fight had finished, each would likely forget the other's existence again.

It should have been alienating, but Sun had always found it comforting. Back home, cities gave her a rare chance to feel normal, and in them, no one gave her undue attention because of her birth.

She forced her mind back to the present. "It was clever of you to mention the guard captain," she told Albern. "But I still think you should have boxed their ears for the way they spoke to you."

"I spoke the truth," said Albern. "They were only doing their jobs. I have no doubt the King's law will be keeping a close eye on me while I am in Bertram, but I have grown accustomed to it, and it no longer bothers me."

Sun frowned. "Would that I had your calm."

Her mind drifted back to her parents, and the street seemed to narrow around her. She hunched her shoulders and pulled up the hood of her cloak, wary of being recognized. Albern saw it, and his smile weakened.

"Ah, yes," he said. "I did not mean to call your mind back to troubling matters. But come. Your hood is up, and I doubt they are looking for me. I will continue the tale to keep you distracted while I tend to my business. I mean to introduce you to an old friend—one who owes me quite a bit of coin."

EIGHT

THE NEXT DAY, WE LEFT THE LANDS AROUND HUZEN and made for Taitou, where we had met Kun and his Mystics. We pressed the horses hard and reached the east gate the next day.

We were not surprised to find it even more heavily guarded than last time. Four Mystics stood watch, instead of the two we had encountered before. As we stopped before the gate, one of the Mystics hailed us with a shout. He was an imposing, older man with a frankly magnificent mustache.

"Who are you, and what business have you in Taitou?" he asked in a gruff bark.

"We are friends to the King's law!" I said. "When last we were here, we spoke to your captain, an honorable man named Kun of the family Zhou. We would speak with him again."

The Mystics looked at each other, and then the older one spoke again. "You would, would you? And why would he speak with you?"

Dryleaf spoke then, in the clarion voice of a bard. He was so often soft-spoken that it was easy to forget the power of his oratory. I would not have been surprised to hear him project his voice through a stone wall two paces thick.

"We can only imagine the burden upon Captain Zhou, now that Dorsea is in open war," he called up. "But we have come to lessen that burden. We are all servants of the High King, and her peace is threatened across Underrealm. Kun knows my stalwart companions are fighters. Tell him they have returned and wish to join him, and I promise that you will have done your captain a great boon."

That gave them pause. After a moment, the older Mystic turned to one of the constables and said something we could not hear. The constable darted off out of sight behind the wall, and the Mystic turned back to us.

"Very well," he called down. "I have sent word, and on your head be it if you waste the captain's time. In the meanwhile, come into the guardhouse. It is too damnably cold and wet out here, and you look as though you have ridden a hard road."

"Sky bless your courtesy," I replied.

They raised the gate for us to lead the horses through, and we hitched them to a post before stepping into the guardhouse. The gruff old Mystic joined us there by the fire while Mag led Dryleaf to a chair. Oku padded around the room, sniffing at everyone's boots. The constables tried to look stern, but I saw them scratch him behind the ears when they thought no one else would notice. The gruff old Mystic even crouched down and pulled a bit of dried meat from a belt pouch to feed him.

"Whence have you come?" he asked us as he stroked Oku's fur. "Have you any news of the civil war?"

"We rode straight from Huzen," I told him. "Fighting broke out in the town. The mayor there is loyal to King Jun. Loyalists battle Wojin's forces in the streets."

He gave a heavy sigh and stood. "The tale is the same in many places. Here, though, it is the reverse. I have heard our mayor is in Wojin's pocket, but he has a garrison of Mystics within his walls. He cannot declare for the false king while we have a sword to his throat, as it were."

Dryleaf clucked his tongue. "But that seems precarious for you, if he were to receive reinforcements. Is it safe to remain here?"

The man shrugged. "No one dons the red cloak for safety. Service to Her Majesty is all I desire."

"And a grand service you provide, I am sure," said Dryleaf. He grasped at empty air until the man took his hand. "I am called Dryleaf."

The man shook his hand firmly. "I am Gang of the family Hua, and you are too kind." His gaze turned to Mag and me. "Who might the two of you be?"

"This is Chao, and I am Kanohari."

"And you are here to join the militia?" he asked.

Mag and I gave each other a glance. It seemed Kun had already begun assembling a force here in Taitou. That would make it easier to join him, or so I hoped.

Before we could answer Gang, the door to the guardhouse opened. In stepped Kun, followed by two Mystics in cloaks with their hoods drawn up. Kun wore the same unquenchable smile as when we had seen him last.

"Sky above and dark below," he chirped. "I had not thought to see the three of you again so soon."

I matched his smile with one of my own. "But you did expect to see us. I suppose you understood things better than we did when you asked us to join the High King's fight."

"I have a gift for understanding things," he said. "And yet, I am eager to gain greater knowledge of the three of you, who have returned from your search for your friend. I confess that I am most curious as to why."

"We have reconsidered your offer," said Mag. "We wish to join your fight against the Shades."

Kun's sunny demeanor dampened somewhat at that. "Oh? And what of the friend you sought?"

I shrugged. "She was safe and sound on the coast.

We found her in Brekkur, but she had long been reunited with her family. It was on our way back that the war broke out, and we reconsidered the position we took in our last chat with you."

"Hm," said Kun, tapping his chin. "The strange part is, most folk in Dorsea do not see our battle as being against the Shades. At present, folk either side with Wojin, or they remain loyal to King Jun and his son, who may still be alive."

This put me ill at ease. We had indeed spoken as if we had some inside knowledge of the war that most would not possess. Fortunately, Dryleaf rallied to save us.

"My friends are no masters of statecraft or politics," he put in. "But I have wandered these nine kingdoms a great deal longer than they. From all we have heard, it seems clear to me that the Shades are the true threat and the power behind Wojin's treachery. If the Shades fell, I doubt this civil war would last much longer. And since the Mystics are servants of the High King above all, it seemed to me that you would be most interested in such a course. That is why I suggested to them that we return here and that they enlist in your service."

Kun's smile remained strong as he considered these words for a long moment. His gaze moved slowly between the three of us as if he was trying to read our intentions in our expressions.

"So you are against Wojin, are you?" he said at last.

"Certainly, if he pits his strength against the High King," I said.

"If that is the case," said Kun, "then do you mind telling me why you attacked loyalist soldiers?"

Mag and I were too astonished to speak. And at that moment, one of Kun's Mystics stepped forwards and drew back his hood. The heavy scar on his left cheek was familiar, as was his stout frame, and soon I placed him. He was the young Mystic we had met at the Taitou gates the first time we came here. As I studied him more closely now, I could see that his face shared Kun's features. It seemed they were relatives.

"Lieutenant Zhen," said Kun. "Are these the ones you told me of?"

"They are, Captain," said the Mystic. "I came to the gate in Huzen just in time to see these two—not the old man—attack the guards. They forced the gate open and fled, even while fighting raged in the streets behind them."

Kun fixed a steely gaze upon us. "You followed them to Huzen. Did they ever visit a friend on the coast? In Brekkur?"

Zhen shook his head. "They did not, Captain. That was a lie."

I cursed under my breath. Zhen must have followed us from Taitou to Huzen, looking for us to betray the King's law. He must have had exceptional woodcraft for me to have never noticed him tailing us. It seemed Mag had been right—Kun suspected us from the first.

Kun's brow furrowed, even while his smile remained. "To be clear: did the guards at the gate attack these people, nephew?"

Zhen's expression darkened. "They did not, *Captain.* These two struck first after the guards tried to enforce their orders from the mayor, who is loyal to King Jun."

"Now, hold on," I said quickly. "We were in the middle of a strange town, trapped in a battle about which we knew nothing. We had no idea the guards and mayor were loyal to King Jun. We did not even know about the civil war. We only sought to escape the fighting."

"By harming servants of the King's law," said Kun, nodding as if I was making perfect sense. "Of course, I wish to believe you. But there is, of course, no reason to do so, since you have lied about so much else. There is every possibility you knew exactly what you were doing. And that, I am afraid, is a risk I cannot take. *Guards!*"

The last word was a battlefield bark, so sharp and sudden that I jumped. The door flew open, and four Mystics entered with blades drawn. The constables in the room drew their weapons with grim looks on their faces.

Beside me, Mag had tensed to fight. Dryleaf's head swung back and forth, trying to read the room from the sounds around us. Oku backed up against my legs, whining. But before things could go any further, I threw up my hands towards Kun and the Mystics at the door.

"Wait!" I said, as sharp as Kun had. It stopped everyone for an instant, but that was enough for me to continue. "Listen. When last we were here, we told you we used to be mercenaries. That was true, but not the whole of it. This is Mag, known to many as the Uncut Lady. I know at least some of you must have heard of her."

They froze on the spot, though Kun had given them no order to halt. His eyes went wide as he looked upon Mag with fresh wonder.

"That is right," I went on, more slowly now. "If you have heard of her, you know she did not have to leave a single guard alive at that gate in Huzen. Yet she did them no lasting harm, but only left them with a few lumps. She could kill everyone in this room right now if she wanted to. Or she could do the same to you as she did to those guards, getting us out of here without spilling a drop of blood."

The air in the room felt thick as butter, and still, no one moved—except Kun, who licked his lips.

"I believe she could," he said, "if tales of her exploits have not been exaggerated. Yet neither of you moves. What are we to make of this?"

"We have no wish to hurt anyone," I said. "We told you we came to help, and that is the truth. Take us into your service. With the Uncut Lady on your side, you are that much closer to victory, whatever your aims."

Again the room went silent. Mag, for her part, had not moved since I started speaking. The mask was down, her battle-trance rendering her emotionless, cold, calculating. I hoped she would restrain herself until we were sure there was no other way out of the room.

Still, Kun stared at us. But now his focus was mainly on Mag, and his perpetual smile had faded. I saw calculation in his eyes: factors weighed, measured, and tossed aside one by one.

At last, he managed to summon his smile again.

"I believe that you do not wish to harm us," he said, "or it would have happened already. But neither can I trust you, what with you having attacked soldiers under the king's command. Even your offer now veils a threat of violence, like the peacetime treaty of a warlike king. And I cannot discount the possibility that you might be spies. I am afraid I must ask you to leave. And if you are on the side of the King's law, you will do so without a fuss. If not . . . well. I suppose I shall learn firsthand whether the Uncut Lady deserves her reputation."

I was at a loss. It was heartbreaking to think of leaving Taitou empty-handed. We would be no better off than we were when we fled Huzen, and we would have wasted even more time into the bargain. Worse yet, Kun would doubtless send word of this to the Mystics across the land. We had to persuade him, but I was at a loss.

But Dryleaf was not. Again he spoke as a bard, his voice filling the room and invigorating the heart.

"You are making a mistake, and you are shirking your duty," he said.

The air in the room, already chilled with the outside air, seemed to grow colder still. Kun's eyes flashed.

"You are turning away two fighters who could turn the tide of a battle," Dryleaf went on. "And former military officers who could train this militia you are recruiting."

Kun's smile widened. "Oh?" he said. "You think you can train my fighters into worthy soldiers?"

Mag dropped her mask. I saw the tension bleed out of her, and at the same time, I felt some of it dissipate in the air, making me sigh with relief.

"I can," she said earnestly. "I can turn your farm boys and smiths' daughters into a force of warriors you can *use.*"

Kun deliberated on that for a moment. But then he shook his head.

"It is too great a risk."

"Watch us as close as you like," I said. "What harm could we do if you are vigilant around us?"

Kun's smile showed teeth. "You two should know better than most that a soldier you cannot trust is worse than useless."

I gave an exasperated sigh, but mostly because he was right. "Then give us a chance to prove you can trust us! A week, Captain. Just give us a week."

His brows rose. "A week? And just what do you think you could do in that time?"

That gave me pause, and I shared a look with Mag. To be honest, the words had slipped out of me in desperation. I did not know that I *could* do anything with just a week. But Mag answered to cover my sudden silence.

"In a week, I can train a fighter who can beat one of your Mystics."

Kun's smile broke into a full laugh. "I assume you are joking."

"I am not," said Mag. "Let me prove it."

Inwardly, I groaned. Ten days to turn farmers into fighters who could beat hardened Mystics? I would have balked at the challenge when I was in my prime, and I had not trained soldiers in well over a decade. It seemed impossible. But we had little choice.

"Hm," said Kun, stroking his chin. "I must admit, such a feat would impress me. And yet, there remains the matter of your dishonesty. Why should I believe your intentions or your boasts, when you have lied about your purpose in Dorsea since the first moment I met you?"

Mag fixed him with a look. "You strike me as one who knows the value of truth sparsely given. When first we met, you suspected us. You sent one of your agents to follow us and see if we got up to any mischief. Yet when you spoke to us, you were all smiles and courtesy."

Kun tilted his head. "No circumstance demands ill manners."

"Just so," said Mag. "But we had no reason to trust you. If you know anything about the Shades, you know that they have slithered into many corners across the nine kingdoms. We thought it better to keep our intentions far from our lips, lest word of it reach them. I regret it now, but I would do it again."

All was silent for a long moment. Then, finally, Kun shook his head ever so slightly.

"A bit of the truth is better than none, I suppose. Very well. You shall be provisional officers in my force. In one week, there shall be a trial by combat. You choose one of your soldiers, and I will choose a Mystic against whom to pit them. If your champion wins, you can consider yourselves enlisted. If my champion wins, you will be on your way and trouble me no more."

There it was. A week did not seem anywhere near enough time. But it was what we had.

And Mag, of course, smiled and said, "We have a deal."

NINE

We had arrived in Taitou late in the day, and so we rested overnight before Kun brought us to his forces. He made us pay for a room at the inn, but it seemed unwise to complain. In the morning, Kun fetched us and led us towards his encampment on the northwestern end of town. Dryleaf and Oku came along with us. I was afraid Kun might order them to stay behind, but he said nothing.

We had not spent a great deal of time in Taitou before, but even so, I could tell things were different. There was a tension in the air that had not been there before. People in the streets had a new sense of purpose, an excitement above the day-to-day lives of common folk. Wagons and carts moved weapons from smiths and town stores to Kun's encampment. Smithies rang with the music of hammers, and there was an extra note of urgency in every haggling merchant trying to extract more coin from each deal.

As we followed Kun out the western gate, we saw the land that had become his army's training grounds. His troops were housed and fed in the city, but Kun had commandeered a few farms outside the walls to give them a space to train in weapons fighting, as well as to practice marching and moving in formation.

There looked to be at least four hundreds of soldiers formed into ragtag groups. Some were in lines, while some were paired off and battering each other with blunt swords. As we drew closer, I spotted red cloaks moving among the crowds. There were dishearteningly few of them.

"How many Mystics do you have?" I asked Kun.

He looked over at me, his immortal smile never faltering. "Forty, all told. Only ten of them are of the rank of knight. Those, I have assigned as lieutenants or sergeants in this little force. The remaining Mystic warriors are my unit, to form a strong center on any battlefield we may find ourselves upon."

Mag nodded. "That is wise. And how many soldiers have answered your call?"

"Four hundreds and three scores," said Kun. "Not

so many, but more than my officers can manage easily. I am quite thrilled to have your help, even if you only remain for a few days."

"We are sure you are," I said, letting a hint of sarcasm shine through. "But if you fear we are spies, why would you tell us the composition of your forces so exactly?"

That made Kun laugh. "Oh, really. Any farmer in his fields could get a good count of my soldiers with hardly any effort. If you worry about the security of information, be assured that I do not intend to tell you anything about my aims, intentions, or plans."

Mag's brows rose. "How heartening."

As we came to the training grounds, Kun gave a tremendous barking shout. *"Tou!"*

Everyone within a span of him jerked, all the soldiers turning to look in his direction. Most of the regular militia simply stared, but every Mystic placed their hand over their heart in salute. The closest redcloak came straight to us, and when he reached Kun, he bowed. He was not as old as we were, but he was not exactly young, either. His frame was impressive, and he wore a short goatee, neatly trimmed, with long hair bundled into a tail that fell just past his shoulders.

"Captain," he said. "How may I serve?"

Kun turned to the two of us. "This is Tou, one of my lieutenants," he said cheerfully. "Tou, please meet Albern of the family Telfer, and Mag, and their friend Dryleaf. I have a wager with them, of sorts. They are to be assigned as sergeants, and each is to train a squadron of militia for the coming campaign. If in one week, they can train a fighter who can defeat one of our order in combat, they are allowed to stay on as part of our force. Otherwise, they will have to leave us."

Tou arched an eyebrow at that. "As you say, ser. I will see to it that they drill hard."

"Oh, do not trouble yourself overmuch," said Kun, smiling wider. "They are the ones being put to the test here, not you. After all, I have no cause to doubt *your* loyalty. But do see to it that they stay out of trouble, will you?"

With that, he turned on his heel and walked briskly away. Tou watched him go for only a moment before turning to us.

"I am Tou of the family Shi," he said, extending his hand. "Well met, even if in strange circumstance."

I took his wrist. "Well met indeed," I said.

"You look to be an archer," he said, and then turned to Mag. "And I would guess that you prefer to fight up close?"

"Right you are, on both counts," I said.

"A Calentin archer is always welcome," he said. "Come. A few of my squadrons lack Mystics to lead them, and I have been trying to manage all of them on my own. Let me introduce them to you."

He led us through the training grounds at a slow pace, in consideration of Dryleaf. Nearby, rows of stuffed targets had been lined up for archers. Too, several large practice rings had been outlined for sword and spear training.

Many people were hard at practice now, and I saw redcloaks moving among them—Mystics giving instructions and barking orders. Some paused in their duties and hailed Tou, waving, and he always waved back. He looked to be a popular man and a respected one, and I hoped that would bode well for us.

"Our forces number five companies," Tou went on. "Each company is led by a lieutenant—me, in your case. Lieutenants wield five squadrons of around fifteen, and each squadron is led by a sergeant. Only a handful of the sergeants are Mystics. The rest are veterans of King Jun's army or former mercenaries." He grimaced. "Or I suppose I should say returned mercenaries, for they are all taking coin to fight once again."

"Not the greatest force we have served in, but not the smallest, either," said Mag. "If Kun can find a worthy target to point us at, we may be able to do quite some damage to the enemy."

"That is the hope," said Tou. He cocked his head. "Though as a matter of etiquette, I must ask that you refer to him as Captain Zhou in the future."

Mag nodded quickly. "Of course. Our soldiering habits are rusty, but I will endeavor to polish them."

At last, we came to a stop in front of two groups of people. A gaggle of archers stood to our right, awkwardly firing shafts at the row of targets before them. To the left, some fighters with practice swords and shields were drilling, though their swings were clumsy and slow.

It was our first chance to get a good look at what Kun had to work with, and it was not entirely heartening. Most of these "fighters" looked to be anything but. They were farmers, craftsmen, and shopkeepers. Every so often, I would glimpse the brawny arms and solid frames of blacksmiths or woodsfolk. But they were few and far between, and they were as helpless with their swords as anyone else. Smiths are usually skilled at crafting steel, but not wielding it.

"Green Squadron! Black Squadron!" Tou's voice ripped through the morning air. "Form up!"

The people around us stopped what they were doing and looked at Tou curiously. One by one, they approached and formed into two ragged lines. They were slow about it, seeming more confused than interested.

"Green Squadron," said Tou, addressing the swordfighters and waving his hand at Mag. "You have a new sergeant. Her name is Mag, and she will see to your training from now on. Black Squadron, you will now be reporting to Albern of the family Telfer."

Dryleaf raised a hand. "And where are my soldiers, if I may be so bold?"

That got a chuckle from Tou, as well as from many of the assembled militia. "An oversight on my part, grandfather," said Tou. "I will find a squadron for you as soon as I am able." He turned back to Mag and me. "You will report to me at the end of each day. Muster is at dawn every morning, and while we train, your soldiers are expected on duty ten days a week. Any questions?"

"No, ser," said Mag and I.

"Excellent." Tou gave a small sigh and looked our squadrons over. "Get to work, then. You have much to do."

"Ser!" Mag and I snapped off salutes, which I thought were passingly suitable for how out of practice we were. Tou waved and left us, heading towards his other units.

Each of us went to our squadrons. I eyed the archers before me critically, and Mag did the same with her swordfighters. My mind began to fall into old habits, and I noticed myself picking out those who stood poised and ready, those who seemed lost, and those who seemed lazy.

"All right, recruits," said Mag at last. "We have watched you dance. Now you will learn how to fight."

As we began our training, Dryleaf headed off into Taitou with Oku, seeking information. I led my squadron over to a row of targets, while Mag took hers to the practice rings. Some of the archers began to line up and prepare to fire, but I called them back.

"Hold a moment. You know my name, but I have not learned any of yours. I can hardly instruct you if I must resort to calling out 'You there!' every time."

I pointed to the closest of them, a large man whose black skin and great height spoke of Feldemarian descent. His thick locs were bound into a tail that swayed when he moved. "What is your name?"

He looked uncomfortably to either side of him as if making sure I was talking to him and not someone else. "Chausiku, ser."

"Well met, Chausiku," I said. "If you do not mind my asking, why are you here?"

Chausiku blinked. "Ser? I answered the call to defend Dorsea from—"

"Forgive me, that is not what I meant," I said. "I mean that you look to be at least ten hands tall, and your shoulders are almost as broad as my bow is long. Why are you here, in this squadron, rather than with the swordfighters?"

His dark face darkened still further in a flush. "I am a hunter by trade, ser. I am skilled with a bow already, and I have never wielded a sword, and do not want to."

"Well, you shall have to learn, regardless," I told him. "Bowcraft is all well and good, but if the enemy gets close, you shall be glad of a blade with which to defend yourself. Still, I am glad you are already familiar with your weapon. Who else here already knows something of archery?"

Seven of them threw their hands up, but one woman did so faster than the rest. She was short and slight, with black hair cut to sweep forwards rakishly. Her skin looked only recently sun-browned, as though she were more used to spending her days indoors. Her eyes were sharp and focused on me like a hawk's. I pointed to her. "You. What is your name?"

"Jian, ser," she said, lifting her chin slightly.

"And where did you learn to shoot?"

"My father was a hunter and a bowyer," she said. "I studied bowcraft under him, and I still work with him in his shop."

"A bowyer!" I said, delighted. "I am one myself—or was, until almost a year ago. We shall have to trade techniques sometime."

"I would be glad to, ser," she said. Then her smile twisted. "And I am not afraid to learn how to kill up close, as some others are."

That gave me pause, and I noticed another flush creeping into Chausiku's cheeks—but this time from anger rather than embarrassment.

"Well, I am afraid I must disappoint you, as well," I said, and raised my voice to address the entire squadron. "The most important thing you will learn from me is not how to kill. That is something you will learn as an unfortunate matter of course. But I hope you will focus on another skill that is much more important. First and foremost, I will teach all of you how to stay alive."

Jian frowned and pushed her hair back off her forehead. "It seems to me that the best way to stay alive is to kill one's enemy so that they are no threat."

"And do you imagine your enemy will stand there and let you plant an arrow in their eye?" I countered. "I would say rather that the best way to kill your foe is to stay alive long enough to do it. And besides, there are many more dangers in a campaign than the soldiers you will face on the battlefield. Hunger and cold, and especially disease, have killed far more soldiers than any battle in the long pages of history. Yet the bards will never sing songs of dysentery. Being a good soldier mostly means keeping yourself healthy until battle finally comes. If you do not learn how to survive a forced march, no tricks of archery I could teach you will be of the least use. Do you understand?"

They gave me a scattered chorus of "Yes, ser." Jian mumbled it along with the rest of them, but I wondered if she genuinely grasped my meaning, or if she even wished to. I decided to let it go for the moment. I was new to these people, and it is an inferior officer whose first action is to throw their weight around.

"Very good," I said. "Now, has anyone here fought before? Any veterans at all?"

To my dismay, only one man raised his hand: a man slightly older than me, whose pale skin and flaming red hair and beard marked him as a Heddan. He looked around at the rest of the squadron, and he seemed surprised to be the only one with his hand up. That told me the unit had only recently formed, and most of them had not had time to meet or learn much about each other.

"Well, that is one, at least," I said, trying to hide my disappointment. "What is your name?"

"Hallan, ser," he said crisply, drawing up straight. He spoke with the rolling, lilting quality and strange affects of Hedgemond, and his great beard jumped when he talked. "I'm a veteran of King Kashonnel's army in my youth, though thass nearly a score of years ago now. But I saw action, ser."

"I am glad to hear it," I said. "Do you remember your training drills, Hallan?"

He flashed a grin to reveal bright teeth, but also two gaps in them. "I'm sure they'll come back quick, ser."

His smile was infectious, and I found myself returning it. "Very good. Then let us finish our instructions and get to work. We have much to do and not enough time for it."

TEN

I QUICKLY LEARNED THE NAMES OF THE REST OF MY squadron. But now, these many years later, I cannot remember all of them. That is the way of things, I fear, and the same is true for all the mercenary companies with which I ever fought. Memory is fickle. Unless a particular story stitched one of my companions tightly in my mind, I forgot them eventually.

Mag and I launched into training our soldiers with great vigor. We set them to the drills we had done in the Upangan Blades. Victon had been an excellent officer, quickly able to turn even the greenest warriors into passable fighters.

And the greenest warriors seemed to be what Kun had given us. Both Mag and I struggled to maintain hope through our dismay. Hallan was the only person in either of our units with any experience in a proper fighting force. I could not tell if Kun had stacked the deck against our success or if our soldiers were representative of the entire army. Something told me it was a combination of the two.

From the start, I began to get a feel for the personalities of those in my squadron. Jian, for example, had a bit of a nasty streak and a frightful temperament.

"You shoot for the head too often," I told her once. "Of course, you will kill a foe if you strike them between the eyes, but it is a much smaller target. The chest is a more reliable hit, and it will remove your enemy from the fight just as quickly."

A savage twist came to her mouth, and I could not quite have called it a smile. "That seems sensible. But what about gut shots, then? I have heard those are likely to kill, and painfully. I would not mind letting these dark-damned traitors suffer before ending them."

I frowned. "They are painful, that is true. But still not as good as the chest. If you shoot for the gut, and your aim is low, you are likely to strike the belt or buckle. That may keep your shot from bringing them down. And if you are off by a wider margin, your arrow might pass between the legs and miss. We aim for the chest because it is the largest target, with the widest margin for error."

Again she nodded, and she did not seem to notice my unease. "That is sensible, as well. The chest it is, then." She showed her teeth for a moment and pushed back her rakish hair. "And then if I miss, I may be fortunate and hit the gut after all."

Chausiku was next to her in the line, and his locs swayed as he turned to glower down at her—far down, for she was less than eight hands tall. "Our purpose is not savagery," he said. "We are here to save the kingdom, not become torturers."

Jian turned to face him. "I am here to punish traitors, not to coddle them."

"Enough, from both of you!" I snapped. "Turn your ire into action. Any more arguing, and you shall be running laps around the training grounds."

"Yes, ser," grated Chausiku.

"I am not afraid of running," muttered Jian. But she turned her attention back to the practice targets, and Chausiku did the same.

Hallan had a more challenging time with his drills at first. I stepped up behind him on that first day and watched as two of his shots whizzed by the dummy.

"Rubbish," he muttered, his beard twitching. Then he noticed me standing there and lowered his bow, straightening up. "Ser. What can I do for ye?"

"I am only observing," I told him. "You have good form. How long has it been since you practiced?"

"Long enough that when last I did, my eyes still worked," he groused. "Form's easy enough, iss getting the target sighted thass tripping me up."

"Why do you not have spectacles?" I said. "Taitou may not be a great city, but surely there is a glass-weaver in town."

"Sure enough there is," he said with a nod. "Juss never needed them much, I suppose. I've been a woodsman for years now, and I can see plenty well enough to bring down a tree. And iss simple living, so I never had much in the way of extra coin to pay for glass."

"Well, you shall need them if you are to fulfill your duty now," I said. "And the coin for it can come from the Mystics. I will speak with Tou this evening and arrange it."

Hallan looked pleasantly surprised, and he bowed, his beard pushing into his chest. "Well, my thanks to you then, ser." He grunted. "Spectacles, on my ugly old face. Who'd've guessed it."

It was not long before I came to treat Hallan as my unofficial second-in-command. He had a good head on his shoulders, and he could make peace if tensions rose among the squadron—particularly with Chausiku and Jian. When I relayed an order through him, my soldiers obeyed as if it had come straight from my mouth. I tried not to favor him too heavily, of course, for I feared the others might grow jealous. But in fact, I think it rather endeared me to them. They seemed to believe that if I relied on Hallan, I must be someone of sound judgement.

But while I did my duty in training my archers, I was much more concerned with Mag's swordfighters. Kun's test would be combat in the ring, not a test of archery, and we had to pass.

On the third day of our training, Tou came by for inspection. I saw him heading for Mag's squadron, and I turned to Hallan.

"Hallan, I am going to speak with the lieutenant," I told him. "If you need me, send someone to fetch me."

"Yesser," he said with a nod, and nocked another arrow.

I went running after Tou and reached him just before he reached Mag's unit. He saw me coming and gave a nod without asking why I was there; I suspect he could guess.

Mag was standing at the edge of a ring, and two men were training in the middle of it. She looked up as Tou and I approached, and she snapped off a salute to him.

"Ser."

"Sergeant," said Tou. "How goes the training? Are you in need of anything?"

"I would enjoy more time to work with them and at least one fighter who had seen action before," said Mag. "But since I do not think those are things you can provide, I will not request them of you."

Tou nodded. "Fair enough. Sad to say, we are all somewhat green here. I myself have never seen combat on the field. The two of you may be the most experienced fighters in the whole force." He pointed at the two men in the ring behind Mag. "Who are these?"

Mag pointed to the younger combatant. He was a strong man, wearing a sleeveless shirt that left his bronzed arms glistening. His black hair was cropped close and dripping with sweat. As I watched, he swiped the sweat away, never taking his eyes from his foe.

"That is Dibu," said Mag. "His opponent is Jie. They are among the better specimens in my squadron. I have tried to pair each fighter up with someone close to them in skill so that all of them get the most benefit from each training session."

Dibu lunged, swinging a horizontal strike. Jie got his shield up, but Dibu managed to catch the edge of it. Jie's shield arm flew wide. As he stumbled back, Dibu pressed forwards. His blade circled around and up towards Jie's face.

I tensed, but Dibu controlled the swipe. It stopped just short of Jie's eye. Jie recoiled, and his foot came down in a puddle of slushy snow. While he was off balance, Dibu kicked his gut. Jie fell, his sword and shield clattering from his hands. Dibu stepped up and pointed his blade at the larger man's face.

"Good!" called Mag. "Reset, and do it again. Jie, you must study your battlefield always. Know where your footing is safe, and where it is precarious. Mud can win a fight faster than skill."

"Yesser," said Jie.

He reached out a hand, and Dibu helped pull him to his feet. But when Dibu looked over to see the three of us there watching him, including Tou, he suddenly seemed embarrassed. His bronzed face flushed, and he quickly turned away.

Tou cleared his throat. "That one does not like performing," he said, stroking his goatee. "Yet he focused well enough during the fight. Who else do you count among your best?"

Mag arched an eyebrow and motioned for Tou and me to follow her. "I have one of particular note. Her name is Li. She has never fought in a real battle before, but her mother was a soldier in King Jun's army, and she taught Li many forms. Between that and the girl's natural talent, Li certainly has the greatest skill of anyone in my squadron. I expect to rely on her to help me teach the rest of them."

I could see at once that Mag spoke true. Li was paired up with another woman, and both of them were light of build but wiry. Yet Li was far more quick and nimble on her feet than her opponent, darting back and forth like a serpent. First her blade was above, then below, and then sweeping in from the side. It was all her opponent could do to keep the sword away from her padded armor, and she could not do so forever.

With the speed of liquid thunder, Li spun around

her foe's clumsy strike. The flat of her blade crashed into the small of the other woman's back. She fell face-down in the dirt. Immediately Li straightened, heaved a deep breath, and sheathed her sword.

"A good strike," called Tou. Both women snapped around to look at him. "But you relented the moment you had an advantage. You cannot do the same thing in a real fight."

Li's eyes widened, and she bowed. "Of course, ser. It is just . . . well, I already felled her."

"And an enemy felled can rise once more if you do not finish them," said Mag. "Again. And this time, do not pull back until the fight is over." She waved at the two of them to begin and then turned to confer with Tou and me.

"She moves like you, Mag," I told her.

Mag looked somewhat miffed. "She is quick enough on her feet, I suppose."

"Well, everything seems to be in order," said Tou. "Better than in order, in fact. I still do not entirely understand why the captain made this wager with you, but I find myself hoping you will win."

"As do we, ser," I said. "Do you have any advice for us? Any tips that might secure a victory?"

Tou shrugged. "I have no hidden information, if that is what you mean. The terms are rather clear, and the captain seems confident you shall not beat him. I can do little more than encourage you to do your best, and hope."

I sighed. "Well, if that is the best we can do, then we shall do it. Thank you, Lieutenant."

Tou nodded and left us. I looked to Mag.

"What do you think? Do we have a chance?"

Mag looked at Li, who was again trading blows with her opponent in the ring.

"A chance? Mayhap. Ask me again in a few more days."

ELEVEN

But of course, Mag and I were not the only ones joining together with allies.

To the north of us, close to the Feldemarian border, Rogan had encamped with many of his soldiers. As I have mentioned, they were the ones raiding into Feldemar. They crossed the border in Dorsean uniforms, attacking farms and the caravans of lesser merchant families. In this way, they had been fomenting discord between the two kingdoms and drawing King Jun's attention to the area. This distracted Jun from the coup that Wojin had been planning under his very nose.

Now that open war had broken out in the kingdom, however, Rogan's strategy would change radically. And it was while he was concocting these plans that Kaita found him at last.

Rogan stepped out of his broad tent and into the open air, walking through the center of the camp. All around him, Shades stopped in their tracks and saluted, hands over their fists. He nodded to each, giving them a stern smile that warmed their hearts.

But as he neared the center of the camp, it seemed as if a thought struck him. His steps faltered, slowed, and then stopped. Though no one else had heard anything, Rogan tilted his head back to look into the sky, and the faint smile on his lips fell away.

A raven swooped out of the grey clouds to land on the dirt before him. Some Shades looked on curiously, and then their eyes bugged with surprise as Kaita emerged from the bird's form. But Rogan looked as if he had expected her.

"Kaita," he said. Warm. Welcoming. Grief-stricken.

"Brother," said Kaita through a raspy throat.

She had been ragged five days ago when she received Rogan's summons. She looked worse now. Her clothes were new, but she was dirty and wasted, and gaunt beyond what Rogan had ever seen of her. Still she tried to stand tall, her head up and her shoulders back. But it was a poor showing, and her limbs shook with the effort of attempting it.

Rogan saw it in her eyes, and he motioned her back towards his tent. Kaita followed him without a word. They passed through the camp quickly, and it was all Kaita could do to ignore the stares of the other Shades. Rogan pulled back the flap of his tent, letting Kaita step through first.

He had barely followed her in before Kaita broke. Her face twisted with pain as tears etched burning lines down her face. She paced to the back of the tent and whirled, walking back up to Rogan and glaring up into his face.

"Weeks," she said, managing to keep her voice down so that those outside could not hear her fury. "Weeks I have been searching for you. I went to every encampment I knew of, every stronghold where our siblings have gathered in strength. No one knew where you were, and that is not like you. No one knew how to send you a message, and that is not like you. You left me alone. Alone in the wilderness, with two people hungry for my death, and after you *promised—*"

Her voice broke, and she turned from him. Rogan laid a hand on her shoulder from behind, but she jerked away.

"Do not *touch* me."

"You were never alone," said Rogan softly. "I have heard many reports of your long journey. In Lan Shui, and then Opara, and then Kahuanga, you were with our siblings always."

"But I had no one I *cared* about," snapped Kaita.

"Not after Dellek died in Lan Shui. I did not have Tagata, or you, or Father."

Rogan's face grew stony. Kaita knew he wished to admonish her, to tell her that she should care about all the Shades as if they were family. But he held the words back. Mayhap he knew that was not what she needed to hear.

"We made a plan together, Kaita," he said. "And we agreed upon it in Northwood, before you set out on your long road."

"That plan never satisfied me, and you know it."

"And do you think I was happy with it? Do you think I enjoyed making the promises I did? I would rather have had you by my side all this long while. But Mag and Albern were more important to you, and I knew that, and so I let you go your own way. That is the nature of compromise, Kaita, of being part of a family. You and I both thought you had a hope in Northwood, and then in Kahuanga."

Kaita's chin trembled as she looked up at him. Yes, she had thought she had a hope. Better than a hope. How could she have foreseen that Mag would be able to defeat her lion form? How could she have predicted that Mag would find a way to survive even the trolls? They were monsters of campfire legend.

But her plans had failed her, just as her strength had failed her every time she and Mag came to blows. She could not win, no matter what she did. Dark below, she could not even find a way to kill *me,* and I was no warrior of legend. Even my sister Ditra had survived Kaita's attempts to kill her.

The seed of doubt had already rooted in Kaita's mind. Now, for the first time, it ensnared her own idea of herself, becoming a corruption that threatened to destroy the last shreds of her conviction.

Yet Kaita was not the sort of person to accept responsibility when she could instead cast blame. And so her expression went from lost to furious once more, and again she stepped towards Rogan.

"You never gave me the chance I wanted," she hissed. "I told you from the beginning what I need, what I knew I would require in the end. Now I have spent months in useless flight, and you have lost scores of your precious siblings. They have exposed our plans in two kingdoms, all because you would not listen to me until it was too late. *That* is why I demanded your promise. Because I knew all along what it would come to in the end, even if you were too foolish to see it."

She stopped suddenly, fearing she had gone too far. But no anger came into Rogan's eyes, only a more profound sadness. And Kaita wondered if he knew all the unspoken thoughts that had flitted through her head before she finally lashed out.

"I wanted to give you a chance to change—to learn *why* you must change," he said quietly. "Since before we met, you have tried to do everything alone. You wish to rely only on yourself, to have so much power that no one can challenge you. Once, you were loyal to a family, and they betrayed you. You have feared to rely on others ever since. But those you hunt—Mag, and especially Albern—they know the value of friendship, of companions on whom they can depend. They know what it is to fight as part of something greater than themselves, to serve without the desire of personal advantage."

"I have served the Shades loyally," said Kaita, a note of desperation in her voice.

"And you know I love you for it," said Rogan. "And I know you love me, and some other few of our number. But I am no fool, Kaita. Your own goals have always come first. The moment you saw your opportunity, you abandoned everything to pursue what you had long desired. You would break the world to achieve your ends, and you would cast all of us aside to do it. That is why your foes defeat you, Kaita, over and over again. And you will never win until you come to your senses. You must tear down your walls—I cannot do it for you. But I can tell you that leaving yourself open to betrayal is better than living your life alone."

Silent sobs began to wrack her body long before he finished. In one corner of his large tent was a small desk and chair, and she stumbled over to sit. Rogan knelt beside her, wrapping her shoulders in his massive, powerful hands, and he let her cry. In time she turned and buried her face in his tunic, and he held her like the sister she was to him.

But when at last her tears subsided, and her fists

loosened their desperate grip on his clothes, she looked up at him. Her eyes were clear once more, and there was a hunger in them.

"I hear you, brother," said Kaita. "I am ready to join the cause with my whole heart, and I am ready to accept the help I know I can find nowhere else. The help that our father promised."

Rogan's heart broke, for he knew that she had not truly understood him. And for a moment, he felt the temptation to refuse her. But he could not. He had made a promise—not only to Kaita, but to the Lord. And though he could not see as far as his father, he knew that he must keep faith with both of them if the Shades were to achieve their ends.

Even if it came at the cost of Kaita's life.

Gently he pulled her hands from his tunic, and then he went to the foot of his bedroll. He had a small chest there, which he opened now using the silver key from his belt.

Out of the chest, he pulled a small packet wrapped in brown cloth.

Kaita's eyes lit at once. "You have them with you now?"

"I always do," he said. "And recently, in particular, I have ensured I had an extra store on hand, for I knew you would come to claim them. I have never forgotten you. Even when I could not see you, you must believe me: you were never out of my mind, and I never abandoned you."

Kaita nodded, but it was an absentminded gesture, for her eyes were fixed on the stones. Again Rogan sighed, and he came over to place the packet in her hand.

"They are yours," he said. "As I promised. But now I must demand a promise from you in turn."

Her eyes flashed as she looked up at him. "And what is that?"

"You must use them at the right time," said Rogan. "Do not plunge after Mag or Albern into the middle of a host of foes. You may kill them if you do, but even with the stones, you will not escape alive. Draw them out first. Use the magestones when they are alone, isolated—even from each other, if you can manage it. Strike only when you are certain of survival. Do not throw your life away trying to end theirs."

For a moment, she hesitated, and Rogan feared she would refuse. He had no right to demand this of her, not really. Already he had sworn to give her the stones, without this condition. But as she looked up at him, Rogan saw understanding in her eyes, as well as compassion.

She stood from the chair and stepped forwards, laying her head against his chest. His thick arms wrapped around her shoulders.

"I promise," she said, "for I know you ask out of kindness and concern. And I will make another promise: I vow to live up to the faith you have shown in me, and that I know Father still has for me."

"And he will until the end," Rogan murmured. His voice was thick with grief, but he knew she would mistake it for reverence. "Now go. Tagata leads the greater part of our forces west. Join her there, and you will soon have the opportunity you seek."

Kaita looked up at him in wonder. "Albern and Mag will be there? But I thought they were to the south, closer to the Birchwood."

Despite the pain in his heart, he smiled down at her. "They will meet Tagata, and soon."

She lifted a hand and placed it against his cheek. "Thank you, brother," she whispered. "I will not fail you. And I will see you soon."

Quickly she left the tent. In a moment, Rogan heard the flapping of wings as a raven took to the air.

At last, he let his tears come, slow and silent as they worked their way through the lines of his face. Kaita had given him her promise, for she thought it came from his love for her.

But even that promise had been mandated by the Lord.

TWELVE

After the first five days of training, Mag and I took stock of our situation. We were sitting apart from our squadrons, sharing a meal around a campfire. Dryleaf was with us, and Oku had curled up at my feet. The day's rain had faded to a mere drizzle. Our breath misted in the air, dissipating quickly, and our feet squished upon the slushy ground.

"I think you should present Li for Kun's test," I said. "I have seen her against the others. No one can match her speed, and few even come close."

Mag pursed her lips, but after a moment she shook

her head. "I do not think so. She has the skill, but something is missing inside her. Her attention wanders as often as her gaze. Nimble feet and quick hands are all well and good, but a true warrior needs something more."

I frowned and paused in feeding Oku a scrap. "What more do you think she needs?"

"A killer instinct," said Mag. "She never presses the fight hard enough, even when she has an advantage. And when she is on her back foot, she all but gives up. She knows her foe is not really trying to harm her, and it makes her complacent. No matter how many times I tell her to take things more seriously, she does not muster the fire she needs to truly crush her foe."

Oku had been waiting patiently for me to finish handing him the bit of gristle I had pulled out of my bowl. I fed it to him and scratched him behind the ears. "That is mayhap a good thing while that foe is another trainee," I said, "but I see your point. Let us hope she can summon that instinct upon the battlefield and survive such a test. But who, then, gives us the best chance?"

Mag was silent for a moment, and then she gave a slow nod as if answering a question in her mind. "Dibu," she said. "If anyone can secure our position with the Mystics, I think it will be him."

Dryleaf's bushy eyebrows shot up. "Dibu? He seems a good man, from the brief conversations we have had. Yet I thought he had not touched a blade until just under a month ago."

"That is true," said Mag. "Yet now he nearly matches Li's skill. I noticed on the second day that Tou seemed to favor him, and soon I saw one reason why. I think if I focus most of my efforts on him, he will surpass Li. He certainly has better instincts. Though he is only training, he never lets up until his opponent is defeated." A small smile crossed her lips. "Or until *he* is defeated. After all, I sometimes train with him personally."

I chuckled. "There is the modesty I have missed in you."

She scoffed. "As if such a malady has ever plagued me."

"How have things been with you, Dryleaf?" I said. "You have been often in Taitou, and also wandering around the army's encampment. Have you learned anything interesting?"

"Nothing I think would be especially helpful," said Dryleaf. "I am making more progress in the town than in the camp, but there is less information there than here. My best sources are at a house of the Guild of Lovers. They are always glad to welcome a skillfully told story or a good singing voice. And of course, many within Kun's army visit them often, including some of the Mystics. But you know lovers."

"Not particularly," said Mag, smirking.

I chuckled. "They are reticent with their clients' information, is what he means," I said. "And well they should be."

"Indeed," said Dryleaf. "They will tell me only harmless little items—interesting, but not especially useful, and with no names attached. Everyone knows Kun is training this army to go and fight, but no one knows where, or when, or for what purpose. He could mean to march on the capital, but I do not think so. He does not have enough troops."

"I agree," I said. "I still think our first guess is the best one. He means to pursue the Shades."

"And that means he is our best chance to find Kaita," said Mag. Her bowl was empty, and she placed it on the ground beside her as she leaned back on her hands. Oku immediately began to lick it clean. "We *must* win Kun's trial. Let us hope that he does not deliberate overmuch on his choice of a fighter. If he thinks the trial will be easy, and that any of his Mystics can defeat our champion, he may carelessly choose someone Dibu can overcome."

I worried about Kun more and more as the days went on, however. He had begun to come around our part of the camp often, looking in on us as we trained our squadrons. He never failed to be exceedingly polite, and I never saw his broad smile falter. "How goes the training?" he would ask, and I would grit my teeth and reply, "Excellent, Captain. You can see for yourself how they are improving." And Kun would inspect the practice dummies and nod in approval.

He would even go to one or another member of my squadron and give them pointers. "Notice how Albern raises his elbow higher than you? That gives his draw more strength, and it shifts the string less when he looses the arrow. Try to match him." Even if he did not wish us to remain in his company, he seemed determined to gain as much benefit as possible from our instruction.

Of course, he took even greater interest in Mag's swordfighters. He would pace around the edges of her practice rings and call out advice or encouragement as the bouts went on. It made some of the soldiers quite nervous. Li, in particular, did not at all enjoy his presence, and her attention wandered even more than usual. Once, she almost dropped her sword when Kun barked at her to press her attack. I began to understand why Mag did not think Li was the best choice.

Yet Kun seemed to have the same opinion that I had held at first. As the days wore on, he focused most of his attention on Li. He observed her evident skill with the blade and the way she toyed with her opponents rather than finish them off. I hoped he thought she would be our champion and that Dibu would be a surprise.

Mag began to guide his thoughts further in that direction. Whenever Kun would come by for inspection, Mag would drill Li personally. She would push the girl to her limits, but not beyond them, making her look as though she could nearly hold her own in the fight.

But the moment Kun left, Mag would return to Dibu and resume working with him instead.

Tou was a constant presence during our drilling, wandering around the rings while he brushed his fingers through his goatee. He oversaw three other squadrons, but he spent an increasing amount of time with us. He would even help our troops practice, and I came to learn that he was a powerful fighter. Though he lacked a substantial build, he was surprisingly strong—impregnable in defense and ferocious when on the attack. Mag requested him to pair up with Dibu whenever he came by, and I could see the boy's skill begin to grow by leaps and bounds. Tou knocked him into the slushy ground every time, but Dibu lasted longer and longer against him as days went by. Each time they finished, Tou would confer with Mag and me, giving advice on how to prepare Dibu for the test. Mag was always grateful for his insight.

Though it may sound boastful, I think Tou was quite intrigued by us. I know, certainly, that we became friendly in short order. Tou tried to maintain an appropriate level of separation and distance, but no more than one would expect from one's superior officer.

He was a good sort, but I could tell he placed great faith in military discipline. Though he wanted us to join Kun's army, he had no wish to undermine his superior officer. This put him in a difficult position, but he managed it as best he could. For my part, at least, I wanted to help him, and the best way to do that was to succeed in Kun's challenge on our own merits.

Day by day, we drove ourselves and our troops as hard as we could. But the week seemed to wear away incredibly fast.

THIRTEEN

THE DAY OF KUN'S TEST FINALLY CAME.

Usually our squadrons were mustered for drilling before dawn. That day, Tou let us sleep until an hour after sunup. My eyes snapped open the moment I heard the calls outside my tent. I lay there for a moment, reluctant to move. So much rested on today. Dibu might win, and then we would have taken a significant step towards achieving our aims. Or we might fail, and then we would have wasted another week. We would be no better off than we were at the start: alone in Dorsea, with no idea how to find Kaita. In fact, we would be worse off, for she would have had ten extra days to flee, or hide herself, or gather more allies to her side.

I did not know what we would do if that happened. I feared to think what Mag might do. But there was nothing for it now. I sighed and roused myself, dressing quickly and stepping out of the tent.

Our squadrons were already mustering themselves, as they did every day. As I joined Mag and stood before them, I could not deny a small flush of pride at seeing them form up with precision and speed. Tou seemed pleased with our squadrons' discipline, as well.

I heard footsteps behind us and turned. Kun came marching up, two Mystics to either side of him. I recognized one as Zhen, Kun's nephew, the one with a heavy scar on his left cheek. It had been he who reported on our doings in Huzen.

It occurred to me that Zhen might be the one pitted against Mag's champion. That might be good for us. Zhen seemed a capable man, certainly, but it appeared he specialized in espionage. Mayhap Dibu would have the edge against him when it came to a straight fight.

Kun stopped before us, wearing his usual broad smile. "Well! Good morning to all of you. I must commend you on the presentation of your troops. Few squadrons among our forces show such discipline."

"Thank you, Captain," said Tou and Mag at the same time. Mag stopped short, her mouth twisting, and gave Tou a deferential nod. He smiled slightly and went on. "Your recognition honors us. We await your order."

"Well, I have only one order for you today, in truth," said Kun with a chuckle. "It is the day of the test! I doubt you have forgotten."

"No indeed, Captain," said Tou quickly. "We are ready."

"As ready as you will ever be, I suppose," said Kun. "I am sure we all hope that it is enough. Well." His eyes darted to Li. Out of the corner of my eye, I saw her wandering gaze focus on the captain, her nimble body growing tense. "Who will be your champion?"

Tou looked at Mag, who took a step forwards. "Captain, I have chosen Dibu to represent the best result of our training."

I was gratified to see a look of surprise—on Captain Kun's face, and Dibu's. Li's cheeks flushed red. Meanwhile, Kun's smile faltered for a moment. He looked past Mag to Dibu.

"Well, soldier? Your sergeant has spoken. Step forwards."

Still, Dibu hesitated, looking at Li as if certain he had misheard. Then, at last, he walked towards us, presenting himself as if for inspection. I noticed his bronzed knuckles were white where they gripped his shield and blade.

"Ser," he said. "I am ready."

"I certainly hope so," said Kun. He smiled at the

Mystics to either side of him. "And so I suppose it falls to me to select my champion. I have given much thought to the matter." Again his smile widened. "Let us hope I can surprise you at least as much as you have surprised me. For my champion in today's bout, I select Tou. I expect you to do quite well, Lieutenant."

Beside me, Tou went rigid. My heart sank into my boots. The lieutenant had been sparring against Dibu nearly every day, sometimes for hours on end. He knew Dibu's strengths and weaknesses. Dibu, meanwhile, had been too busy learning how to fight at all to study Tou specifically.

But as I looked to my right, my gaze fell upon Mag. To my surprise, she was fighting to suppress a smile. I wondered what under the sky could be going through her mind.

"And so we begin!" said Kun brightly. "Have you a favorite fighting ring, Dibu? I will let you choose, since I think most would agree you are the underdog."

"I . . . do not, Captain," said Dibu slowly. He nodded at Tou. "The bout may take place wherever you wish, Lieutenant."

I expected to hear defeat in his voice, the apathy of knowing an unfavorable outcome before it arrives. But to my surprise, he sounded thoughtful, as though he was already trying to think his way through it. That lit a new spark of hope in me. It seemed Mag had been right about Dibu's instincts, at least. I did not doubt that if Li had been chosen as our champion, she would merely be going through the motions now, convinced she could never win.

We proceeded to the nearest ring. Tou and Dibu traded their swords for practice blades. They spent a few moments at either end of the space, swinging the blades to get the balance. Dibu kept his eyes on his weapon and his shield, inspecting them closely, as though he might find the secret to victory in the grain of the wood or the dull shine of the steel. But Tou's gaze was locked on Dibu, and his jaw kept working.

"Now, I expect you both to give your best effort," said Kun loudly. "But of course, you are ordered not to cause each other any serious harm. You are both assets of the Mystics, after all, and therefore of the High King. Do not deprive her of a loyal sword arm, nor the soldier to wield it."

"Of course, Captain," said Dibu. Tou echoed him as if it were an afterthought.

"Well then," said Kun. "Begin!"

Tou and Dibu stalked close, both turning slightly to the right so that they ended up circling each other. Slowly the circle shrank until they were a pace apart.

Dibu struck first, his sword arcing around in a powerful side swing. Tou deflected it with his shield. But Dibu seemed to expect it, bringing the blade back around and trying to hit his side. Tou's blade was there to block it, and then he launched a counterattack.

Dibu blocked three strokes in a row, and he did not give ground, but held Tou off where he stood. My heart leaped as he went on the offensive again. Tou was the first to fall back one step. Then he pressed Dibu, who took two steps back.

Each blow clanged harder against shield or sword. Every swipe came faster. Gradually Tou stepped up his speed. But Dibu matched him blow for blow. His mouth was a grim, determined line.

Then Dibu did something I had never seen from him before, something Mag had not taught him. He launched forwards with his shield, which crashed against Tou's. Tou held, but then Dibu's leg swept out, kicking Tou's feet from under him.

The Mystic fell to the ground. Our squadrons gave a great cheer.

But Tou did not lose his head. He rolled away quickly, and Dibu brought his sword down on the ground where he had been. It put Dibu ever so slightly off balance, giving Tou just enough time to regain his feet. Now his brilliant red cloak and black hair were soaked with mud, and he was breathing heavily.

I glanced at Kun, and I saw his smile turn icy.

"Enough, Tou!" he barked. "This is a test, not training. End it!"

Tou's jaw clenched, and I felt my hopes plummet. He had treated this like a practice bout, gradually fighting harder to teach Dibu as much as possible. But he was a military man first and foremost. He would obey his captain's order, and his captain had ordered him to win.

Tou lunged to attack. I heard a gasp ripple along our squadrons. Few among them had seen him unleash all his skill, but they could see it now. Every swing of his sword was as fast as blinking. He struck his shield against Dibu's with every other stroke, knocking it aside, trying to find an opening.

Dibu was on the defensive now. Almost every blow forced him back. But whenever I feared he would step out of the ring, he sidestepped to keep himself inside. Every time, it gave him a new lane of retreat, more room to work.

I realized what he was doing. He was trying to tire Tou out. He knew he could not win an even match. But if he could hold off Tou's attacks long enough, he might conserve enough energy to balance the odds.

Mag had been right. Not only was Dibu a natural fighter, but he was smarter than I had expected.

Yet his wits did not seem to be enough. Twice he almost went down as Tou battered his shield. The third time, Tou brought the edge of his shield against Dibu's, cracking it down the middle. The next swing knocked the shield clean off Dibu's arm, and he winced with pain.

Tou's foot lashed out, catching Dibu in the gut. He stumbled back, dropping his sword a pace away. Even as he tripped, Tou caught him in the shoulder with the flat of his blade. Dibu's padded armor held, but he cried out with pain as he spun and slammed face-first into the ground.

Without thinking, I clutched Mag's arm (which

was like seizing an iron bar). But when I looked at her, she still wore the smile she had had before.

"Wait," she whispered.

I looked back just in time to see Tou glance at us. There was an apology in his eyes, but there was also a resolution.

He lifted a foot to step towards Dibu and demand the yield.

Dibu's hand flashed out, seizing his broken shield where it had fallen. He flung it across the mud, and it cracked into Tou's shin. The Mystic slipped on the slush and went crashing into the ground. Dibu sprang, and when he came up, his sword was in his hand.

In an instant, he was standing with one foot on Tou's sword wrist, the tip of the blade at his throat.

Everything went completely silent. I believe I was even holding my breath. Dibu, on the other hand, was panting heavily, and his close-cropped hair was soaking with sweat and mud.

"Do you yield?" said Dibu, between gasps.

Tou looked up at him, brows raised in surprise, clearly impressed.

"I yield."

Our squadrons erupted in cheers and yells. They flooded into the ring, surrounding Dibu and pounding him on the back, ignoring the winces they drew through his embarrassed smile. I half thought they were going to lift him and carry him out of the ring on their shoulders.

"Troops!" barked Mag suddenly. "Attention!"

Everything fell silent again as our squadrons turned, hands slapping to their sides.

All eyes went to Kun, who still stood on the side of the ring. His eternal smile had returned. But I saw ice in his eyes as he looked down at Tou, who still lay on the ground. A long moment passed.

"Clearly, I should have chosen another champion," he said at last. "But, well. What can one do in the face of such disappointment?" Then he turned to Mag and me. "Congratulations. The terms of our agreement have been satisfied, and you are now militia serving under the Mystic order. And what good fortune for all of us, for we march to war tomorrow."

He gave Tou one last look. "There will be a council in my tent at sundown. I expect to see you there, and not covered in mud."

Kun turned on his heel and strode off, his two Mystic guards at his side.

We waited a respectful length of time—mayhap not until he was out of earshot, but certainly until he was out of sight. Then I turned to Mag and arched an eyebrow. She smiled, and together we turned back to our squadrons.

"As you were," I said.

The cheers resumed. Now they did lift Dibu by the legs, hauling him into the air and carrying him off. Dibu let out halfhearted cries of protest. He turned back as they bore him away, looking at Tou, who had not yet risen. It seemed Dibu wanted to help his opponent to his feet, for honor's sake, but the rest of the squadron would not have it.

Well. Dibu deserved his celebration. And so I walked to Tou and reached down. Tou sighed, took my wrist, and let me haul him to his feet. He did his best to dust himself off, but with the heavy mud and slushy snow clinging to him, I am afraid it did not do much good.

"It shall be a while before I recover from that," he said.

"He barely touched you," said Mag.

"It was not my body that suffered injury, but my pride." He stopped wiping the mud off and gave us both a stern look. "It is important to me that you both know: I did not let him win. That was a clever ploy on his part."

"Trust me, I am aware," I said. "I saw the look on your face when you went for him. And neither of us holds your effort against you. You were following your captain's orders."

"We are only happy Dibu prevailed," said Mag. But she could not entirely hide another smile. "And if we are being honest with each other, I think you might be somewhat happy about it, too."

Tou's cheeks flamed, and he cleared his throat as he turned away. "It will certainly be good to have the two of you around for the coming fight," he said, absently running a hand through his goatee, which streaked it with mud.

"Hm," said Mag.

"In any case, thank you," I said, and held out my hand. Tou took my wrist, and we shook firmly. "You have been of immense help during the training, and our squadrons have reaped the benefits. Though you lost the match, you also shared in the victory."

Tou shook his head slowly. "I do not know what madness is upon you that makes you want to be part of this war so badly," he said. "But the High King's forces need all the help we can get, and yours more than most. I only ask that you do not make me regret it."

"I promise," said Mag. "You will be glad we are here when it comes time to fight."

FOURTEEN

AFTER DIBU'S TRIAL, WE HAD LITTLE TIME TO CELEBRATE. Kun had ordered a march for the next morning, and that meant the rest of our day would be spent in furious preparation. Before setting our squadrons to their tasks, Mag and I conferred with Dryleaf.

"Where do you think we are going?" I asked.

"Who knows?" said Mag. "I am sure Kun would not tell us even if we asked."

"Yet he may have told others," said Dryleaf. "You two must see to your preparations, but I will be of little use in that. Let me instead see what I may learn. I should tell the Guild of Lovers, in any case—I am certain they will want to know, and doing them a small favor may repay us all in the end."

"An excellent idea," said Mag, nodding. "Let us know if you learn anything."

Dryleaf gave her a smile and set off towards Taitou, Oku trotting at his heels. Mag and I went to our squadrons and began prodding them into action to pack their things.

Now, even as we had been preparing for Kun's test, the rider had been making her way across the land in search of us.

Her road had grown much more difficult since the civil war broke out, but she was smart enough to keep from being seen. She avoided cities and the major roads, as we had done. Some time ago, she had visited Taitou and learned that we had been there, but she left before we returned. Now she guessed we were lurking somewhere in the nearby wilderness. That was where she had been searching for the past week. But she did not have my skill at finding paths through the wild, and so the going had been slower. She slept in ditches and under trees, muttering complaints about the fact that Mag and I would not sit still and let her catch us.

But because she was being so careful, and quite by accident, she discovered the Shades.

She was leagues north of Taitou, creeping through

a wood called the Brackenbough (which, I am sure, would have amused Dryleaf greatly). Day was fading to night. Sheer luck kept the Shades from seeing her. She was only a few spans from the edge of their encampment deep in the woods, but she did not know it.

Suddenly a thought struck her. We might have set up a camp and built a fire, and mayhap she could see the smoke from far off if she climbed a tree. She tied off her horse and found the tallest tree she could. Grunting and cursing, she hauled herself up hand over hand until she had cleared the tree line surrounding her perch. And just as she had hoped, she saw the smoke of a campfire.

But then she saw many more columns of smoke. Not just one campfire. Nearly a dozen.

The rider frowned. She knew the fires were not from Mag and me. But now she was curious why so many people should be camped deep in the Brackenbough.

She made her way back down to the ground, but she did not mount her horse again. Instead, she set off into the woods on foot. From her belt she drew her short sword and her club, one in each hand. Then she moved forwards with every bit of stealth she could summon.

But she never reached the camp. Two figures appeared in the forest ahead, forcing her to stop.

The rider drew up behind a tree. She stuck out one eye, taking a few moments to study the figures before her. They stood a span apart so that they could just see each other through the woods.

Sentries. But what were they guarding?

Then the rider noticed their outfits of grey, with blue cloaks pulled tight about them.

She knew what that meant. She had seen Shades before. From the campfires, it seemed to be a decently sized force. Mayhap two hundreds. That was more than the rider had ever seen in one place.

"Dark below," she grumbled.

She slid behind the tree again and then snuck away south, quiet as a rather large mouse. Soon she had rejoined her horse and untied it from the tree branch.

Now she had a choice to make. This discovery troubled her, and she could not simply ignore it. Such a force of Shades moving through the kingdom could threaten all of Dorsea, and that was more important than Mag and me.

Taitou was to the south, and she knew that town held a small garrison of Mystics. If anyone could deal with this situation, the redcloaks could.

The rider blew out a loud, exasperated sigh, sending it misting up into the wintry air. Then she climbed into the saddle.

"Come on, boy," she said, patting her horse's neck. "We make for Taitou. One more delay I will take out on the wanderers' hides, whenever we find them."

Dryleaf went about his business in Taitou, while Mag and I set to ours in the encampment. We had drilled our squadrons on packing their kit, but they still needed our attention and an occasional sharp word. By the time the sun was lowering towards the horizon, I was nearly worn out. Dryleaf found Mag and me just as we had reunited and started supper.

"I hope your day was fruitful," he said.

"The only fruit borne today was a thistle," I said, "and I feel its needles all up and down my back. Why is it I can travel hundreds of leagues with the two of you and feel fine, but after spending one day helping others prepare for a journey, I feel ready to quit?"

Dryleaf chuckled. "Ask any parent if they were ever as tired before children as they were after."

Mag smirked. "We are their officers, not their parents, and they will have a rude awakening if they forget it. But what of you? What were you able to learn?"

The old man shook his head with a smile. "I should have predicted this, but the Guild of Lovers already knew about the march. They have a wagon ready to follow the army with some half-dozen lovers. Two of my friends, Orla and Nikau, will be coming along. In any case, the lovers must have heard of it from some of the Mystics who are closest in Kun's council—who I would have difficulty befriending, of course. It appears the march was a complete surprise to most of the redcloaks. Even Tou had not known of it."

I met Mag's gaze. "That means Kun was afraid of word getting out," I said.

"And that likely means he is going after the Shades,"

said Mag, tapping her fingers on her thigh. "This is something, at least. You could learn nothing else?"

"Only that we are marching north," said Dryleaf. "No one knows exactly where."

"North," I mused. "I know of nothing important that way. Other than the town where you grew up, Mag."

Her mouth twisted towards a frown, as though she had almost said something but then thought better of it. "That place is anything but important."

Just then, Tou approached us. He gave us all a quick nod and touched Dryleaf gently on the shoulder to let him know he was there. "I have returned from Captain Zhou's war council."

I glanced at the sun, which had only barely begun to sink below the horizon. "It seems to have gone rather quickly."

Tou nodded, but he looked troubled. "It did. My company will be marching in the vanguard with the captain's Mystics. He instructed that your squadrons be at the forefront, behind him."

That was a surprise, though I quickly realized it should not have been. "He wishes to keep an eye on us," I said.

His mouth twisted. "I am only passing down the order." But I could see in his eyes that he thought I was correct. "When we muster in the morning, you know where to be."

"Yes, ser," I said, snapping a salute where I sat. Tou nodded and left.

Mag's eyes were alight with excitement. "Good for us, I say. I would rather be at the front—anything to get to the Shades faster. We can help root out the Shades and end this war, Albern. I feel it."

I chuckled. "End the war? Why, Mag. You sound almost as though you are truly committed to the fight now. I thought it was only a cover for us to find Kaita."

She did not answer, or even change her expression. But her fist jabbed out and struck me hard in the shoulder. My whole arm went dead, and I cursed and fumed as Mag went to help Dryleaf fetch his supper.

That evening, a wagon trundled up to the camp as we were almost ready to end our night. It was covered entirely in a brilliant blue cloth of a beautiful weave. Mag and I stopped and watched it approach. Hallan and Dibu were with us, each of them discussing some final matters before the morning's march. As the wagon drew near to us, I spied the driver—a tall, brown-skinned man with lustrous black hair down to his shoulders, supple, muscled arms, and large, strong hands. He looked like a man of Calentin, which held my attention. As the wagon slowed, he nodded to us.

"Good eve, friends," he said. His voice was like warm, smooth liquid pouring down the nape of your neck. "We seek a friend of yours. An older gentleman named Dryleaf. Do you know him?"

"Is that Nikau?" Dryleaf thrust his head out of his tent. "Nikau, darling boy! You found me."

Like a mirror of Dryleaf, a woman poked her head out of the blue front flaps of the wagon. She was a slim, delicate young thing, with pale Heddish skin and hair that flamed red like Hallan's, but curly and more lustrous. She leaned her elbows on the front edge of the wagon and beamed down at Dryleaf.

"There he is!" she called sweetly. "We have arrived, dear friend, and we thought to seek a song from you before we slumber. Any journey should be blessed by merriment before it begins, or else who knows what darkness might befall it?"

"Who, indeed? Thank you, my boy," said Dryleaf as Dibu helped him climb out of the tent and stand up. "It would be my utter joy to share songs and stories with you tonight, and on the road as well."

"Am I to guess that you are from the Guild of Lovers?" I said.

"We are," said the man with a knowing smile. "I am Nikau, as Dryleaf said."

"And I am Orla," said the woman, holding a hand towards me. I took it and kissed it. Her fingers were as soft as cream, and almost the same color. "Entirely enchanted."

I cleared my throat. "As are we. I am Albern of the family Telfer, and this is Mag. These are Hallan and Dibu, two soldiers in our squadrons. Dryleaf has sung your praises ever since we arrived in the town."

Orla climbed down from the wagon and wrapped her arm through Dryleaf's, laying her head on his shoulder. "If that is true, I feel simply cheated. How could he sing without me there to hear it?"

"We shall have plenty of chances to hear him on the road, love," said Nikau with a smile. He kept studying me. I wondered if he was as curious about me as I was about him and if he could see my Calentin features through my lighter complexion. "A pleasure to meet you both. Do not hesitate to seek us out, should you wish our services. It would be our honor to comfort the friends of Dryleaf, who we have come to love so well."

"I shall, ah. Certainly consider it," I said, scratching the back of my neck. "My friend Mag, however—"

Mag smirked at my obvious discomfort. "I am not a bedder. But your offer is generous and well-spoken."

"That is well enough," said Nikau, giving her a nod, and then me a wink.

"You are coming with us?" said Dibu. "On the march?"

Nikau gave him an easy smile. "We are. And if it means I get to see those arms of yours each day, I, for one, will do so with pleasure."

Dibu thrust a tongue into his cheek hard to fight a smile, and he shook his head. "I thank you for the compliment. But . . . we are marching to war, or so we all believe. Is it not safer to ply your trade here?"

"Ye need not worry for that, boy," said Hallan, folding his arms. He gave Nikau a nod, and Orla a wink. "Lovers are much as safe in war as they are in any town or city. Their laws forbid them from taking sides, and so why should anyone seek to harm them? Their trade's neutral, and a help to either side. And I can say from some experience that a lover can hardly find better clientele than when traveling along with an army."

"All very true," said Orla, smiling at him from Dryleaf's side. "And I do love a soldier with experience."

Hallan bowed low, his beard pressing into his chest. "I'll recommend some to you, then." His eyes flitted to Nikau. "And mayhap you'll make some recommendations as well."

"I am sure they will hardly be necessary," said Nikau, placing a hand on Hallan's arm. "But for now, we had better see to our arrangements. Come, Orla. I will not build your tent for you."

Orla laughed, and it was like music. "Of course you will, if I ask it," she said. "But I am coming." She leaned in to give Dryleaf a quick peck on the cheek. "Await my return, dear one. We will come to hound you for a song as soon as we may."

She danced away towards the back of the wagon. Behind her, some other lovers descended to the ground, and they began to see to the horses' needs and set up tents near the army's. I noticed Mag's and my squadrons looking at them with interest, and I strongly suspected they would be glad for Dryleaf's presence during the long march before us.

Mag was shaking her head with a slightly amused

expression. “At least our march shall not be dreary—wherever we end up marching to.”

“No, it certainly will not,” said Dryleaf, beaming.

We all sang and spoke and laughed and drank that night, and the next morning we set out from Taitou before dawn. Tou’s company marched just behind Kun’s Mystics, as ordered. Dryleaf found a place in the army’s train near the lovers, among the wagons and carts of the camp followers that accompany any force on a campaign.

Mag and I were marching to war for the first time in many years. Though we walked in grim company, for the first time in a while, I found myself excited to take the next step in our journey.

The rider was headed south towards Taitou on a narrow, little-used hunting trail. The day was cold, and the warmth of her mount was little comfort against it. Sharp hills cracked the land around her, like broken fingers arching towards the sky in pain. Dark mutterings poured in a steady trickle from her lips, promising baneful revenge against Mag and me when at last she caught up to us.

To the south, a flight of birds launched itself into the air, screaming.

The rider stopped. Her eyes narrowed. She moved off the trail into the hills, hiding her horse behind some boulders. Retracing her steps, she found a place where she could watch the path while keeping herself hidden.

It was not long before a column of soldiers came into view. The rider leaned forwards, narrowing her eyes.

At the head of the column, she saw Mystics. Some were on horseback, but most were on foot. Behind the redcloaks were other folk. They looked like artisans and farmers, and almost none of them were mounted. But they carried weapons and shields, and sometimes one or two pieces of armor, though it was ragtag and scattered among them.

Militia, thought the rider.

And then she saw Mag and me. We were close to the head of the column, riding our horses in plain sight.

The rider froze. But only for an instant before she was cursing under her breath and racing back towards her horse.

"Dark-damned, steer-loving, slipshod nuisances," she said, and carried on in like manner as she mounted. The moment she was in the saddle, she dug in her heels with a great cry, riding towards the hunting trail at a gallop.

Kun and his Mystics spotted her while she was still spans off. Immediately the Mystics formed up, drawing weapons and hefting their shields to form a wall in front of Kun. Knights barked orders, directing more of the column to advance and join them.

The rider slowed her horse to a walk, throwing empty hands into the air.

"Hail!" she cried. "My weapons are stowed, and I bear no ill intent. Kindly do not shoot me."

Mag and I came marching forwards with our units. The rider studied us, eyes narrowing in a glare, but she could see that we did not recognize her. And why should we have? She was wrapped head to toe in clothing against the cold. Not even a shock of hair stuck out from her hood and mask.

"That is far enough," Kun called out amiably. "Who are you, and what do you want?"

"Two things," said the rider. "The first is more important. I have come looking for you, for I guess that you are the Mystic garrison from Taitou. I have news for you about the Shades."

The effect on all of us was immediate. Mag and I glanced at each other, and most of the gathered soldiers gripped their weapons tighter.

The woman's voice instantly struck me as familiar. But it was far away and muffled, both by her mask and by the heavy snows all around us. My mind raced, trying to place it, but I could not.

Kun's smile only widened.

"I am curious about your news, as well as why you think I should trust it," he called out. "But you said you wanted two things. What is the second?"

The rider's voice went sour. "I am looking for three people in your company."

Kun's smile vanished. "Are you now." It was not a question, but more of a statement of annoyed anticipation.

"I am," said the rider. "I seek Dryleaf, an older man. And two whom I see before me: Mag, called by some the Uncut Lady, and especially Albern of the family Telfer."

Mag frowned, and a flush crept up into my cheeks. Yet still I could not place her voice.

The rider smiled to herself, drawing a dark enjoyment from our reactions.

Kun, meanwhile, had turned a baleful glare on us. "I see," he said. "Why does it not surprise me that the two of you are connected to this stranger, who rides out of the wilderness with knowledge of the Shades?"

Mag never took her eyes off the rider. "I do not recognize her, Captain."

"Nor I," I added. It did not seem wise to mention the familiarity of her voice, for I did not think Kun would be much pleased. "Who are you, stranger? Show your face."

"Stranger?" The rider snorted. "How would a stranger know your names, or recognize you? You know me, wanderers, even if you do not know that you know me."

She dismounted before removing her mask and pulling back the hood of her cloak.

I had nocked an arrow. Now it dipped immediately. Mag put her spear up at once. Both of us took a tentative step forwards, unable to believe our own eyes.

"Yue?" I gasped.

FIFTEEN

SUN STOPPED DEAD IN THE STREET, HER MOUTH AGAPE.

"Not Yue from Lan Shui?" she said.

Albern's smile was broad and smug, and Sun knew he was immensely enjoying the look on her face. "The very same. Come, keep walking. We have a ways to go."

"But . . . but she . . ." Sun struggled for words, trotting at Albern's side. "What on earth was she doing there? What about Lan Shui? She was a *constable!*"

"She was, but she—"

"Now hold on," said Sun. "I learned much about

Yue from you. And if there is one thing I know, it is that she would *never* have abandoned her duty to Lan Shui. She took it so seriously that she was ready to arrest you and Mag just for looking suspicious!"

"Oh, her duty to her king was her highest priority," said Albern. "And that had not changed."

"But she abandoned Lan Shui!" cried Sun. "Why would she do that?"

Albern stuck a tongue in his cheek, biting down on it as if he was trying desperately to quell the grin plastered on his features. "You see," he said slowly, "I was telling you a story, in which I was just about to relay my conversation with Yue, and during which time I asked her these questions, and Yue—"

"All right," growled Sun. "Get on with it."

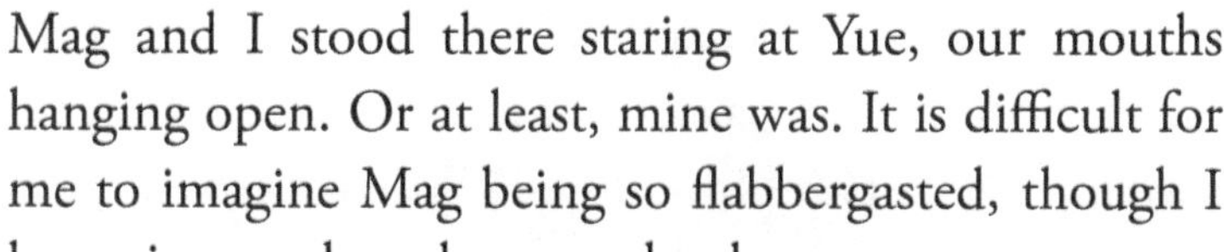

Mag and I stood there staring at Yue, our mouths hanging open. Or at least, mine was. It is difficult for me to imagine Mag being so flabbergasted, though I know it must have happened at least once.

"Careful," Yue told me after a moment. She could not entirely banish a sardonic smirk. "Winter it might be, but there are still enough flies to be caught in that gaping hole in your face."

"Yue," I breathed. "What under the *sky* are you doing here?"

Mag arched an eyebrow. "And what in the dark below, while you are answering questions."

"Ha," said Yue.

"Pardon me," said Kun. His smile had returned, but it was sharp as a razor's edge. "You are carrying on a conversation as though you are the only ones invested in its outcome. Let me kindly remind you that you are not."

"Of course, Captain," I said at once. "Forgive me. This woman is a friend."

"Though how in blazes she found us is another matter," said Mag. Suddenly she frowned. "Albern . . ."

Her voice trailed off, and I realized what she was thinking. Kaita would have known Yue from Lan Shui, and she might know—or have guessed—that we were friendly. As a weremage, Kaita could hardly ask for a better opportunity to get within striking distance of us.

"Yue," I said slowly. "You remember what we were seeking when we left Lan Shui."

"Of course," she said, irritated. "You left to find the werema—ah." Her brows lifted. "The weremage. And now, here I am."

"A weremage?" said Kun. "What is this about?"

Yue turned to him and bowed. "Captain. I was formerly a constable in the town of Lan Shui. It is a modest place, some leagues southeast of—"

"I know it," said Kun. "Go on."

Yue nodded towards us. "These two traveled through the town some months ago. There was a weremage who caused some local trouble, and they helped me resolve the issue. But the weremage was never found." She scowled at the two of us. "They are afraid I might be her, which is an uncommon display of good sense."

Kun's brows shot for the sky. "You certainly seem familiar with their antics."

"And I guess that you are as well," said Yue, bowing again. "But they are right, ser. I could be the weremage in disguise."

Mag opened her mouth to speak, but I gripped her arm to stop her. She could offer to test Yue—she had learned how in Calentin. But I did not think it wise to reveal that knowledge to Kun, for it might lead to awkward questions.

Fortunately, Kun solved the problem for us. "Prudence is always a wise course. Zhen—forgive me, *Lieutenant* Zhou? Test her, if you would."

Zhen, Kun's nephew, stepped forwards. He sheathed his sword as he approached Yue and stood before her, a pace away. Yue held her ground, but her jaw clenched as she looked at him.

"A test?" she said. "I have never heard of this."

"Most have not," said Zhen. "It is taught to some within the order, and it is quite foolproof."

Yue lifted her chin. "Very well. What do you need me to do?"

"Nothing," said Zhen. "But I must strike you. Nothing too damaging, I promise, but it will daze you for a moment."

She fought a scowl. "You are certain this works?"

"I am," said Zhen.

Yue sighed. "Very well. Do what you must."

Zhen nodded. Then he stepped forwards and slammed his hands into Yue's temples with two powerful chops. Her head reeled back, and she blinked hard against the pain. But her eyes did not glow, and soon her vision seemed to clear. She glared at Zhen.

"That hurt."

I laughed out loud. "Yet it was worth it—at least to me."

I went running forwards to embrace her, Mag only a pace behind me. I struck Yue hard and wrapped her in a hug.

"But why *are* you here, Yue?" I said quietly.

"To find and aid you two, of course, you great idiot," she growled.

"Excuse me," said Kun. "You keep forgetting the rest of us are here, and it begins to border on offense."

"Apologies, Captain," said Yue, stepping towards him. "I have sought these two across Dorsea. If they have joined your efforts in this civil war, then I would pledge my service as well."

"Would you now?" said Kun. "Sky save me. I am nearly drowning in recruits, seemingly whether I wish them or not."

"You could hardly ask for a better sword arm than hers," I told him. "Mag and I will vouch for her."

"That is no surprise," said Kun. "I imagine you

have friends scattered all across the nine kingdoms, turning up when one least expects it."

I did not miss the subtle dig. That could also have been a description of the Shades. I thought hard, wondering how I could convince him to let Yue stay on.

Yet I need not have worried, for Yue stepped forwards. The Mystics beside Kun tensed, but Yue stopped while still two paces away. In a tone I had never heard her use before—proud yet deferential, strong but respectful—she spoke.

"Captain Kun," she said. "I am Yue of the family Baolan, former constable of the town of Lan Shui. I am kin to Constable Aroha in Opara, to Constable Pinti in Yota, to Constable Zho in Danfon, and to Constabular Captain Stubhart on the High King's Seat. If letters can be sent to them, they will all vouch for me, as will Constable Ashta in Lan Shui itself. Also, my uncle Joshin serves the Mystics with honor in the city of Bertram, and my grandmother Brinna was a chancellor in Pinkeng in the south until her retirement five years ago. Long has the family Baolan served the King's law, and I have no greater aspirations in this life or any other. I am the servant of Jun of the family Fei, the true king of Dorsea, and his kin, and through them the High King.

"I have fourteen months of training with sword, shield, and club, and nine years' experience using them in service of the people of Dorsea. With these companions, Albern and Mag, I have fought and defeated vampires, and I would throw myself into the maw of a thousand worse horrors to protect the nine kingdoms."

She fell to her knee right there in the slushy mud, and she bowed her head to Kun. "I decry the false pretender, Wojin, who now sits the throne, and all who swear fealty to him. I know of the Shades who threaten the nine kingdoms, and I pledge myself to their defeat. I have fought them already, and I will fight them again if given the opportunity, and I will not stop until their evil is driven from the land.

"If I may aid in your enemies' defeat by the strength of my arm, it is yours. If I may bring you to victory by what courage I have, I pledge it. And if I can uphold the order of the nine kingdoms by either my life or my death, I give them both into your service, as I did when first I donned the red armor of my station."

We all stood frozen. The air fell to silence. Some nearby militia had drifted closer as she spoke, and now everyone present stood in silent astonishment. Kun studied her. His perpetual smile had fallen away, and yet that did not worry me. I could tell he was impressed.

He dismounted, stepped forwards, and took Yue's shoulder. Firmly, but not roughly, he pulled her to her feet.

"I accept your service, Yue of the family Baolan, and I count myself honored to do so," he said. "If every soldier who marched for the High King were of your caliber, I do not doubt the war would be over within a month."

His smile returned, and he looked at Mag and me over Yue's shoulders.

"If all the two of you end up doing is bringing me her aid, I will consider myself well served, and more than compensated for losing our wager."

I bowed. "Thank you, Captain."

His gaze returned to Yue, and he arched an eyebrow. "Vampires? I shall need to hear that tale. But not now. I will summon you for counsel after supper, to hear this information you have on the Shades. Be ready."

Yue saluted with a fist over her heart. "Yesser."

He gave her a sharp nod and then turned to Zhen, who still stood close by. "That is enough of a march for today. Order the column to make camp for the night."

So saying, he set off back to his Mystics. Yue turned to Mag and me, and she folded her arms under her chest.

"Well," she said. "Now that I have saved you from trouble *again,* we should talk."

"We should, but I would be remiss not to send for Dryleaf." I turned to Chausiku, who stood close by. He and the rest of my squadron had observed all these proceedings with wide eyes, and more than a few of them with mouths hanging half-open. "Chausiku. Fetch Dryleaf from the train, if you would. He will want to be here."

"Ser," he said with a nod. For a moment longer, he stared at Yue, Mag, and me, but at last he set off, his tail of locs swinging behind him.

"Hallan," I said. He snapped sharply to attention, beard bristling. "See that everyone gets themselves well situated. Keep the tent lines straight this time, and call for me if you need me."

"Ser," said Hallan with a nod. He turned to the rest of the unit. "You heard the sergeant! Line'em up nice, little ones, or I'll have you digging latrines tonight."

Mag turned to her squadron. "Dibu, Li, can you see to arrangements?"

"Of course, ser," said Dibu with a nod. Li echoed him after a moment, and then slung her pack off her back, her wandering gaze momentarily fixed on Yue.

Yue was now looking at us with one brow cocked. "Sergeants, are you? A mark against my estimation of the captain, if he elevated you so."

I laughed. "I am sure it will reassure you to know that we forced him into it. But dark below, Yue. What brought you here?"

"That is a bit of a tale," said Yue. "As I recovered from my injuries in Lan Shui, I had time to think. When I became a constable, I did it to protect the kingdom. Now it seemed you were doing more for the safety of Dorsea than I was. That was an untenable thought. And by the time I had finished healing, Lan Shui had been quiet and peaceful for many weeks. Ashta, it turns out, is more than capable of dealing with day-to-day affairs. She had even hired a new constable to help her, and I felt . . . unnecessary. So I turned my command over to her and tried to follow you to Opara. But when I reached it, I learned that you had come, and then left, and then come and then left again."

"Wait," said Mag, holding up a hand. "Who told you all that?"

Yue shrugged again. "The Rangatira's constables. A cousin of mine named Aroha serves there."

I raised my brows. "Do all of your kin take the red leather?"

"Those who do not take the red cloak," she said, glowering. "May I tell my story, or will you continue to interrupt me at every opportunity?"

"We make no promises," said Mag.

Just at that moment, Dryleaf came hurrying up, his arm in Chausiku's. At his heels came Oku, and as soon as the hound spotted Yue, he came bounding forwards with great leaps and barks. Yue looked down at him with a frown she could not quite maintain.

"You still have the mutt," she said.

"Yue," I said reproachfully.

"Oh, all right," she said. She scratched him behind the ears as Dryleaf came hobbling forwards, his arms outstretched.

"Yue!" he cried. The moment Yue took his hands, he seized her around the neck and pulled her down for a hug. I saw tears shining in his eyes as he embraced her. "Dear, dear, *dear* girl. When young Chausiku here told me it was you, I hardly dared to believe him."

"Hello, old man," said Yue. She returned his hug, squeezing him mayhap a bit harder than she should have, what with his age. "I am glad to see you safe, but dismayed to find you still following these fools as they traipse across all the nine lands."

"They have taken excellent care of me," chuckled Dryleaf, wheezing slightly in her grip.

"Of course they have," said Yue. "They know that if they let anything happen to you, I would flay the skin from their bodies."

Dryleaf laughed aloud before pulling back and reaching up to cradle her face in his leathery hands. "But sky above and dark below, what brought you all this way?"

"I was just telling them," said Yue. "But I do not mind repeating myself. It has been a long road, and conversation rare. Mayhap after a meal and a, er . . . a rest." She glanced back at Mag and me.

"Of course," I said. "I imagine you have a tent? If not, I am certain one can be provided. I think Kun rather likes you, after that speech."

"Yes, that *was* impressive," said Mag, smirking.

"I am sure it was," put in Dryleaf. "You do not know Yue as I do. Her talents lie far beyond simple skill with a blade."

"They do indeed," said Yue. But she licked her lips nervously. "And speaking of which, there is something I would take care of, now that most of the important business has been seen to, and before we talk further, or before Kun summons me to his council. Before I lose my nerve, at any rate."

That confused me, and I saw my expression mirrored in Mag and Dryleaf. "What is that?" I asked her.

Yue's gaze flicked to me, and then away. "I made you an offer in Lan Shui, and you said you would take me up on it when next we met. Well, now we have met. So, shall you set up your tent, or shall I set up mine? It has been . . . a very long road."

I do not mind telling you that I was struck utterly speechless for a moment. In wild desperation, I looked to Mag and Dryleaf. Though I am no prudish child of merchants, I doubted my cheeks had ever been so dark.

Mag raised an eyebrow. "Well? Go on, then. You know what to do, yes?"

Dryleaf patted me on the shoulder. "Be careful, my boy. Her injuries were severe, and she may still be recovering."

I could only splutter and look up at Yue. *Me* be careful with *her?* She was a head taller and had to outweigh me by two stones, at least.

But then she reached out her hand towards me. And I saw her grow suddenly hesitant, timid—almost shy. There was a question in her eyes, and a fear of what my answer might be.

Well. I was not such an old man yet, and blood ran in my veins. And Yue was, as I have told you . . . a powerful woman.

I took her hand and led her to where Hallan was building my tent for me.

SIXTEEN

Of the rest of that evening I wish to say little, so let us resume the tale after some time had passed. After a while, Yue went to Kun's council. When she returned, Mag and I learned that Kun had assigned her as sergeant to another squadron of soldiers in Tou's company. But to our dismay, Yue would not tell us much of what else they had discussed, for Kun had commanded her to secrecy. All she would say to us was that the army would march west in the morning.

"West?" said Mag. "Why west?"

"Because that is where the Shades were going, as best I could tell," said Yue.

"But there is nothing to the west," said Mag. "Dorsea's large cities are all to the south, and Feldemar's to the north. These are wildlands."

"I only know where they are heading," said Yue, shrugging. "I know nothing more of their aims than you do."

The next day, Kun turned his march away from the rising sun. And now that he had some definite idea of our enemy's movements, he pushed his troops hard. We found ourselves on a forced march, and suddenly Mag's and my experience with campaigning became invaluable.

A fighting force lives a very different life on the march than at home. Wise officers give their soldiers a routine, and wise soldiers follow it. Though it may sound silly, lives may be lost because of the smallest of forgotten details. A battle may turn because you did not build a tent line straight, which led to an injury in the night, which held up the march for an hour, which allowed your enemy to surprise you. Or you may arrive to battle exhausted because many in the camp were woken by the commotion of the night before.

There are also smaller tricks to make the journey easier for each soldier. On the first night of our westward march, I came upon Jian unloading her whole pack and laying out all its items.

"You would do better to save your effort," I told

her. "I doubt you will use half those things tonight, and then you will only have to pack them again in the morning."

She paused, frowning down at her pack and pushing back her rakish hair. "But I did not bring much. It only takes a few moments."

"A few moments now may seem trivial," I told her. "But in the morning, you will be even more tired and sore than you are now. Then you will throw your things haphazardly into your pack, which will bounce on its straps all day, tiring you further."

"Trust him, girl," said Hallan, whose own tent was nearby. His fiery beard jumped as he pointed up at me. "He's legged more leagues and fought more fights than even me, though he be younger."

Jian shrugged. "Very well. I suppose I will listen to so *very* many years of experience."

"Fair enough," I said with a smirk. I went on down the line to inspect the rest of them, giving Hallan a nod of gratitude as I went. He waved it off with a smile and began to clean his new spectacles.

Mag and I impressed these little details upon our squadrons as best we could. I noticed that when we did, Tou listened attentively as he stroked his goatee. Before long, I caught him passing our words on to the other sergeants in our company. I suspect he even conferred with the other lieutenants and passed them the same information, for I soon noticed most of the army doing as we had instructed our squadrons.

A hard march through the day under Kun's watchful eye and a tent shared with Yue at night. Life had taken on the routines of the mercenary days of my youth, and I found myself not displeased.

At the end of the day after Yue joined us, we made camp at the northern edge of the Carrweld Forest. Mag had been quiet throughout the day. I wondered if she was thinking of Shuiniu, the village where she had grown up. It was just there, just a little ways into the forest. As we had ridden throughout the day, I had kept an eye to the south. Whenever I saw a road or a hunting trail, I wondered if we could have followed it south until it reached Mag's old home. We could not take the time to visit now, of course. Kun would never allow it, and we were on contract now—we were bound to remain with the army until our next stop in a town or city, on pain of punishment. Yet I was filled with a sudden desire to go to Shuiniu, to see the streets that Mag walked as a child, to visit the people who had known her when she was young.

"You are very quiet," said Yue, driving such thoughts away. "What troubles you?"

We were sitting side by side as we ate our supper. Everyone had left us to eat alone, which I appreciated—I had been surrounded by bodies and shouting voices all day during the march. Now it was quite pleasant to take in a quiet moment with Yue's comforting presence by my side. The evening was milder than they had been of late. Though the sky was dark with clouds, there was no rain, and we had found a log to give us a dry place to sit, free of the slushy snow that covered the ground.

"Oh, nothing very important," I answered, glancing around to make sure Mag was not near. "That forest there is called the Carrweld. Mag grew up in a town there, and I wondered if she was homesick."

Yue snorted. "Strange. It is hard to imagine her growing up anywhere. Something about that woman feels eternal, as though she sprang out of the ground full grown."

I shook my head. "You exaggerate. But then, you are not the first to do so. Many people see her remarkable skill at fighting and ascribe all sorts of other wild notions to her. I suppose I have been guilty of it myself. Mayhap that was why I was so surprised, though I should not have been, to learn she had had a whole life before we ever met."

"Of course she did," said Yue. "We all do. You scarcely know anything about me in the time before we met, and I know precious little of you, aside from what happened to you in Northwood. Though I imagine you were a troublemaker even before then."

That cast a dark pall over my mood, and Yue saw it. She frowned, leaning forwards to get a better look at me.

"What?" she said. "What is it?"

I had a sudden urge to avoid her gaze. "The battle of Northwood was a dark day," I said. "But the time before it was hardly better. I had not thought of it in some time."

Her brows rose. "It must have been bad for you to compare it to Northwood."

"It was," I said. "I lost—" I cut myself short. "It was," I said finally.

Yue waited through a long moment of silence. Then she nudged me with her elbow. "You lost what? Your favorite dog?"

Oku's head came up, but I ignored him. "No, nothing. I should not have said anything, least of all now."

Despite my reticence, Yue seemed to hear much in my words. "Ah," she said carefully, leaning back, her hands on the log. "You lost some*one*. Someone . . . special?"

I placed a hand on her knee and finally looked her in the eye. "Forget it," I said. "I am enjoying myself now. There is no need to dwell on the past."

"Albern, you are allowed to have had lovers before me," she said. "I had many before you."

"Of course you did. Of course we both did. But it hardly seems the thing to talk about now, does it?"

She shrugged. "And why not? If their memory lingers, I do not mind you speaking of them to me, if it helps."

I sighed, reaching up to scratch at my stubble. I had not had a chance for a proper shave since we left Taitou. "Nothing lingers. It is fine. I have spent enough time thinking about him. I am ready to look ahead. Sky above, how can I complain? It is nothing like Mag in Northwood, losing the love of her—"

My words choked off. I tossed my head back and forth, failing to convince even myself that my mood was light. Yue, who did not seem fooled in the slightest, leaned closer and fixed me with her gaze. Again, I could not meet her eyes.

"Albern, whoever he was, you do yourself no favors by trying to convince me he was unimportant. I think you are trying to pretend for my benefit, but if so, you are a fool. Ours is not some moons-flying romance, you astonishingly foolish man. I am not looking for such a thing anyway. At least not now. Certainly not with someone who still holds a torch for their last lover."

"Of course not," I said. "I know that. You and I are simply . . . it is . . ."

"Enjoyable," said Yue, with the slightest smirk. "So enjoy it. Let yourself feel what you must, and when that feeling is sorrow, take comfort in me." She stuck her tongue in her cheek. "I plan to take comfort in you."

I had just started to take a pull from my wineskin, and now I almost choked on it. "Sky above, Yue," I gasped.

"There we are," said Yue. "Now, come. I am tired after another long day's march, and I want to get to sleep early." She stood and reached down to pull me up. "But not too early."

I sighed and let her lift me to my feet. "Fine," I said. "But only for your sake. I will take no joy in this."

"I am about to make you a liar," she said, heading for the tent.

But before I followed her, something caught my eye. I looked to my left and saw Mag standing there. She was a little apart from Dryleaf and our squadrons, who were all clustered around a fire, listening to the old man tell a story. Nikau and Orla were there, the lovers distracted from business by whatever tale Dryleaf was spinning.

But Mag did not seem to be listening to him. Her back was straight, her arms at her sides, and her gaze was fixed unerringly on the Carrweld. I knew from long experience that she could hold her body still as a statue when she wanted to. But now I saw a twitch in her hands. They hung loose and open, and her fingers would jerk forwards and then back. Forwards, and then back.

She did not see me. I doubted she saw anything but the darkness beneath those branches.

Almost I went to speak with her. But Yue called out to me, and I turned to follow her into the tent at last.

SEVENTEEN

OUR MARCH NOW TOOK US INTO OPEN WILDERNESS, with no real roads to speed our journey. Still, we made a good pace west, clearing almost four leagues each day. On the third day, we turned from our somewhat northwesterly course to aim southwest, passing from a land of broken hills to one of rivers and marshes. Kun seemed to know the region well, for he led us unerringly around the worst delays in the land.

On the fifth day, we reached a town called Kuan Shu on the banks of the River Marsden. There we found a bridge, and after crossing, we camped beyond the western borders of the town that night.

Captain Kun did not let us spend any time within the walls speaking to Kuan Shu's inhabitants. I believe he did not wish us to spread any word of who we were or what our mission was. But he sent his nephew, Zhen, and some other Mystics into the town, probably to seek information about the Shades.

On the sixth day, Kun stopped the march about an hour earlier than expected. While we halted on the road, waiting, Kun and his advisors deliberated ahead of us. I was about to ask Tou if he wanted to see what was the matter, when Kun sent out the order to make camp for the night.

The sun was still a good hour or two above the horizon. I could think of only one reason why we would halt early. If Kun thought we were to meet our enemy in battle soon, he would want to keep his army as fresh as possible.

But I kept these thoughts to myself as I directed my squadron in building their tents. Then my attention caught on a messenger approaching from the head of the camp, where Kun's tent was being built. The woman went to Tou and spoke quietly with him before leaving at a brisk pace, heading farther back down the column. Tou stood looking after her for a moment, fingers on his chin, before he sought me out and motioned me over to him.

"Trouble?" I asked.

"No," said Tou. "Only a summons to speak with the captain. I may not be gone long, but just in case, would you have one of your soldiers build my tent for me?"

"I will see to it myself," I said. "And your stakes will not be as shaky as they have been in recent days."

His expression lightened, and he rolled his eyes. "Not everyone is as . . . seasoned a campaigner as you are."

I placed a hand to my chest, raising my eyebrows in mock affront. "A jibe at my advancing years? I thought you a better man."

Tou chuckled, seemingly against his will, and flapped a hand towards his pack. "Just build the tent."

"Of course," I said, smiling. The smile lasted until he was gone, and then a worried crease came to my brow. My thoughts were troubled as I built Tou's tent and then my own, and then I knelt to light a fire after Chausiku brought some wood.

Tou finally returned as the last light was fading in the sky. His face was grim as he approached me by my fire.

"Get Mag and Yue and come speak with me," he said.

"Yes, ser," I said, and went to do as he had bid.

When I found Mag, she and Yue were sitting with their squadron and eating. Dryleaf was there with them, as were Nikau and Orla. The lovers spent time with us every night, at least for our evening meal, before they went and plied their services among the army. Yue, it seemed, was in the middle of a tale about our fight with the vampires.

". . . and then they split up," Yue was saying as I approached. "*Split up,* the fools. Unfortunately, Albern was the one to find me, which meant I had to save my own hide. The vampire got a good chunk of my shoulder with its claws, but I managed to shove it into the flames and burn it to death."

"*After* I had already pierced it with an arrow," I put in.

Yue looked up, the surprise on her face too exaggerated to be genuine. "Albern! I did not see you coming."

"Mm," I said. "I am afraid you must finish your tale later. The lieutenant needs us."

The mood of those around the fire darkened in an instant. Without a word, Mag and Yue got to their feet. But as Yue was stepping away, Dryleaf reached up and took her hand.

"Should I come with you?" he asked.

"Tou is in a hurry," I said. "But I promise we will speak with you after."

Dryleaf nodded. "Very well. I eagerly await it." Then he turned to the rest of those sitting by the fire. "And in the meantime, mayhap I should tell you *my* part in this tale of the vampires. It was quite amusing—Albern was so impressed with my wisdom that he thought I could see without my eyes."

Orla wore a joyful expression. "I would not be surprised, dear one," she said, gently rubbing the back of his hand. "The sky bestows many blessings on those who command the magic of talespinning."

A few chuckles rang out behind us as we walked away. I smiled ruefully in the growing darkness. "Why do all your stories seem to make me the butt of the joke?"

Yue slapped my rear end. "Because you are so excellent for the role."

My face flamed, and I hoped they could not see it in the sparse light of the campfires we passed. Mag, however, ignored our flirting.

"Do you know what this business is with Tou?" she asked.

"I do not," I said. "But the moment the march stopped, the captain summoned all the lieutenants. And I noticed that we did not march as long as we could have today."

"I noticed that, too," said Mag.

Yue glanced back and forth between us. "What does that mean?"

"Captain Zhou may be trying to save our strength," said Mag. "And there is only one reason he might do that, which is to have us ready for a battle he believes is imminent."

Yue sighed. "I see."

"Let us see what Tou has to say before we consign ourselves to gloom," I said. "There may be another explanation."

There was not.

"The captain believes we will meet the enemy soon," said Tou, skipping any preamble. "We have stumbled upon signs of the Shades' march."

We stood there in dour silence—Mag, Yue, me, and the other two sergeants in Tou's company. They were both Mystic knights, but for the life of me, I can no longer remember their names.

"They are marching in the open?" I said at last. "That is unusual, from what we have heard."

"So it is," said Tou. "But they are both in the open and not, you might say. These are wildlands. It is unlikely anyone would see them, and less likely that anyone who saw them would know what they were seeing."

"Where are they coming from?" said Yue.

"The captain has a theory," said Tou. "Recently there have been rumors of Dorsean raids into Feldemar. King Alim of Feldemar has sought reparations. But King Jun knew nothing about the raids, and he refused responsibility for them. Diplomats on both sides were trying to sort the situation out. Now the captain thinks he knows the truth: these attacks were carried out by the Shades. They posed as Dorsean soldiers to foment discord between us and Feldemar."

Mag and I glanced at each other again. "That seems a sensible guess," said Mag. "We have had several encounters with the Shades so far, and they are fond of getting others to do their fighting for them."

"And so now we expect to meet these Shades on the field?" I said.

"The captain thinks so," said Tou. "And in very little time. We do not know their destination, but we mean to keep them from reaching it."

"Good," said Mag. "What does he need from us?"

"Only to be ready," said Tou, scratching his goatee. "And to make sure your squadrons are ready as well. You all have good heads on your shoulders and at least some experience in a fight. The same cannot be said for everyone you command. See to their readiness. Prepare them for what is to come."

"Easy enough," I said. But immediately, I winced. "Or rather, easy enough to understand. Of course, it is no simple thing to prepare someone for their first battle."

Yue arched an eyebrow at me. "Hm. I wonder what was wrong with me, that when we first met, I thought you had such a silver tongue."

I rolled my eyes at her before addressing Tou again. "We will see it done, ser. Let us know if there is any other way we can be of service." Then I turned and looked Yue dead in the eye. "And my tongue may not be silvered, but it has received no complaints of late."

I turned on my heel and left, while Mag nearly collapsed, trying to hold back her laughter. Yue went beet red and failed to muster any retort.

EIGHTEEN

I WOKE THE NEXT MORNING WITH A MISSION—ONE not given to me by Tou.

Quickly I broke my fast by the campfire nearest my squadron's tents. Then I headed towards the west end of the camp, where Kun and his Mystics slept. A few curious eyes followed me as I walked past, but I ignored them. Most of the time, if you act as though you are supposed to be wherever you are, few will question you. Such was the case then, for no Mystics came to ask me what I was doing.

At the westernmost end of the camp, I saw the

signs Kun had found. A wide trail had been tramped into the ground. It intersected with our path from the north, and there it turned west and headed in the same direction as our march. I gathered all the information that I could. Their number seemed to be around two hundreds, which was less than half of our force. That was close to Yue's best guess at their numbers. I saw no hoofprints at all, which was a heartening sign. If they had been a mounted party, we could not have hoped to catch them. It seemed to me that they had been here only a day ago. But I could not be entirely sure, nor could I tell anything else; Kun and his Mystics had already wandered about the place, disturbing many of the signs.

I turned and headed back towards my part of the camp with the same air of indifference as when I had come. Once again, no one hailed or challenged me. When I reached our row of tents, I saw that Mag was already up and breaking her fast by the fire. She greeted me with a lazy wave. I sat by her and pulled out a packet of dried meat. I had already eaten, but no seasoned soldier refuses a second helping.

"Good morn," I told her. "I have been busy already."

"So I gather," she said. "Looking into the signs of the Shades?"

"Just so. We are only a day behind them, I think. And they are marching west, on the same path as us."

Mag frowned. "West. I still do not understand it.

This is not the quickest way to reach any city of import. If they mean to make trouble in Feldemar, they would do better to go north, and if in Dorsea, then to the south."

I shrugged. "Mayhap they mean to practice some smaller mischief, as in Lan Shui."

"What is that about Lan Shui?" came a sleepy, grumbly voice. Yue hauled herself out of my tent. Her short yellow hair stuck out in all directions, black in the roots after so long without dye. "Do not tell me we are heading back home after I spent so long riding away from it. I might just throw a fit."

"I do not think so," I said, chuckling. She came to sit beside me. I brushed a hand lightly up her back, and she stole some food from my pouch.

Mag, meanwhile, did not look convinced by my idea. "I doubt they are doing anything like the ritual that summoned the vampires. Why would they need so many soldiers? The Shades in Lan Shui numbered less than a dozen."

"A fair point," I said. Then I arched my brows. "Though mayhap Yue struck closer to the truth. What if their destination is not on this side of the Greatrocks? They may be making for the Sunmane Pass, there to cross the Greatrocks and pursue some mischief in western Dorsea."

Mag's eyes widened. "No. They do not mean to cross the pass. They mean to occupy it."

Yue frowned. "Occupy it?"

But I understood Mag at once. "Of course. There are only two passes through the Greatrocks. If the Shades could occupy one of them, they would cut the kingdom's trade and travel in half."

"Why only in half?" said Mag, her expression going dark. "I would wager that another force makes for the Moonslight Pass in the south. They will cut Dorsea in two."

Yue and I looked at each other, and then at Mag. "We have to tell Kun," I said.

Mag snorted. "Would he even listen to us?"

"He could hardly ignore you," said Yue.

"You might be surprised," said Mag. "He has suspected us from the start. We only march in the vanguard so he can keep an eye on us."

"But this could devastate the kingdom," said Yue. "What do you mean to do about it, if not tell the captain?"

"She is right," I told Mag. "We have to try, at least. Mayhap if we present a plan of action, along with our guess, we may be able to convince him."

Mag's eyes flashed. "Do you think we could get our hands on a map?"

"I have one," said Yue, to our surprise. "It is nothing fit for kings, but I brought it for my journey, when I was trying to determine where you fools might have gone."

"Yue, you are a gift," said Mag. "Please, fetch it at once."

Soon we had it laid on the ground near the fire.

Mag took a piece of charcoal to draw on it, and her brow furrowed as she studied it. She circled a spot. Twenty-five leagues west of our position, there was a narrow pass between a wood to the south and a cluster of hills to the north.

"This place," she said. "It is the northern edge of the Greenfrost. We march right for it, and so do the Shades. It would be a perfect place to attack them. But Kun's army has no hope of catching them before they reach it. Not unless we send a smaller force to ambush them, to delay their march until the rest of the army can catch up."

"It will be a hard trek even so," I said. "But with us guiding Tou's company, we could get there in time."

"Then let us bring this to the lieutenant at once," said Yue, "before Kun begins the day's march."

We found Tou with little trouble. He was finishing his morning meal, and he arched an eyebrow at us as we approached.

"Good day," he said. "What is it? You look as though something important has happened."

"Not yet," said Mag.

As quickly as we could, we outlined our plan. Tou listened attentively, curling his fingers through his goatee and frowning.

"The Sunmane Pass," he said. "I admit, it makes more sense than anything else we have guessed at. But they would have a hard time holding it with no place of strength to defend."

A chill went through me. "They may have a stronghold in the peaks," I said.

Tou met my gaze, nonplussed. "Oh? I know of no such places in those mountains. How could they keep it hidden?"

My throat went dry. "I . . . I have seen something similar before. In the mountains west of Northwood. It is where I first saw Shades, though I did not know who they were at the time."

I was afraid Tou might have heard something of that stronghold and know that there was more to my tale. But to my immense relief, he only nodded. "Well, then. I think you are right. This must be brought before the captain." His expression soured. "Though I wonder if I should bring it to him myself. He is . . . not overly fond of the two of you."

"An understatement if ever there was one," said Mag lightly. "But you will need Albern and me to guide the company if we have any hope of catching the Shades in time."

Tou tilted his head. "You know the area well?"

"She is Dorsean," I told him, "and grew up not far from here. And I was trained as a ranger in Calentin. Though I do not know this land well, I can guide a force through any wilderness if I know where I am going."

Mag's mouth opened and then clamped tight again. I hoped I had not overstepped, saying more than she had wished. But she did not look angry, only conflicted.

"All right," said Tou. "The troops have risen, and most will soon be ready to march. We must speak to the captain at once. Come."

"Ser," said Mag, Yue, and I together.

We followed him through the camp to Kun's tent. A small table had been set up, and Kun was enjoying a meal upon it. Upon another, smaller table beside him, he read reports and letters. As he noticed our approach, he looked up, gave us a beaming smile, and wiped a bit of grease from the corner of his mouth.

"Lieutenant Shi," he said. His eyes roved across the rest of us. "And your sergeants. To what do I owe such a pleasure?"

Tou drew up smartly and gave a salute. "Captain. Mag and Albern have shared some thoughts with me this morning, and I thought it best to bring them to your attention."

"Indeed?" said Kun. "I am sure I cannot wait to hear what is going on in their inimitable minds." He stood and motioned to one of his attendants, who began to clean the remainder of his meal. "Let us speak in my tent."

We followed him inside. Like those of most military commanders, his tent was a grander thing than the one- and two-person tents of the rest of the camp. He had a space in the middle for a desk, upon which had been laid a map of Dorsea, larger and more detailed than Yue's.

"Now then," said Kun. "I imagine this has something to do with whatever Sergeant Telfer was poking his nose into this morning?"

So, someone had reported my investigation to the captain after all. I tried not to look like a guilty child who had been caught stealing an extra slice of apple tart. "Yes, Captain," I said. "I was curious about the Shades and what their aims might be. And I am somewhat skilled at woodcraft, so I thought I might be able to glean some information."

"Lieutenant Zhou is also quite capable in such matters," said Kun. "Tell me: do you think you discovered anything he did not?"

"I am certain he saw everything I did, Captain," I said. "Yet Mag and I might have been able to guess more from the information."

Mag stepped in. "Ser, we believe the Shades are making for the Sunmane Pass. If they can prevent travel through it, and if an equal force can do the same in the Moonslight Pass to the south, they will deal a devastating blow to Dorsea. It will help Wojin hold the throne, and even if he were usurped, Dorsea will be utterly unable to aid the High King against Dulmun."

Kun's brows shot for the tent's ceiling. "That is quite an assumption. Do you know something of the Shades' intentions?"

The meaning behind the question was obvious. Kun rarely missed an opportunity to needle us with the possibility that we were on the side of the enemy. I ignored it, and as Tou rolled out Yue's smaller map atop the larger one, I pointed to the marks we had made with charcoal.

"It may be an assumption, Captain, but I believe it is a good one," I said. "Mag was the first to think something was wrong. She was born and raised in Dorsea, and it bothered her when she saw the direction of the Shades' march. They are headed due west, yet there is nothing valuable between here and the Greatrocks—nothing except the pass itself."

"And two hundreds is more than enough to hold the pass and keep anyone from using it," said Tou. "At least we think so, if the Shades have a stronghold in the Greatrocks."

I blanched as Kun gave him a sharp look. "A stronghold? And what makes you think they have one?"

Tou paused, turning to look at me. "Well . . ."

I took a deep breath. "Captain Zhou. What do you know of Jordel of the family Adair?"

A long moment of silence stretched as he studied me. Tou now seemed uncomfortable, as though he regretted bringing us here. Mag's gaze remained locked on me, studying my face. I suspected she worried for me—after all, she was one of the few who knew all the details of my time with Jordel. More details than I would share now, certainly.

But I was also keenly aware of Yue's gaze upon me. It was only a few days since we had spoken of Jordel, though I had not named him then. Her expression was a mix of curiosity and pity.

At last, Kun spoke slowly. "I did not know Jordel. But I have heard much of him."

"Especially since Northwood fell, if I am not mistaken," I said.

Kun's smile sharpened, and he lifted his chin. "What makes you say that?"

"Because I was with him in the Greatrocks," I said. "I fought by his side when we discovered the Shades there. And I laid his cairn when he fell, and I wept at his grave."

The air in the tent was thick enough to cut with a knife. Kun did not so much as blink, and I could read nothing in his smile.

"Hm," he said. Another moment passed, and then his smile softened. "Well. This is all interesting information that I certainly wish I had had earlier. I wonder if I can believe it. Though if you were trying to trick me, I hardly think you would admit involvement in the death of the last Mystic captain you knew."

For weeks now, I had kept my temper through such remarks. Kun never stopped prodding us, trying to get a reaction. And I understood why, and I forgave him for it. But now I felt my blood rush in my ears, creating a whine at the very edge of my hearing, and a terrible rage thundered in my chest.

"Captain," I said, my voice louder than it should have been, "I will not stand idle while you speak that way. You have your jibes at Mag's and my expense. We hear them beneath your courtesy, and we know you know it. But you will keep your needling words far from the subject of Jordel."

Tou's eyes were wide, and he looked as though he wanted to do something but did not know what. Meanwhile, Kun's smile had again grown sharp and icy. "Oh, I will? Or what? What will you do if I do not comply?"

"There is no 'or,'" I said.

"Albern," said Mag, gently but firmly.

"No!" I barked, cutting her off. Her brows lifted, but I ignored her and turned back to Kun. "There is no 'or.' You will stop because you are a man of honor, and respecting Jordel's memory is the honorable thing to do. If I were a Shade in disguise, intent on your ruin, it would still be right. If I were an assassin with designs on the High King herself, it would still be right. You will not speak ill of the dead or of—" My voice caught, but I forced myself to go on. "—Or of one who loved him. You *will* hold your tongue, not for fear of anything I might do, but because it is right, and because you are worthy of such restraint."

Everything lapsed into silence again. Tou still looked ready to spring into action the instant he felt sure of what action to take. My limbs shook as anger and anxiety coursed through me together. I was prepared to fight, to flee, or to break and weep on the ground, and I could not have told you which I wanted to do most.

But Kun did not look angry. His smile had not gone, but it had eased.

"At last, some honesty," he said quietly.

I frowned. "Ser?"

He dropped his gaze to the map and leaned over the table on clenched fists. "The two of you wrap yourselves in lies. You have since the moment I laid eyes on you. Nothing you have said to me has come without some cloak of falsehood, or a shawl of deceit at the very least. And that is fine. I do not need unshrouded honesty from everyone who serves me. But it makes me suspicious, as is my right." He looked back up at me again, studying me close from beneath his thick black brows. "Yet now I hear you speak with truth ringing from every part of you—your tongue, your eyes, and your heart. It is refreshing."

There was a long pause while I took this in. "Thank you, Captain," I said at last. "So you believe me?"

"I do," said Kun, smiling. "And your sharing of truth deserves the same in turn. I had not meant to tell you this yet, but now I wish to inform you of something Lieutenant Zhen learned in Kuan Shu."

Lieutenant Zhen straightened suddenly, his eyes widening. "Ser—"

Kun waved him to silence with one hand. "Zhen, please. They deserve as much, now that they have laid their hearts bare, as it were." He turned his gaze to us. "Wojin has been deposed."

"What?" said Mag, Yue, and I at the same time.

"Yes," said Kun, nodding. "Reports are murky as to how. But agents in the capital city of Danfon, led by other Mystics, overthrew the pretender king. Even now, he is being held captive there."

"Then who sits the throne?" said Yue.

Kun glanced at her. "His Majesty—formerly His Excellency—Senlin of the family Fei. King Jun was, it seems, killed. That much was true in what Wojin said, if nothing else was."

"But this is wonderful news, ser!" said Tou. "Should we not proceed to Danfon at once to help the new king stabilize his claim?"

"You forget yourself, Lieutenant," said Kun, though his smile remained plastered on his face. "We are Mystics. Our duty is not only to Dorsea, but to the High King, and through her, to Underrealm itself."

Tou bowed his head at once. "Of course, ser. Please accept my apology."

"It is accepted," said Kun. "And to answer your question: no. I do not think that Danfon is where we are most needed. King Senlin remains a loyal servant of the High King, and I have faith that he will consolidate his power in the capital and across the kingdom. But he will not be able to do so if the Shades succeed in cutting Dorsea in two by claiming the mountain passes."

Mag's eyes were alight. "So you believe us, then?"

Kun's smile widened. "Yes. I believe you. Your guess as to the Shades' intentions is better than any of mine. And knowing the lieutenant, you came up with a plan of action before you brought this to me. What is it?"

Tou glanced back and forth between Mag and me, as though he could hardly believe it. But he recovered quickly, clearing his throat. "Well, Captain. Sergeant Mag pointed out this area here." He indicated the spot Mag had marked earlier. "A smaller, faster force could be sent ahead to circle the Shades, ambushing them in the Greenfrost. That could hamper their march long enough for our main host to catch up with them, wiping them out before they reach the Greatrocks."

"Hm," said Kun, thinking. "It would be a hard march."

"Albern and I can serve as guides, ser," said Mag quickly. "I know the area, and Albern's woodcraft is unmatched—or, that is, I am sure it is comparable to Lieutenant Zhou's."

Kun chuckled. "You need not look after my nephew's honor so closely, Sergeant. Very well. I will let the two of you guide this force. Lieutenant Shi, your company will march on the route they have indicated."

"Yes, Captain," said Tou, giving him a bow.

"And I will be coming with you," finished Kun.

That gave all of us pause. Tou looked surprised, but Mag looked suspicious.

"Your . . . presence would be most welcome, of course, Captain," said Tou slowly.

"Oh, not just mine," said Kun. "My entire unit. All of the Mystics in our force, save those who are sergeants and lieutenants in the other companies. After all, if you intend to slow the Shades' march, you will need the strongest fighters you can get." He turned to Mag. "With Lieutenant Shi's company and my unit, we shall have just over a hundred of troops. Will that let you stage an ambush that can halt our foes' advance?"

Mag grinned. "I could do it with half that, ser."

Kun's eternal smile turned just as wolfish as her own.

NINETEEN

Days later, unaware that the Shades' position had been discovered, Kaita wrestled with weighty thoughts.

Mag had guessed correctly. The Shades, having fulfilled their purpose on the border between Dorsea and Feldemar, now made for the Sunmane Pass. Most of the western senators had not been loyal to Wojin, and they would wish now to support the new king, as soon as they could muster the armies to do it. The Shades might not be able to prevent that from happening, but they would want to delay it as long as they could.

These matters were much on Kaita's mind. But something else also troubled her thoughts. She wore no furs against the cold—it was nothing compared to Tokana—but she still had on her cloak. She never took it off these days. And as she considered the road ahead, her hand stole into the cloak, probing an inside pocket. There sat the package of brown cloth Rogan had given her.

She could feel the magestones calling to her. Sometimes she even peeled back the edges of the cloth to look at them, as though to reassure herself of their presence. They glinted back at her, dark as the pupil of a giant's eye.

Wild thoughts flitted through her mind whenever she looked at the stones. Rogan had never wanted to give them to her. What if he had lied? What if he had given her fakes? She should eat one, test it, just to be sure, just so that she could know—

Footsteps approached her tent. Kaita snatched her hand away from the stones as the front flap opened. Tagata entered, bent double to fit.

Tagata was a shadeborn, like Rogan. Ten and a half hands tall she stood, and her shoulders were as broad as two ordinary folk abreast. On her back she carried a massive greatsword, which was as tall as Kaita herself. But her most frightening ability was neither her strength nor the surprising speed with which she could move. It was the tattoo inked on the back of her neck, the mark of her lord's favor. That mark could banish death itself, letting her recover from even the most grievous wound in a matter of moments.

She was a killer, born and bred and given a dark blessing. Yet, like Rogan, she was not always cruel or violent. As she entered Kaita's tent, her eyes held nothing but fondness and concern. And as she saw Kaita resting only in her cloak, she gave a little smile.

"Are you not cold, little one?" she said. "But then, I suppose you would not be, after your days in Calentin."

Kaita felt a flash of anger at the mention of Calentin, but it quickly subsided. She knew Tagata meant nothing by the jest, and she did not know as much of Kaita's story as Rogan did. So she smiled in response and beckoned Tagata to sit beside her.

"I find the cold bracing," she said. "But I am not opposed to piling on a few extra furs when I have someone with whom to share them. There are few things as pleasant as sharing warmth and comfort when the world is cold and dead."

"I agree with you there," said Tagata, taking the seat Kaita had offered. Their shoulders pressed together, and even through her thick cloak, Kaita could feel the warmth of Tagata's shoulder. She was like a furnace. It was something she had noticed in all the shadeborn she had ever met, as if they burned with some inner fire that no winter could hope to douse. Kaita leaned into her, resting her head on her shoulder.

Rogan had always told her to love all the Shades

like her own family. But in truth, Kaita held most of them in disdain. They were like sheep, like the very people who had made her suffer early in life. She gave her trust and love only to those who deserved it—ones like Tagata, and Rogan himself. Ones who were useful, because they were strong.

But they were also very, very clever. And even as Tagata wrapped an arm around Kaita's shoulders, sharing more of her heat through the cloak, she glanced down at Kaita to give her a quick look-over.

"Are you well?" she said. "Is there anything you wish to speak with me about? Anything that worries you?"

Kaita sighed through her nose. "You should say what you mean. I have not taken the magestones. I gave my word to Rogan. And yet in return, he has sent me to march with you, directly away from where I wish to go."

Tagata frowned. "We must make for the pass. If the western senators can muster—"

"I know the reasons," snapped Kaita. She paused, took a breath, and forced herself back to calm. "Of course, this host can hardly turn around and head east. But I could. I could go on the hunt for Albern and Mag again. I have the power to end them at last."

"You must have faith," said Tagata. "If Rogan told you this was the right thing to do, you must trust him. He would not deceive you."

"I trust in him, just as I trust in our father," said

Kaita irritably. "Yet what else am I supposed to think? The last I heard, Albern and Mag were to the east. Yet he sends me to march west. Does he know where they are better than I do? If so, why does he not tell me? Why not tell me *where* and *when* I shall meet them, rather than a vague promise?"

"He would never say it unless he believed it to be true," said Tagata.

"And I wish to trust in that," growled Kaita. "But how can I? How can he know?"

Tagata hesitated. At first, Kaita thought she had no answer. But when Tagata spoke, it was almost as if the words were being forced out of her. "He has . . . methods."

Kaita drew back, feeling her arm and shoulder cool as she looked up into Tagata's face. Tagata, meanwhile, did not meet her eyes, but looked studiously at the tent flap.

"Tagata?" said Kaita. "What do you mean?"

Tagata licked her lips, considering. "He . . . that is, I mean Rogan, but Father as well . . . they have . . . a sight."

She paused. Kaita remained silent, waiting. She felt a curious certainty that Tagata should not be telling her this, and that she should not press the matter, for that might drive Tagata back to silence.

"I do not know quite how it works," said Tagata. Now she spoke more quickly, as though cracks in a dam were widening. "But they can see things. Threads of time and fate, like the future in a tapestry."

"No one has that power," whispered Kaita.

"They do," said Tagata. "I do not know how it works. I do not know where they gained it. Rogan often says that we are all equal to each other—but I cannot be his equal, for this gift is beyond me. I barely know of its existence, and I know nothing of its origin. It seems to me that it is . . . unclear, some of the time. Yet from what I know, it is infallible."

"And what do you know?" said Kaita.

But Tagata shook her head. "I should not have said as much as I have. I will not speak more of this. I only tell you so that you know your faith is not misplaced. If Rogan said you would achieve your aims this way, but did not explain why, then I am sure it is because he has seen it."

Kaita wanted to ask one of the thousand questions whirling in her mind. But before she could prod Tagata to speak on, they heard shouting outside the tent.

Instantly they were on their feet, Kaita casting her cloaks and blankets aside. They threw themselves out of the tent just as a Shade came running up to them, her eyes wide, and pointed east.

"Commander!" she said to Tagata. "One of the eastern outriders has delivered a report. There is a force following us."

"What?" snapped Tagata. "How many? How close?"

"That is unclear, commander," said the messenger. "He saw the smoke of many campfires, but could not see the foe."

Tagata paused for a moment, considering. But a furious excitement sparked in Kaita's heart.

"It is them," she said in a whisper. "It must be."

Tagata frowned at her. "If there are many campfires, it cannot only be Mag and Albern."

"No," said Kaita. "Not just them. They have allied with others, other servants of the High King, to pursue me. Or to pursue us, for I doubt they know I am here. You were right. *Rogan* was right. I should never have doubted."

"You can be forgiven, I think," said Tagata. She turned back to the messenger. "Send word all through the camp. Muster for the march, and be ready to press hard. We must reach the Greatrocks before they catch us."

"Yes, commander," said the messenger, and she ran off to carry Tagata's words through the camp.

"I should go east," said Kaita.

Tagata's eyes went wide. "*No,* Kaita," she began. "You cannot—"

Kaita stopped her with a raised hand. "Be at peace. I do not mean to fight them. But I am your only weremage. Let me scout their position and estimate their number. When I am done, I will come straight back."

Tagata did not seem entirely convinced. The giant frowned down at her. "Will you promise me?"

Kaita gave her a small smile. Not all the Shades had earned her love, but Tagata had done so long ago. "I will do better than that," she said quietly.

She reached into her cloak and pulled out the small packet wrapped in brown cloth. As Tagata stared in shock, Kaita placed it in her hand and folded her thick fingers around it.

"Keep them until I return," said Kaita. "They would slow me down in my flight. And without them, you know I have no chance of striking at Mag and Albern in the heart of their allies."

"Kaita . . ." murmured Tagata.

Wordlessly, Kaita stood on tiptoe and pulled Tagata's face down to kiss her on the cheek. Then she turned, and her eyes filled with magelight. An instant later, a raven took wing into the grey, cloudy sky.

Kaita had to flap hard, for there were no updrafts to cast her sailing through the air. But she relished the burning in her wings, the feeling of blood coursing its feverish way through the tiny veins of her bird form. Her months of fleeing from Mag and me had left her exhausted, but she had had a week of easy travel with the Shades to recover. Now flying felt like a return to honest work after being too long idle.

At last, she spotted Kun's force. She studied it from high up in the air. Her best guess was that around three and a half hundreds of troops lay below her, not counting the camp followers behind. That was almost double the size of the Shade force. Worse yet, she spotted some dozen or so red cloaks wandering among the press—Mystic officers directing the militia.

So. The Mystics were aware of the Shades' march

and were hunting them across Dorsea. And they were only half a day's march behind the Shades. At least they had no horses, other than some few officers' mounts and pack animals. Tagata and her troops should still be able to reach the Greatrocks before they were caught, though it would be a near thing.

Kaita was about to swoop lower. She wanted to see if she could identify the leader of this little army. She especially wanted to catch sight of Mag and me, to confirm what she already suspected. But just before she bent her wings to dive, an arrow flew up from the host. It pierced a raven, a real raven, through the breast. The bird plummeted to the ground.

Dark take them, thought Kaita. They were shooting birds in case they were weremages. Even as she watched, a falcon drew too close and was shot down.

Well. In truth, that was all she needed to know. If this host was taking precaution against weremages, that must mean that Mag and I were there. We would have told them about her. She could not get closer to confirm it, but she had all the proof she required.

She turned and powered her wings back towards Tagata and the rest of the Shades.

Of course, Tou's company had left the rest of the host days ago, and Mag and I had gone with him. Under our guidance, the company had marched south for half a day before swinging west. Then, we had raced along a small valley that ran south of the Greenfrost. Kun had directed the rest of his forces, under Zhen's command, to pursue the Shades with all possible speed and distract them.

That was why Kaita only counted three and a half hundreds of soldiers, and she reported that number to Tagata.

That was why she only saw a dozen or so redcloaks—the rest were with Kun, who marched with Mag and me.

That was why the next day, Kaita only kept an eye on the force behind, and never flew ahead to scout the Greenfrost for danger.

And that was why the Shades were utterly unprepared when we found them in the forest the next day.

TWENTY

We marched at a breakneck pace, sleeping six hours each night and pressing ourselves hard during the daylight. Each time we stopped, Mag and I consulted Kun's map again. We evaluated each day's progress and made plans for the next. I put every ounce of my woodcraft to its utmost use, and Mag wracked her mind for every detail she could remember of the countryside.

If Kun's soldiers had not been so green, I doubt we could have carried off the march in time. When soldiers have never seen combat, their first outing seems like a thrilling adventure. They will march and train harder, and they find it easy to call upon inner reserves of strength and energy.

These things fade once they learn the reality of war. But since ours had not yet absorbed that lesson, we were able to push them hard enough to catch up to our foes.

Our force reached the woods a day before the Shades. The Greenfrost is so named because it is filled with trees called pycnandra, which secrete a greenish sap. When winter comes, the trees freeze over, and the sap turns the ice green. Then it is like wandering through a forest of emerald and jade statues. They were still frozen when we passed through the wood. It was a breathtaking sight, though we had little time to appreciate its beauty.

The path where the Shades entered the Greenfrost to the east was winding and sinuous. But halfway through the wood, the road straightened, and then it ran straight as an arrow's path until it reached the western end of the forest. It was on this straightaway that Kun planned our attack.

Tou's company had five squadrons: three of archers, including mine, and Mag's and Yue's with swords. And then, of course, there were Kun's Mystics, all carrying swords and shields, and each wearing chain.

We deployed two squadrons of archers on the south of the road and my unit to the north. Kun would signal the attack by firing a flaming brand into the air, and the archers would loose. Our bowfire would sow confusion in the Shades' ranks, miring them down. Then would come the second strike. Kun's Mystics would attack straight down the center, with Mag's squadron supporting him on the left and Yue's spears on the right.

Kun knew we would not be able to stop the Shades entirely, not with only a hundred of fighters. His idea was to make them retreat instead. We wanted them to run north, where the Greenfrost gave way to a vast, broad land with many hills and dells.

"Captain," said Yue, when Kun told us the plan. "Will they not vanish into the hills? How will we keep track of them?"

"Indeed, we hope they try it, because it will not work," said Kun. He nodded to Mag. "Mag here knows this region. The land there is too gentle to block sight very well. Nor will it let them funnel us into a trap, nor will the gentle slopes give them much of a high ground to defend. The hills only look impressive from a distance. Once inside, they will never leave again."

It was a cunning ploy, and Mag and I were impressed. I think Kun could tell we approved, which seemed to please him, despite himself. Something had changed in his attitude towards us. I did not get the sense that he trusted us, but no longer was he always suspicious of us. He spoke frankly with us as he laid out his plan.

"I wish to impress upon you both," he said to Mag

and me, "that your squadrons will be in the path of the Shades' retreat. You must withdraw the moment they move in your direction. I hope you understand that I am not placing you in this position out of any wish of harm to you. With your experience, I know—or hope—that you will be able to lead your squadrons in a disciplined retreat."

Mag cracked a smile. "You can say what you mean, Captain, if you mean to imply we are cowards."

Kun's small council erupted in laughter, which we all quickly cut off. The humor was a good thing—all our faces had been grim, and there are few things more harmful to a fighting force than for its commanders to be too moody.

"Hardly," said Kun, smiling as usual. "Discipline and speed are all I ask of you. Maneuver west, swing around, and join the rest of us in pursuing them north."

"As you wish, Captain," I said.

"Good," said Kun. His smile lost some of its luster. "All that is left, then, is the waiting."

As any soldier with experience will tell you, the waiting is the worst part.

I gathered my squadron and moved with them to the north, positioning them in the forest where Kun had directed us. Mag and her unit came with us. Our troops kept their eyes cast down at the ground, and their fingers were pale where they gripped their weapons. Only Hallan seemed to be in better spirits, and that was only compared to the rest. His mouth was set in a firm line; he told no jokes, but kept his now-spectacled gaze on the beautiful jade forest ahead.

We stopped at Mag's position, and I turned to her to clasp wrists.

"Take care of yourself," she said. "If you are killed, I shall be very cross with you."

"And the same to you," I said.

I glanced over her shoulder at her squadron. Li stood there. Her gaze wandered like always, but her hands were shaking. Beside her was Dibu, who was as still as a rock.

I stepped past Mag.

"Listen to me," I said, loud enough to cut through their stupor. "I know your minds. I was there once. We all were. Even Mag, hard as it is to believe it."

Gently I punched her in the shoulder. She responded with a chop under my bicep, and my whole arm lanced with pain. I shook it hard to get the needles out.

"That is my drawing arm, you sow," I growled. Despite themselves, her squadron chuckled. "Yes," I told them. "That is how you should be feeling. Not thrilled, for you are not fools. But neither should you worry overmuch, for you have one great advantage in the battle you are about to fight. You have her. You have all heard stories of the Uncut Lady. Sky above, Dryleaf has told you plenty of them in the last weeks."

I hooked my thumbs in my belt and threw my shoulders back. "Well, tonight Dryleaf is going to need you. He will need you to tell *him* tales about your sergeant so that he can add them to his trove. I have fought with Mag on more battlefields than most of you have years in your life. She will not let you down. She will do everything in her power—and that is considerable—to lead you home safe from the field. Do the same for her, and each other, and you will be fine."

As I spoke, I watched them straighten. They turned to look at Mag, and then back to me. And in that brief moment, fear turned to resolution.

Once more I took Mag's wrist, and then I pulled her in for an embrace. There was nothing left to say, and so I led my squadron off.

We were half a span away from Mag's squadron when Jian cleared her throat. "Well, Sergeant. Have you any inspiring speech for us? I half thought Mag would speak on your behalf the way you spoke on hers."

"And what did you think she would say?" I retorted. "You have little to hang your hope upon. You are, after all, stuck with *me.*"

That got a halfhearted laugh from all of them. I stopped and turned, for we had reached our position.

"No, but in all earnestness, the most comforting thing I can say to you is that you do not need any comforting today. For most of you, this is your first battle. And it may be the safest one you will ever see.

You have an easy job today: shoot an enemy when they do not know you are there and flee before they can retaliate." I raised one finger. "But there *is* something you must remember. You must listen for the moment when I sound the retreat. And you must stay close to me, and to your squadmates, when we pull back. Pay attention to your surroundings, and always keep an ear out for my call. What is far more important than killing the enemy?"

"Staying alive," they all said in chorus. I had drilled it into them hard enough.

"According to you," added Jian, after a moment.

Chausiku's nostrils flared, and his locs shook as he turned on her. "Dark below, Jian—"

"Be calm, you tree trunk," she told him, pushing her rakish hair off her forehead. "It was a jest."

I rolled my eyes. "All right. Find a tree to hide behind. And get ready."

TWENTY-ONE

It was I who loosed the first shot.

That makes me sound like the quickest archer on the field. But if I am being honest with you, it is because I forgot that Kun was supposed to give us a signal to attack.

The Shades came marching down the forest road from the east. Their dark forms slid in and out of view between the emerald trunks of the trees, like imps half-glimpsed in the wild. I watched them come, wrapped thick in their cloaks of blue. None were on horses, and they all bent wearily under their packs and bedrolls.

They looked to be far more tired than our company, for we had been able to leave most of our equipment and supplies back with the main force.

Near the head of the column was a giant of a woman who gave me pause. It was Tagata, as you might be able to guess, but of course, I had never seen her before. She was massive, towering over the Shades all around her, with muscles thick as anything. She wore no extra clothing against the rainy chill, and her skin glistened with a sheen of sweat in the afternoon air. I swallowed hard.

The first shadeborn I had met was Trisken, who slew Jordel. When I first saw Rogan, I recognized in him the same strength, the same viciousness. I saw it again in this woman now. That meant shooting her would be useless, even if I were to plant an arrow in her eye.

Therefore I chose the closest Shade to me as a target instead. He was a young man, mayhap in his twentieth year. His pale cheeks were rosy with heavy breaths that misted in the cold. He was not wary, nor was he looking about for any sign of attack. He would not even know he was in danger before he was dead.

I sighed and waited for the right moment. But as I said, I forgot about Kun's signal. Fortunately for me, Kun and I had the same idea of when the right moment was. I must have loosed my arrow at the same instant that Kun fired his flaming brand into the sky. At the same time that my shaft sank into the young man's neck, and he fell to the ground, gurgling, a searing hiss sounded in the air.

Shouts erupted from the woods all around us as our soldiers saw the signal. Flights of arrows ripped through the air to land among our foes. The Shades recoiled into each other and drew their weapons. But their movements were slow, sluggish, burdened with the weight of leagues behind them.

All but the brute woman. In an instant, her greatsword was in her hand, shining in the thin sunlight through the clouds. She gave a battle cry that shook the trees, and the Shades jumped in response. Suddenly there was vigor in their steps, and they tried to form into ranks.

We loosed another volley—the third, for me. Our hail of arrows struck the blue cloaks, and I watched them fall. We were silent—what use a battle cry when you are almost a span away and drawing no closer? Our only sound was the hissing song of death flying on wings of fletching.

Then Kun led his charge, and the air filled with their roar. A score and a half of Mystics came charging from the trees, and at their flanks were Mag's squadron and Yue's spears.

Snow turned red as blood splashed across it. The Shades reeled back. Their allies behind them tried to shove them forwards again. But they only pushed them onto our blades.

I saw Li there. She stood side by side with her fellows, but she was hesitant, the tip of her sword shaking. A Shade lunged at her with a savage roar. Li blocked his strikes, but she did not retaliate. And as she stepped back, her foot slipped in the blood-red snow.

Before the Shade could finish her off, Dibu was there. His sword hacked into the Shades' raised sword arm. The man screamed, but only for a moment before Dibu stabbed him through the gut.

Another Shade ran up. Dibu traded two blows and then slammed the edge of his shield into her face. She reeled back, nose broken. Dibu's sword hacked at her neck, nearly severing her head. She flopped to the ground.

With a moment of space to breathe, Dibu turned and hauled Li to her feet. She was still shaking, but she nodded at him. Together they plunged again into the fray, driving the Shades back.

But alone among the Shades, the brute held. Kun's Mystics broke like a wave around her. And she, like a boulder in the surf, held them off until they had to withdraw. Her greatsword came around in a grand sweep. A handful of redcloaks struck the bloody slush, never to rise again.

A curse slipped out of me. I had lost sight of Mag in the press. Hopefully, she would recognize the woman's power from my descriptions of Trisken. If she could strike at the tattoo I guessed was on the back of her neck, we might bring her down, which would be a grievous blow to the Shades.

And then a raven swooped out of the sky, and I forgot all about Mag and the brute.

The raven plunged straight into the Shades' midst. No natural bird would have landed there during a battle. And if I needed any more confirmation, it came in a flash of magelight. Soon Kaita was visible among the press, shouting orders to her fellows.

I could not take my eyes from her. My drawing hand had stilled, and no shafts flew from my string. Hallan paused in his firing, looking at me strangely. He reached over and seized my shoulder, shaking it.

"Sergeant!" he cried.

I roused myself from my thoughts. Kaita could wait.

Where was Mag? Still, I could not see her. But there was the brute woman, holding the Shade line firm.

"Everyone!" I cried. "If you are a good enough shot not to hit our allies, loose your arrows at the giant!"

I pointed her out—as if they needed help to spot her—and then drew and fired my arrow. Six more shafts joined mine. Two missed, but that still sent five arrows slamming into her chest, her neck, her arms.

The brute reeled back. The Shades around her buckled in dismay.

Now the Mystics pressed forwards. Three sank blades deep into the brute's torso. I watched her cough up blood.

My gaze darted back to Kaita. She looked at the brute woman, and she screamed. In anger? In grief? I did not know, for I could not hear.

One ambitious Mystic swung his blade for the brute's neck. But she was not as grievously wounded as he thought. With a roar, she caught his sword in her hand. It sank into the flesh, but she gritted her teeth and bore it. Then she seized the Mystic around the neck and crushed his face with her forehead. His whole body went limp, and he fell to the ground.

The other redcloaks drew back, nervous. That gave the brute the moment she needed to stand. Even as I watched, her skin began to stitch over the gaping wounds in her body. She drew in ragged breaths and hefted her greatsword again.

But another volley of arrows fell upon the Shades, and more of them dropped to the ground. The brute looked back at her allies, and I saw her hesitate. She did not know if there were more soldiers in these woods, waiting to pounce.

As the muscles in her jaw spasmed and then clenched as hard as iron, she raised her greatsword and pointed it north.

"Retreat!" she cried, and the word shook the very air, though her voice was thick with the blood in her lungs. "North! Retreat!"

I looked to Kaita again. She had taken up the call as well, shoving the Shades around her towards the trees—towards us.

And then I saw Mag.

She and her squadron had begun to fall back, retreating before the Shades as Kun had ordered. But

Mag had stopped. She was looking at Kaita, who stood amid the Shades a span away.

Their eyes met across the battlefield.

Both of them stood motionless, gazes locked. Around Kaita, the Shades fled straight towards us, towards the trees that promised safety. Around Mag, her squadron wavered, unsure, not wishing to abandon their sergeant.

"Mag!"

My voice cut through the battle. Mag swiveled to look at me.

But there was Kaita. Mag turned back.

"Mag!" I barked again. Her gaze drew inexorably back to me. "Not yet."

She heaved a great sigh. And she nodded, turning to her squad. I saw her order the retreat, though I could not hear the words.

"Retreat!" I called out. "West, into the woods!"

My unit looked ready to melt with relief, for the Shades were now only half a span away. They began to head west, but I hesitated a moment more, looking back towards Kaita.

She had not moved. She was looking at Mag, even as Mag's unit withdrew. And in that moment, it was as if I could hear the silent words in her mind.

Not yet, I had said. And now I heard Kaita promise, *But soon.*

I turned and followed my squadron. The Shades fled north towards the hills, just as Kun had planned, and we gathered to wait for the rest of our forces to catch up.

TWENTY-TWO

"And was she correct?" said Sun.

"Hm?" Albern was studying the streets and barely seemed to have heard Sun's question.

"Kaita. Was she correct? Was it soon that she and Mag faced each other at last?"

Albern sighed. "Still eager for the end. Well, be assured, it is coming. It was not long at all before it happened."

"Thank the sky," said Sun. "Let us hear it, then."

"Ah-ah," said Albern. "You shall have to wait a little while. We have arrived."

He stopped, and Sun groaned as she skidded to a halt beside him. They stood in front of a building that looked like a simple shop but for the thick wooden beam barring the front door.

"This place?" said Sun. "It looks to be closed. You should keep telling the story while we wait for it to open."

"It is meant to look abandoned," said Albern, chuckling. "Yet it is very much occupied. Come."

He led her around the back of the building. In the rear was another, smaller door. Sun had seen this sort of shop before. Behind the door would be a stair leading up to an apartment. Albern knocked in a strange pattern: three times, then a pause, then once, then another pause, and then twice more.

Moments passed as Sun looked nervously around. They were in a narrow intersection in the alleys between buildings. Though it led to open air in all four directions, Sun could not help a slight feeling of being trapped.

"Keep talking while we wait," she whispered. "At least tell me what Kaita—"

Snap. A latch turned inside the door, and it cracked open. But Sun could see that a thick chain was affixed to the inside of it, which kept the door from opening too far.

Through the crack, she saw a man. His face was of a medium brown and wrinkled—though not as heavily as Albern's. He wore a thin mustache and a scrub of beard that only held to the edge of his chin, but which was neatly trimmed. His clothing had a sort of look Sun was well familiar with from up-jumped courtiers back home: fine quality, but too ostentatious. His hair fell to his shoulders, black but heavily streaked with grey. His eyes were sharp as he took in Albern, and then his glance flitted to Sun. When he spoke, it was with a heavy south Heddish accent and cadence.

"Albern," said the man. He undid the chain and opened the door wider. "You're late."

"Only by a few days, old friend," said Albern. "I had some important business to attend in Lan Shui."

The man sniffed. "Iss always important business with you. I s'pose you should come in."

"We would not want to trouble you."

"Did I say you're troubling me? Come, iss bloody warm in this sun."

He closed the door and undid the chain before opening it again. He waved a hand to indicate they should climb the stairs. It was less the gesture of a well-mannered doorman and more the furtive command of an irritated parent summoning their children in for dinner.

At the top of the stairs was an apartment, as Sun had expected. A large central room took up much of the space. Cabinets and shelves of crockery lined the walls, and a hearth dominated the back right corner, though it was now empty and cold. A large wooden table stood in the center. On this was a map of Dorsea and Selvan, with some of the other kingdoms poking in at the edges. Sun spied some markings on the map in various colors. But before she could get a good look at them, the man threw a thin blanket over the map to cover it.

"Something to drink?" said the man.

"Mayhap a bit of wine," said Albern. "Not too much, though. We need to keep our wits about us today."

The man's eyes sharpened at that. "Some trouble in the city?"

"Not if we avoid it," said Albern. He sounded unconcerned, but his words reminded Sun of her family. A worried knot formed in her stomach.

The man snorted. "Fairly said." His gaze turned upon Sun, and she felt as though she was being inspected like a murky ledger. "You as well?"

She felt her cheeks flame. "I . . . I will have some wine, yes. Thank you."

"Welcome."

The man went to one of the cupboards and pulled out a bottle, tugging the rag from its neck. He produced two glasses and filled them, handing them over. Sun thought it strange that he was not having any himself, and her hackles rose—but then he went to the table in the center of the room. A half-full glass already stood there, and he filled it the rest of the way. Still, she waited for him to drink before she took her first sip.

"How goes business?" said Albern. "Have you had any more trouble along the western coast?"

"Fah," spat the man. "The western coast is nothing *but* trouble these days. Well, trouble and money, which is the only reason I still deal there. But most of the northern pirates have scuttled into dark holes with the hunt on, and so it isn't as bad as it might be."

"That is good to hear," said Albern. He drank deep of his wine. "And how about closer to home?"

For the first time, the man gave a smile. It was crafty and seemed to hide many secrets, but it was still a smile. "Much better, especially with your help. And speaking of . . ."

He went to another cupboard on the opposite side of the room from the wine. Inside, Sun could glimpse several iron cases that she recognized as lockboxes for coin, as well as piles of bags made from black velvet. He danced his fingers along the bags as if the tips could tell the contents merely by touch. At last, he selected one and hefted it, tossing it in the air twice. Satisfied, he returned to the table and upended the pouch.

Gold scattered across the thin blanket covering the map. Sun guessed there had to be more than a hundred weights. She could not stop her eyes from widening. The man spread a hand expansively over the coins.

"Payment rendered for services well performed," he said. "I threw in a little bit extra. Loyalty may be iss own reward, but I find something a bit heavier provides even more motivation."

"And we thank you kindly," said Albern. He began to scoop the gold up, dropping it back into the pouch without counting it, and then he glanced over his shoulder at Sun. "Would you like a separate pouch?"

Her throat went dry. "I . . . A separate one?"

"Why, yes," said Albern. "Half of this is yours, you know."

"I . . . What am I supposed to do with it?"

Albern blinked. "Money can be exchanged for goods and services."

Over his shoulder, the strange man turned away, but not quite quick enough to hide a smirk. "Glad to see yer keeping witty company these days."

Sun's cheeks, already dark, flushed darker still. "I *know* that," she snapped. "I mean, what am I supposed to do with it *now?*"

Albern shrugged. "Tie it to your belt and keep it under your cloak, I suppose. You would not want to lose it to a cutpurse. And try not to spend it all today—I have one more place to visit, and you may find a profitable use for it there."

"But I . . ." Again Sun looked at the size of the purse in Albern's hand. "That is too much to carry around. It will pull my belt straight off!"

Albern turned to give the stranger a look. The man sighed before turning and stepping behind a half-wall that obscured the rear left of the apartment. In a moment, he reappeared, carrying an odd sort of wallet. It was made of well-worn leather, and it had thick, long straps. The man tossed it to Albern, who caught it deftly and turned to Sun.

"You may buckle this around your chest," he said. "It will keep the purse slung against your right shoulder. You will appear to have a slight hunch under your cloak, but it is more comfortable than having the pouch hang from your belt. Or you can fit it into your saddlebag."

"Thank you," said Sun, taking it from him. Then she turned to the stranger. "I can pay you for this."

He gave her a thin smile. "Pray don't worry about it. Call it another bonus—for him, not for you. Mayhap in time, you'll provide enough services to earn such rewards."

Sun did not know quite what to say to that, particularly since she did not know what services had been performed for all this coin in the first place. She scooped her gold into the purse and strapped it over her shoulder. It did indeed hang comfortably on her, and she decided to keep it there rather than put it in her saddlebag. She had never held this much money before in her life. Of course, she had *seen* this much, but it had all belonged to her family, and they never let her touch it or choose how to spend it.

"I believe thass all the dealings we have for today," said the strange man. "Do let me know if you see to that business along the south Selvan border, old man."

Albern snorted. "Scarcely older than you."

"But you *are* older than me."

Albern chuckled and reached out his left hand. The man took his wrist, and they shook. Then Albern motioned Sun to the back stairs before descending them himself. Before she followed him, Sun turned to their host.

"Thank you," she said. "For the coin, and the wine. I am Sun, of the . . . that is, just Sun."

His eyes flashed, but he did not ask about the words she had abandoned. "Iss been my pleasure, Sun. If I can ask: have you met any of Albern's other friends?"

Sun blinked. The question seemed to hold hidden meaning, but she had no idea what it might be. "We . . . met a woman named Dawan in Lan Shui," she ventured.

"No, no," said the man, shaking his head. "Here in Bertram. Never you mind. Juss look after yourself—and him. That man's worth a fair spot of coin to me."

The words were quite mercenary, but Sun thought she caught concern in the man's eyes. It reminded her of Dawan's parting words, a quiet plea the medica had whispered in her ear when Albern was not listening. Nodding, she turned to follow Albern out of the apartment.

Only when they were back outside did she realize that the stranger had never given his name. Sun's mouth twisted, but she decided to leave it.

"Well," she said instead. "I suppose you have no intention of telling me what that was all about?"

"You suppose quite correctly," said Albern. "But you may learn in time."

"If we *have* enough time," said Sun. "I fear that there are not enough years left in your life to tell me of all the years that came before."

"Oh, come now," said Albern, nudging her shoulder. "In only a few days, I have told you the story of many months. You will catch up eventually, and should not feel too badly about being so slow."

Sun whirled on him. "*Me* slow? You are the one—"

But Albern laughed and stepped for the mouth of the alley, back towards the street. Sun followed him, fuming, but mostly for show. She enjoyed the easy rapport she and Albern had built together, and which had seemed to come to them quite quickly. It reminded her of the old man's conversations with Mag.

And as she thought of that, it occurred to Sun that such familiarity might be a double-edged sword to Albern. Surely he enjoyed the return to a time where he had a traveling companion he could jest with, and who would return jokes as easily as she took them. But at the same time, she must be a poor replacement for Mag and a constant reminder of what he had lost years ago.

Her mood dampened. Pulling her cloak tighter about her, she started to follow Albern into the street.

But then she leaped back, dragging Albern with her. Two riders on horseback thundered through the place he had been standing. Sun took an angry step after them, opening her mouth to call out.

She froze as she saw cloaks of black and gold—the colors of her family.

"Albern!" she whispered, her voice full of fear.

"I see them," he muttered.

Together they moved into the alley's shadows, watching as the riders hit a bend in the street and passed out of sight.

"A good thing you are wearing that borrowed cloak," said Albern softly. "They did not recognize you."

"Yet they must know I am in the city!" said Sun. "Why else would they be in Bertram? We have to leave."

"There are a thousand reasons they might be in Bertram." Albern's voice was calm, as though he was trying to talk down a rearing horse. "We knew they might have sent out scouts in many directions, hoping to catch you in a wide net. This might be no more than that. They were not keeping too careful an eye out, or they would have looked more closely at your face."

"I . . . I should get new clothes," said Sun. "And mayhap some sort of mask. The hood may not be enough."

"As soon as we may." A sudden smile crossed Albern's lips. "After all, we have the coin for it."

Despite herself, Sun gave a little smile in return, and her fingers rose to slide along the straps of her new purse. "I . . . I suppose we do."

"They have no way of knowing you are here," said Albern. "Not for certain. We are not in danger yet."

Sun blew a heavy sigh out through her nose. "Mayhap not. But let us keep it that way. We should leave Bertram now. We have enough coin for the next leg of the journey. Whatever your other business here, you can return for it later."

Albern hesitated, and his gentle smile faded away. "I cannot. Someone is expecting to meet me here today, and if I do not appear, it will cause trouble. I am sorry, Sun, but I have to see this through. I hope you will come with me."

A rising tide of panic threatened to make her vomit. "How urgent can these errands be? When we were in Lan Shui, you made it seem like Bertram was one of many choices. Was that true? Or did you always mean to come here, no matter what I said?"

Albern did not hesitate in the slightest. "Both," he said. "We could have gone another way if you wanted. My errands here could have waited a few days, or even as much as a week or two. But I always intended to come to Bertram eventually. And now that I am here, I must finish my business in the city. If you wish to leave Bertram at once, there are places I can arrange for you to go. You can return when you and I are both assured it is safe. But if you stay, I do not think you will regret it."

The offer to send her away was tempting. She feared to stumble into another of her family's guards out here on the bustling streets. And she thought of herself far away, spending her days in an inn, with plenty of coin to pay for food and ale while she waited for Albern to fetch her.

But then she thought of being alone. Of Albern's

absence. And what if her family found her regardless of her caution? Then Albern would not be there to help her escape them.

That was not such a tempting thought, after all.

Albern seemed to spy the indecision in her eyes, for he spoke again. "Remember what I told you not long ago. My family tried to pull me back into their clutches, but they failed. You will not be taken anywhere while I draw breath. Something you should do, by the way."

She sucked in a deep gasp of air and then let it out in a rush. For a moment, she felt lightheaded. But then her head seemed to clear, and she came to a decision.

"Very well," she said. "I will stay with you. But for the sky's sake, please do your business in the city quickly."

"As quickly as I may," said Albern. "And if you wish, I will not continue the story until we know we are safe again."

"Do you jest?" grumbled Sun. "I need something to distract me. Say on."

TWENTY-THREE

WELL. YOU REMEMBER THAT WE HAD DRIVEN THE Shades into the hills north of the Greenfrost. While our company set up camp in the wood, Kun gathered Tou and the sergeants for a small council after the battle. His customary smile was absent. Soldiers had died that day. He found a large rock to use as a makeshift table and laid a map of the area upon it. With one hand wrapped around his chin, he studied it as he spoke to us.

"Our foes will not go far tonight," he said. "They are already weary, for they have pressed their march hard, and now they have wounded to tend to. We can wait for the rest of our force to arrive in the night, and then we can wipe them out at our leisure. Let the company rest and recover themselves. What were our losses?"

"None from Black Squadron," I said. The other archer sergeants gave the same reply.

"None from Green," said Mag. "A few cuts and bruises, but nothing to slow anyone down."

"I lost three, ser," said Yue, in a voice sharp as flint. "And four wounded."

My gaze snapped to her. Her face was stony, and her eyes were not quite on Kun, but staring over his shoulder into the far distance.

Kun sighed. "The bodies?"

"The rest of Blue Squadron is seeing to them now," said Yue. It sounded as though she was about to say more, but she did not.

"Very well," said Kun. "As for my unit, six Mystics fell. Eight more were wounded, but only two very badly. That leaves just over a score at fighting strength. I will have to share the burden of the center line in future battles."

"Understood, ser," I said. Mag looked troubled, and she remained silent.

"At least their lives were not given in vain," Kun went on. "A score and a half of our foes lie dead. My best guess is at least that many more are grievously wounded, which will slow down the rest of them. It is never easy to lose a comrade. But our fellows who ventured into the darkness today made the enemy pay dearly in blood. We who survive must honor them."

"Yes, ser." This time the whole council spoke in unison.

"Good," said Kun. "Lieutenant Shi, see that sufficient sentries are posted to prevent any surprises. The rest of you see to the arrangements of your units. If any soldier has snuck wine or ale into their packs, let them enjoy it moderately—and have them share with their fellows as well. Everyone deserves a drink tonight, if they wish it. Dismissed."

"Captain," I said, throwing up a hand. "One more thing, if I may."

Everyone had been turning to head away, but now they all stopped. Captain Kun looked at me, surprised.

"Sergeant?"

"Ser," I said. "A woman led the enemy today. A tall brute of a fighter."

Kun's expression darkened. Most of the Mystics who had died had fallen at her hands. "I noticed her."

"Then I am certain you noticed her healing from the wounds we dealt her. I have faced one like her before, ser. They are favored soldiers among the Shades, imbued with some dark magic given to them by their lord. As long as the enchantment holds, they can heal from any injury, even fatal ones."

I watched as Kun's jaw clenched twice. "Formidable indeed," he said.

"But not invincible," I said. "I spoke to you before of Jordel of the family Adair. It was he who discovered how to defeat them. The one we faced in the Greatrocks had a tattoo on the back of his neck. That was what contained the enchantment. Jordel destroyed the man's tattoo, and that made it possible for him to die. If we should engage the brute again, we should seek to destroy the tattoo first. It will not be easy, but if we can manage it, we can bring her down."

Kun's gaze roved across the little council. "You all heard him. Relay the instructions to your troops, as I will relay them to my Mystics. Sleep well."

With a chorus of "Ser," we set about our tasks. As Mag, Yue, and I headed for our squadrons, I glanced back over my shoulder. Kun was bent over his map. Still he wore no smile, and his brow was furrowed as he studied the parchment.

I tried to put him from my mind as I turned to the others. "Yue. Are you all right?"

"I am fine," she said.

"We know what it is to lose people in your command," Mag said gently.

"Then you know nothing you can say will ease my mood," said Yue. "Let us see to our duties. I want something to do."

We reached the middle of the camp, which was still being built around us. Before parting from Yue, I stepped up to her and placed a hand on her arm to keep her from running off. It took a moment, but she met my gaze.

"I am here," I said quietly. "Do not forget it."

Yue scoffed. "As if you have ever let me, since the day we met," she grumbled. But her words were not as fiery as she tried to make them sound.

I pulled her into an embrace, and then I went to see to my squadron. They had already put up their tents and were building fires, around which they had gathered with Mag's unit. Hallan noticed me as I walked up, and his beard jumped as he nodded.

"Sergeant." He and some of the others started to rise from where they were sitting.

"At ease," I said, motioning them all to stay down. "Let us get those fires going and have a meal. The captain also gave explicit orders: if anyone has anything finer than water to drink, they are commanded to enjoy it and share it with their fellows. But do not get too drunk."

That got a few laughs from them, as well as half-hearted cheers. Jian dug into her pack and pulled out a large, full skin. She waved it in the air with a grin.

"Wine, Sergeant?"

"Sky above, yes," I said, taking the skin from her.

It was far from the best I had ever had. But as I am sure you have realized since we met, anything you drink after a fight tastes ten times better than it should. I took a deep pull and handed it back to her.

"Thank you, Jian. You handled yourself well today."

"Thank you, Sergeant," she said, taking a swig. Then she turned and offered it to Chausiku, who sat close by. "Some for you?"

Chausiku looked somewhat surprised. "Yes. Thank you."

"Captain's orders," said Jian with a shrug, pushing her hair back. "So, what do you think, now that you have seen a real fight?"

As he lowered the wineskin, Chausiku's expression darkened. "We survived. I call that a good result."

"As do I," said Jian amiably. "I even killed one of the bastards. And with a gut shot as well. I aimed for the chest as you said, Sergeant, but I am glad I was off."

Chausiku did not answer, but rose with a glower and walked away. I frowned at Jian. "What pleasure do you gain from goading him?'

She grinned. "I suppose I enjoy the reaction. It is so easy to get from him."

I sighed. "Jian, you still seem to think this is some kind of game. You want to punish those you see as evil, but you see your fellows as competitors, not allies. When a battle does not go so well, you will wish you were with friends instead of people you have only mocked since the day you met."

Her expression soured, and she took another pull from her wine. "It will be a dark day indeed before I need someone to coddle me."

I shook my head and left her, walking to where

Hallan was getting his campfire going. A cloud of thick, acrid smoke poured from the logs he had stacked together. Hallan cursed and coughed into his thick beard, pulling off his spectacles and swiping at his eyes. My nose began to sting as I approached him.

"Hallan?" I said. "Are you all right?"

"Fine, ser," he wheezed. "Iss this damn wood. Burns like darkfire."

"It is the pycnandra," said Dibu. He was there with Li, who was staring at the burgeoning flame. She did not appear to notice anyone around her, but was lost in her own wandering mind. "Their sap is what turns the trees green when they freeze. But it burns like poison."

Mag approached, coming from the line of her squadron's tents. "I knew someone was trying to burn the greenwood. You can smell it from a span off. Find something else for fuel, or we will all be hacking and coughing through the night."

"Oh, they tell me now," grumbled Hallan. He yanked the logs out of the fire and doused them in a puddle of rainwater on the ground before rising to find other fuel. But before he could leave, I saw Tou approaching.

"Squadrons!" I called out. "Officer present."

Mag's and my units stood and snapped to attention. Tou came to a stop, folding his hands behind his back and giving us all a nod.

"Good eve, all of you," he said, his voice carrying

through the evening air. "I have come to relay the captain's compliments. You all carried yourselves well today, and the plan was as successful as could be expected. You have his thanks, as well as mine."

"Ser," we replied in chorus.

"As you were," he said. "Enjoy your rest tonight, for you all deserve it."

As most of them returned to their seats, he came to me and Mag. Mag raised a hand in greeting.

"Lieutenant," she said.

"Sergeant," said Tou. "In particular, I wanted to relay my appreciation to you. You were on the front lines, but you did not lose even one sword. That is worthy of high praise."

Before Mag could answer, Dibu stood from his seat and stepped up to join the rest of us. "It is worth more than praise, Lieutenant," he said, folding his bronzed arms behind his back. "Watching her was like witnessing an Elf-tale. She was everywhere in the fight. Her spear was like lightning from the sky."

Mag's jaw clenched. Tou seemed to notice it, for a small smile crossed his lips as he stroked his goatee and cleared his throat. "No doubt she was impressive, and yet she was not the only one who gave a good showing. You fought well today, soldier. Even better than you did against me in the trial."

Dibu's mouth worked. "Thank you, Lieutenant. Your training has been invaluable."

"Good training still requires a good student," said

Tou. "It is a rare pleasure to find one who so easily takes lessons to heart. And that goes for all of you."

He placed a hand briefly on Dibu's muscular arm before stepping past him to Li. She still sat on the ground, and she was staring at the fire Hallan had been trying to build. Its embers were dead now, but she did not seem to have noticed.

"How are you, Li?" said Tou, more quietly now.

The sound of her name seemed to break her reverie. Li looked up at him, eyes lost for a moment. "I . . . am fine, ser."

"You survived your first battle," he said. "You should be proud."

She gave a brief, humorless laugh. "How can I be proud of something I had little hand in? Were it not for Dibu, I would be a corpse burning with the others. He saved my life and killed two of the enemy to do it."

"Yet you rose again," said Dibu, stepping up beside Tou. "And you claimed one foe for yourself before the end of the fight. The lieutenant is right, Li. You should be proud."

Li nodded, but from her expression, you would have thought she did not even hear them. Tou gave a little sigh and stood, turning to Dibu once more.

"Well, I do not wish to take up too much of your time. I only wanted to pass on the captain's praise. Dorsea is indebted to you all for your service today. And so am I."

Dibu swallowed hard and bowed his head. "Ser."

Tou gave Mag and me a quick nod, and then he set off to do his rounds with the rest of the squadrons. When I turned to look at Mag, she was fighting hard to contain a smile.

"What are you grinning about?" I asked her.

"Hm? Oh, nothing," said Mag. "Only it seems we are in the captain's good graces at last."

"And about time," I said. "One step closer to Kaita."

That caused her smile to evaporate at once. "Yet not quite close enough."

"Not yet," I told her. "But soon. Come now. Let us get our people situated, and then get ourselves to bed. I will sleep like a rock tonight."

"As if you ever sleep any other way," said Mag.

I snorted and shoved her shoulder, and she shoved me back (which sent me stumbling three paces). I went and checked on my squadron's tent lines, made sure they knew their watch schedule, and then started making my way to my tent. I still had not seen Yue, but I knew it would be best to leave her alone until she was ready. But on my way to bed, I spotted Chausiku. He stood a little apart from the rest of the camp, away from the fires, staring out into the Greenfrost with his hood drawn up. I approached, and as he heard my footsteps coming, he looked over at me.

"Ser," he said, nodding.

"Good eve," I said. "You should be getting yourself to sleep."

"I will, ser," he said. "But my mind is racing now, and I am trying to let it wear itself out."

"I confess I sometimes need the same." I stood beside him, folding my arms over my chest for warmth. "Today was your first taste of battle, and you did well. But how are you, really? I know you did not enjoy it, as Jian did."

Chausiku snorted. "That I did not. I cannot understand that woman, and I doubt I ever shall."

"Give it time," I said. "You are united in purpose, even if you view the purpose differently."

"I know that to be true, yet I find it hard to believe," said Chausiku with a sigh. "Her bloodlust is unnerving. I answered Captain Zhou's call because I care about Dorsea, and I would not see my nation betray the High King. But I could have gone my whole life without killing another person, and I would have been happier for it."

"Would not we all," I said, "if only the world were gentle enough to allow it. Yet still, you and Jian may find common ground in the end. I hesitate to hope for it, for it may require the war to go on for a long while. But if it does, do not be surprised if you find yourselves becoming fast friends."

"Like you and Mag?" said Chausiku with a smirk. "I confess I cannot see it."

"Well, mayhap not like us," I admitted. "Mag is easier than most to be friends with."

"And yet she is so terrifying in a fight," said Chausiku with a shudder. "I could hardly believe it. She deserves every legend I have ever heard of her. How *did* you become such good friends, anyway, when she is so much younger than you?"

That made me laugh. "It will surprise you to learn that she is, in fact, a little older than I am. We met when I had not quite seen my twentieth year, and she was already as good a fighter as she is today."

Chausiku's eyes were wide in his dark face. "Really? I would have thought she was a decade younger than you, at least. I would believe you if you said you were twice as old as her." Then, suddenly, he looked uncomfortable. "Meaning no insult about your appearance, of course, Sergeant."

My easy smile widened, and I shook my head. "I am sorry to disappoint you, soldier. Some people hardly seem to age, and some . . . well." I waved my hand up and down the length of my body.

Chausiku snorted, trying not to laugh. "Well, in any case, you are lucky to have her for a friend. And now I think my mind has indeed tired itself out. I will see you in the morning, Sergeant."

He turned and left me. It always amused me how shocked people were when they learned the truth about Mag's age compared to her looks.

But Mag *had* aged, I knew. I remembered her when she was younger, and I knew her now. She *was* different, if not as different as I was.

Sometimes being close to a tale keeps us from seeing it clearly. A soldier on the battlefield might slay two foes and think the battle is close to won—but the general on the hilltop can see foes sweeping around the flanks and taste the coming defeat.

But sometimes, being close to the tale is what shows us the truth of it. We can see clearly the sunlight on a fish's rainbow scales, while someone on the shore sees only an ugly trout through muddy, churning waters.

That is how it was with Mag and me. Certainly, she was someone you had to see up close to believe—if you *believe* in stories, that is.

Ah, well. I turned my steps towards my tent, and soon I was abed. I was alone for a long while, as Yue spent time with her squadron, mourning their losses with them. But even before she returned, I slept poorly. Roots kept digging into my head, and I could not seem to get rid of them, no matter how I tried to shift on the forest floor.

TWENTY-FOUR

Now, I have commented on Mag's appearance before this. But it is worth noting that she always looked younger than she was, even when she lived in that village called Shuiniu.

Ten years before Mag and I met, she had just begun her apprenticeship under Duana. Of course, she did not have a hand in the brewing straight away. As is the case with many apprentices, she spent her first several months taking care of odd jobs around the brewery. She would sweep up shavings, fix small things that had broken, and haul water and grain from one place to another as required. All the while, Duana would explain the craft to her, indoctrinating her into the finer aspects of the art.

And Duana would tell stories. It seemed she was a talespinner, of sorts, though none so fine as Dryleaf. But mayhap that is one reason Mag and I became such good friends. She always loved stories, and she would listen with rapt attention as Duana told tales of long ago. She heard stories of the time before time and the founding of Underrealm, the dark days of the Wizard Kings, and many great heroes and terrible villains scattered throughout the countless years of history.

And then, one day, Duana said something that made Mag frown and stop in the middle of her work.

"What is that?" said Mag. Her eyes were wide, and her hand stilled where it had been wiping a brewing vat with a rag.

Duana looked at her in mild surprise. With a giant wooden spoon, she had been stirring a large cauldron as it came to a boil. Now she glanced at the spoon, the cauldron, and the beginnings of her next brew. "What is what?" she asked.

"The word you just said," said Mag.

"Meldin? That is the name of the Dragon in the tale."

"Not the name, that other word. The D . . . Dr—"

"Dragon?" said Duana. "What about it?"

A shadow seemed to come over Mag's face, her expression a cloud of confusion. "What is that? Is it an animal?"

Duana studied Mag, who seemed held as if frozen in ice. And the old brewer felt a powerful, mournful sadness enclose her heart. She often forgot how many little things like this Mag did not know, things that most children learned from bedtime stories.

But then, most children heard those tales from their parents, and Mag had had no such opportunity.

"They were not animals," said Duana quietly. "They were . . . something more. Do you know of satyrs or centaurs?"

Finally, Mag moved, but only to give a tiny nod. "You told me of centaurs."

"Then you know they have bodies like animals, but they are clever of mind like we are," said Duana. "Dragons are something like that, but far greater and more terrible. They are more akin to Elves."

Mag nodded quickly, eager to please. "I know of Elves."

Duana smiled again. "Good. If you have heard of them, you can get an idea of Dragons."

"Are they the same size as us, like Elves?" said Mag. "Or are they smaller, like imps?"

"Neither," said Duana, and despite herself, she felt a tremor of fear. "They were vast in size. The span of their wings was like the length of the ships that sail the deep ocean, and they could swallow a horse in a single bite. From their mouths, they could spew a noxious fume that choked the lungs and dissolved the flesh. But they could also command firemagic and set their breath ablaze, and then the fume became darkfire. They could burn whole towns in blasts of flame."

She saw suddenly that Mag was trembling where she stood. Her eyes had filled with tears, and she had dropped her washcloth to the ground.

"Here now," said Duana, rushing to her. She wrapped her arms around Mag's shoulders and held her close, while Mag clutched the front of her shirt and buried her face in her chest.

"Will they come for me?" said Mag, her voice incredibly small.

"Never," said Duana. "They all vanished from Underrealm long ago."

Mag stopped shaking, and she looked up at Duana with a frown. "Where did all of them go?" she said quietly, fearfully.

"We do not know," said Duana. "But we need not concern ourselves with it now. No one has seen them in hundreds of years—not since the very earliest days of Underrealm."

Mag nodded, scrubbing tears from her eyes with the back of a dirty hand. "All right," she said.

Soon Duana had her back to her chores, and Mag's mood rose as she got to work. But it was a long, long time before Duana ever ventured to tell her another tale of Dragons.

TWENTY-FIVE

But let us return to the Greenfrost.

In the hours before dawn, the rest of Kun's army arrived at our camp. Zhen, Kun's nephew, had marched his troops through the night. I was asleep when they arrived, but I woke when I heard the commotion at the east end of camp. There was a tense, silent moment in my tent while I tried to hear whether it was sounds of battle or not. When I heard no shouting or clashing steel, I guessed that Zhen must have arrived. Beside me, Yue was peaceful in sleep, breathing gently through her mouth. I shook her.

"Yue," I said. "Wake up. The reinforcements have arrived."

"Whuz," she mumbled, sitting up in the darkness and rubbing at her eyes. I could barely see her in the dim firelight leaking through the tent.

"The rest of the troops," I said. "Kun may need us. We should get up."

"All right, all right," grumbled Yue. She began to pull on her clothes. I had slept in mine, so I donned my boots and slipped out of the tent into the open air.

The earliest signs of grey had begun to edge into the sky above me as I studied the road to the east. It was filled with people now, marching troops all looking weary but resolute, with wagons and pack animals behind them. As I studied them, a woman ran up. I recognized her as one of the captain's messengers.

"I have a message for Lieutenant Shi," she said, "but he is not in his tent."

"He is not?" I said, frowning. "I will look for him. May I relay the captain's message?"

"I suppose," said the woman. "It is nothing secret. Captain Zhou wishes to send scouts to locate the Shades. They are to be selected from Lieutenant Shi's company since they have had several hours of sleep now. The captain needs to discuss the plan with the lieutenant."

"Understood," I said. "I will send the lieutenant along as soon as I find him."

She nodded and ran off. Just then, Mag emerged from her tent.

"Mag!" I said. "Good morn, or close enough to it. The captain sent word—"

"I heard," said Mag. "Where do you think Tou has gone?"

I shrugged. "I hardly think anything sinister can have happened. The sentries gave no alarm, and everything else seems to be in order."

Mag's mouth twisted. "Let us check his tent to be sure."

We jogged there as the murmur of voices grew towards the east end of camp. Some troops were throwing themselves straight onto the ground, as though they meant to sleep before even building tents. I thought they might change their minds once the slushy snow soaked their clothes.

Tou's tent was empty, as the messenger had said. I turned to Mag with a shrug.

"Mayhap he is at the latrines," I said. "Foreign water can ruin any soldier's rest. At the very least, we know our squadrons are likely to be the ones sent to scout for the Shades. I think we should rouse them to get ready for the captain's order."

"Let us do it, then," said Mag, who still looked worried. "But we need to find Tou as quickly as possible."

"We can search for him while our troops are readying themselves," I said.

Our squadrons' tents were lined up next to each other, with the flaps facing an open lane between them. Mag took her squadron's tents on the left, and I took mine on the right. We went down the line, throwing open the tents and ordering our soldiers to wake and ready for the day. Hallan and Chausiku snapped awake at once, while Jian complained at me until I cut off her words with the tent flap. Mag went down her line, until about halfway down when she reached the tent that belonged to Dibu.

She threw open the flap and froze. I saw it, and I paused. Slowly I approached from behind Mag, my brow furrowing.

"Mag? What is—"

"Lieutenant," said Mag, trying desperately and failing to keep laughter out of her voice.

"Sergeant," came Tou's bleary voice from inside Dibu's tent.

My eyes adjusted to the dim campfire light, and I could see him staring out at us, alongside Tou, both of them shirtless and wrapped together in a bedroll. They looked to have just woken up.

"Orders from the captain, ser," I called out, my expression deadpan. "He requests your presence to discuss the assignment of a scouting party to hunt down the Shades. We are mustering our squadrons in anticipation that it might be us."

"Very good," said Tou in a resigned voice. "I shall be along presently."

"As you say, ser," said Mag. Her gaze swiveled to Dibu. "You have a quarter-hour, soldier."

She let the tent flap fall, and we collapsed in on ourselves. Seizing each other's shoulders, we shook with laughter that we tried frantically to silence. We were reduced to stumbling through the rest of the tents, throwing up the flaps and gasping out *"Muster"* before choking back another peal of hysterics. Yue came to us when we had almost finished, and she scowled down at me.

"What under the sky has gotten into you?" she said. "You look fit to erupt, and I do not like the way that vein is throbbing in your forehead."

I said nothing, but only pointed back down the line as I kept giggling. Tou was just emerging from Dibu's tent. His cloak was in his hand, and he whirled it on against the cold before marching off towards his tent.

Yue stared at him for a moment, frowning. "Oh," she said slowly. Then her face lit with understanding. *"Oh."*

"I knew it," said Mag. "I knew it from the first."

"Knew what?" I said. "The two of them? Wait." A realization struck me. "Is *this* why you put Dibu against him for the test?"

"I did not know the captain would choose Tou, so of course not," said Mag. "I picked Dibu because he was the best I had. But I was *elated* when the captain chose Tou."

I buried my face in my hand. "You are the most conniving—"

"I already told you I had no idea who the captain would choose," said Mag, folding her arms with a smug grin.

"Are the two of you done with petty gossip?" said Yue with a scowl. "Our squadrons are supposed to be assembling for muster."

"You are right," I said. "Let us get them in line."

It was not very long before it was done. Tou appeared, and Kun walked beside him. Kun's smile was back, and it looked no less bright for the early hour. He nodded to the sergeants, and the whole company gave him a salute. Tou studiously avoided looking at Mag and me, and I am confident our foolish grins never left us.

"Good morning," said Kun. "Today, I hope to bring this expedition to a close. We are going to advance into the hills, and we are going to bring our enemies to bay. To ensure our success, I mean to send a scouting party ahead to hamper the Shades' march in any way possible. Lieutenant Shi?"

Tou gave him a nod and then addressed us, fixing Mag and me with a steely gaze. "Black Squadron. Green Squadron. You will form the scouting party. Head north into the hills, track the Shades down, and follow them. Each of you fetch one horse from the train. Use them to rotate messengers back to camp, informing the captain of the Shades' movement."

"Ser," said Mag and I together. I believe we kept our tone somewhat professional.

"The main force will advance behind you," said Kun. "I am giving the reinforcements two hours to rest from their march, and then we will follow you into the hills. We will catch the Shades and wipe them out. A swift and fitting end for those who have betrayed the High King and all the nine kingdoms." Suddenly he paused, and though his smile remained, his brows furrowed. "Sergeant Baolan?"

Mag and I looked at Yue in surprise. She had her hand raised, and she kept her eyes fixed on the captain. "Blue Squadron is available for the scouting party as well, ser."

Kun's smile softened. "Thank you, Sergeant Baolan. Green Squadron and Black Squadron will serve for the purpose, though your willingness is appreciated."

"We owe them a debt of blood, ser," said Yue fiercely.

"And you will pay it," said Kun. He stepped closer to her and lowered his voice so that only Tou and we sergeants could hear. "I am not holding you back to slight you. You lost people yesterday. That is a tragic honor, but an honor nonetheless. Let the fresher squadrons take the fore now."

"Ser—" began Yue.

"No, Sergeant," said Kun, but gently. "This is an order. And if you need any further assurance, think of the fact that I am keeping my Mystics with the main force as well. Do you think that an insult to them?"

Yue's nostrils flared. "Of course not, ser."

"Then be at peace." Kun stepped back and once again spoke to the whole company. "You have your orders. Dismissed!"

"Yes, ser!" we cried in chorus.

Mag turned to me. "Ready for another day on the field?"

I glanced sidelong at Yue, who was fuming and not looking at either one of us. "I suppose so," I said. "But quickly—before we go, we should speak with Dryleaf. I would guess he has been worried about us while he followed along in the train with Zhen."

With Yue, we hurried to the east end of the camp, where Zhen's troops were getting themselves arranged. In the rear of the column, with the other followers, we soon found Dryleaf by the sound of Oku's excited barks. As soon as the hound scented us, he came bounding forwards with a loud baying of joy, and Dryleaf followed behind. Orla and Nikau were with him, each of the lovers holding one of his arms, but for comfort rather than to help him along.

"Are those my friends?" he called out, feeling his way forwards with his walking stick. "How have you fared without me here to protect you?"

"Well enough, old man," said Mag with a laugh, taking his shoulder and guiding him to us. "We appreciate your service in guarding the reinforcements."

"One does what one can, I suppose," said Dryleaf. His head swung back and forth. "Albern? Yue?"

"We are here," I said, placing a hand on his shoulder.

Yue still looked dour, but she said, "And safe enough. Do not worry yourself."

"Not for a moment," said Dryleaf. But the relief on his face gave lie to the words.

I looked to Nikau. "Were things well on the march?"

"Well enough. We did not press ourselves as hard as you did. But we missed you." He put a hand on Yue's arm. "Nothing is as fun when all the most interesting folk have left."

Yue could not restrain a grin, and she scratched the back of her head. Dryleaf's smile widened as he spoke. "Well, here we are, reunited. What fresh dangers do we expect to face now?"

I gave a glance at Yue. "Kun is sending Mag and me to scout for the Shades," I said. "Once we have pinpointed them, he will bring the rest of the force north to wipe them out."

"Into the hills, you mean?" said Dryleaf. "I spoke with Lieutenant Zhou while we have been marching west to catch up with you, and he told me the lay of the land."

"They should be easy to find," I said. "Especially with the wounded we left them with after our last scrap."

Dryleaf's face grew worried. "That is good. But take care that you do not grow overconfident. I know one reason we brought them to bay here was so that the landscape would give them no advantage. But our enemies are wily and may yet have tricks up their sleeves."

"We will be careful," said Mag.

"Too careful, in some cases," muttered Yue.

Dryleaf's head turned towards her quizzically, but when she said nothing more, he let it be. "Good, good. You should take Oku with you when you go. The poor boy has been frantic with boredom during our march."

"Gladly will we do so, now that you have a chance to rest," I said. "Oku, tiss." The hound darted to my side and sat, looking up at me expectantly.

"Rest, yes," said Dryleaf, sighing. "I will treasure the next few hours in my tent. But give them a happy ending, and come back to me safe."

"Safe and victorious," said Mag. "That is a promise—or as close to a promise as one can give in war."

A shadow passed over Dryleaf's face, but if doubt was in his heart, he did not speak of it before we left him.

TWENTY-SIX

From the moment we started our trek north, I could see the truth of what Kun had told us about these hills. They were gentle and easy, mere ripples in the land, like a slightly rumpled blanket. I chose to climb them as we went, rather than sticking close to the trail the Shades had left in the wet ground. It slowed us, but it gave us a better vantage point to see the land around us, and hopefully to spot the Shades from afar.

Their course wound through the dips, and the furrow they had cut in the land was easy to see: a black slash of mud through the shoots of new grass. We advanced as quickly as we could. Three soldiers in each squadron held torches aloft—one in the front, one in the back, and one in the middle, lighting the way for their fellows. Hallan held the front torch in my squadron, so I stayed a good several paces away from him to keep my eyes sharp in the darkness. We climbed over one hill and down the other side to an open space through which our enemies had passed. As we crossed the Shades' trail, Oku ran back and forth across the black swath in the land, sniffing at their steps. A drizzle began to drift down upon us out of the sky.

"Hold," I said. Our squadrons stopped at once. "Jian, Chausiku. With me. Hallan, you are in charge of Black Squadron until I return, but listen to Mag."

"Albern," said Mag, frowning. "Where are you going?"

"To the top of the next hill." I pointed to the marks. "They stopped here for a while before pressing on. I would guess they sent out scouts looking for a better place to camp. Once they found it, they did not go too much farther before stopping overnight."

"I should come with you," said Mag immediately.

"No," I said. "Jian and I are quieter. And if we encounter the enemy, we will not be fighting, but running back to you."

"Then I can help cover your retreat."

"Mag, no. I am going ahead, and that is that. We will signal you to follow if we find them."

Her mouth worked. But I could see she did not wish to have an argument while the Shades could be getting farther away, especially not in front of our squadrons. I turned to Jian and Chausiku again.

"Come on." Oku padded up to my side, but I held out a hand to stop him. "Kip, boy. Stay with Mag." He whined and sat back on his haunches.

We crept up the hill, the mud helping to keep our footsteps muffled. When we neared the top, I held out a hand to tell them to slow down. We approached the summit at a crawl.

Nearly an hour had passed, and the sky kept lightening in the east. I was trying to use that to our advantage. We crept to the top of the hill on our bellies, and I followed the track of the Shades' progress.

There. I pointed so that Chausiku and Jian could see it, too. Outlined against the grey sky far away, I could see a figure. It was only a black silhouette from this distance and with so little light to illuminate it. But as we watched, a cloak fluttered, the motion making it stand out clearer against the sky.

"A sentry," I said. "A posted one, not a rear scout. That means they are camped just over that hill."

"Should we eliminate them?" said Jian at once.

"It might raise the alarm," I said. "Better to bring the others forwards and form a plan together. Jian, go to fetch them."

She rolled her eyes and growled, but she did it.

Soon both squadrons came to the bottom of the hill, where I conferred with Mag.

"They are over that crest," I said, pointing. "Across another open space, and then over one more hill. I would guess the distance at four spans."

"Excellent," said Mag. "If they are encamped, mayhap we should leave them be for now."

"I would agree, but dawn is imminent," I said. "I cannot imagine they will stay there past sunup. Therefore I think we should either hold them in place or drive them in the direction we wish them to go."

"How do you mean to do that?" said Mag.

"If we circle to the east and attack them from there, they may think the whole host is coming from that direction," I said. "Then we can tell Kun to attack from the west, and drive the Shades straight into his arms."

"A good plan, save for one detail," said Mag, raising her brows. "Kaita's raven form."

"Dark take me," I said. "I forgot about that."

"There is nowhere to hide from her in these hills," said Mag. "Once they are alerted to our presence, we will not be able to conceal ourselves from her sight."

"Well, first things first," I said. "Jian. Go back to the captain. Inform him of where the Shades are, and tell him we are devising a plan to hold them in place for his advance."

"Send Chausiku!" said Jian at once. "He is faster than I am by far."

I gritted my teeth. "You will be riding a horse. Chausiku's legs give him no advantage in that."

Jian's cheeks flamed, though she tried to hide it. "I mean that he is a better rider," she said. "I have scarcely even touched a horse in my life."

"Fine," I said. "Chausiku?"

"Yes, *ser,*" he said, glaring at Jian. He set off, loping towards the horses we had brought, and soon was galloping away south.

"That leaves us where we started," said Mag. "How do we hold them in place?"

An idea struck me. "Kaita is a problem, but she may also be the solution. We should not try to hide at all. Let her see how few of us there are—and let her see that you and I are here."

Mag's eyes lit. "She will attack, hoping to kill us. Clever. But what if the other Shades convince her to flee?"

I shook my head. "I doubt it. After all she has been through in search of us, I cannot believe she would resist such a tasty morsel now. We will appear alone and isolated, with only a paltry two squadrons to defend us." I turned my gaze across our units. "Little does she know we have the two best squadrons in the army."

Their chests puffed with pride at that. Jian wore a savage grin.

"Very well," said Mag. "You should advance with one or two archers and bring down a sentry from afar. Make a stink about it so they raise the alarm. Then retreat to the rest of us as quickly as you can."

"Agreed," I said. I turned to Hallan once more. "Hallan—"

"I've got them, ser," said Hallan. Then he turned an exasperated eye on Jian. "And you should take this one with you. She's eager enough, thass sure."

"I suppose she is," I said. "Jian, with me. Stay quiet, and do as I say, or I will throw you to the Shades myself."

Her face went pale. I suspect that when she asked to stay, she had not thought she would be going to antagonize the enemy with only me by her side. I will confess I took some grim satisfaction from her expression, but I only let myself enjoy it for a moment.

Together we set off into the drizzle and the mud. Instead of northeast, where the sentry was, I guided her due north to a hill west of the Shades' camp. By creeping around the southern edge of the hill, I hoped to keep out of the sentry's sight for as long as possible. And we would be in the hill's shadow, weak as it was, so that hopefully he would not notice us until it was too late.

Despite her evident anxiety, Jian followed closely in my footsteps. Soon we were at the bottom of the hill where we had seen the guard last time. I could glimpse a bump I thought was their head, far above us. I turned to Jian.

"Here we are," I whispered. "I am taking the kill, and then we are getting out of here. Do you understand?"

"S-Ser," she stammered.

"Good," I said. "Stay here."

I crept up the hill pace by pace. Slowly the sentry came more fully into view. They must have been tired, for they faced only south, never turning to look left or right.

Poor fool, I thought.

I nocked, drew, sighed, and loosed.

The arrow pierced straight through their head with a soft *thunk.* I saw a splash of blood erupt, only barely visible as red against the lightening sky.

I turned and ran back to Jian as fast as I could.

HROOON

A horn sounded behind us. Soon it was joined by others, and then they sang in chorus, screaming the alert, warning of danger.

"That worked perfectly!" I cried as I reached Jian. "Now run for your life!"

TWENTY-SEVEN

After the ambush in the woods the day before, Kaita and Tagata had led their forces into the hills to the north. Their troops were in disarray and greatly hampered by the wounded they had to drag with them in their retreat.

But Kaita cared for only one of them.

"Tagata!" she cried, pressing through the Shades to go to her. Tagata's wounds were healing themselves, the Lord's magic melding flesh and skin together. But Tagata had suffered so many grievous injuries that it was a slow process, and she winced and growled through her teeth with every step.

As Kaita came running up, Tagata raised a hand to forestall her worry. "I am fine," she said. "The Lord's blessing will not fail me."

"This is my fault," said Kaita. "I should have scouted ahead."

"You kept your eyes on the force following us, as we both agreed," said Tagata. "Our enemies were clever, and we underestimated them. If you wish to take the blame for that, you must share it with—"

Her right leg buckled beneath her, and she fell to the ground. Kaita tried to support her, but it was like catching a falling boulder.

"Tagata!" cried Kaita. "Are you all right? Does it hurt?"

"Not the healing, no," said Tagata through gritted teeth. She tried and failed to regain her feet. "But until the wounds have gone, I can still feel every one."

Kaita looked desperately around. They were in the hills now and could not see very far in any direction. But though the rolling land blocked sight, it was hardly defensible. The slopes were gentle, and they could be scaled or descended with little effort. She growled in frustration.

"I am going to take a look around," she told Tagata. Then she raised her voice to bark at the Shades surrounding them. "Halt the march! Stay here until I return."

Gently she removed Tagata's arm from her shoulder and stepped away. Magelight flashed in her eyes, and a moment later, she powered into the air on raven's wings.

At once, she could see things were even worse than she had feared. They were only a few spans into the hills, but nowhere was there any position better than their current one. The only glimmer of hope came from the fact that, looking south, she could see flashes of firelight in the woods. Her enemies had made camp in the Greenfrost and were not yet giving chase.

She dove back to the ground and resumed her human form. Tagata looked up with blood on her lips.

"Are they close?" she said.

"They have set up camp in the wood," said Kaita. "And we should do the same. There is no better place to march tonight, and we must get as much rest as we can. You need to heal, and the rest of us need to be fresh tomorrow. They will not simply let us sit here unmolested."

"Mayhap we should march a little—" Tagata grunted at a stab of pain. She fell back to one knee, clutching the hilt of her greatsword as its tip sank into the ground.

"And that is enough of that," said Kaita. "Everyone! Set up camp. Sentries on every hill surrounding this dell. Someone raise Tagata's tent for her, *now.*"

Her voice cracked like a whip, and the Shades leaped to obey. Kaita went to Tagata and took her hand. Tagata tried to smile at her through the pain wracking her body.

"You need to rest," said Kaita. "Promise me you will."

"It seems I have little choice," said Tagata. "I will be fine in the morning."

"Should I stay with you?"

Tagata shook her head, sending her heavy auburn hair cascading over her face. "I will be fine. And you will get no rest if you are with me. The healing process is not always pleasant, and less so, the worse my wounds."

Kaita browbeat the others until they had Tagata's tent up, and then she helped her inside. But she found little rest for herself that night. Sleep would not come, and after two hours, she gave up. She settled for taking flight once more, swooping low over the camp of Kun's army in the Greenfrost. The glow of our fires refracted through the emerald trunks, like a crystal that breaks sunlight into many colors.

She could not tell which tents were mine or Mag's. Yet she could almost feel us below her. More than anything, she wanted to descend upon the camp in a fury, to find us and destroy us. The magestones were back at the camp, and Tagata was wounded. Kaita could eat them, and she would never be discovered . . .

But Mag and I were among allies, and Kaita had made promises to Rogan. She was worthy of trust, and she had to prove it. And so, many long hours later, she finally returned to her tent and passed the rest of the night in sleep almost as restless as my own.

When she woke, just before dawn, she emerged into the open air to find Tagata standing there.

The shadeborn's eyes were closed and her shoulders back. Her face tilted slightly up, as though the scent of some treasured dish wafted to her on the breeze. Firelight played across her features, deepening the crags and scars splayed across them. All signs of her injuries were gone—the Lord's blessing had done its work through the night. And now, as Kaita approached, Tagata's eyes opened, and her expression turned grim.

"I received a message," she said. "From the Lord."

"When?" snapped Kaita, eyes wide. "In the night?"

"Yes," said Tagata. "He had dark tidings—yet the darkness holds a glimmer of hope. But come. We should speak of this privately."

She threw back the flap of her tent, and Kaita led the way inside. Sitting so close, she could again feel the heat radiating from Tagata. It almost made her want to cast off her cloak.

"What are these tidings?" said Kaita.

"We will face our foes in battle again soon," said Tagata. "And we will lose."

For a moment, Kaita could not speak, but only stared at Tagata in shock. "What do you mean, we will lose?" she said.

"They will heavily outnumber us," said Tagata. "No strategy we could concoct will work in these hills, and we cannot outrun them. However, this will not be our end. Some of us, at least, will be able to escape."

"Then let us escape *now,*" said Kaita. "They have not come to attack us yet. There is still time."

"We will not find a way out until the time is right," said Tagata. "The Lord did not know how we would get away, but he said we would see a sign. It shall be a fiery wyrm."

Kaita could only stare in shock for a moment. "Is he—" She stopped herself, for she had come dangerously close to insulting the Lord. "I do not understand. I would think you were joking if I did not know better."

"I assure you I am not," said Tagata. She looked at the tent flap mournfully. "We will lose many of our kindred today."

Kaita shook her head. "I do not understand this sign. Does the Lord mean we will see a *Dragon?* That is impossible."

"I doubt it means that," said Tagata. "He tells us what he sees, but it is as I told you before. Things are not always . . . entirely clear."

Her frustration mounting, Kaita took several deep breaths in an attempt to find calm. But it only seemed to further stoke the fires of her anger, like bellows to a forge.

"This message . . . I know it is related to the sight you told me of," she said slowly. "But this seems worse than useless. It seems to promise a hope that I cannot envision."

"Rarely do I understand the Lord's signs when he relays them to me," said Tagata. "But you must keep faith. Every victory we have seen so far, every stride we have taken in our mission across Underrealm, has come because of the Lord—from his cunning, and from his sight that pierces the veil of time."

Again Kaita shook her head. "You say you have followed his wisdom before, and it has not led you astray. Because I believe in you, I will choose to believe in this. But if our enemies should come upon us, and I see no other choice, I *will* devour the magestones, Tagata. Whether Mag and Albern are alone or not. I will not let them kill me—or you—without using every tool at my disposal to kill them first."

She half expected Tagata to be angry with her. After all, she was threatening to break the promise she had made to Rogan, and through him, to the Lord. But Tagata only looked upon her with profound sadness.

"Your choices are your own, dear one," she said quietly. She placed a hand on Kaita's shoulder. "But I hope you will rethink this. Woe betide you if you take the stones outside of the ordained time. His love will be no protection to you, then."

Kaita quailed for a moment at the strength of certainty in her voice. But then she shook herself, steeling her resolve. "I have said what I have said. Let us muster the troops and march from this cursed land."

HROOON

Horns blew outside the tent. Kaita and Tagata both whipped their heads towards the sound. It came from the south, where their sentries were posted on hills overlooking the land all around.

"And let us do it as soon as we possibly can," muttered Kaita.

The horns were still sounding as Kaita took her raven form and launched into the air. Tagata stood beneath her, head tilted upwards, watching her take flight. The sky was still mostly dark, and Kaita blinked hard, trying to make out shapes on the ground below. The campfires had made her night-blind.

There. Two figures running west across the hills. Kaita's heart leaped. Two figures? That could be . . .

She dove closer and recognized me. The person beside me was not Mag, but some other soldier who was unknown to her.

Fierce bloodlust thundered in Kaita's veins. I was practically alone. She would not even need magestones to—

Then she spotted Mag and our squadrons not far off. A quick count told her our number, and she wheeled out of her dive.

Her heart burned with conflict. Only two squadrons. That was barely anything, compared to the force that had attacked them yesterday. Mag and I, with just over two dozen friends. That was isolated, was it not? It was close enough. She could attack us with the strength of magestones, and her promise to Rogan would be—

She growled in her mind. It was close enough to

the terms for Kaita, mayhap. But not for Tagata. And Tagata had the stones. Kaita did not think she could lie straight to the shadeborn's face even if she wished to, and she did not wish to.

But mayhap there was another way. She circled back and landed in the Shade camp, resuming her human form and running to Tagata.

"They are here!" she cried. "Mag and Albern. They are just over that hill, Tagata, and they have only two squadrons with them. We could crush them with little more than a thought."

Tagata looked around the camp. "We have wounded kindred, Kaita. They will not be able to join us in a chase."

"Leave them here," said Kaita. Tagata's nostrils flared, but Kaita raised her hands. "They will be safer here, anyway. We can draw the threat away from them. They will be able to escape when we—that is, if they need to." She swallowed hard, for she had almost announced aloud that they were expecting to lose this battle.

But she could see that she had convinced Tagata. The shadeborn turned to the camp, and her great, bellowing voice rang out.

"Kindred!" she cried. "Our enemies await the kiss of our blades over those hills. We will destroy them in the Lord's name! To arms! *Death!*"

"Death!" cried the Shades.

The camp became a scramble. All who could walk

fought to be the first to don their sword belts, to heft their shields and ready their armor.

"I will keep watch over our enemies," said Kaita. "Look for me in the skies. I will guide you."

"Be safe," said Tagata. "And Kaita."

Kaita froze as Tagata reached into her pocket. When her hand came out, it held the brown cloth packet. She placed it in Kaita's much smaller hand.

"Take them," said Tagata softly. "If you see your chance, you take it."

"They . . . they will slow me down," said Kaita, hardly daring to breathe.

"You do not require speed," said Tagata. "They are on foot, and you fly with the winds. But you should have them with you if the chance presents itself. I trust you as Rogan does. As our father does."

Kaita could not contain herself. She threw herself up, her arms wrapping around Tagata's neck, and kissed her deep. One massive arm wrapped around her, crushing her into Tagata's chest. When they parted, Kaita's eyes were shining.

"Thank you," she whispered.

"No one is more deserving," murmured Tagata. "We are doomed to lose today's battle, but you may have your chance for revenge. Do not let it slip away."

Kaita nodded and turned. Her eyes flashed with light again. She shrank, her clothes sinking beneath the flesh along with the brown cloth packet. It was an awkward lump in her chest, but she managed it.

Feathers sprouted, a beak sprang from her jaw, and the raven form was complete. She launched into the sky again, pursuing Mag and me across the land.

TWENTY-EIGHT

MAG AND I LED OUR SQUADRONS IN A RUN TO THE west. It was tempting to draw the Shades back along their own trail, but I was wary of them seeing through our trap. So we stayed near the trail but swung slightly to the north. If Kun followed the Shades' course, he would see their army chasing us, and then he would be able to strike.

I kept an eye on the grey sky above us, and so I was not surprised to see a raven swooping after us. Kaita would keep us in her sights, I knew, and guide the Shades to hunt us down. I grinned.

The grin faded from my face as a hail of arrows flew towards us from the south.

"Down!" I cried.

Our soldiers dropped into the mud, but not quickly enough for three of them. One of my archers and two of Mag's swordfighters pitched over, arrows embedded deep in their bodies. A shaft struck the ground next to Oku, and he leaped aside with a yelp. One of my archers who fell was the middle torchbearer. His torch tumbled down the hill we were on, rolling awkwardly side to side as it descended. The flaming pitch burned the sparse dew off the new grass, and some of it caught as the torch kept rolling.

I looked up to where the arrows had come from. A party of Shade archers had run ahead of the rest of their force. They had stuck to the lowlands and moved faster than we had, and now they had a clear shot at us atop the hill.

Mag saw it at the same time. "North!" she cried. "Move north!"

We ran up and over the lip of the hill, coming down the other side. But a murmur was on the air, coming towards us from the east. More Shades, advancing quickly.

"Dark take them," I said.

"Retreat to the west!" said Mag.

"Hold that order!"

Mag's gaze snapped to me, and I pointed to the hilltop east of us.

"We should deliver one volley as they come over the top. It should pin them for a moment, at least, and give us more time to flee."

"Very well," said Mag. "Green Squadron, line up behind the archers. Watch for a flank."

"Ser!" barked her squadron.

"Black Squadron, draw!" I cried.

Arrows flew to strings and drew back. We held for a long, tense moment as the murmur of voices grew louder on the air. Oku was beside me, bristling and growling.

I saw a helmeted head appear over the eastern hill.

"Loose!"

A dozen arrows darted through the air, slamming into the first line of Shades. Nearly every one found its mark.

"Again!" I roared, drawing and firing my arrow.

My squadron joined me, and another hail of death fell among our foes. The Shades fell back with cries of dismay. In a moment, they were out of sight behind the crest of the hill.

Mag and I motioned our soldiers west with sharp hand movements. We did not want to cry a retreat and let the Shades know we were fleeing. Silent as shadows, we fled across the mud, looping around the hill on its western side.

"We have to draw them back closer to the trail," I said to Mag in a low voice. "Otherwise Chausiku will never be able to lead the captain to us."

She only shrugged and raised her brows. "You are the ranger. Lead on."

"I am *not* a ranger," I growled. "Squadrons, follow me!"

"Certainly acts like a ranger, though, doesn't he?" said Hallan to Jian, who barely restrained a smile.

The sun broke the eastern horizon at last, peeking its shining face above the tops of the hills. And its light came just in time to illuminate a party of Shades ahead of us. It was the archers who had fired upon us only moments ago. They pulled up short, shock on their faces. They had not expected us to loop around the hills and meet them so soon. I counted no more than a dozen, and they were scant paces away.

Mag leaped forwards, silent in her battle-trance. Her squadron drew their blades and roared with anger as they rushed the archers. Oku charged beside them, baying with all his might. The Shades loosed a ragged volley before trying to turn and flee, but my archers riddled them with arrows. Only three managed to get away by splitting up and vanishing into the hills. The rest fell dead, pierced with arrows or hacked apart with swords or Mag's spear. Oku brought one down, jaws clamped around her ankle and then her throat. But Mag lost another soldier in the skirmish, and the Shades' desperate bowfire took two of my archers and wounded another. We each had a dozen fighters left, including ourselves.

"South," I gasped, as I hauled my wounded archer

to her feet. She gritted her teeth as she leaned on me and tried to run as best she could.

The murmur grew louder to the north. And as we drew near to the Shades' trail once more, the murmur became a roar. I risked a look back and saw the Shades emerge over the hills behind us. There were at least a hundred and a half of them, and they came charging across the mud at us with bared steel. At their head was the brute woman, and above them swooped Kaita in her raven form. She was drawing closer, and I knew it could not be long before she would take the field in one of her animal forms.

Mayhap we can at least kill her before the end, I thought.

"Keep going!" I cried. "Run! As long as you can! We have to give the captain time to—"

Another roar filled the air, hundreds of voices screaming in bloodlust and fury.

The Shades ground to a confused halt, even as I turned my gaze to the east. The rising sun fell into my eyes, and I had to shield them with a hand. When I could see again, the sight nearly made me weep.

Three hundreds of soldiers swept down from the eastern hills. At the head of the charge were the red-cloaks, with Kun himself holding a sword high in the air. Their fury shook the ground as they swept down upon the Shades.

"Retreat!" roared Tagata. "Get back to the hills! Retreat to our siblings!"

Kaita watched from the sky as the Shades turned and fled. Tagata waited until the last, holding the rear of the formation as they ran into the hills. The Mystics' militia were coming right towards her forces, and they outnumbered the Shades two to one.

Kaita cursed in her mind. She had been too focused on Mag and me and had forgotten to watch out for the rest of our allies. Now the Shades were going to fall—mayhap even *Tagata* would fall—and it would all be Kaita's fault.

But no. She had to cast such thoughts aside, for they would not help her fix anything. Kaita swooped low, looking for any way the Shades could escape. They made their way north through a narrow gap between two hills. It was the closest thing to a defensible position that Kaita could see. Tagata formed up squadrons of spears before the opening, to hold it against the Mystics as they attempted an offense. But it would not last long—soon, the Mystics would simply move up the hills and around the sides of the Shade formation.

Kaita swung wider, looping in the air and looking for anything to help. There seemed no hope of escape in these cursed hills, and a last stand would serve little purpose. But there had to be a way. Her hunt could not end like this. Tagata's tale could not end like this.

She tilted her wings to bank left, and she felt the odd bulge in her chest.

Kaita's heart nearly stopped.

The magestones. They would give her the strength of hellskin. Kaita had never seen it, of course, but it was supposed to be terrible. What use would the Mystics' weapons be against her hide? How could their shields withstand her claws?

Even if they managed to bring her down, she should at least be able to kill Mag and me before the end.

It was not the promise she had made to Rogan, but darkness take that vow. Rogan was the one who had sent her on this pointless march, promising she would have her chance. That was clearly false, whether or not Rogan had meant to lie to her. If she would never have a better opportunity, then she would take what she could. Who cared if she died in the end if she fulfilled the purpose that had sustained her all these years?

But then her eyes fell upon the fiery wyrm.

She recognized it in a flash, though she had not been searching for it. It was a blazing trail of fire down a hill to the northeast of the Shades' position. My fallen archer had dropped a torch, and it had tumbled back and forth as it rolled down the hill. The grass had caught fire, and tongues of flame had licked the turf as though an artist had painted it with a great brush. It looked for all the world like the shape of a flaming wyrm stretched out upon the hillside.

The Lord had told Tagata that they would see this sign. And that the sign would lead to escape. Was it possible?

Kaita swooped lower, feeling lightheaded. The blazing trail ended behind a cluster of grey boulders pressed up against the side of the hill. But there was nothing there, not that Kaita could see.

Wait. *There.*

Kaita could not see it until she landed on the boulder. It was a cave entrance, though it could only be seen from among the rocks. Anyone walking by the hill, or even on it, would not see the tunnel until they were nearly inside it.

In an instant, she was winging her way back to Tagata.

"Charge!" cried Kun. He wore his smile still, but it was fierce, alive with the thrill of battle. He and his Mystics pressed towards the gap between the hills. It was their third charge against the Shades, and I knew it would be the last one.

"Loose!" I cried. Our arrows flew over the Mystics' heads, landing among the enemy and casting many of them to the ground. The rest of the Shades wavered, and they broke almost the instant Kun's Mystics slammed into them. As one, they turned and scattered, blue cloaks fluttering in the air behind them as they ran north in the mud.

Mag and I guided our squadrons close behind Kun's as he ran in pursuit. But almost from the moment I pressed through the hills, I felt that something was wrong. There were a paltry few dozen of the Shades in front of us.

Then I forgot such thoughts as another roar filled the air.

Zhen, Kun's nephew, cried aloud as he led his company from the east. Kun had sent him east to loop around behind our foe. Now they were flanked and cut off. Four hundreds of our soldiers met in the center of the battlefield.

The Shades turned back and forth, wavering. They did not know whether to face the charge from the south or the one from the east. In the end, it did not matter. They died to a one, their blood staining the muddy ground beneath them as it pooled.

The battlefield fell to silence—that sudden, shocking stillness that comes after the worst violence, the most brutal carnage. It was broken only by a ragged cheer from our forces before everything fell to quiet again. I fell on my back in the mud, panting heavily. I felt like I had run many leagues in our flight from the Shades, and every step had felt even worse with the sucking mud clutching at our feet.

"Oh no, you great idiot," came Yue's voice. "Come here."

I heard her heavy footsteps approaching. I groaned, but I smiled and raised a hand. Yue seized it and hauled me to my feet. Her arms wrapped around me and mine around her. We shared a kiss, which was both poisoned by and sweeter for the death all around us.

"Why, Sergeant Baolan," I said in mock surprise. "Were you worried about me?"

"Dark take you for a fool," she said. "You are not running off and risking your life like that again, and the captain's orders be damned."

"Careful," I said. "That is dangerously close to mutiny."

"Then I am a mutineer," she said, and kissed me again.

But as the thrill of the fight left me, and our little army began to collect itself and take our toll of the dead, my thoughts grew dour. I remembered what I had noticed when we had first run into this killing field.

And it seemed I was not the only one.

"Where did they go?"

The battle-trance was gone. Mag's voice was quiet. Almost fearful.

Yue looked over at her. "What was that?" she said.

"The Shades," said Mag. "We had them surrounded, yet there cannot be more than two scores of them here. I see neither the brute nor Kaita. Where did all of them go?"

I studied the ground. Tracks led into the field from the south, where Kun had attacked. There were tracks from the north, where the Shades had come in the first place. And tracks came in from the east, where Zhen had led his company in the final charge. But there were no tracks leading out of the little dell at all.

A darkness came over my heart, but I tried to shake it off. This was a victory. I was determined to treat it as such.

"We do not know," I said. "But we have time. Time to figure it out, and to finish the rest of them. I have not forgotten Kaita."

Mag did not look convinced. She shuddered as though a sudden fear had seized her. But at last, she nodded and turned to attend to her squadron.

My grip on Yue tightened.

TWENTY-NINE

KAITA COLLAPSED AGAINST THE ROCK WALL OF THE cavern, her whole body heaving in deep, shaking breaths. All around her, Shades seized their chance to rest after their desperate flight.

When Tagata learned of the tunnel, she had asked for volunteers to serve as a rear guard while the rest escaped. So many had volunteered that Tagata had been forced to choose thirty of them. The heartbreak it caused her was still plain on her face.

Kaita had guided them all to the tunnel entrance, and they had pushed their way in as quickly as they could. They had vanished beneath the ground mere moments before Zhen's flanking company would have seen them. Filled with battle fury, Zhen missed spotting the Shades' tracks leading to the tunnel. Then his troops had trampled over the signs, obscuring any hint of how the Shades had seemed to vanish into thin air.

The tunnel had turned west and continued beneath the hills for a long way, plunging deep into the earth before leading to a massive cavern. The Shades had torches, but the ceiling was so high their light did not reach it. Stalagmites thrust up from the ground everywhere, like a vampire's twisted, pitted fangs. But the space was drier than the soaking outside, and hidden, and surprisingly warm compared to early spring's chill.

Just over a hundred Shades remained—less than half of those who had started the march. And there were nearly four hundreds of their foes outside, searching for them and ready to cut them down.

Kaita looked over to where Tagata stood. The shadeborn seemed indefatigable. She had not fallen to the floor gasping, like her siblings. She stood solid in their midst, head bowed in mourning. Kaita knew her well. Tagata would blame herself for every soldier who had fallen on this long trek. The Lord had foretold the outcome, and he held her blameless for it, but that did not matter to her.

Slowly Kaita forced herself to her feet and went to the shadeborn's side, placing a hand on her arm, which burned like an oven.

"Tagata," said Kaita quietly. "You saved everyone you could."

"Not enough of them," said Tagata. She lifted her head at last, still avoiding Kaita's gaze, and took a deep breath. "But now we must look forwards. Help me see to everyone's arrangements. I want fires if we can find the fuel. None of us should have to sit in the dark, alone with our thoughts."

"I think I should scout the caves," said Kaita. "We do not have endless supplies. We have to find a way out of here, and I doubt we will be able to leave the same way we came in. The redcloaks will likely make camp in the same dell where they—" She bit off her words.

Tagata's expression darkened. "Where they slaughtered our kindred," she rumbled.

"Yes," said Kaita. "But we will avenge them. I swear it. Let me take my mountain lion form and search for a way out of this place, and then we can plan our retaliation. The Lord told you this place was an escape. There must be a way."

Tagata gave her a small smile. "Who ever thought you would be the one coaxing me to have faith in our father? But you are right, of course. Go then, dear one. I will care for our kindred."

They shared a brief embrace, and then a glow filled Kaita's eyes as she took her mountain lion form. The caves seemed to fill with light in her vision, the sparse torches letting her see almost as well as if it were day.

She remained standing there by Tagata for a moment, drinking in the warm air. Her nose filled with the scents of the Shades behind her, and a thousand other smells as well: long-stale dung from animals who had passed through, and fresher deposits from bats. There was no sign of any larger animals having been here recently, which was a relief.

Soon there was nothing more to be learned without setting off to explore. She rubbed her lion head against Tagata's waist and received a gentle caress along the throat. Then she loped off into the darkness.

There were three tunnels other than the one they had used to enter. Picking the first one to her right, she ran down it, eyes and nose open. The passage twisted this way and that. Sometimes it dropped sharply down, and sometimes it rose so steeply that she had to climb, her claws digging into the limestone of the walls.

For a half hour she crept along the passage, her hopes high. The tunnel did not dive deeper into the earth, which was a good sign. If it did not finish in a dead end, then there was a good chance Kaita would find an exit.

And then, slowly, several strong scents began to creep into her nose. The first was fresh air, thick with snow, and her heart leaped. But then she smelled other things. Wood, but with an acrid and bitter undertone. That would be the pycnandra trees.

And she smelled people: a great many of them, and their horses, and wagons, and goods of all sorts.

It was Kun's force. Kaita had little sense of direction beneath the earth, but this tunnel must have looped around to the southwest. It emerged into another hidden place in the hills, right beside where Kun and his army had made camp.

Kaita's heart sank to her paws. But she pressed forwards anyway, just to be sure. The tunnel ended just as the other one had, behind a pile of boulders that blocked sight. Scrambling and scrabbling with her claws, Kaita climbed up, poking her head over the top of the boulders.

There. The Mystics and their allies were barely more than a span away, off to the east. She could see the redcloaks massed towards the north end of the camp, while the army's train was to the south, closer to the caves where Kaita now stood.

Once again, she could almost *feel* Mag and me close by. We were there, right *there.* If she only took one of the magestones, she could plunge into the heart of the camp, find us, and . . .

But no. There was still her promise to Rogan. Kaita growled, and the sound rumbled thick in her chest.

This tunnel was useless for escape unless the Mystics eventually left—in which case, the Shades could more easily leave through the same passage they had first found.

Discouraged, she trotted the long path back to the large central cavern. By the time she reached them, they had set up their camp, tents all in neat rows as they had done above ground. Kaita came trotting up to Tagata and resumed her human form.

"That tunnel is no use," she said, pointing south. "It leads straight to our enemies, like the first. At least they have not discovered its entrance, or not that I could smell."

"In dark circumstances, we must cherish small blessings all the more," said Tagata. "Thank you, Kaita."

"I will go explore the other passages."

She turned to go, but Tagata held up a hand. "Wait," she said. "You should rest. The others tell me you were wakeful through much of the night, and you have run far and overused your magic since before dawn."

"I am fine," said Kaita, shaking her head. "I will rest once I find us a way out of this mess."

"Eat some food, at least," said Tagata. "You cannot tell me you are not hungry." She smiled as Kaita's stomach rumbled aloud.

"Mayhap a bite would be good," said Kaita reluctantly.

Tagata chuckled and ushered her over to one of the noisome campfires the Shades had built. There were only two, for they had had to make them out of dried dung, and there was precious little of that to be found. Kaita sat, her body nearly screaming in relief after its exertions, and they began to tuck into a little meal together with their fellows in the darkness.

THIRTY

Back on the surface, Mag and I had reconvened with Dryleaf and Yue in the wake of the fighting. Kun ordered our camp moved from the Greenfrost into the hills. The move took somewhat longer than it should have since we were all weary with the day's battle. But Kun felt it necessary to consolidate our presence in the hills, at least until we determined where the Shades had disappeared to. Now, close to midday, we ate a meal by our campfire, the same as Kaita below the earth, though of course, we did not know that.

I could see the deep dissatisfaction in Mag's expression. Her mind lingered on the Shades. It was a beautiful day around us, sunlight filtering through the grey clouds to shine from the snowy hills. But her mood was ugly, and she spoke little, only giving brief answers when we tried to broach conversation.

"Where did they all go?" she muttered after a time, placing her bowl on the ground. It was not even half-eaten. Oku's ears perked up.

"They cannot be far, Mag," I said gently. "There is nowhere around here to hide for long. We will find them."

"And in the meantime, there is plenty to do," said Yue. "We have wounded to see to, and troops who need our guidance." But she sounded disgruntled, and she poked savagely at the logs of our fire with a long stick.

"All of that is well and good if it helps us find Kaita and end her," said Mag. "Yet now it is only a delay. She has evaded us before, and it seems she has done it again. But this time she brought a whole army into the shadows with her."

Dryleaf's hand rested on Oku's head, scratching him behind the ears. Oku sat patiently, enjoying it, but his gaze was riveted on Mag's abandoned food bowl. "You fear losing her forever," said the old man. "But I do not think that is how your hunt will end. One day you will have the confrontation you desire, even if it is not here in these hills."

Mag's fist clenched. "No," she said. "It *will* be here. It *must* be."

"Mag, come now," I said. "Why is it so important that—"

"Because I am *tired,* Albern," said Mag. Her voice cracked, and hearing it froze me. "I am tired of having her dangled in front of my face, luring me along like a carrot does a mule. I am tired of wandering endlessly across the nine lands. I want this to be over. Now. I am tired of—"

She turned away, looking towards the center of camp.

"Mag . . ." I said slowly. "I did not—"

"I do not know what comes next," she said, almost whispering. "I have no plan for it. But I want one. I have been trying to think of it, trying to picture it. I cannot. It is as though my road ends with Kaita, vanishing at her feet. It makes my life feel so small, and I am tired of that, too. I want an after."

She stood.

"And I am going to have one."

"Mag?" I said sharply. Yue and I scrambled to our feet as she stalked off. I helped Dryleaf up and brought him along. "Where are you going?"

"To speak to the captain," she replied.

"Mag, wait," said Yue. "Why?"

"I am going to find her."

"What, alone?" I said. "Mag, you are not going anywhere without us. Or me, at least." I gave Yue a furtive glance.

"Us," she said, frowning at me. "She has the right of it. It would be better than sitting here on our rears."

"That is the spirit," said Mag, still walking at a breakneck pace.

"Mag," said Dryleaf. His voice was almost too quiet to hear. But Mag's gait hitched for a moment, as though she had nearly paused but forced herself on. "My dear girl. Do not risk too much with rash action."

"I risk nothing," said Mag. "Every time I have faced her, I have defeated her without taking a scratch."

"Of course she cannot harm *you,*" said Dryleaf, who was breathing heavily now with the pace of our walk. "But what about everyone else?"

At last, Mag stopped. She wheeled on him. "And why do you think I am doing this?" she snapped. "What do you think this whole journey has been for? I started chasing Kaita because of what she did to my home, to my . . . to my Sten. In Lan Shui, she killed many. In Kahuanga, she started a war that killed even more. Even now, though we win each battle, dozens fall every time. It seems clear that I can protect no one by moving slow, by ensuring each step is safe. So I am done with it. I am ready for the end, and I am sick of people telling me to wait!"

"Mag," I said reproachfully. The look on her face was so fierce, I had an urge to put myself between her and Dryleaf.

"It is all right, my boy," said Dryleaf. He patted my arm. "Strong words are of no concern to me. But I beg of you, Mag: if you want to know what comes after Kaita, then turn aside from her. I have suggested it before, though I knew you might not be ready to hear it. You *need* to hear it now. You have allies, friends. You have the good Captain Zhou and this little family that has taken you into the fold. It will not replace what you lost in Northwood—but you are wise enough to know that nothing will ever replace that. Build something new instead. It will be no less dear simply because it is different."

"Mayhap I will," said Mag. "But after. Northwood is not over. Not until she lies dead at my feet."

"And will that help Sten?" said Dryleaf quietly.

"It has never been about Sten," said Mag. "I know that. I am not a fool. It was always for me."

And she turned and set off towards the captain's tent again.

Yue followed her, and I started to do the same with Dryleaf. But he patted my hand and shook his head. "Leave me, boy. I will be of no help, and I may only anger her until she says something foolish to Kun. I will find my way back to our fire with Oku's help."

"All right," I said. "We will return as soon as we may."

I ran after Mag and caught her as she reached Kun. He was in conference with Tou and the other lieutenants, including his nephew, Zhen. The group of them all looked up at us in confusion.

"Sergeants," said Tou, looking confused. It was a breach of protocol to approach him while he was in conference with the captain.

"Lieutenant Shi," said Mag. Then she turned from him to Kun. "Captain Zhou. I request permission to investigate the Shades' disappearance, along with Sergeants Telfer and Baolan."

"Sergeant," said Tou, speaking sharply now. "That is something to discuss with me first, and with the captain only if I approve."

"Apologies, ser," she said, nodding to him. "But time is of the essence. Hours have passed since we saw them. Wherever they are now, we can be certain they are moving farther away. If we do not find the trail, we may lose them."

Kun had looked at her all the while with a surprised smile on his face. Now he cocked his head. "We are well aware of the situation, Sergeant," he said. "Your offer is appreciated, but unnecessary. Lieutenant Zhou will lead the search for the Shades' trail."

"You should use Albern's talents as well, ser," said Mag.

"Sergeant!" said Tou. "Return to your unit and—"

"That is all right, Lieutenant," said Kun, raising a hand. As Tou subsided, Kun looked upon Mag again. "You have some personal stake in this, Sergeant. And you know how I value honesty. Tell me why this means so much to you."

"A weremage marches with the Shades," said Mag at once. "She killed my husband."

"Mag!" I said, more in shock than dismay. It was

no business of mine what she did with the truth, but she had withheld it on our road so far.

"She and her fellows invaded Northwood," Mag went on. "She murdered him in front of my eyes. I have been hunting her ever since. Truth be told, Captain, I joined you in hopes that you would come into conflict with her, and now you have. She is almost within my grasp, yet I can feel her slipping away."

Kun never took his eyes from her. His lips twitched, and I could see heavy thoughts behind his eyes. Then, at last, he spoke.

"Killing the weremage will accomplish little in the war for Underrealm," he said. "She is an asset of the enemy, yes, and a powerful one. But only one. Meanwhile, you, Sergeant Telfer, and Sergeant Baolan are three highly trained and invaluable officers in our war effort. Risking the three of you to locate the enemy is unacceptable. If you have any skilled trackers in your squadron, I might consider sending them, if you propose it to your lieutenant first."

"Captain—" said Mag.

"No, Sergeant," barked Tou, stepping in front of the captain. "You have pushed things quite far enough already. Your captain has given you a command. He has even deigned to explain his reasoning behind it, which you are not owed. Turn and march back to your unit *now,* or you will face discipline."

I had never seen the lieutenant so angry. Mag looked as if she wanted to argue more, but she subsided. Kun's expression was firm, but I saw pity in his eyes. If I am being honest, I agreed with his decision. An army is nothing if it lacks unity, and soldiers cannot be running off to settle personal vendettas.

Gently I put a hand on Mag's arm. "Come."

She turned without looking at me and stalked back to the tents. I waited a moment more, bowing my head to Tou.

"Apologies, Lieutenant. She . . . It happened very quickly."

His nostrils flared, but he did give me a brief, sharp nod. I took that as the best sign I was going to get, and together with Yue, I followed Mag back to our tents at the heads of our squadrons.

"How did it go?" said Dryleaf.

"Not well," I answered him. "The captain was not amenable to Mag's decision."

"And is that the end of it?" said Dryleaf.

"Not on your life," said Mag firmly.

Yue frowned. "What do you mean? The captain gave his order."

"I am going out anyway," said Mag.

"You cannot be serious," said Yue. "After he told you no?"

Mag looked at me. "Albern? What do you say?"

I hesitated. "I . . . I am not sure, Mag. We asked the captain. Why do that, if you meant to disobey?"

"Because I thought he would say yes, of course," said Mag. "And he should have, because I am right.

Your skills are wasted sitting here in camp. He says we three are too 'valuable' to lose. Well, what good is value if he does not use it?"

"Yet if he sends us out alone, and we do not return," countered Yue, "then we are worth nothing in the next fight. I understand your frustration, Mag. But I understand the captain as well, and you must do the same. He is our superior officer. We are soldiers."

"I left the mercenary life for a reason," said Mag. She turned from Yue to me. "I want to go after her, Albern, and I need you to come with me."

Slowly I shook my head. Rarely have I felt more torn. "Mag. Kun said . . ."

"And since when do we care what others tell us?" said Mag. She nodded at Yue. "Yue tried to tell us what to do in Lan Shui. We disobeyed, and we saved the town."

"This is not Lan Shui," said Yue.

Mag shrugged. "Yue, you are an honorable woman and a dark-damned good fighter. But if you had had your way, Lan Shui would now be empty of everything but vampires and corpses. I do not mean that as an insult. You did what you thought was right. But we had knowledge you did not. That is exactly what we face now. We know better than the captain, not through any fault of his own, other than mayhap not enough trust in us."

"He does not trust you enough, and so you mean to betray his trust even further?" said Yue. "How do you think that will help anything?"

Mag, however, kept her gaze on me. "If you worry about us shirking our duty, we do not have to. We are mercenaries. Let us resign."

"We agreed to see this campaign through," I said. "Kun would brand us as deserters and outlaws. He would have no choice—imagine if everyone in this force thought they could simply turn tail for home after a bad day. If we wish to leave when we return to Taitou or reach another city for resupply, that is one thing. But we cannot abandon our contract out here in the wilderness when another battle could be just around the corner."

I do not mind admitting that Mag was frightening me. I knew she was angry—I could feel the fury emanating from her—but she did not yell, nor did she even scowl. It was as though she restrained her rage just beneath the surface. It gave me the uncomfortable feeling of facing her battle-trance, but from the sharp end of her spear.

"Very well," said Mag. "If we cannot break contract, I am afraid we must disobey orders. I mean to seek the Shades' trail the moment the sun is down, which should be early."

"We cannot, Mag," said Yue. "Albern, tell her we cannot."

I struggled for words, searching for some way to make Mag see the foolishness of her actions. Still, she held me in her gaze, and the look in her eyes was so intense that I felt incapable of gainsaying her.

Yue stepped between us, breaking my eye contact. "Albern, you are a great fool, but not this great of a fool," she said softly. "Do the smart thing. Stay here with me tonight. Let us go and invite Nikau to stay with us—he has been trying hard enough to get inside our tent. Forget this madness."

"If that is more important to you than finding Sten's killer," said Mag, "then I suppose I cannot stop you."

Floundering, I turned to Dryleaf, who still sat motionless by the fire. "Dryleaf?" I said weakly.

But he only shook his head. "I am sorry, my boy. I have said all that could be useful. You know I think this is madness. If that does not sway you or Mag, nothing else I could say would do so."

Mag stepped around Yue and put a hand on my shoulder, gripping it firmly. "Albern. In Northwood, we promised each other. Together until the end, until Sten was avenged. In Lan Shui, we said it again. Are you still with me?'

"Are you with *me?*" I said. "Why must your way be the only one?"

"Because my way leads to Kaita," said Mag. "You would have us sit here and wait, and that is nothing either of us promised the other."

I have lost battles in which many of my friends died. I have borne the bitter sting of watching my commander surrender to the enemy in the middle of a corpse-littered battlefield. But rarely have I ever felt so defeated as I did in that moment.

"All right, Mag," I said quietly. "I made my pledge. If you are going, and if I cannot say anything to sway you, then yes. I am by your side. Until the end of the road."

A beautiful smile splashed over her face as if it had been thrown there. She released a sigh, and I realized how afraid she had been that I would refuse her. But that was never a possibility, really. She turned to Yue.

"Well?" she said. "We are going. Will you turn us in to the captain? Or will you come with us? I want your sword by my side, Yue."

Yue barely seemed to hear her. She was only looking at me. "Albern?" she said. "You agree with her?"

"I do not," I said. "But I promised, Yue. I cannot abandon her now."

"Hm," snorted Yue. "I thought that promise went two ways." She turned back to Mag. "Very well. If I am outvoted, I suppose I will come, too. I am no faithless friend. But we had best be quick about it, and quiet."

"We will," said Mag. "Then our course is set. Tonight, the moment the sun has gone down. The moons are full, and their light should be good for wandering."

"All right," I said. "But we should leave Oku. If we want to be as quiet as possible, it would be best to have just the three of us."

"A good idea." Mag knelt and took Oku behind the ears, scratching him fondly. It was an uncommon display of affection from her, as though she was in high spirits. But I could not shake some persistent feeling that it was an ill omen.

"Kip, boy," she said. "Stay here with Dryleaf until we come back."

His wide, watery eyes looked into hers, and he cocked his head. When she stood, he went to the bard and lay down by his feet. But he kept his head raised, and he did not stop looking at her. A low whine issued from his throat, and it grew louder when we started to walk away.

As we went to ready ourselves for the night, I glanced back once. Dryleaf's blind eyes had closed, and his head bent low, pushing his long beard into his chest.

That evening, Kun sat inside his tent at one of his small desks. A letter was in his hand—a report to the Mystic chancellor of northeastern Dorsea, relating the army's activities in the region so far. But his hand had long ago stilled at the quill, and his eyes stared at nothing. He wore his usual smile, but it was absentminded. He was thinking of Mag and me, of course, and Mag's earnest plea to go and find the weremage.

So she lost her husband, he thought. That made sense to him. It brought many other strange things about her, and me, into a new clarity.

He thought of his sister. Dear, sweet Min. He had cared about her more than anything else in the world. He still saw her beautiful dark eyes whenever he looked at his nephew Zhen.

What would he have done, had she died from a blade instead of the wasting sickness that took her? Would he have lived his life the same way? Would he still wear the red cloak now?

He turned to the door of his tent and called out, "Bring me Lieutenant Shi."

The decision made, his quill sped across the letter again. By the time Tou arrived to speak with him, Kun had finished. He sealed the letter and handed it to the same messenger who stepped into the tent to present Tou.

"Lieutenant Shi," said Kun brightly. "Please, sit."

"Captain," said Tou, taking the seat opposite. "Thank you."

"Of course. We all spent enough time on our feet today." Kun's smile widened. "I have been thinking of your sergeant's little . . . outburst today."

Tou's face darkened. "Ser. I spoke with them immediately after our council. I assigned Mag's squadron to latrine duty for the next three days, and I gave Albern and Yue strict warnings about—"

Kun cut him off with a raised hand. "All appropriate reactions. But I find myself thinking of Mag and her purpose for being here. Purpose drives us, Lieutenant. None take the red and rods but those who have a desire to protect the nine kingdoms—or none should, at any rate. Some soldiers in this force have joined for the coin, but most are here for some other reason. I am sure there are as many reasons as there are soldiers in our force. But those purposes align in one factor: a love of Dorsea. That is what makes them invaluable to us, and through us, to the High King. And we should not disparage the varied reasons that brought them under our command, if those reasons may be aligned towards our common goal."

Tou ducked his head. "Of course, ser. But . . . forgive me, but why do you tell me all this?"

A long moment passed in silence. Then Kun sighed. "I mean to let your sergeants go hunting for the Shades."

Of all the things Tou expected to hear, that was not among them. "Ser?"

"I mean it," said Kun. "Sergeant Telfer is an excellent tracker. Lieutenant Zhou is better, but not by much, as he told me himself. And if Albern should manage to locate the Shades, he may need Mag's help. She was right. Zhen is already out there seeking the enemy. Better to double our chances."

Tou's jaw kept clenching and releasing. But if he harbored any doubts, he kept them to himself. After all, it would hardly be becoming to argue with his captain after he had just disciplined the rest of us for insubordination.

"Very good, ser," he said. "Shall I give them their orders in the morning?"

"You had better do it now," said Kun, glancing at the tent flap. "Night has fallen. They will want to leave first thing in the morning, I imagine, and so they will want to turn in as early as possible."

“I believe the three of them have already gone to bed,” said Tou. “I will tell them now in any case, even if I have to wake them, so they can prepare whatever they will need. Thank you, ser.”

He stood from the table, saluted, and left. Kun watched him go, still smiling. He pinched the bridge of his nose and pushed back, rubbing at his eyes, the smile never fading.

But it vanished when Tou came running back to his tent only a few moments later.

THIRTY-ONE

"Ugh," said Sun. "You mean he caught you?"

"I am afraid so," said Albern. "Well, *caught* is not quite the right word . . . but you will see what I mean a bit later in the story."

"Before you tell it, though, I have another question," said Sun.

Albern's brows shot for the sky. "Do you indeed? Mark this moment—the first time you asked me to stop telling the story so that we could talk about something else."

"You are most amusing," said Sun, no hint of a

smile on her face. "But the question is, in fact, about the tale. When you spoke of Mag hearing about Dragons for the first time . . ." A shadow seemed to cloud the day, and they both shuddered until it passed. "You mentioned she had no parents. Why not?"

"Well, she must have *had* parents," said Albern. "Everyone does, after all. But if they ever did tell her tales of Dragons, she had long since lost those tales by the time she met Duana and came to Shuiniu."

Now, I told you that Duana was a veteran of the Dorsean king's wars. This was not, of course, King Jun, whose death had sparked the civil war in which we found ourselves. Duana was older. She had fought under Jun's father, Wolin of the family Fei, and had served him with honor.

But when Duana came back from the war, she had many scars, and not all of them were of the skin. I am sure you know of veterans who suffer from maladies of the mind. Sometimes Duana would find herself growing anxious when there was no reason to be, breaking out in cold sweats and jerking at the smallest sound. It would come and go in waves, like a fever that resurges after starting to break.

This might have been why Duana knew the signs of Mag's distress when she first told her of Dragons. She knew how unreasoning such terror can be, and how small and weak Mag must have felt before the images in her mind. Thoughts are but wisps and gossamer to most people, but to some, they hold a terrifying power—and sadly, that power is usually wielded most harshly against those who should be in control of it.

The townsfolk in Shuiniu understood this, as do most in the nine kingdoms. They would leave Duana alone if that was what she required, or stay with her and hold her hand through her tremors if she asked them to. But most of the time, when Duana's attacks would grow too much to bear, she would take a long stick and go walking through the woods. That forest was called the Carrweld, as I have mentioned before, and it was peaceful. Beneath the trees, with birds singing and only the sound of her footsteps to accompany her, Duana would find peace again. Her body would gradually calm, her shakes ceasing, her breath coming free and easy.

But one day, the woods were not so peaceful. One day, just as Duana had overcome her fear, she heard something moving in the underbrush nearby.

Duana's pulse raced again—but this time, it was under control. She gripped her walking stick in both hands, holding it before her in readiness.

The sound came once more. The creature was coming closer. Grimacing at the walking stick in her hands, Duana hoped she was not about to face a bear. But it sounded too small for that. Then a worse thought crossed her mind—it might be a cub, and the mother could be close.

Duana was about to turn tail and run for town, hoping she could outdistance the thing, when she spotted the face.

It was a girl. She was in a low bush, barely two paces away, and she was staring at Duana. Her face was so streaked with dirt and grime that Duana had missed her at first. She had wild, ratty hair filled with mud and sticks and who knew what else.

Duana knelt at once. She held out a hand, moving it ever so slowly and speaking in a gentle, coaxing tone.

"Well, hello there," she said. "I am sorry if I startled you. Can you come out?"

Huge eyes blinked at her from that dirt-covered face. Ever so slowly, the girl pushed out from the bushes on either side of her.

She was naked, and the rest of her body was as filthy as her face. All sorts of detritus and dirt was worked into her hair, and all up and down her skin. But that skin was remarkably well-kept otherwise. Duana saw no signs of injury upon her, not even a scratch. But in her hand, she held a sharpened stick like a spear. Fresh blood stained the tip, and it looked as if there were many more coats beneath it.

"Hello," said Duana again. "I am Duana."

Those great brown eyes blinked. "Duana." The girl's voice was halting, but loud, strong.

"Yes," said Duana. She settled back on her haunches while placing a hand to her chest. "I am Duana. And you?"

The girl pointed to Duana's hand on her chest. "You."

"Me," said Duana. Then she pointed at the girl. "And you." Again the hand on her chest and then pointing to the girl. "I am Duana. And you?"

The girl blinked twice more. Then she pointed at Duana. "You. Duana. I." She placed a hand on her chest.

Sudden, clear certainty came into her eyes.

"Mag. I am Mag."

"Dark take you to its depths, and dark take me for a fool for believing in you!" bellowed Sun.

Albern looked entirely alarmed, and he glanced at the crowd surrounding them on the street. Fortunately, no one seemed to have paid much attention to Sun's outburst, for the bustle of a thousand conversations did much to drown her out.

"I am sorry?" said Albern.

"You should be!" said Sun. "All this time, I thought you were leading me somewhere with all this talk about Mag's peerless fighting."

"You did?"

"I thought you were going to *explain* it. You made it seem as if one day, you were going to tell me how Mag learned to fight!"

"I did?"

"You did, and you know it," growled Sun. "You gave

me hope, and now I find that you are not going to tell me anything about it at all."

"Am I not?"

Sun reached over and pinched his nose, much to Albern's very evident shock. "Stop answering my questions with more questions."

"Am I? Or, that is, I will try." Albern's voice came out thin and nasal through her fingers.

Sun released him. In truth, she was not all that angry, and she was enjoying his reaction to her sudden outburst.

"You lied to me as well," she said. "You told me that Mag's fight against Ciaran was her first fight. Yet she came out of the woods with blood on her spear. Clearly, she had fought before."

Albern could not help a little smirk. "I am usually quite careful in my wording. And what I said, precisely, was that her scrap with Ciaran was her first fight against another *person.*"

"Albern," said Sun, letting a whine come into her tone, "you cannot be serious about this. Are you trying to tell me that Mag walked out of the woods as a mysterious little child, already knowing perfectly how to fight, and without a scratch on her under all that dirt? Is this your idea of the brilliant tale of the murky past of one of Underrealm's greatest figures? Because I must tell you that it is *horrible.* I have not felt so cheated since my tutor first taught me how to gamble and then stole my allowance for

three months straight. My parents banished him from our home when they found out, but they let him keep the gold for his cleverness."

That made Albern laugh. "Now, *that* is a good tale. A premise, a development, and a resolution that is unexpected yet inevitable. Pithy, too. Certainly more economical than this overlong yarn I have been spinning you." He fixed her with an appraising look. "But as for your other question—Sun, what would you like me to say? I am relaying a tale. Would you like me to tell the story of what happened, as best I know it? Or should I make something up? Mayhap you would prefer a tale in which Mag set out to sail the Eldest Deep, battling all of the dark creatures of those terrifying waters, until she found a sea-hag who imparted upon her the secrets that allowed her to become an invincible fighter. That would be a fantastic story. I am certain they would pay me a great heap of coin in any tavern where I chose to spin it. However, it does not happen to be the truth. So. Which story would you rather hear?"

Sun folded her arms as they walked, staring at her feet in a pout. "That is an entirely unsatisfactory explanation."

Albern smirked. "Well, I shall endeavor to do better in the future."

"Get back to your ill-fated scouting expedition in the night," said Sun, waving a hand at him. "I do not want to hear anything more about impossibly perfect children coming from nowhere."

Albern's mouth twisted. "You may not feel the same way, by the end of the tale."

THIRTY-TWO

As night drew on and the moons rose higher in the sky, Mag, Yue, and I slipped out of Kun's encampment, searching for any clue as to how the Shades had escaped. It was a fine night. Both moons shone full above me, and the clouds had parted, letting the land flood with silvery light. In those days, my eyes were sharper, and I could pick out the details in the land as we went.

I went to the dell where we had wiped out the Shades, or at least the rear guard who let the rest of their fellows escape. The tracks looked much the same—the only things different were the signs of Kun's force moving south after the battle, and one set of new tracks from Zhen, whom Kun had assigned to search for the Shades.

"There is nothing new, Mag," I said. "I might have a chance at spotting something in the daylight, but—"

"Albern," said Mag. "Come now. You have to try, at least. Give me that much."

I sighed. "I do not know what more I can do. I can think of no way they could have vanished like this. It is like Elf-magic."

"Let us retrace our steps during the battle, then," said Mag. "We came from that way." She pointed to the west.

"No, we came from there," I said, pointing to the hilltop where the Shade archers had fired at us. "Honestly, Mag, sometimes you are like an infant lost in the woods."

A shadow passed over her expression, but I did not notice. I had frozen in place, staring up at the hill.

"Albern?" said Yue. "What is it?"

"That hill . . . that is where the Shades fired at us," I said. "They killed one of mine. He bore a torch."

"I remember," said Mag. "They got two of mine as well."

"I see where the torch rolled down the hill," I said. "But I do not see the torch itself."

We all looked up at the spot together. There was the mark that looked like a wyrm. It was less clear now, for the flames had long since burned out. But there was a black trough burned in the green shoots of new grass, and it looked for all the world like a dragon twisting as it dove to the ground, wings folded back against its body.

"Someone could have found it and picked it up," said Yue.

"Look at the boulders," I said. "It should have rolled down them, but it did not. There are no burn marks, no traces of pitch on the rocks."

I walked forwards, Yue and Mag trailing behind me. And as I climbed up, I discovered the same thing Kaita had seen earlier that day: the hole behind the boulders, invisible unless you were almost inside it. The trail of the rolling torch vanished into the shadows.

"Dark below," I said.

"In the strictest sense," said Yue.

"We have them," said Mag.

"Yes, we do," I said. "All right. Let us return to Kun and—"

"What? No," said Mag, looking at me as though I had gone mad. "They cannot be far inside. We have to go in. Kaita could be just a span away from us at this very moment."

"Mag, you cannot be serious," I said. "You told Kun you wanted to find the Shades so he could point his troops at them. Was that a lie?"

"It was not," said Mag. "But Kun refused me. Now

we have found them on our own. Let us slip in, kill Kaita, and then return. No one has to be any the wiser."

"Mag," I said, shaking my head. "Even if we can get in and find Kaita, and even if we can kill her—and neither of those is likely—what makes you think we could get back out again?"

"Albern is right, Mag," said Yue. "I agreed to come out here, but I did not agree to throw myself blindly into the midst of our enemies."

"Then let me do it," growled Mag. "I can deal with Kaita easily enough if I can only get my hands on her. Albern, listen to me. How many times have we faced Kaita on the battlefield? When she knows we are coming, or when she sees we are within striking distance, she always flees. She did it in Northwood. She did it twice in Tokana. And neither of us can catch a bird, or even a mountain lion, for that matter. We *have* to take her by surprise. If we do not, she will only escape again. Please."

I sighed. Mag did have a point. It is perilously tricky to hold a weremage in place when they wish to escape you. And if anyone could slip into the midst of our enemies, kill one of them, and get out again, it would have been Mag. But I was not confident that anyone *could* do it, not even the legendary Uncut Lady.

"When *will* you turn back, Mag?" I said. "What if it grows more dangerous? What if they raise the alarm? What if they kill you, or one of us?"

"That will not happen," said Mag at once. "I will not let anything happen to the two of you. And yes, I promise you: if they raise the alarm, I will turn tail and flee with the both of you." A sudden smile twisted her lips. "I will probably run faster than you, Albern, for age has made you slow."

I laughed despite myself, choking it back and trying to maintain a stern expression. "All right. If I have your vow, I will come with you."

"Then it is settled," said Mag, clapping her hands. "Do not worry, friends. I will lead the way."

So saying, she lowered herself into the darkness behind the boulders. I heard her land lightly on the tunnel floor, and then she hissed up from the shadows for us to follow her.

Yue moved to go down, but I stopped her with a hand on her shoulder. She met my eyes, squinting to see me in the moonslight.

"Are you sure about this?" I said. "Mag and I could go on alone. You could return to camp."

"I would feel faithless if I turned from the two of you now," said Yue, though her usual fire was missing. "I only . . . Albern, you do not have to go along with her in everything."

"I know that," I said. "And deep down, she knows it, too. But while I am joining in her foolishness, I am glad you are with me." I leaned in and kissed her.

Smiling despite herself, she shook her head. "You are soft, Telfer. But fear not. I will harden you. Come on."

She dove into the darkness while I flushed and tried to concentrate on finding a way to slide down that would not break something vital. When eventually I landed catlike beside Yue, Mag had already taken a few steps down the tunnel. The moonslight vanished almost immediately, leaving us in total darkness beneath the earth.

"I have torches," I said, reaching for my pack.

"No," said Mag quietly. "If they see us coming, they will raise the alarm for certain. We shall have to feel our way along."

Yue groaned. "Mag, one of us could trip, and the sound of the falling might alert them anyway. Do you honestly expect us to push forwards into the darkness without a light to see by?"

Mag paused for a moment, thinking. "I suppose if they have posted sentries, they will have torches of their own. But still, I do not want them to see us coming. If you must light a torch, stay far behind me. I will push forwards in the dark, and if I see anything, I will run back to you and alert you."

"Fine," I said. "But if you wish to sneak up on them, you have to take off your armor. Leave it here at the entrance, and we can recover it when we come back."

"I can move quietly with it on," she groused.

"Not quietly enough," I said. "Come, Mag."

"Fine." She undid the straps that held her scales tight to her body and shucked them off, dumping them by the tunnel entrance with a heavy clank. Then she turned and stalked off into the darkness, one hand on the wall to her right. Soon she had vanished.

"All right," I said. "Get your flint, and let us have some light."

In no time, Yue and I had the torch going. Once it was lit, I used it to light a second, which I gave to Yue. Together, side by side, we headed down the tunnel after Mag. She was gone in the darkness ahead of us, and we kept our pace slow, to let her have plenty of space from the glow.

But it was not long at all before Mag came running up to us out of the tunnel ahead, emerging into the torchlight so suddenly that my heart jumped. We stopped short, and my hand strayed to my sword.

"What is it?" I said, my voice hushed. "What is wrong?"

"Nothing," she whispered. "I spotted a Shade guard ahead. He has a lit torch, which made him easy to see from afar."

Yue and I shared a glance. "Well, if there was any doubt that they went this way, that ends it," said Yue. "Now what?"

"He looks to be standing at the entrance to a larger cavern," said Mag. "If we can remove him, I believe we will reach the Shades' main encampment. Then we can find and slay Kaita."

I sighed. "It might be easiest with an arrow. But if there are other guards within sight of the first, it may raise the alarm."

"That is a risk we shall have to take," said Mag. "I cannot approach him undetected, for he trains his eyes on the tunnel. And if he raises the alarm, you get your wish: we retreat to Kun and the others."

"Hooray," I said, my expression deadpan.

Mag smirked. "Spoilsport. Now go and end this fool."

"And there is no chance I can persuade you to go tell Kun, now that we know for certain the Shades are here?" I said, knowing the answer already.

"None at all," said Mag cheerfully.

"All right," I said. "Take my torch and give me some space."

She did as I asked, and I advanced into the darkness of the tunnel. Soon I saw what Mag had seen: a faint glow of torchlight reflecting from the rocky walls around me. It made my going easier, and I was able to take more care with my steps, reducing the sound of my passing to no more than a mouse's scurry.

Soon I had the Shade in sight. He did indeed seem to be standing at the entrance to a much more massive cavern. That had to be where the rest of the Shades were. This guard was staring down the tunnel, and it felt as if he was looking right at me. But he held his torch in his hand, rather than finding some way to prop it against the wall behind him. It made his vision in the dark almost worse than useless.

I sighed and nocked an arrow. The angle would be hard. I could not fire too high, or I would strike the tunnel ceiling. But if I fired too low, the curve of the flight would carry the arrow into the floor instead of my foe.

I drew. I sighed. And I loosed.

The arrow sank perfectly into the Shade's throat. Jian would likely have scolded me if she saw me aim for anything but the chest, but I was trying to keep things quiet.

The torch fell from his hands, and he clutched at his neck, seizing the dart and trying in vain to stanch the sudden gout of blood. Slowly he collapsed to his knees, and then to the floor.

I held still for the longest moment I have ever experienced in my life.

No alarm sounded.

Sighing in relief, I turned and stalked back down the tunnel. Mag and Yue's faces were tense as they watched me emerge from the shadows.

"The door is clear, and no alarm raised," I said. "But we had best be quick. They have to change the guard sometime, and then we will be discovered."

Mag and Yue set their torches down. We could retrieve them on the way back out. We continued down the tunnel until we reached the place where the guard had stood. I could see now that his head had been shaved close to the scalp, but he had a long, stringy beard. He stared up at me as I passed, his mouth slightly open. I ignored him.

THIRTY-THREE

Now we could see the vast cavern beyond the tunnel. It stretched for spans in both length and width. Laid out near its center was the Shades' camp. There were several lines of tents, with two low campfires that I could see. Some figures walked around, but they seemed to be either fetching food or heading off to relieve themselves in some distant corner. I saw no posted guards. Kaita must have been convinced that hiding beneath the earth would keep them safe.

I tapped both Mag and Yue on the shoulder and drew them behind a large, jutting rock formation. I began speaking to them in sign, afraid of letting out even a whisper in this place. The Shade camp was a span off, but sound carried far on the harsh, rocky surfaces all around us.

"What now?" I signed.

"We need the officers' tents," signed Mag. "Kaita will be there."

"What in the dark below are you two doing?" whispered Yue.

"Shhh!" I hissed. "We are signing. Do you not know sign?"

Yue grimaced. "I . . . do," she said aloud. "But I have not practiced in—"

I put a hand over her mouth. *"Please* be silent. Follow along as best you can." I turned back to Mag and resumed in sign. "The camp is like most camps. The officers will be in the group of tents near the other end. Past the soldier tents."

Yue signed haltingly. "Past the sword tents?"

I blew an exasperated breath out my nose. *"Soldier* tents," I signed again, emphasizing the motions.

Recognition dawned in her eyes. "I am hungry," she signed confidently, though I believe she meant "I understand."

"Let us circle their camp," signed Mag. "I will go in. You will keep watch. If you see an enemy, fire an arrow at the ground near me. I will hear it and know to run. But they may hear it, too, so only shoot if there is great danger."

I did not like it, but I had no better ideas. "All right," I signed. Then I reached out and gripped her shoulder. "Be careful," I whispered. "Remember, you promised you would run if we had to."

"I remember," she whispered with a smile. And then she signed, "And you should not be talking out loud."

"All right," I signed back. "Let us go."

Sneaking around the camp was the easy part. The Shades were in the center of the cavern, and we never drew closer than a span away from them. I worried about our every footfall and the scuff of our limbs against protruding rocks, but I likely need not have. Even from this distance, I could hear the noises of the Shades, and they were much louder than any noise we were making.

We did not have to go too far before reaching a good position. Mag gave us one last nod before setting off towards the camp. She left her spear with us, exchanging it for a long knife Yue wore on her belt, which Mag now affixed to her own. Silent as an Elf, she crept forwards. I kept my eyes on her, holding my breath whenever she ducked out of sight and releasing it when she emerged into view again.

The first tent was the easiest. It was near the edge of the camp, and the flap side pointed outwards. I was afraid Mag might move straight into it, but she was wise. She stopped two paces away and waited, watching and listening. No Shades wandered near the tent, and Mag must not have heard any sounds from inside, for she soon crept forwards once more.

Like a shadow, she vanished inside. I could not hear it, but I could almost imagine the soft *shunk* of her blade sliding through the Shade's eye, the brief sounds of struggling as she held them down while their body jerked, lapsed, and then lay still forever.

Mag emerged into view again. I could see blood on her hands. I held a brief hope that Kaita had been in the tent, but it did not seem so, for Mag did not return. But at least she had killed a Shade officer. That was something.

Mag did not wait as long before the next tent, and her impatience was almost our ruin. As she began to approach it, there was a commotion close by. Mag threw herself to the ground. Yue and I tensed, and I nocked an arrow.

From a tent five paces down the row, a Shade emerged. She stood tall and stretched, scratched herself, and blinked hard in the light of the campfire. Then she turned and walked towards the camp's edge. Her path brought her perilously close to Mag, but she passed by, and Mag remained unnoticed. Soon the Shade had vanished into the darkness on the other side of the camp, and I lost sight of her.

Yue and I released a long breath at the same time. Mag stirred, rose from the floor where she had flung herself, and crept forwards on all fours. The flap of the second tent rose and then fell again, and Mag was inside.

This time the kill must not have been as clean, for I saw the tent jerk briefly. But it lasted only a moment, and then Mag came out again.

I leaned forwards, hoping she would come creeping back towards us. There were only a handful of officer tents in the cluster—there were fair odds, at least, that Mag should have found Kaita in one of the first two. But it did not seem so, as she turned and crept towards a third tent.

"Dark take it," growled Yue. "This cannot last forever."

But things seemed to be going well so far. Who knew but that Mag might wipe out the Shades' leadership in one fell swoop, and Kaita along with them. The only foe she would not be able to dispatch so quietly would be the brute woman. But Mag was smart enough to know that. She would not even try.

She *was* smart enough to know that, was she not? I certainly hoped so.

As Mag neared the third tent, I settled back on my haunches to wait. It was growing uncomfortable sitting on the cold, hard stone of the cave. But my whole body jerked with fright as a cry went up from the opposite end of the Shade camp.

"Awake! Awake! Foes! Awake!"

My gaze flew to the source of the noise. I could not see who was shouting. Mag, sky bless her, did not hesitate. She turned and began fleeing back towards Yue and I, keeping low.

The Shade camp erupted into frenzied activity, like an anthill kicked by a restless child. Blue-cloaked warriors poured from the lines of tents, drawing their weapons and looking wildly around.

There. Finally, I could see who was shouting. At the other end of the camp, the brute woman came into view. She towered over those around her, and her shaggy mane of hair swung back and forth as she scanned the darkness.

"Enemies!" she roared. "Enemies in our midst! They are murdering your officers. Find them!"

"What in the dark below?" hissed Yue. "How did she see Mag from the other side of the cave?"

"I do not know," I growled. "But we have to get out of here."

Mag reached us just at that moment. "I do not know how they saw me," she said. I could hear the frustration in her voice.

"And I gather you did not find Kaita," I said.

"No." She almost spat the word.

"Well, we will have another chance. But not now. Run!"

We fled through the shadows, sprinting for the cave entrance. I was terrified we might find it guarded. Mayhap the Shades had discovered the slain guard, and that was how they knew we were here. But there was no one there. The corpse lay right where we had left it. And with all the Shades rushing to the officers' tents, no one was looking in our direction. I scooped up the fallen guard's torch as we ran by.

"I do not understand," said Mag.

"Mayhap it was the weremage," said Yue. "She could have been . . . oh, sky, I do not know, a bat or something. Mayhap she saw you and told the large one."

"She would have come after us," I said. "Or raised the alarm herself."

"Well then, you know more about it than I do," snapped Yue.

"We have to get back to camp," said Mag. "If we tell Kun, and he summons his troops quickly enough, we can still wipe them out before they have a chance to run."

"Oh, *now* she wants to tell the captain," I said.

All three of us could not help a bark of laughter as we sprinted through the blackness.

Kaita heard screams. Her head snapped up. She whirled in the darkness and sprinted back down the tunnel towards the Shade camp.

All day she had been exploring the passages tirelessly, but she had nothing to show for it. One of them had gone on for what felt like a league before abruptly reaching a dead end. She had not gone far down the third, the one she was still in now, but it had not seemed promising. She could not smell any fresh air, and it had seemed to plunge ever deeper and deeper into the earth.

But all these thoughts fled her as she pelted down the tunnel towards her allies. Soon enough, she came leaping into the grand cavern, where she found the Shades in chaos. Tagata was there, standing near the officers' tents near one end of the camp. In her arms, she cradled the corpse of one of her captains, one whose name Kaita could never remember.

Magelight flared, and Kaita resumed her human form. "What happened?" she cried. "Tagata, are you hurt?"

"I am not," growled Tagata. "But they killed Harnel and Selnir."

Harnel, that was it, thought Kaita. "Who killed them?"

But even as she asked the question, the answer came to her in a flash. She knew she was right when she saw the mounting fury in Tagata's gaze.

"Mag and Albern," growled Tagata. "As I was resting, I received a message from the Lord. He told me they were here, *now,* slaying our kindred. Thank goodness I received word from him before they took more."

A chill ran up Kaita's spine. If she had stayed and rested, as Tagata had urged . . . they might have found *her*. It could be *her* corpse in Tagata's arms right now. She wondered bitterly whether the Lord would have foreseen that, and whether he would have warned Tagata in time.

But then again . . . if Mag and Albern had come, then they were alone. They were isolated from their allies. Kaita had the magestones, and she could—

"Tagata," she said quickly. "When did they leave? I could still catch them while they are alone."

"No, dear one," said Tagata softly. "Too much time has passed. They will have returned to their allies now. I am sorry."

"Dark take them," growled Kaita. "Will I never get my chance?"

"You will. Have faith. But for now, there are more pressing matters." Tagata's expression grew grim. "They are going to bring the Mystics down upon us. Everyone is preparing to march, but we do not know where. We cannot leave the way we came. That is where the Mystics will come. Have you found another exit?"

"No," snarled Kaita. "Only paths farther down into the earth, and the southern passage that leads right to—"

She stopped short as an idea struck her. And she could see the same thought reflected in Tagata's savage smile.

"Ready the march," said Kaita. "We make for the south passage."

Mag led the way back to Kun's camp, with Yue and me close behind. On the northeastern end of the camp, Chausiku still stood his sentry post.

"Hail!" called Mag in the darkness. "Three rods."

"And two wings," called Chausiku. He had raised his bow at the sound of her voice, but now he lowered it again. Relief was plain in his expression as we crept up out of the darkness. “I am glad to see you safe, Sergeants.”

“As are we,” I said. “No trouble here while we were gone?”

“None,” said Chausiku. “No one seems to have noticed a thing.”

My mouth twisted. “That is well. But remember—do not lie on our account. If anyone asks you what happened tonight, you tell the truth, do you hear?”

Chausiku lifted his chin slightly. “I hear you, Sergeant.”

It was not an agreement, but I decided to let it be. With any luck, he would not need to face such a choice at all.

A campfire still burned at our end of the camp, where our tents were set up at the end of our squadrons’ lines. Mag made to walk straight past them, heading for Kun’s tent. But a sudden shout stopped us all in our tracks.

“Hail, Sergeants!”

We froze. Then, slowly, we turned. From the shadows between our tents stepped Kun. Behind him was Tou, a furious expression on his face.

The captain’s smile was as thin as new-frozen ice.

“And where, pray tell, have the three of you been?” he asked sweetly.

THIRTY-FOUR

"Captain," said Mag.

"Am I?" said Kun.

Mag, Yue, and I exchanged a glance. "Ser?" said Mag.

"Am I your captain?" said Kun. "Because one obeys one's captain. And yet the three of you have gone to scout for the enemy alone after I explicitly ordered you not to."

That, of course, is the sort of statement for which there is no safe response, and so we said nothing. At Kun's side, Tou looked furious enough to burst into flames. Only deference to his captain seemed to be keeping him silent. I did not doubt he wished to say many loud, angry things to us, and would when Kun had gone.

"Well?" said Kun. "You are all uncustomarily silent. Sergeant Telfer, at least, has a clever tongue that hardly ever stills. What am I to make of you? This is the sort of thing that carries heavy penalties. Limited rations certainly, mayhap stocks, if we had them. Lashes would not be out of the question if anything disastrous should occur as a result of your transgression. Even execution, were the consequences dire enough. I say this not to hound you with empty threats, but to convey the severity with which I must now consider your case."

Mag rallied, speaking in a calm voice. "Ser, we apologize for going against your orders. But our venture bore fruit. We found the Shades. They are trapped, and we can wipe them out if we act quickly enough."

Kun studied her for a moment, his eyes sometimes flitting to Yue and me on either side of her. When he spoke, it was not in response to her.

"Do you know that, when you first arrived, I was positive you were Shades?" he said. "I was convinced of it. The first thing that shook my conviction was Sergeant Baolan's arrival. And then we fought together against the enemy, and I watched you kill them with my own eyes. My last vestiges of doubt vanished, and I thought that was the end of it. Yet now I see things clearly for the first time after a long while spent in the darkness."

"Ser," I said, "we are *not* Shades."

"Oh no," said Kun. "I am even more certain of that now. You are something less evil than Shades, but no less dangerous. You are vigilantes. Folk who think yourselves above the rest of us, who see yourselves as being removed from the petty concerns of the nine lands."

"Respectfully, ser," said Yue, "I love Underrealm with my whole heart, and I will defend my honor on—"

"Be silent, Sergeant!" roared Tou. He bit off the words almost as sharply as they had erupted, and I gained a new appreciation for just how hard he must be clamping down on his temper. "Do not try to defend your honor when we have caught you violating the captain's trust."

Yue's jaw spasmed once, but she fell silent. Mag spoke again, still calm.

"Yet it is true, sers. We do love Underrealm."

"Not as much as you loved your husband," said Kun, and he too was calm. "I do not say this to hurt you. It is no evil thing that you loved him more than a nation. Underrealm is not even a real thing, nothing you can touch, or see, or hold in the darkness when fear and grief press themselves upon you. It is more useful than true. Yet within the false idea that is a kingdom, there are real people. Many of them are as worthy as your husband, though you do not know them. And by your actions, you endanger them. This war that poisons Underrealm is of little concern to you as long as you satisfy your pursuit of revenge—and yet in that pursuit, you are willing to leave others in grief, countless folk who now must seek their own reparations for the loss of loved ones."

He paused for a moment and sighed, and his smile faded a bit. "I changed my mind, you know. I sent for Lieutenant Shi tonight. I told him to assign you to hunt for the Shades tomorrow, as you requested. If you had been less foolish, you would now be free to pursue your aims. And if I had not come around to your way of thinking, I would never have noticed your betrayal."

The captain's words struck me hard, and I could see I was not the only one. Mag's eyes had widened, and her stance had become tense. I could feel the conflict inside her, self-doubt worming its way into her mind.

Again she mustered herself. "Yet we found the enemy. If we act quickly, we can destroy them. But we have to rouse the troops now."

Kun's gaze grew knife-sharp, and his smile grew just as thin as before. "Why?"

Mag blinked. "To . . . to root them out of—"

"Why *now*, Sergeant? Why not in the morning?"

There was a long, deathly silence. Then, at last:

"Because they discovered us," grated Mag.

"Oh?" said Kun, eyes wide with mock surprise. "Did they?"

Again, a silence stretched wide enough to drown in. Finally, I growled out, "Dark take it, Mag, now is not the time to go dancing around half-truths. Captain, we infiltrated the camp and slew two Shade officers and a guard. But they spotted us."

"With each revelation, the situation grows more dire," said Kun, "and your offense more severe. Not for the first time, I find myself confident that you tell the truth. If you were lying, surely you would not keep digging yourself deeper into the grave."

"We are sorry, ser," I said. "But this can be turned to our advantage. If we move now, we can root them out of their hole and end this expedition. Please, ser. We know we were wrong"—I stared hard at Mag to quell any disagreement, though to my surprise, she looked docile—"but give us the chance to make it right."

His smile widened. "Well. At least you express some remorse. And I suppose I cannot deny someone a chance at redemption, whether they deserve it or not. Of course we must march on them, and at once. I have half a mind to leave your company here to guard the camp as punishment. But Lieutenant Shi is quite angry enough already, and I have never believed in punishing an officer for his subordinates' mistakes. Not to mention that if we must fight, I would rather have the Uncut Lady to the fore."

This, at last, seemed to be what Mag needed to hear. She straightened, her grip tightening on her spear. "Thank you, Captain. You will not regret this."

"I hope not," said Kun. "If I do, be assured that you will regret it far more. Lieutenant Zhou will remain behind with one company to guard the supply train. The rest of you get ready to march. I want us to leave within a quarter-hour. Dismissed."

We turned and strode away. But we had barely gone half a span before I heard a growl behind us.

"Sergeants."

I swallowed hard, and we all turned to face Tou. He was still livid, his eyes boring into each of us in turn. His hands were clasped behind his back as if he was restraining himself.

"Lieutenant Shi," said Mag.

"I do not know what changed between Taitou and here, but you had better change it back," said Tou sharply. "I trusted you, and I thought you trusted me."

"Ser," I said, "it is not that we did not trust—"

"Be silent," snapped Tou. I fell quiet. "You went off against orders because you thought you knew better, and your concerns were more important. Everyone knows you two are the most experienced fighters in the army. They have known it since you arrived. But I respected you because you did not *act* superior. You never lorded your skills or your history over the rest of us. Now it seems that was all a ruse, and you held yourselves above us all along."

He stepped up to Mag. "You are not above us," he said. "Just because you could take anyone here in a fight, that does not mean you are better than we are.

We know the strength of trusting the people we fight beside, and that is a greater strength than any one person can match. Even the Uncut Lady. I thought you understood that already, but you had better learn the lesson now."

Mag did not look at him but stared over his shoulder into the distance. Tou remained standing there for a moment before he turned and marched away.

"Get your squadrons ready," he called back over his shoulder. "You will not be even an instant late for muster."

An uncomfortable moment passed before Mag looked at us and shrugged. "They will feel differently once we wipe out the Shades," she said.

"Let us hope that is how tonight ends," said Yue.

"We had better go tell Dryleaf we are safe," I said.

Mag shook her head. "Only to tell him we are going back out into danger again? He is probably asleep. Let him rest. We will complete our mission, and then we can come back with tidings of victory. Besides, you have heard the lieutenant—if we are late, he may flog us."

I gave an uneasy look towards the supply train at the south end of camp. "I suppose you are right," I said. "Very well. We will not wake him until we have happier news to report."

Yue snorted. "He may sleep long, then."

THIRTY-FIVE

It was a cold night, and the wind whistled low. Yue growled at it in response, thumping her hands against her arms to stave off the cold. She had joined her squadron of spears, helping them get ready for the fight. She found herself irritable, and she did not know exactly why. Mayhap it was partly because her unit badgered her with question after question about the coming battle.

"Will we face them underground or above?" said one.

"I think underground, but I cannot know for certain," said Yue.

"Will we be on the front line again?" asked another, eyes wide. Her wound from the battle in the Greenfrost was still healing.

"I do not know," growled Yue.

"Sergeant, should we bring—"

"I do not *know!*" barked Yue.

They all fell silent around her. She closed her eyes and put a hand to her forehead.

"I am sorry. That was . . . I spoke to you like Ashta and Sinshi back home. I should not have then, and I should not have now."

"It is all right, Sergeant," said one of them slowly.

"No, it is not," growled Yue.

The wind picked up, needling them all with frozen rain scouring their skin. Again Yue pounded her arms to warm the blood.

"In Lan Shui, I was in charge," she said. "And I knew most everything about my job. Nothing went on in my town that I was not aware of. But here, everything is different. I am not them." She tossed her head in the direction of Mag and me, who were busy with our squadrons. "I am a fighter, and I have been one for most of my life, but I am new to *this* kind of fighting. Before I met you all, the closest I came to war was when the vampires attacked my town. And waiting for them to come . . . I suppose that the threat seemed great, but at least we had a plan to fight them." A spark seemed to light in her eyes, and her squadron saw it. "But that was not why I felt confident. I felt confident *because* of them." Again she nodded to Mag and me.

One of her soldiers snorted. “Mostly because of her, I suppose.”

“No,” growled Yue. “Both of them. Albern may not be . . . well, he may not be Mag. But he is no slouch, either. I would lay ten gold weights on him against anyone in this little army, except Mag herself. I thought he was a dark-damned steer when first I met him. And do you know what? He *is* a steer. But he is a *good* steer. He is *my* steer. Not just kind of heart, but skilled and wise as well. If there is anything wrong with him, it is that—”

She cut herself off. Her squadron stared at her curiously.

“What, Sergeant?” said one.

“It is that he cannot keep his fool mouth shut when he should,” snapped Yue. “Much like others I could name. Now heft those spears. We have a battle to fight.”

But before she went to fetch her weapon, she looked at me again, and then at Mag. The wind blew a curtain of rain before her, blocking us both from view.

It was a cold night, and the wind whistled low. I shivered against it, pulling my hood tighter around my face.

My squadron stood in the darkness around me, rubbing or slapping their arms as we waited for the order to march. I walked among them, seeing that they and their equipment were in shape. Here and there I caught a loose buckle or strap and helped to tighten it, and I ensured no one carried anything they did not need.

Chausiku had been called back from sentry duty, replaced by an archer from Zhen's company. From what the other archer had said, Zhen was not pleased to remain behind while we marched off to glory. I was not sure whether the captain was leaving him because he wished to protect him, or because he felt Zhen was a lieutenant he could trust absolutely. Either way, if I could have chosen to remain behind, I would have. Fighting a desperate, deadly battle in narrow tunnels beneath the earth was far from my idea of a good time.

"Remember," I said. "We will be going in first, but only until we make contact with the enemy. As soon as we see them, we are to loose a volley and then run like Elves are after us. Green Squadron will take it from there."

"Yes, ser," said Jian fiercely. She was projecting all eagerness for the coming battle, but I could sense the nervousness beneath. "And mayhap we will have the chance to loose one or two extra shots into the traitors."

"Hopefully, it will be over too quickly for that," I replied.

"Will they not see our torches coming in the darkness?" said Chausiku. His anxiety was much plainer to see than Jian's.

"They might, but there is little we can do about that," I said. "They could do one of two things. They might attempt to hold the tunnel against us, for it is narrow and will render our numbers no great advantage. Or, they might seek a pitched battle in the large cave where they have made camp.

"If they try to hold the tunnel, Jian may well get her wish. The captain will not send our fighters to die against that brute woman who leads them. Instead, we will pepper them with bowfire until we whittle them down enough that they have to retreat. Either way, it will likely end with a pitched battle in the large cave. There, we should be as safe as we were in the battle in the Greenfrost."

Hallan's great red beard jumped as he chewed on a piece of meat, pulled from a pouch as a midnight snack before our foray. His eyes would rest upon me for a moment before darting away. He seemed less than pleased. I had not told him about my plan with Mag before we left. It was strange to feel such disapproval from the man, who was usually the friendliest archer in my squadron.

"Easy enough, ser," he said gruffly. "Anything else?"

"No, that is all," I said. I turned to speak to the rest of them. "Tonight has held more than its share of bad decisions, and for my part in them, I am sorry. But we are all making the best of a bad situation."

Hallan spat. "S'pose you did what you thought was best."

"We did," I said. "And with luck, we will be proven right in the end."

"Hm," said Hallan.

The wind whistled colder, and I shivered again.

It was a cold night, and the wind whistled low. Mag's squadron buckled on their swords and hefted their shields. Dibu and Li swung their arms nervously, trying to stave off the cold just like the rest of us. But Mag seemed unaffected by the weather. The sharp wind's only effect on her was to send her cloak and hair swirling. Frozen rain tried to slice at her face, but it could not find purchase, and soon it melted and ran down her cheeks. Her gaze was fixed to the northeast, where the cave and the Shades waited.

"Is everyone ready?" said Mag.

"Yesser," said Dibu.

"Good," she said. "We will be right behind Black Squadron. That means we will be the first to meet the enemy, when it comes to blades instead of arrows. Let me take the fore then. Focus on staying alive."

"They say this is it," said Li. Her voice shook. "They say this should be the end."

"It will be," said Mag, fervent but quiet.

She thought of her words with Dryleaf, about our plans to leave Kun's army at the next large city we reached. She motioned Li and Dibu closer and spoke quietly enough that only they could hear.

"I have a question. Do both of you mean to see this war through?"

Li's wandering eyes focused, and her brow furrowed. "What do you mean?"

"This war for Dorsea," said Mag. "For all of Underrealm, I suppose. Will the two of you stick with Kun as long as it takes?"

"I plan to," said Dibu, folding his strong arms. A moment later, Li nodded in agreement.

"That is good," said Mag flatly. "You are both good at this. One should not be overly proud to be a good soldier, but one should not be ashamed of it, either. And you could both be great one day if that is what you want. But not me."

Li snorted. "Ser, you must be joking. You are the greatest among—"

"I mean that it is not for me anymore," said Mag. "I used to enjoy it when I was . . . well, not young. But younger. And when I looked back on those memories, I thought I would enjoy myself again now. But I do not. I am not meant for this sort of life anymore. One day, you might not be, either. When that day comes, I want you to try to recognize it. Because I will not be there to tell you. You are going to have to look out for each other." She gave a sad smirk. "And for the lieutenant, I suppose."

Dibu's cheeks flushed.

"Well, not like that," said Mag. "Although, I suppose like that, too. Come. It is time to march."

The cold wind picked up, blasting them all. Nothing about Mag shivered but her cloak.

THIRTY-SIX

And so we marched. Four of Kun's companies set out, leaving behind the fifth under Zhen's command. Zhen himself stood at the northeast end of camp and watched us march away, his eyes never leaving the column.

I do not know how long he waited, as we all faded into the darkness before him. But I know it could not have been too long.

We reached the entrance to the tunnel in short order. I approached it with some trepidation, afraid that we might find the Shades had come out and formed up for a defense.

Yet the snowy field beside the boulders was empty. No soldiers waited for us with drawn blades, nor were there tracks to show they had come out at all. They were still inside.

We halted, and the column drew up. Kun summoned Mag, Yue, and me to him. Tou was also there, arms folded, glare fixed upon us.

"Well, Sergeants," said Kun. "Where do we go next?"

I pointed. "Behind those boulders is the entrance to a tunnel leading to the enemy."

"We should take care, Captain," said Mag. "They may be guarding the entrance, hoping to hold it against us."

"Indeed they might," said Kun, smiling. "What I would not give for a wizard of any stripe. But very well. It might be best to drop a torch down first and see if we can spook them. If they fire arrows at it, we will at least know if they are waiting, and we can plan from there."

"Yesser," said Mag. "Let me do it."

"Certainly," said Kun, waving her forwards.

Mag took a torch from Dibu and crept up the hillside until she was above the boulders. She waited for the space of a heartbeat, and then she dropped the torch inside.

We all waited in dead silence. But nothing happened. I could see the light glinting around the edges of the boulders at the entrance.

"Nothing, Captain," said Mag, her voice floating towards us in the night.

"Very well," said Kun. "Two should drop down with shields and hide behind them at once. Two others should drop ropes at the same time, in case we need to pull them out quickly."

"Bring a rope," said Mag. "I can go in first alone."

Before we could answer, Mag dropped into the darkness. I heard her boots land on the tunnel floor, and then another long silence.

"Nothing, Captain," repeated Mag. This time her voice was heavy with the echoes of the tunnel. "They are not here. We can proceed."

Kun turned his gaze on me in the darkness, and though he still smiled, his eyes were steely in the moonslight.

"Very well, Sergeant," called Kun. "But while I can sympathize with the impulse to put yourself on the front line, you do yourself no favors by disobeying my orders."

"My apologies, ser," called Mag. "I will not do so again."

"I wonder if I can believe that," muttered Kun

We began to filter into the tunnel. My squadron went first, as Kun had planned. I dropped into the tunnel beside Mag before my archers, and in the brief private moment we had, I fixed her with a look.

"Mag, you have to stop," I told her. "I know you feel guilty, and I understand. But you *will not* get yourself killed trying to make things right. Do you understand me? I will not have it. If you cannot think of your own safety, at least think of me, and of Dryleaf."

"I *am* thinking of you," said Mag. "Do not worry about me."

I shook my head. "Do not give me a reason to."

Then Jian dropped into the tunnel next to us, and I had to bite my tongue. I waited until all my archers were inside, and then we waited a moment longer until Mag's swordfighters had followed. Our squadrons would press down the tunnel, but not too quickly, while the rest of the army trickled in behind us.

Hallan walked near the front, torch in hand. No one else in my squadron held a torch, and Mag's unit hung well back with their torchbearer, so we had only scant light to go by. But that seemed better than giving the enemy many targets to fire at in the darkness.

That long, slow advance down the tunnel was one of the most nerve-wracking experiences I have ever had. It was not like the anticipation of any everyday battle. We *knew* they were ahead of us, lurking in that darkness. They could not help but see us—we had a torch. Yet we had no choice but to advance straight towards them, helpless in the dark.

We had no grand strategy, not like Kun had devised before. There was no room for it. This would be brutal, messy, and violent. We would fight and die in darkness, in the flash of torchlight glinting off blood-soaked blades. It would be a hard task to clear the

Shades from this place, especially if the brute woman took the fore. If that happened, we would have little choice but to pit Mag against her and pray to a sky we could no longer see.

Yet there was no sign of our enemy. We were close now to the great cavern. But no arrows came hissing out of the darkness to fall among us.

When I guessed we were a span away from the large cavern, I stopped. Something about this felt wrong. The Shades would gain no benefit from fighting us in the vast space ahead. It would have made far more sense for them to fight us here in the tunnel, funneling us into a small space. As I sat there in the dark, pondering the mystery, Mag crept up, and not far behind her came Lieutenant Tou and Captain Kun.

"What is it?" said Mag.

"The cavern is up ahead," I said. "Yet there is no sign of them. I cannot read the tale of it."

"Mayhap they are trying to hide," said Tou. His anger at Mag and me was forgotten for the coming battle—or at least he had put the anger away on a shelf in his mind, to be retrieved later. "Mayhap they have holed up deeper in the cave, hoping that we will think they have left."

"I do not think so," I said slowly. "I would call that foolish, and nothing they have done so far has shown foolishness on their part."

"What do you think, then?" said Kun.

"Mayhap they have set an ambush inside the entrance," said Mag. "They left the tunnel open so that we would think the danger was gone, or at least so that we might grow lax in our caution. They hope we will press into the cavern with speed, and they can strike us from the sides when we are in an open space."

"That could be," said Kun. "Very well. Sergeant, take your squadron forwards. Proceed into the cavern cautiously, and keep a shield wall up around you. If they hope to catch us unawares, we must endeavor to disappoint them."

"Why not let me go in alone?" said Mag. "I will provoke as much of a reaction as my whole squadron, and there is no reason to risk more lives unnecessarily."

"Do not be a fool," I snapped. "Mag, even you cannot guard all sides of you at the same time."

"You know how fast I am," said Mag. "If they start to fire upon me, I will retreat into the—"

"Enough," said Kun. "Albern is correct. Take your squadron, Mag. Be careful, and if they fire upon you, retreat."

A moment passed, with Mag's jaw working furiously. "Yes, Captain."

She set off, leading her squadron down the tunnel towards the entrance to the cavern. My archers and I followed behind, all of us with arrows nocked.

Dibu held the torch in Mag's squadron. The others surrounded him with their shields turned outwards, so that the group of them edged into the cavern like an exceptionally watchful turtle. I tensed, expecting a hail of arrows to fall among them. But no attack came.

A long moment passed as Mag kept leading them farther out into the space. But it was, indeed, empty.

Chills began to creep paths down my spine. I shook them off and pushed into the cavern to join Mag.

"Where in the dark below did they go?" she growled.

"An apt choice of words," I said. "Hallan, give me that torch. I need to have a look around."

I took it and went to inspect the place where the Shades had built their camp. There was a great deal of detritus around, small pieces of cloth that must once have held food, as well as some bones and other scraps from finished meals. But there were no tents, no bedrolls, nothing but a few smoldering remnants of the campfires they had managed to build from dung.

"They left," I said quietly. "But where could . . .?"

Quickly now, I moved to the wall and began circling the perimeter of the cave. Very soon, I found what Kaita had already seen—three other tunnels leading out of the main cavern. I paused at the southern one. There I saw the smooth stone floor streaked with many muddy boot prints. The Shades had left this way.

I ran back to the center of the cavern. Kun was there now with Mag, and more than a hundred of our soldiers had filtered into the cavern behind him. The captain's smile had grown very, very dangerous.

"Ser," I said. He turned his gaze upon me. "The Shades left through another tunnel, this one leading to the south. Either they found an exit that way, or they took it and hoped they would find one. Either way . . ."

The captain nodded. "Yes, Sergeant," he said. "It seems we have little choice but to chase them even farther into the darkness. Your archers will take point again. Forwards!"

We advanced into the tunnel. But this time, I moved with more speed. I was not as afraid they would turn and try to fight us in the tunnel—if that had been their plan, they would simply have done so at the entrance. No, I suspected they were making for an exit with all speed. But they would still be hampered by their wounded. We could come upon them in the open and cut them down as they fled. We only had to press a little farther, a little faster, a little deeper into the darkness.

The passage twisted, it turned, it climbed. Once, we had to put our weapons away and haul ourselves hand over hand up a short rock wall. The cold of the outside world was long forgotten, and I bemoaned my heavy winter cloak that was now soaked with sweat instead of rainwater.

I could see the footsteps plainly in the torchlight. They began to look more hurried, as though the Shades had started to run through the darkness. And then I felt it—a cool breeze wafting towards us. The icy air of the outside world once again kissed my skin, giving relief against the heat.

"Captain!" I called out down the tunnel behind me. "An exit!"

And then the breeze came again, carrying other things this time.

To my nose, the scent of burning. And to my ears, the sound of screams.

My heart nearly stopped.

No, I thought. *Sky above, no. Please.*

THIRTY-SEVEN

THE MOMENT HE REALIZED WHERE WE WERE, CAPTAIN Zhou pushed past me. He abandoned his Mystics, Mag and me, our squadrons, everyone. He ran out of the cave entrance, scrambled over the boulders that hid it from view, and went sprinting into the destroyed remains of our camp.

"Zhen!" he cried out. "Report! Lieutenant Zhou! *Nephew! Report!*"

He did not hear the voice he sought. Instead, a Mystic knight appeared. Her left hand clutched her right shoulder, which was bleeding heavily. The arrow stuck out of both sides of the wound, and the woman gritted her teeth through the pain.

"Captain," she gasped. "Thank the sky you—"

"Lieutenant Zhou," snapped Kun. "Where is he?"

The knight went very still. "Captain. He . . ."

Kun pushed past her, ignoring her grunt of pain as he jostled her shoulder. He ran to the north end of camp, where Zhen's company of soldiers had been.

Had been.

Nearly the entire force lay dead. Arrows had pierced them; axes had hewn them. The Shades had come out of the hills from the west, and they had found most of Zhen's company still asleep. Our enemies had cut them down even as they struggled to emerge from their tents. Some were alive, moaning and crying out in the snow. Few of them would survive the night.

And there was Zhen.

He was near the front line, where the fighting had started. He had not slept after we left. He had meant to stand vigil through the night, waiting for his uncle and the rest of us to return. But then he had heard the sounds of fighting to the west, and he had raced towards them. Two new, much larger wounds now joined the angry scar on his cheek. A blade had pierced his throat, and an arrow stood straight up from his chest like a flagpole. His face was a battle-grimace, determined, resolute.

Doomed.

Kun fell to his knees. His hands shook as he held them out. His nephew, his sister-son, stared past him into the empty black sky, seeing nothing through those familiar eyes. Slowly Kun scooped him up, gripping the boy by the shoulders and pulling him into his lap. There he held him tight, taking off his own cloak to wrap around the boy, as if hoping to bring some warmth back to the rapidly-freezing skin.

Mag, Yue, and I had gone running through the camp like Kun. But we ran for the train, where we had last seen Dryleaf.

Everything was chaos. The Shades had slaughtered drivers, they had broken wagon wheels, they had spilled every store of food and drink into the snow.

The army's very guts lay spread upon the ground. Losing Zhen's company was a devastating blow, but the loss of the supply train was mayhap even more damaging. Kun would have none of the supplies he needed to carry on. The Shades had taken or destroyed nearly everything, everything but—

My heart melted with relief as I saw the blue silk coverings of the wagon from the Guild of Lovers. It was untouched. The Guild was protected, both by edicts of the High King and by laws older than Underrealm itself. After all, what use to kill lovers in war, when their rules keep them from taking sides in a conflict? I had not been sure the Shades would respect such boundaries. But they had, and the lovers favored Dryleaf. Mayhap . . .

We ran to the wagon. "Dryleaf!" I cried. I seized the flap and threw it open.

At once, I fell back, landing hard on my rear. Knives flashed at me out of the darkness, the light of campfires glinting off their steely edges. I scrambled up, holding my hands high, while Mag and Yue did the same. From inside the wagon came a great peal of barking.

"Hold!" cried Yue. "We mean no harm."

Orla and Nikau saw us, and they lowered their knives. The other lovers took the cue and did the same, though they still watched us warily. Oku came bounding out of the wagon, whining and sniffing at my boots.

"Orla," I said. "Dryleaf. Did he—"

"He is here," she said, scooting aside. Nikau pulled back a blanket, and there was Dryleaf, cradled among the lovers.

I gasped, and Yue put a hand to her mouth. Dryleaf had taken a nasty blow to the head. They had wrapped bandages around it, but it was bleeding heavily, and the cloth was almost soaked through. The old man's eyes were closed, and his breath came slow and labored.

Mag looked upon him, her whole body solid and unmoving as a rock.

"They took the camp by surprise," said Nikau in his smooth, liquid voice. "The first we knew of the attack was when an arrow struck someone running by.

As they died, they fell upon Dryleaf and knocked him to the ground. He hit his head on a log. As soon as Orla and I realized what was going on, we carried him into the wagon, and we have been here ever since. The attackers left us alone."

"Thank the sky," I said. "How long has he been asleep?"

"Not long," said Orla quietly. She brushed her slim, pale fingers against his cheek. "He stayed awake a long while. We had some dreamwine, and we gave him as much as he could stomach to help with the pain of his wound. He . . . ." She fell to silence.

"He what?" snapped Mag. Orla recoiled, and Mag sighed and bent her head. "Forgive me. What were you going to say?"

"He kept asking for the three of you," said Nikau. "He was afraid, and he kept asking us what was happening, but we did not know what to tell him."

Orla began to weep.

Just then, Dryleaf stirred and started to come awake. His hands reached out, grasping. Nikau took one of his hands, and Orla clasped the other where it came to rest on her dress, stroking the back of his gnarled old fingers.

"Mag," moaned Dryleaf. "Albern. Yue. Where are they?"

"We are here, Dryleaf," I said. "We came back."

Dryleaf burst into tears. "Oh, thank the sky," he said, almost whispering. "Where are you? I cannot tell, your voices, they . . ." Tears took the rest of his words, and he shook in Nikau's smoothly muscled arms.

I looked around at the lovers in the wagon. "May I—?"

"Of course," said Nikau. He motioned for the rest of them to clear some space, and I clambered into the wagon at once. Yue followed more slowly, but then we were there, and Dryleaf clutched our hands, gripping us as if he wished never to let us go again. There was not enough room for her in the wagon, but Mag stood at the back, reaching in and holding Dryleaf's leg so that he would know she was there as well.

"We came as soon as we realized what had happened," I said softly. "I am so sorry we left."

"I was afraid you had fallen," said Dryleaf, holding tightly to my hand. "I thought they had killed you all before they came and attacked us. I could not tell where they had come from, not after I fell."

"We are fine," said Yue. "They fled from us and circled around to come after you, the cowards."

Dryleaf said nothing, but only kept weeping, holding on to both of us. Yue looked up at the lovers.

"We can take him now," she said. "Thank you."

"Yes, thank you from the bottom of all our hearts," I said. "Nothing we could do would ever repay you."

"We would never let harm befall him," said Nikau. "He is a treasure."

"He is that," I said.

Yue bent and scooped him up in her mighty arms.

Careful as a mother holding her babe, she carried him out of the wagon, while Dryleaf clung to her. Mag moved woodenly out of the way. As Yue walked with Dryleaf to his tent, Mag stared at both of them, unmoving. With a final murmur of thanks, I left the lovers and went to her.

"Mag, this was not your fault," I said.

"Oh?" said Mag. "You told me that in Northwood, and I knew it was true then. I do not think it is true now."

"We could not know that Kaita had found a way to—"

"Of course we could have known," said Mag. "Or we could have guessed, or prepared for the worst. We thought—no, I will stop hiding behind that coward's lie—*I* thought she was mine for the taking. Like an animal I merely had to put down. I was so focused, so foolish, that I forgot she has a cunning mind and a will to match ours. I was the one who alerted the Shades to the fact that we knew where they were hiding. I led Kun's force away from the camp. Dark below, Albern, I was the one who brought Dryleaf on this fool's errand, when he clearly has no place amid a war."

A shiver passed through me. She had reminded me of something—a truth that now pressed itself upon me with an urgent, frantic need.

"Mag. We have to go."

Yue had set Dryleaf down while she tried to recover what she could of his possessions. Now she looked up at me. "Go? What do you mean, go?"

"I mean leave," I said. "We have to. We have no choice. Kun will blame us for this. And he will . . . he will be right to do so. But Mystic justice . . . I will not submit myself to that. Yue, I am so sorry."

Yue shook her head—not in defiance, but slowly, like a bear trying to clear the cobwebs of winter after waking in the spring. "But I . . . but the law. The King's law."

"Please, Yue," I begged. "Nothing you did tonight was evil enough to deserve what Kun will do to you. Please do not submit yourself to it."

"Let me stay," said Mag. "It was me. I pulled both of you along with me. I practically forced you to go. Let me stay. The three of you leave, and let me take the punishment."

"No, Mag," I snarled. "If you will use guilt to connive me into coming along on your schemes, then I will use guilt to force you to flee with me when they go awry. We promised, *until the end of the road.* You forced me into those caves on that promise. Now I will force you to flee because of it. If you stay, I stay. We run together, or not at all."

Mag's jaw set. But she would not consign Yue and me to death along with her, and I knew it. "Then get up," she said sharply to Yue. "And bring Dryleaf. The longer we wait, the more time we give Kun to recover and come looking for us."

Our horses, as well as Dryleaf's, were with the Guild wagon. Yue changed Dryleaf's bandage—I was relieved to see the bleeding had slowed—and then helped him to the wagon, where he said his good-byes. All the lovers gave him gentle words and soft touches of farewell, especially Nikau and Orla.

"Again, we thank you," said Mag. "You are eternally in the favor of the Uncut Lady, and if you ever require my help in any matter, it is yours."

"And there is something more mundane I must ask of you now," I told them. "Do you have any spare tents or bedrolls? We cannot fetch ours before we leave. We can pay you."

"We have no tents," said Nikau. "But there are plenty of bedrolls, and they are of good quality."

"Here is something for them, and for any other more immediate needs you might have," said Mag.

From her saddlebag, she pulled a fat purse, practically bursting with gold, and handed it over. I knew it was nearly everything she had left, but I held my tongue. This was a lighter penance than she wished to pay, I knew.

Nikau took it from her solemnly. "I feel you overestimate our deed. But thank you." He nodded to her and then to me. "I hope we have the good fortune to meet you again." Orla embraced us one by one, unable to summon words of her own.

Our good-byes said, we headed towards the south end of camp, walking and leading our horses by the reins. Only Dryleaf was mounted, hunched over his saddle horn, his shoulders drooping, and his head bowed.

"I feared I might find you here, but I hoped I would not."

My head snapped up. Mag, Yue, and I ground to a halt.

Tou stood there. Beside him were Dibu, Li, Chausiku, and Jian. The four of them looked shocked, as though they could not believe their own eyes. But Tou's face was one of snarling wrath, his eyes ready to kindle into a blaze.

"Lieutenant Shi," said Mag. Her voice was almost too steady, as if she was trying to summon her battle-trance but could not quite manage it.

"Turn yourselves around," said Tou. "Make for the north end of camp, where the captain's tent stands. When he has finished mourning his nephew, I know he will want to pass judgement on the three of you."

I closed my eyes. So Zhen had died. *Dark take everything,* I thought. *He deserved better.*

But Mag kept her gaze fixed on Tou. "You know we cannot do that, ser."

"You told me," said Tou, spitting the words. "You told me when you joined us that I would not regret your presence. And now you are *deserting?*"

His rage cut me to my heart. But that was not the worst of it. Far worse than Tou's anger were the expressions of Chausiku, of Li, of Dibu. They were like children watching negligent parents walk out the door, not able to understand that they intended never to return. I searched for something to say, any words I could summon that would make them see, make them understand why we had to go.

I could find none.

"Please, ser," said Mag. "Believe me when I say that I will regret my time here more than you can know, and not for my own sake. But I will not let you stop us from leaving."

Now Tou *did* spit. "Then do it. Make your move, you dark-damned traitor."

Mag stepped forwards. Tou unsheathed his blade. Dibu and Jian drew their swords a moment later, half-heartedly, torn. Li and Chausiku simply stood and stared.

As Tou advanced, Mag flipped her spear around and jammed the point into the ground. When Tou swung his blade at her, she ducked beneath it, darted up, and struck him under the chin with her fist.

A *crack* broke the air. Tou fell to the ground, senseless.

Everything was silent. Mag stared down at his fallen form. Dibu, Li, Jian, and Chausiku all watched her for a long, quiet moment. Finally, she looked up at them.

"Just step aside," she pleaded.

One by one, they looked at each other. It was Jian who spoke first, stepping forwards to stand over Tou.

"No," she said simply. "We cannot stop you from leaving, but I do not think we will give you the easy way out."

One by one, Mag knocked them out cold. They fell to land in the mud, some of it still red with the blood of those slain by the Shades.

I stepped forwards. I knelt and lifted each of them, sliding their cloaks beneath them so they would not wake up lying soaked and freezing in the mud. After a moment, Yue bent to help me.

Then we mounted our horses and rode south from the camp as fast as we could.

THIRTY-EIGHT

You can imagine what was going through my mind as we fled into the night, cold, miserable, and alone. After all, I told you of how I was exiled from Tokana when I was close to your age.

But it may interest you to know that this was not Mag's first time, either. She, too, had had to run from her friends after a fight she would rather have avoided. It is how she left Shuiniu, the town where she used to live before we met.

Several years had passed since her first scuffle with Ciaran. In that time, Mag had kept her head down and her fists still, happy to be a brewer under Duana. In truth, the fight with Ciaran meant little to her. It had been a petty dispute, and to her mind, it had been settled.

But Ciaran never forgot it. Nor did he ever forgive Mag for it. He was one of those petty, small-minded folk who hold tight to grudges, letting them fester and rot. He did not care if he had to wait years to get back at her if it meant he could be confident of victory in the end.

As part of his revenge, and because people like him always desire power, he sought to become mayor. He was good at manipulating those around him, and so he achieved it before too very long. It would be overstating things to say that anyone in Shuiniu really *wanted* to give him the position. But many folk, if they are somewhat simple or easily frightened, can lend their support to an utter scoundrel because he promises to solve the problems they think they have. Never mind that he always makes things worse instead—all that matters to him is that he gets there. And once planted, such villains can be very difficult to root out.

At first, his appointment seemed to have little effect on the town or Mag. Business was good for Duana, in both the brewery and the tavern, and it did not change much from year to year. But Duana had begun to get old. No longer could her aging body keep up with the pace of the work. She entertained the idea of letting Mag run the tavern, and even broached the subject once or twice, but Mag had little interest. She loved brewing more, as did Duana, and they both wanted to spend their time at their craft.

So when someone in the town offered to buy the tavern for a good price, Duana gratefully accepted. It seemed the perfect arrangement. She and Mag could brew in peace. And the security of their livelihood seemed assured. There was no one else in Shuiniu foolish enough to try competing with Duana's skill, and the tavern would always need ale. They would have more than enough custom to live on.

But almost as soon as the tavern had changed hands, the new owner stopped purchasing Duana's ale. Instead, they began to ship it in from more distant towns, and even some cities.

At first, Duana and Mag could not understand it. It cost far more to transport the ale such a long way. And yet the tavern's new master did not charge any more for his drinks than he had done in the past. It did not seem possible to continue the practice. Not even the cost of rooms and board would make up the difference. And when they tried to find out why the tavern master had stopped buying Duana's ale, they were met with sullen silence, if he would see them at all. Nor could they sell their ale to the townsfolk. Most people cannot afford to purchase kegs at a time, nor do they have the means to store them.

There were, of course, any number of things they could have done. If nothing else, Mag could have built a small bar beside the brewery, and I am sure the folk of Shuiniu would have come to drink at the new bar as they had from the old one.

But while they were trying to determine their course, the truth came out. The tavern's new master was in Ciaran's pocket. Ciaran had arranged the purchase, paying the greater part of the price. That gave him power over the tavern, and so he ordered it to stop purchasing Duana's ale. He also paid a subsidy to the tavern's owner to keep prices the same despite the cost of shipping ale in. Ciaran had spent his whole life hoarding whatever wealth he could, and he was good at it. This new scheme was no more trouble to him than remembering to get dressed in the morning.

Mag was furious when she heard the news, and she immediately went to confront Ciaran, without telling Duana. She accused him of undermining Duana for petty revenge.

Ciaran gave her an ugly grin. "This is simply good business," he insisted. "After all, the town elected me, in part, for my skill at earning coin. Certainly, I have acquired more of it than you and your master, and so the people trust me more in these matters than you. Can you not see that trade with the broader world is the only way to prosperity? If some in Shuiniu, such as yourselves, must fall by the wayside, well . . . that is the price that must be paid, for the good of the many."

"You give them piss and insist they be grateful," said Mag. "And if anyone gave your ledger half a glance, they would see that you are not even earning more coin for the town."

Her hands clenched to fists, which made Ciaran somewhat nervous. But his grin widened, and he spread his hands.

"Any cunning merchant knows that sometimes you must lose coin today to gain more tomorrow. After all, those who travel here to bring their ale bring coin with them, and they spend it in the town."

"At your smithy and the tavern you own, mostly," said Mag.

Ciaran licked his lips. "And why not? I pay the subsidy for the ale. I am risking the coin, and I should reap the benefit. I have to look after Shuiniu's best interests, even if it is harder on my coin in the short term."

Mag barely kept herself from striking him. "How does *this* serve the town's best interests?"

His eyes flashed, and his mouth twisted in an ugly sneer. "It seems unwise," he said slowly, "to continue purchasing anything from someone like Duana, who would employ a girl as violent as you."

Now, there are countless ways that Mag could have responded. She could have withdrawn, and together with Duana, made some other arrangement. If she had been thinking clearly, she would have seen that Ciaran was trying to goad her.

But Mag was not thinking clearly at all, not at that moment. In fact, as she described it to me, the world had turned a peculiar shade of red.

"Violent?" she snarled. "I will show you violence."

And she did. Her eyes went blank, and her expression dead. It was the battle-trance, and Ciaran recognized it, and his whole body quaked in fear.

She trounced Ciaran, right there in his home. She slammed his head on his desk, scattering parchments and missives he was in the middle of, and then she threw him into a bookshelf that fell over onto him. She dragged him out from under the mess, and then she drove her knee into his gut and struck him across the face, splitting his lip. Then she let him fall helpless at her feet.

Ciaran was stunned for a moment. But as he regained his senses, he gave her a savage grin from the ground, blood staining his teeth.

"How dismayed I am to learn I was right about you," he said. "Assaulting the mayor is a grave crime. I could have our constables take you away to jail you in a city. But I think I shall be merciful. I shall merely levy a fine upon you—and your master. It will be substantial, of course, commensurate with your wrongdoing. How I hope you and Duana will have the coin to pay it."

Mag's eyes went wide, and her hands went slack. What could she do now? She could hardly kill Ciaran. His actions might be base and treacherous, but they were hardly worthy of murder. He was not truly evil, like Kaita, but only an up-jumped snake who enjoyed power and dominance over others.

And in this moment, he had won.

Ciaran watched all these thoughts play across her expression, and his face grew crafty.

"Of course, such a fine could be hard to lay upon you," he said. "If you were to flee from Shuiniu forever, for example. I wager you could get away with it. It might take me time to summon a constable. And it would hardly serve the town to fine Duana if you were no longer here to share in the punishment. The tavern master might even see fit to purchase from her again if you were no longer in her employ."

The message could not have been more clear if he had written it into a contract. Mag was to leave and never return. All Ciaran wanted was for her to be gone. He had no grudge against Duana except through Mag. If Mag left, forever, then Shuiniu would return to business as usual.

At least for a time. For peace never lasts, with men like him. They are always hungry for another victim. Anyone weaker than they are, to give them a false feeling of strength.

But Mag did not know that, and she had little choice. So she took a step back from Ciaran, who was still on the floor, propped up on his elbows. He knew he had won, and slowly he levered himself to his feet. He wiped his bloody mouth on the back of his sleeve.

"You will never see me again," said Mag, her voice shaking. "At least not here. I do hope that we meet each other somewhere far away from Shuiniu. It will be my pleasure to teach you another lesson then, though you will be too stupid to learn it."

Ciaran spat. "Get out. Before I rescind my mercy."

Mag left, never giving a backward glance to Ciaran or his house. She took her time wandering through the streets of the town, for she knew this would be the last time she would see them. In too short a time, she found herself back in Duana's brewery. Duana was drinking a mug of her own brew, drawn from the last batch she had made before the purchase of the tavern.

She looked up, and she must have seen the dismay on Mag's face. Quickly she tried to stand from her stool, but she slowed halfway up, wincing at a pain in her leg.

"Mag?" she said. "What is wrong?"

"I . . . I have to go," said Mag.

Duana's face fell, even as her eyes filled with understanding. "You went to see Ciaran, you dark-damned—"

"Too late for chastisement," said Mag. She swiped at a sudden mist in her eyes, though she tried to make it look like she was only wiping sweat from her brow. "And too late to warn me not to do it. Ciaran has banished me. If I try to stay, he will levy a fine against us that we cannot hope to pay."

Duana slammed her mug on the table, sloshing some of the ale over the side. "Dark take it, Mag! You should have known better—"

"I know," said Mag. She said it quietly, but still, it cut Duana off as if she had shouted. And as she looked upon her master, Mag could no longer hold back the tears, and they poured steadily down her cheeks. But she managed to hold her voice steady. "I am sorry. I could have . . . I do not know, but we could have thought of . . . of something."

That was as much as she could safely say without breaking down, and so she stopped. And seeing her distress, Duana sighed. She went behind the table and poured another mug of ale, which she placed in Mag's hand. Mag drained it before Duana could sit back down, but she went to fill it on her own, and Duana settled into her chair.

"Well, never mind any of that," said Duana. "As you said, it is too late to chastise you or to urge another course. What is done is done. And . . . and in the end, this is likely for the best."

Mag's head whipped towards her, a hurt look on her face. "You . . . want me to go?"

"I do not want it," said Duana. "But what we want, and what is best, are not always the same thing. You know you are unusual, Mag. Everyone in town knows it. It is one reason Ciaran has always hated you—for he is petty and trivial, and so utterly unremarkable, and he sees the chasm of difference between the two of you."

"You are more skilled than I am," said Mag. "You cannot say I am remarkable when you can do this." She hefted her mug, which was already half gone.

"That is not what I mean, and you know it," said Duana. She turned her gaze east, and suddenly it was as if she saw across a great distance, through the walls of the brewery and into a far land beyond. "You and I both know you are not like most people. I saw it when first I found you in those woods, and I have seen it ever since you came to live with me. I saw it again when you trounced Ciaran the first time. Selfishness made me keep you here as long as I have. But I think you are meant for other things, Mag. Things far beyond the meaningless bounds of this unimportant town."

Again Mag's throat had grown thick, and words were hard to come by. "It was important to me."

"I know it," said Duana softly. She swiped at her eyes, as Mag had done before, and stood. "But we have both already said how looking back is worthless. Come. I will give you what I can spare. I only wish I still had the tavern, so that I could give you a horse."

They gathered Mag's things, such as they were, and soon she was ready. They shared one last mug—so far as Mag knew, she would never have another cup of Duana's ale again—and then they said their farewells. Mag never told me exactly what they said to each other then, but some things it is better not to know.

And when it was done, Mag set off into the wilderness of the Dorsean forest, alone and penniless. She did not know it was the start of a road that would lead her to me, and one day to Sten. But it would also take her to Northwood, and to that night in the Greenfrost when all hope seemed lost.

THIRTY-NINE

"I HATE THIS STORY," DECLARED SUN.

Albern arched an eyebrow at her. "Do you now?"

"I do," said Sun. "Most every story I ever heard of Mag was a happy tale, an adventure from which she emerged victorious. Yet now you are only telling me of what seem to be her very worst sorrows. And you are hammering me with them, as if they were nails and I were a stubborn plank, again and again. It is as though you want to be absolutely sure I understand how abjectly miserable she was."

"Well," said Albern, "what did you expect when you asked to hear how she died?"

Sun's eyes went wide. "Wait. Are you telling me that story now? When I asked you to tell me, you did not say you were going to do it!"

Albern snorted. "I did not say I would not, either."

Sun snatched handfuls of her hair, for she had a sudden urge to rip it all out. "But Albern, this is all wrong. This is not *anything* like how I heard Mag died. I thought it had to do with . . ." She swallowed through a dry throat. "With that other matter."

Maddeningly, Albern only shrugged. "And not for the first time, I must ask you, Sun: who do you believe? Skalds from your home, or the man who was there?"

Sun folded her arms in a huff. "And yet you will not even say it. Tell me the truth: is this the story of how Mag died?"

Albern stopped beside her in the street. He turned and looked her straight in the eye. Sun felt transfixed by him, by the sorrow she saw in his dark expression.

"Yes," he said. "This is how she died."

They stood there for a long, silent moment in the middle of the street. Passersby moved around them with muttered complaints. The lowering sun cast heavy lines of black shadow across Albern's eyes and cheeks, and his unmoving face bore down into Sun. She felt dumbstruck.

"But . . . so this is the end of the tale?"

"Were you not eager to hear it?" said Albern. "You wanted to get here. Why do you object now?"

"Because . . . because I . . . I do not know why!" said Sun. "But what kind of storyteller lets his listener know how the tale will end?"

"Sun," said Albern slowly, "you *know* Mag dies. You have always known that. One of the first things you ever asked me was how she died. So how can it ruin the tale for you, if you have always known that would be the ending? Any tale would end with the hero's death if talespinners did not cut themselves off at a happier moment of victory. And how many stories have you asked your family's skalds to tell you again and again, no matter how many times you had already heard them? Why did you want to hear those stories after the first time, if you already knew what would happen?"

"That is different," said Sun. But she said it quietly, and she was not sure she believed it. "I felt like . . . those stories had a point, or they seemed to. Whether they ended well or poorly, there was a reason for it all. But I can see no reason for Mag's suffering in the Greenfrost, no greater purpose served at all."

"Well, neither did we at the time," said Albern. "But you have struck on something there. Even in a tale's darkest moments, it is the storyteller's job to make the audience feel as though their time is not being wasted—that there might be some hope at the end of a weary road, or at least some semblance of satisfaction. I am sorry you feel otherwise now. But stay with me a little longer, and when I am done, then you can tell me if you are still disappointed."

Sun sighed. "That prospect holds little hope for me, either. This tale is why we started traveling together. If you finish the story, does that mean we are done?"

Albern's expression, which had been stern and craggy, softened at once. He clucked his tongue for his horse, and together they started walking down the street again. "No," he said. "No, of course not. I will not abandon you, Sun, not if you do not wish me to—and mayhap not even if you do, depending on the circumstance. And if it is any consolation, after this tale is done, I may have others, and you may wish to hear them. But because you have asked me so many times for the end of the story, I wanted you to find out—the way Mag needed to find out—that the end is not something we should rush. We should let it come in its own time. If we rush it, we may regret it."

He fell silent then, and they walked together for a short while without speaking. But even as Sun was pondering his words, a hand clapped down on her shoulder from behind.

"Mistress," came a rumbling, familiar voice. "The Lord and Lady Valgun command you to attend them at once."

Sun felt as though the whole world had fallen in on her in an instant, as if all the buildings along the street had collapsed on her head. She looked up into the face of Niall, one of her mother's bodyguards. He stood a good head taller than she was, and his dark eyes squinted heavily down at her from his nut-brown face.

Dimly, her mind took in other details. There was Ursa, Niall's right hand, and Frida, diminutive and quiet, but lightning fast in a fight. The women stood on the other side of Albern, one of them with a hand on his horse's reins. Albern himself stood stock-still, his gaze darting everywhere. Sun's mind raced in circles until she felt ready to faint.

"Mistress," repeated Niall.

Ursa had fixed a steely glare on Sun, while Frida's look was almost pleading. She was one of the kinder warriors in her parents' employ, but Sun knew she would not hesitate to bring Sun back home by force if that was what was required.

"I am fairly certain she does not wish to come with you," said Albern.

"You are not involved in this, old man," snapped Niall.

"I am feeling rather involved," said Albern.

And then he drove one heavy boot straight into Niall's groin.

Niall collapsed as though struck with a sledgehammer. Even as Frida reached for her weapon, Albern brought his hand into a vicious chop at her throat. She fell back, gasping and hacking, while Albern slammed the top of his head straight into Ursa's nose. Sun heard a *crunch,* and then Albern seized her, and she was following him down the nearest alley, both of them dragging their horses along.

"Sky above!" cried Sun. "Sky above, what have we done?"

"Strictly speaking, *you* have done nothing," said Albern. He was breathing heavily—his burst of motion seemed to have taken a toll. "Those three are used to getting their way. None of them expected resistance. But they will not be stunned long. Well, not the women, anyway." His hand fumbled in a pouch at his belt.

Risking a glance back, Sun could see he was right. Ursa and Frida had nearly struggled back to standing. Niall, on the other hand, still lay whimpering on the cobblestones, clutching between his legs. But then Sun and Albern darted around a corner, and the guards were out of view.

"We are leaving the horses," said Albern. "They should lure your family's guards away. I will send word to a friend to have them rounded up."

"But what are we—"

"Now, Sun."

She slapped Vika's flank. The horse whinnied loudly and ran down the alley to the street. Cries erupted from the crowd there. But Albern had stopped at a door leading into the back of a building. His left hand came out of the pouch at his belt, fingers gripping an iron key. In a flash, he unlocked the door and threw it open. He pulled Sun in after him and shut the door again.

They both waited in the darkness for a tense moment of silence.

The heavy pounding of boots came to the door. Sun's blood froze.

The boots continued down the alley, where the horses had fled. Soon all had faded to silence.

"Dark below," wheezed Albern. "That was a good run. Lucky we were already close to this place when they found us."

"Lucky indeed," said Sun. Her body seemed to be responding properly to her impulses again, but all she wanted to do was collapse. Instead, she looked around at the space they were in. It was a small room, with shelves running along the walls. Only a little bit of light leaked in under the door through which they had entered. Another door to their right led deeper into the building. "But what *is* this place?"

"The back room of an inn that has been unoccupied for some time," said Albern. "Come, let me show you the common room."

Sun frowned in confusion, but she followed him nevertheless. The door to the right opened into a space behind the tavern's bar. The bar was a large, impressive construction, all of black walnut with a fine grind and polish, but rough edges from the tree's natural growth. High rafters converged in the center of the room above them. A large brass chandelier hung from where the beams met, currently empty, but ready to hold dozens of candles. High windows let shafts of sunlight pierce the room and kept it well ventilated. It seemed a grand place for parties, but Albern had spoken the truth—no one looked to have been here in weeks, mayhap months.

"How did you know this place was here?" said Sun. "And how did you have the key?"

"Well, you will already have gathered that I have many friends in Bertram," said Albern. "This place belongs to one of them. They are planning to reopen it soon, and one of my errands in the city is to help them do so. Why, look at that—there is even a cask of ale here. Would you like a drink?"

"Sky above, *yes,*" said Sun.

She went to the bar, dusted off one of the stools, and sat, while Albern moved around to the back and went to the cask. It was a quarter cask, but that was more than enough to enjoy themselves, depending on how long they stayed here.

Albern tapped it and fetched two glasses from beneath the counter—they were free of dust, which told Sun someone had brought them recently. Soon the drinks were ready, and Albern handed Sun's to her.

"I hope that encounter proved to you one thing," he said. "Your worst fear has come true, but you have survived it. Your family found you. And yet you remain free. Let us drink to that."

Sun could not help a small smile. "Very well. To freedom."

They raised their glasses and drank. Sun took one

swallow and lowered the cup, pulling a face. It was not the worst swill she had ever had, but it was undoubtedly the worst she had tasted since meeting Albern. The old man had a gift for finding the best cup of beer around, but this seemed to be an exception.

"Dark below," spat Sun. "With ale like this, it is no wonder this place closed down."

Albern barked a laugh. "A good point. This cask is a gift to celebrate the tavern's purchase, but mayhap it should not have been given. The best thing I can say about this ale is that it can get us drunk. And that is good, because the story is about to take a dark turn."

Sun stared at him. *"About* to take a dark turn?"

She had meant it as a joke, but Albern's expression grew mournful. "Darker, I suppose."

After Mag led Yue, Dryleaf, and me out of the hills, we went due south to lose ourselves in the Greenfrost. I took up the rear of our sad little procession, doing my best to hide our tracks from any pursuit. But privately, I doubted they would come after us. Kun would be enraged at the death of his nephew and dismayed at the gutting of his army. But he was a captain first and foremost. His highest priority now was getting the rest of his troops to safety before they starved to death. He might send a squadron after us at most, but I doubted we would earn even that mean of an honor.

And, I reflected sadly, he no longer had Zhen to

send after us. I did not know anyone else who would be able to track me, if I did not want to be found.

The night was already half gone when we left. I pushed us to walk until dawn had begun to lighten the sky to the east. Then, at last, I stopped and had us set up camp, building a little fire. With daylight coming, we would not need to fear anyone spotting the glow through the trees.

We were now mayhap a league south of the road where we had first ambushed the Shades. The Greenfrost glimmered in the swelling daylight around us. But where I had once thought the trees looked like eminent sculptures all in emerald, now they were like stern tombstones in jade, bending over us and fixing us with silent stone eyes of judgement. I tried not to look at them.

We cleared snow from a spot on the ground near the fire, and there we set Dryleaf down to rest. We gave him every cushion we could summon, our softest saddlebags, and every extra cloak or blanket we had. He now looked like a prince lounging in a large bed of cushioned pillows. But his body and clothes were still grimy with travel, and fresh blood stained the bandages wrapped around his head.

Mag sat close beside him, never taking her eyes from him. Yue was off to the side, staring unblinking into the fire. I could imagine the torment in Mag's mind, but I could not begin to guess what Yue must be thinking.

Dryleaf stirred. His hand sought Mag, and when he found her, he squeezed her arm gently. "I am afraid I am rather slowing you down at this point."

"Never," said Mag. "If anyone harms our little troupe by being here, it is me."

"Enough, Mag," I snapped. "In a contest of guilt, there is no winner. We all . . . we all need to sleep. We have been on our feet for nearly two days straight. Let us rest. Then we can figure out what to do."

I thought she would argue with me. I expected her to. But she only looked even more defeated, and that frightened me more.

"Very well," she said softly. "I will take the first watch."

"Let me do it," I said. "It will let me inspect our surroundings and get the lay of the land, as well as make sure we have left no trail leading to us."

"Please, Albern," she said, still not looking at me. "I would not sleep, anyway. At this moment, I feel as though I will never be able to sleep again. Let me have a few hours alone to . . . to try to master my thoughts."

I blew a long breath out through my nose. It turned to mist at once, flying up around my head like a Dragon's breath. "Fine. But if you fail to wake me for my turn, I will not let you stand another watch for a week. Do you hear me?"

Mag nodded. "I hear you."

"Promise me, Mag."

She looked up at me. The firelight danced across her face, but I could see no reflection of it in her eyes.

"Do you not believe me, Albern?"

I tilted my head. "Of course I do, Mag. But I know how you—I know *something* of how you are feeling right now. I will not allow you to give up. Nor will I allow you to try and find more ways to punish yourself. Now, I am weary, and I want to sleep. Promise me, so that I can lay my head down without fear."

"I promise," said Mag. Small. Defeated.

Lying, as it turned out.

Another misty breath wreathed around my temples. "All right. Good night."

I pulled my bedroll off my pack. But before I laid it out, I went to Yue and put a hand on her shoulder. "Yue, I—"

She shoved my hand away. "Leave me alone."

I shook my head. "Yue . . ."

"Dark take you, Albern, you were wise enough to leave me be when I lost soldiers in battle. Be wise enough to get away from me now. I am not going to do anything stupid, if that is what you are afraid of. I just want to be alone."

I ground my teeth and turned from her to look at Dryleaf. He no longer held Mag's arm but had his hands tucked under his armpits for warmth beneath the blankets. Silent tears left slow tracks down his cheeks.

"Of course," I said softly.

I went to the other end of our little campsite and laid out my bedroll. Soon I was tucked inside it, huddling for warmth, my back to the fire and to my friends. Eventually, I heard Yue do the same, laying out a space to sleep and soon filling the clearing with little snores.

I fell asleep not long after that.

I woke up close to sundown.

And Mag was gone.

FORTY

Mag waited by the campfire until the rest of us had fallen asleep. That was not long. Dryleaf's injury sent him back and forth between senselessness and an agitated dozing. Yue and I were bone-tired and soul-weary. Before long, Mag rose from her place by the fire.

A moment's trepidation held her. What if someone came upon our camp while she was gone? But I had told her Kun would not pursue us. And she believed me. She always believed in me.

Even if I could no longer believe in her.

Oku got to his feet and trotted to her, a low whine issuing from his throat.

"Kip, boy," said Mag.

Oku paused, one front paw hanging in the air.

Mag knelt, scratching him behind the ears. Then she pulled him into her arms, sinking her fingers into his fur, holding him close and relishing his warmth. Oku pushed his nose between her elbow and body, nuzzling into her.

"I am going," she said quietly. "You have to stay here, and you have to stay quiet. Do you understand?"

Oku drew back and looked up into her eyes.

"Of course you do," she said. "You are a good boy, are you not?"

He took two slow steps back, and then he sat. He did not move or make a sound as she strode away from our camp.

Before long, she had emerged from the northern end of the Greenfrost. As I have told you before, she was never good at tracking. But even she could see the signs of an army marching across the landscape. There was the trail, the deep furrow that Kun's force had left as it marched out of the woods and into the hills. She could even see, faintly in the distance, the smoke of campfires rising into the sky above the tops of the hills.

She sighed, set her course, and started walking towards them.

Far away, and yet not so far as all that, Rogan sat at

a table in a tent, looking at a map of Dorsea. He was alone—or as alone as he ever was. His thoughts lingered on Kaita, and they left him despondent.

Suddenly he felt a presence. The flap of his tent flew back, and a figure strode into the tent.

Rogan looked up, and his heart nearly stopped as he recognized the Lord.

"Father?" he said, frowning. Something was . . . wrong, but his mind was slow to identify it.

Then the Lord came and placed a hand on his shoulder.

Rogan shot to his feet. *"Father!"* he cried, his voice shaking the tent canvas. "You . . . how are you here? You cannot be here! You—"

"Be at peace, my son," said the Lord. "I am here because I must be. Have faith."

"Of course, Father," said Rogan, bowing his head. "Forgive me, I . . . oh, Father."

He leaped forwards and wrapped his arms around the Lord, crushing the smaller man into his chest. And though Rogan, like all the shadeborn, was always as warm as if a furnace burned in his chest, he felt an even greater warmth seeping from the Lord, suffusing him, granting him a peace of mind and a comfort that he had long missed.

"It has been too long, my favored son," said the Lord quietly.

"It feels like forever and an age," said Rogan, withdrawing slightly. "Are you absolutely certain that this is safe?"

"As certain as I can be, and as safe as anything is," said the Lord. "Besides, it could not wait. Much has become clear to me. I finally know the reason, Rogan. I know why we had to send Kaita to her doom, though it was agony to us both."

Rogan's eyes shot wide. "Why, Father?"

"You will soon see. Fetch horses, but only for the two of us. We must move quickly."

As I woke from the day's sleep, I leaped up with a shout. "Where is Mag?"

My cries startled Yue awake. "What?" she grumbled, blinking against the fading sunlight.

"Mag!" I shouted. I should not have been yelling so loud, but I did not care. I ran around the edges of the camp, screaming into the Greenfrost. "Mag!"

Dryleaf had come awake. He tried to push himself up from the ground, but he could not do it until Yue came running to help him. His head swung back and forth, blind eyes blinking anxiously.

"Albern!" he called out. "What is it? What is happening?"

"Mag is gone," I growled, stomping back towards the camp. "Dark take her, I knew it, I *knew—*"

My attention caught on Oku. The hound was trotting back and forth towards the north end of the camp, sniffing the ground and whining.

"What is it?" I ran to him, and he pointed with his

nose. The ground there had been swept clean—I had done it myself when we found the campsite, to ensure no one would follow us here. But now there was a fresh set of tracks. It set out from our camp, walking away north between the trunks of the trees.

"Dark-taken sow!" I roared. "How dare she? She . . . she—" I bit my own words off, unable to find words for my rage.

Yue had come to stand beside me, and though she was no better a tracker than Mag, even she could not miss the set of bootprints leading north through the mud.

"We have to go after her," she said.

I bit my tongue nearly hard enough to sever it. "We cannot," I growled at last. "Not both of us. Yue, I am so sorry. I do not deserve to ask anything of you. But please, someone must stay here with Dryleaf. I need you to keep him safe while I rescue Mag."

"Rescue her?" said Yue. "How do you mean to do that?"

"I think she has gone to Kun's camp," I said. "To turn herself in and face punishment for everything that has happened. I can . . . I should be able to . . ."

Yue's face had gone stony. "Be able to what, Albern?"

I shook my head slowly. "I do not know," I said. "Mayhap I can sneak in and . . . help her escape somehow."

"And what if she is guarded?" said Yue. "What will you do to any soldiers watching over her?"

I looked at her, aghast. "Yue. I would never harm them. If there is no way to get her out . . ." I swallowed hard. "Well. If I cannot get her out, then I will get caught trying. I promised her, Yue, that I would stay by her side until the end of the road. I cannot break my word. Not to Mag."

Yue studied me for a long moment. At last she said, quietly, "All right, then. If you promise you will not harm a servant of the King's law, then I will stay and watch Dryleaf."

"I promise."

Dryleaf was trying to rise to his feet. "Albern," he said, groaning the word. "You have to . . ."

The effort was too much for him, and he subsided, sinking back into the bed we had made for him. I ran to his side. "I am here, Dryleaf."

"You have to save her," said Dryleaf. "I have told you before. She needs you, far more than either of you think."

"I do not know if I believe that," I said. "But I will—"

"You *must* believe it," insisted Dryleaf. "You are not her lackey, Albern. Stop acting as if you are—for both your sakes."

I studied him. His expression was so focused that I felt he was staring right back at me. At last, I nodded.

"All right," I said quietly. "I will remember it. And I *will* save her."

One should never make a promise like that. I felt

as if I were lying to his face. But I refused to leave him without hope.

I stood and turned to Yue. "Stay safe until I return."

"Just see to it that you *do* return," she growled.

For a moment, I hesitated. Then I nodded, turning to go.

"Oh, come here, you fool."

She seized me and pulled me in. It was not the most affectionate kiss we had shared, and certainly not the most passionate. But it was something, at least. I had feared that whatever had grown between us had died, after what had happened with Kun, and I would have understood.

"I will see you again," I said.

"You had better," she said.

I turned and ran north, following Mag's trail. Oku padded beside me, silent and true.

Tagata and Kaita were curled around each other in a bedroll, in a tent, a league to the west. Their boots, cloaks, and other clothes were scattered all around, as were three skins that had once contained wine. Parts of the bedroll were torn and ripped, letting in the cold air. But Kaita only had to press herself closer to Tagata's massive, bare form to banish the chill from her skin, and so she slept content.

Until Tagata stirred, pushed herself up on one elbow, and gently shook her shoulder.

"Hmm?" said Kaita. She looked up, blinking hard at Tagata's face. The shadeborn's hair stuck wildly out in all directions, much like Kaita's own. "Oh, again?"

She pulled Tagata down for a kiss. Tagata smiled and gave in for a moment, but then she pressed a hand to Kaita's cheek to stop her.

"No, dear one. I have received word from the Lord. Come. We must leave."

Kaita groaned. The wine had not quite worn off, but it was starting to, and it threatened a noticeable headache. "Now?" she complained. "Well, tell the troops to get ready and then come back to me. We can take a short while to ourselves, while they prepare to march."

"Not our kindred," said Tagata, chuckling. "Just us. You and me."

"Why?" murmured Kaita, pressing against Tagata's chest again. "What do the two of us—"

Her eyes shot wide. She jerked up, gawking at Tagata in the darkness.

"You cannot mean . . ."

Tagata smiled. "Get ready," she said, reaching for her vest. "And make sure you bring the magestones."

Soon they were dressed, and they emerged into the frigid cold together. Kaita followed Tagata to the east. And every few steps, her fingers stole into her cloak to probe the brown cloth packet.

I came sprinting out of the Greenfrost, Oku beside me. I could still see Mag's trail. It stood out fresh on top of the many other tracks from recent days. She was not making even the barest attempt to hide her passing. She had to know I would be able to follow her. Did she think I would not go into Kun's encampment? Did she believe me faithless, that I would abandon her to her fate, and not try to stop her, or to save her?

A chill struck me.

Did she think Kun would be so quick to execute her that I would not even have the chance? That when I failed to save her from her fate, I would be forced to turn tail and head back to Yue?

That was a darker thought than I wished to contemplate, and certainly a darker one than I wanted to imagine in Mag's mind.

I put on a fresh burst of speed, hardly even glancing at her trail anymore. It went straight north. That required no skill to follow. I knew where she was going, and I would go with her until the end, even if it were only to find her already—

I stopped.

Mag's tracks turned. They were no longer heading for Kun's camp, but had swung west.

My gaze followed, and I frowned, wondering what Mag could be looking for in that direction.

And then I saw another massive furrow in the muddy ground. One like the trail of Kun's army, but smaller, and heading west through the hills.

The tracks of the Shades. They had left it when they retreated, after destroying the supply train.

My eyes shot wide.

No.

Mag marched west.

She had known what she was looking for when she left the Greenfrost. She had known the Shades were to the west. And so she skirted the edge of Kun's encampment until she saw the signs of their retreat. She was no tracker, and she never had been. But she could read the signs of an army marching across the land.

She was following those signs still. There was determination in her step, but no speed. She was resolute, but she was not eager. This path was inevitable. It was always going to come to this, in the end. She had once deluded herself into thinking there was another way, but she knew now that that had been an impossible dream.

Like her life with Sten.

She swallowed past a sudden lump in her throat and rolled her shoulders. And she trudged on. She would not stop, not now. Not until she reached the end of the long road.

Alone.

She wondered, briefly, if I would ever forgive her.

Above her, a raven called in the darkening sky. Mag ignored it at first. If the bird sought carrion, it would soon have its fill.

Then she stopped.

It was late for ravens to be out.

The bird landed in the mud in front of her a span away. Magelight flashed in its eyes, and Kaita resumed her human form.

And then behind her, over the low hill west of their battleground, came another figure, this one lumbering. More than two heads taller than Kaita, and with a massive greatsword slung across her back. The brute woman.

Mag heaved a mighty breath, letting it out through her mouth to wreathe into mist around her.

She hefted her spear and swung her shield onto her arm.

FORTY-ONE

KAITA COULD NOT BELIEVE IT. HERE WAS MAG, AT last. Alone, isolated from her friends. Kaita had kept her promise to Rogan, who received his instructions directly from the Lord himself.

The Lord had known. He had always known, all this time, how it would end. His foresight was perfect. And what was more, he really did love Kaita. Despite all her doubts, all her questioning, he saw her value, and he had granted her the boon she most desired. She would never doubt him again.

A savage grin spread across her face.

“The end of our road,” she called out to Mag across the muddy field.

“And not soon enough,” said Mag, her tone casual. “Are you going to turn into the cat, or the bear? Or have you grown tired of tricks? I will kill you like this if you want.”

Behind Kaita, Tagata snarled at Mag’s threats. But Kaita laughed and turned to her. “Dear one, there is no need to worry. Look at her. Alone, without anyone to rescue her.”

“I am not the one who will need rescuing,” called Mag.

Kaita ignored her, keeping her gaze on Tagata. “Stay here. You know I have our father’s strength now.”

“But I came here for you,” said Tagata, scowling past her at Mag.

“And you *are* here for me,” said Kaita. “That is what is important. You can be my witness. But let me do this on my own and help me celebrate when it is over.”

Tagata’s nostrils flared as she heaved a sigh. But then she nodded and took a step back. “Very well.”

Kaita bowed her head towards Tagata. Then she turned back to Mag. Her hand stole beneath her cloak again, as it had done often on the journey here. But this time when it came out, a single magestone was clutched between her fingers.

Mag went very still. And Kaita saw it. This was not the indifference of the battle-trance, the certainty and neutrality that came with her fearless war mask.

This was hesitation. Uncertainty. Kaita had never seen it in Mag's demeanor before, and it thrilled her beyond reckoning. For once, for the *first* time, she was the one in control, and Mag was not confident of the outcome of the fight.

A small, quiet pitter-patter of rain began to fall on them, strengthening by the moment.

Kaita stood straighter, spreading her hand at her side to catch as much of the setting sun's light as possible, even as clouds moved across the sky to obscure its dying glow. It warmed her skin, reminding her of Tagata as they pressed against each other in the tent.

Kaita smiled. And she slid the magestone between her lips.

It crunched between her teeth so sweetly, so gently. There was the slightest resistance, like a carrot that had been steamed to perfection. And then the black crystal melted on her tongue, sliding down her throat like sweet honey. It vanished there, in her center, her core, only to come surging back a moment later. Kaita could feel it coursing through her veins, filling her flesh and her skin and every part of her with pure, raw power.

Power. She thought she had known it before. She thought she knew strength in the burly frame of the bear. She thought she knew killing swiftness in the lightning paws of the mountain lion. But she had known nothing. She could feel it within her—every form she knew, every animal she had taken into her canon, now stronger, faster, more nimble.

But beneath it all, in her very essence, she could sense something new. A form she had never seen before, had never even imagined. Now it presented itself to her, offering up every detail, letting her see it in its entirety, the way a weremage must see a creature when they learn its form. Every part of it was now as familiar to her as the raven in which she had journeyed endless leagues.

This was power. This was safety—the strength to destroy any enemy who ever crossed her. No one could ever banish her again. No one could ever cast her aside for being useless, not with this form inside her.

It was everything she had ever wanted.

She let the form flow into her. And she began to change.

Her eyes turned black, and then they began to glow. A sickening darkness seeped out of them and consumed the fading sunlight. Her skin swelled. It flowed out like water and then hardened, turning rigid as glacial ice, and like ice, it was white and translucent. She fell forwards on all fours. Her shoulders and arms swelled like those of an ape of the northern jungles, but half again as tall and three times as heavy. Her face jutted forth, and huge fangs erupted from both top and bottom jaws. Where the skin formed into solid white armored plates, it also grew jagged spikes that erupted out all across her form. Between the blades, the surfaces were rough like tree bark made of razors, so that nothing could touch her without coming away bleeding.

Kaita gave herself one moment—only one. She closed her eyes, inhaled, and then exhaled again, tensing and flexing every muscle in her new body.

She could not believe it. To know that *this* was the strength of magestones. *This* was the power of the Wizard Kings of old. How had they ever lost it? How could anyone have taken this away from them?

No one could stop her now. She should have taken the stones weeks ago. She *could* have plunged straight into the center of the Mystic army. Who could have stopped her? No blade could pierce her hide. No one could live once she had set her sights on them and pronounced their death.

Her eyes snapped open, and they focused on Mag.

A moment ago, Mag had looked uncertain. That was gone. Her face was a deadpan mask again, the battle-trance with which Kaita was all too familiar. Kaita hated it, hated Mag for it.

The rainstorm above them had worsened, and now lightning cracked in the sky. Thunder rocked the ground, sending waves through puddles of rainwater. And Kaita roared to meet it, and the sound was like every demon in the darkness below. She charged, and it was more terrible than the worst storms of winter.

Kaita's first swipe came faster than the lion, too fast for Mag to dodge. She raised her shield instead, hoping to roll with the blow as she would have with the bear. But it was too strong, and with a crash, she was flung back, sliding five paces through the mud.

For a moment, Kaita stood there, flexing her great clawed fingers, marveling at them. She had never been so fast, never so strong. Why would the Lord not grant this gift to all his wizard children? Underrealm would not stand for a month, not against even a handful of them.

Mag got to her feet. The mud clung too thick for the rain to wash it off. Still, her face was the impassive mask, not a muscle in it twitching.

But that was fine. Kaita did not need to see Mag's fear. She did not need her to scream or to weep.

It was enough to watch her die.

Kaita launched herself across the snow. Mag tried to dodge aside, but Kaita turned, quick as lightning. Her left rear limb struck out, a crushing blow that slammed into Mag's back and flung her facedown into the ground.

When she came up, her lip was split open. Rainwater mixed with the blood, sending it racing down her chin to splash into the mud.

Kaita's heart sang.

Again she lunged, and then again, each time swiping, snarling. Mag tried to avoid her blows, and sometimes she managed it. But Kaita was simply too fast now. She struck Mag once in the ribs, and something cracked. Her claws raked down Mag's spear arm, sending more bright blood to stain the churning ground.

Though it was Kaita's own claws doing the cutting, she almost could not believe it was working. Never in the past had she so much as nicked Mag's skin. From what she knew, no one ever had.

Mag backed off two paces. She was breathing hard now, though her mangled spear arm did not shake. Her lip still bled down her chin and onto her shirt, but her expression had not changed.

As Kaita stood there marveling at her success, Mag leaped. Her spear came up, and she jammed it straight into Kaita's neck.

It struck the chitinous armor. And there it stuck. Kaita could barely feel it—like a playful pinch from a lover.

She bared her dagger-long fangs, a snarl and a smile all at once.

Her claws raked Mag's body. The spear went spinning away. Mag's shirt of scales kept her from being gutted. But the claws punctured it in places. Blood soaked into her undershirt. And now her spear was behind Kaita, far out of reach.

Kaita stepped forwards, planting her claws in the ground on either side of Mag's head. Mag looked up into her ink-black eyes.

I was running through the snow in the fading afternoon light, Oku by my side. Ahead of us, I could hear the inhuman screams of some unknown creature. A new form of Kaita's, I guessed, though I could not imagine what sort of animal would make that sound.

My lungs seemed to be screaming nearly as loud, but I ignored them. I had to keep going. Mag was in trouble, and she was alone. That mattered more than any pain.

She is alone. She is alone, and I promised.

And in a bitter corner of my mind, a voice snarled, *But she promised, too.*

And then I came over the top of a hill. I was just in time to see Kaita plunge pace-long claws straight through Mag's chest and into the ground.

FORTY-TWO

I STOOD THERE FOR AN ETERNAL MOMENT, UNABLE TO understand, unwilling to believe. The only sound was the rain slamming into the muddy ground all around us.

I almost ran forwards. Oku wavered, looking between Mag and me, waiting for the command to attack.

But those claws . . . Mag's blood . . . .

Never had I seen a weremage in their hellskin form, but I recognized it from the tales I had heard. And if Kaita could do this to Mag, I stood no chance. I hated myself for it, but something kept me from flinging myself into certain, pointless death by Mag's side.

I threw myself behind a nearby boulder, where I waited, panting from my desperate run. Oku darted into hiding beside me. Gritting my teeth and squeezing the stitch forming in my side, I edged out around the boulder far enough to see.

Kaita had Mag pinned to the ground. Blood flowed out of her, turning the mud into a dark slush. I could see it was not her first wound. Her lip had split, and a deep slice ran down the length of her arm.

None of it made sense. It was impossible. In more than two decades, I had never seen anyone so much as break her skin. And now she . . .

She is dying, I thought.

I did not want to believe it, but it was true. Any fool could see it. And Mag had to know it. But still her face was impassive, expressionless. She had her shield on her arm, and so she reached up to slam it into Kaita's twisted face.

It was like striking a mountain. Kaita did not even flinch. Her left hand was still plunged deep through Mag's body. Now, with her right, she snatched the shield in her massive claws and crushed it. The wood shattered to kindling. Shards of it plunged into Mag's flesh. Kaita's claws constricted further, and I watched them sink through Mag's skin, into the muscle, threatening to cut the arm off. Mag's blood flowed into the mud like a river.

The whole time, Kaita never stopped looking straight into Mag's face. She snarled and growled with every new cut. But Mag remained stone-faced. She did not flinch as the raindrops fell right in her eyes, as another blast of lightning tore the sky in half above her.

With her left arm in Kaita's claws, only her right arm was free—the mangled, sliced arm that had been wounded before. But one hand had been enough for the bear or the lion. So she formed her fingers into a knife, and she jabbed it towards Kaita's eye.

Kaita was too quick. She twisted her neck, and Mag's fingers struck her cheek instead. The bones snapped like twigs. Kaita's spikes gouged Mag's palm.

Kaita grinned, though it was more of a hateful snarl.

She released Mag's shield arm. All her fingers curled into a fist except the forefinger, leaving one great, razor-sharp claw extended to a point.

Slowly, ever so slowly, she drove the claw through Mag's throat.

Mag's lifeblood bubbled out, gushing around the claw. Her shield arm fell to the ground, and then her spear arm. Her feet slid through the mud as her legs relaxed. But her eyes never left Kaita, even as the light inside them dimmed.

Forever.

Kaita waited a long moment, as if to be sure. Then she straightened. She looked as though she could not believe it was over.

I had almost forgotten myself as I lay hiding behind that boulder. It was as if I was not even there, as if I had become disembodied, floating over the scene like a moon in the sky, observing but unable to intervene.

But now I had a horrible thought. What if Kaita sensed me? Smelled me? Heard me?

Yet as moments kept stretching, nothing happened. If she had been the lion or even the bear, she might already know I was here, despite the rain. This creature, this hellskin form, seemed to be built entirely for strength, speed, and invulnerability. Its senses were not keen enough to detect me.

Kaita stepped back and resumed her human shape. She turned and walked away. And now I saw that the brute woman stood nearby. I had been so focused on Mag that I had not noticed her at first.

The two of them embraced. Kaita took one last look back at Mag's fallen form. And then finally, they both turned and strode off west, to where I knew the rest of the Shades would be waiting.

Steady tears poured down my face, and I could not restrain my deep, sobbing breaths, though I tried to keep them quiet. Oku kept whining softly. I held a steady hand on his head, my fingers deep in his sodden fur, though I could not tell you whether it was for my comfort or his.

Finally, slowly, I stood from my hiding place and went to Mag. She still stared upwards, right where Kaita's horrid face had been. Oku trotted around to her other side.

I fell to my knees in the mud. Rainwater poured over me, soaking through my clothes, but I did not care. I could not deny what had happened, but neither could I believe it, and I would not accept it. Mag was never supposed to die. Eternal, Chausiku had called her, and he was right. She was too strong, too incredible—larger than life and certainly too remarkable for death. She was never supposed to go.

Especially if it meant leaving me here on my own.

I reached down and brushed her hair out of her eyes, and then I closed them. I fell forwards onto my elbows, my forehead planted in the mud, and my tears spilled to freeze on the ground.

Oku whined and edged forwards. With his muzzle, he prodded at her broken fingers. When she did not move, he pushed harder, lifting her hand to rest on her lap, like he was trying to get her up. When she still did not move, he licked her hand, cleaning off some of the blood.

"No, boy," I said, choking on the words. "She is gone. Sky save us. I should never have taken her from Northwood. I wish I had never left Strapa. I wish I had never met—" I stopped, for I could not quite bring myself to say it.

And then Mag's body jerked.

She gasped, the sound of her breath wet and bubbling through punctured lungs. Her back arched until I thought her spine would snap. Her head barely touched the ground. Every limb jerked and spasmed, her hand striking me in the chest. I could only stare at her in horror.

"Aaahhh!" she screamed from her ruined throat.

"Mag!" I cried.

Dark below. I had been sure she was already dead. This was even worse. Now I would have to sit with her through her agonizing last moments, and I would have to watch. It was Sten all over again.

And then I saw her fingers.

With sickening, wet cracks and pops, they bent back into shape. I saw the bones sliding beneath the skin, muscles and tendons tensing, squeezing, twisting. In a few moments, the hand had returned to normal, though it was still covered in blood and cuts from Kaita's bladed skin.

Then her slashed arm began to seal itself together. Fresh blood poured from every wound, but slowly the flow was stanched as the skin rejoined, covering them over.

I hovered my hands over her, wanting to help but not knowing how. My wondering gaze went from wound to wound, the gaping holes in her chest, the slit in her throat. All of them were healing. Her sealing wounds pushed out the splintered wood from her shield. Then the gaps closed to hide the blood and flesh beneath.

Finally, the wounds were gone, leaving nothing so much as a scar.

Nothing so much as a scar.

And then, all at once, many things made sense for the first time.

FORTY-THREE

We were in the mountains of Tokana, and Mag and I had found our first troll. Dark take her, she had taunted it, accusing it of working with the Shades. The troll roared and slammed its hands into the earth before storming towards her.

"No chance of peace, then," said Mag. "I suspected as much."

"Mag!" I cried, but too late. She crouched and leaped towards the thing.

It struck her a backhanded blow and sent her flying over a nearby house.

She landed where I could not see her, among the debris of another destroyed home. Her spine snapped. Broken, jagged beams from the wrecked house pierced her side and her leg.

Mag gritted her teeth and stifled her scream as best she could. Her arms were useless, and her spear and shield fell to the ground. For a short while, she sat there, heaving agonized breaths through her teeth.

Then her spine cracked and popped, pushing itself back into place. Mag cried out as she felt her bones rearranging themselves inside her, her nerves reconnecting to flood her mind with agony.

She could use her arms again. She reached up and seized the jagged end of the wooden spar. As she pulled herself off it, she whimpered at the feeling of the twisted wood ripping through her insides.

The wounds were already sealing when she fell to the ground on all fours. Soon there was no hole in her side. The slices along her palms vanished.

Shaking, she got to her feet and inspected herself. Scooping up some dirt from the ground, she scrubbed at the fresh bloodstains until they were dry. Then she snatched up her weapon and shield and ran back towards me and the troll. By the time she found me, there were no signs of injury. And in my panic at the troll, I did not notice the new bloodstains in her clothes.

* * *

We were in the mountains near Opara. Shades had ambushed Mag, Tuhin, and me. Mag had gone running off with Oku beside her, hunting the Shades in the dips and crags of the land. She had killed three already, and they were starting to figure out she was among them.

A Shade heard her coming and drew. Mag rounded the corner, and his arrow took her in the eye.

Her body went limp in an instant, like a puppet with cut strings. Oku howled in rage and leaped at the man. The Shade dropped his bow and drew a long dagger, trying to fend Oku off. They danced around each other, neither managing to land a blow. Oku paced around the Shade, growling, while the man tried to find a chance to plunge his blade home.

Behind him, Mag's body shuddered. Slowly, she got back to her feet. She gritted her teeth as she seized the arrow and pulled it out.

Her eye was still healing when the Shade turned, too late, and saw her. His face filled with horror as she plunged her spear into his heart.

She fell to her knees, shaking her head in a futile attempt to clear it of the pain. Tears poured from her remaining eye at the horrific feeling of her brain repairing itself inside her skull, and then of the bone growing back into place. As her mind started to clear, she probed the Shade's body with shaking hands. Her fingers found a waterskin.

"Thank the sky," she muttered, voice wobbling. She poured the water over her face and head, washing away the blood as best she could.

By the time she returned to me, I thought the blood covering her had spilled from the Shades she had killed. But Oku trotted by her side, looking up at her and whining, and I did not understand why.

We were in Lan Shui, and Mag was alone, fighting two vampires in the burning house that had once been a Shade hideout. We had named one Shoulders. The other was the largest, so Mag had dubbed it King.

She kicked Shoulders over a chair. Flames caught along its skin, and it screeched in pain as the fire consumed it. She followed up with her spear, impaling it against the wall.

Shoulders lashed out in its death throes. Its clawed hands and feet raked across Mag's arm, her shoulders, her neck. But Mag, secure in her battle-trance, did not flinch. She watched its body wither and die, vanishing in flames like parchment.

King smelled the passage down into the basement with the magestone blood. He knocked her aside, breaking one of her arms in the process. Mag fell to the ground, impassive, silent.

And by the time Yue and I found her, her wounds had sealed themselves, and her arm had returned to normal.

"One left," she said, pointing to the basement door. And we followed her down without question.

Mag was in the woods outside Shuiniu. She was naked and alone. She could not speak, for she knew no words. And she was hunting dinner.

A deer stood in the forest, a half-span ahead of her. In her hands was a sharpened stick—a poor substitute for the spontoon she would one day own, but still deadly in her grip.

She stalked as close as she dared. When she could not draw any closer without the deer hearing her, she threw the spear. The instant it left her hand, she was already sprinting forwards.

The spear plunged into the deer's flank. The animal screamed, even as Mag leaped through the air towards it. Landing feet first, she bowled it over and seized the spear. She yanked it out, shoved it into the deer's neck, and held the buck down while its body jerked in its final spasms.

She had crouched down, ready to feast, when she heard a snarl. She whirled faster than blinking, but not quite fast enough. Her fingers sank into fur as she clutched the throat of a panther.

It knocked her to the ground as she had done to the deer. But Mag was prey to no creature. Her hands became knives. She could not reach its eyes, but she struck it under the legs and in the jugular. It yowled in pain.

But before she could drive it off, its jaws clamped down on her throat. It gave a vicious jerk of its head, and her neck broke with a sickening *snap*. Mag's body went limp.

The panther held her for a moment. Then it dropped her and padded over to the deer. For a moment, it sniffed, inspecting the corpse, before digging its fangs into the hide and beginning to eat.

Mag's body jerked.

Her neck snapped back together, and she gave a strangled cry of agony. She closed her eyes, deep breaths forcing themselves in and out, while the wounds in her neck slowly sealed over.

She rose.

The panther turned. It stared up at her, its amber eyes glinting in the sunlight that broke between the tree trunks.

It must have known this was a fight it could not win, for it turned and fled deep into the woods.

Mag heaved a sigh and returned to her deer. Once again, she crouched, ready to eat. But this time, she kept a wary ear out for any other creature approaching her.

And then she heard something. Footsteps, coming closer.

She went to investigate. And she stumbled upon Duana, out for a walk.

It was the battle of Northwood, and the beginning of my long, long journey by Mag's side, seeking revenge against Kaita.

Sten had died. Mag had attacked Kaita with all her

fury, but the weremage had escaped. Now the two of us stood against a fresh wave of Shades. But the people of Northwood had rallied around us, and there was a pitched battle in the streets.

I saw Mag surrounded by her enemies. I saw her kill, but I also saw them cut and pierce her with their blades.

A club struck me unconscious. And Mag saw me fall.

No, she thought, in the part of her mind behind the battle-trance. *Not Albern. Not him, too.*

She shoved through the crowd and scooped me up. Holding me under one arm, she carried me through the battle and to safety. Behind a building that hid us both from sight, she set me down and felt for a heartbeat.

It was there, and it was strong, thank the sky. Her battle-trance fell away, and she breathed a sigh of relief. But it turned to a hiss of pain as her wounds started to seal themselves.

When she was whole, she picked me up again. The battle was starting to wind down. She found Elsie and placed me in her charge, to be healed on the floor of the tavern's common room. When I awoke and saw her, I stared at her in wonder.

"Before I went down," I said, "I saw you surrounded. I thought I saw you wounded."

(I *had* seen her wounded.)

She stepped forwards and held out her arms. "They

did surround me. I fought my way free. Do you see any wounds?"

(At least she did not lie to me. Not then, anyway.)

I did not see any wounds, and so I sighed. "You are frightening sometimes, Mag."

"Only sometimes?"

She smiled, and it hid every bit as much sadness as the mask of her battle-trance.

She was the Uncut Lady still. So far as any of us knew.

Sun stared blankly at Albern across the bar. Surreptitiously, she glanced down at her mug. How much of it had she had? Was this her second drink, or third? Was the ale the reason the old man had ceased to make any sense?

"What exactly are you saying?"

Albern's mouth twisted. And though he had revealed the tale's great secret to her, there was no joy in his expression, none of the restrained smile of a skald who enjoys the reaction of his audience. There was only a profound mournfulness.

"I am saying what you think I am saying, but you are reluctant to hear it. Do you begin to understand now, Sun? That was the moment I learned a lesson I have been trying to impart to you all this time—not just today, but since we met in that tavern.

"Mag's story, the legend that surrounded her, the

impossibly grand tale of the Uncut Lady . . . it was never something we were meant to *believe.* It was a good story. It bolstered the spirits of all who knew her, and especially those who fought beside her. It made our lives grander to hear it, even if we doubted it was true. Because deep in our hearts, we knew it could not have been. And as you will see, the story itself was a protection of sorts. It hid a truth Mag did not wish to reveal."

Sun felt lost in wonder. There were a thousand things she wanted to ask, but all her questions seemed limp and useless in the face of this knowledge.

She was surprised to find that she believed him without question. Often before this, she had doubted Albern's tale, even though most of it seemed possible. This new revelation seemed entirely impossible, and yet she did not doubt it for an instant.

"Mag was never the person I thought she was," Albern went on. "In some ways, she was less than the legends, and in other ways, she was more. Yes, she was an incredible fighter, but not as great as the stories made her out to be. She *had* suffered wounds. She had even died before. Many times. But she always came back. And with every death, she learned, and she became faster, and stronger, and even better in the next fight."

"But . . . but *how?*" said Sun, finding her voice at last. "How is it possible? Where did she gain such power? And why?"

Albern fixed her with a look. "I know the answers

to those questions. But I am not yet ready to give them. Can you accept that?"

Sun met his gaze for a long, silent moment.

"Yes."

"Good," said Albern. He sighed. "Then for now, let us return to that cold night in the rain."

FORTY-FOUR

"Mag?"

I could only stare at her in wonder. I had no idea what under the sky was going on. Mag's screams had subsided, but she still whimpered and groaned through clenched teeth. Her wounds were still stitching up, her body snapping itself back into shape. She was in agony. And what could I do about it? I could not even touch her without provoking a fresh cry of pain.

Her eyes focused for a moment, and then they found me. But she quickly turned away. "What are you doing here?" she gasped. The words were horribly mangled and garbled—her throat was not yet fully healed.

"What in the dark below do you mean?" I demanded. "I came after you, you absolute fool. What were you thinking, coming out here alone?"

"Why would I ask you to come?" she said. "Look at me. You would only have died."

"And you *should* be dead," I said. "Mag, what is—"

A horrible realization struck me. I seized Mag's shoulder and hauled her over to lie on her stomach. She tried to resist, tried to grip my wrist and render me helpless, as she had countless times before. But beneath her sealing skin, her muscles were still horribly mutilated, and she had no more strength than a toddler.

Once she was lying facedown, I seized her hair and shoved it up, pulling it side to side. I inspected the back of her neck, and then, when I found nothing, I tried higher up on the scalp.

"There is nothing," said Mag through gritted teeth. The muddy ground muffled her words. "Nothing, Albern, I swear."

I ignored her and looked carefully for myself. But she was right. There was nothing. I rolled her back over, and she glared at me as she came to rest on her back again.

"This magic," I said. "It is the enchantment of the

Shades' master. How did you come by it? How long have you had it?"

"I do not know," she said, still clearly in pain, her teeth gritted.

"Do not lie to me, Mag!"

"I do not know, Albern!" she pleaded. "I have been . . . like this, since I could remember."

"But . . . but why?" I said. "How did it start?"

"I do not know," she said. "I have some . . . some vague, hazy memory of the middle of the woods, near that town called Shuiniu—the one I told you about, that was not far from Taitou. There I lived alone for many years, hunting for food in the forest. It was a long time before I met other people. I did not know how to speak when they found me. I only knew my name, and how to kill."

Another chill went through me. "Mag. How long ago was that?"

She took a deep breath and met my gaze. "Twenty years before we met."

Slowly I shook my head. "That is impossible. You were only twenty years old when we met, or around that age. Do not try to tell me you came out of the woods as an infant, already knowing how to fight."

"No, Albern," she said quietly. "I am telling you I came out of the woods like this. *Exactly* as I am now. In every way."

I suddenly felt dizzy, and I sank back onto my rear in the mud.

Chausiku had seen it. He had told me, but I had laughed him off. He said she was far younger than I was, and I told him she aged well.

She did not age well. She did not age at all. She looked exactly the same now as she had when we met. But for years, I had kept telling myself that was not true, because it could not be. I told myself I saw subtle differences, things only I could see because I knew her so well. But that was a lie, something to let my mind feel secure in the face of the inexplicable.

I had thought Chausiku could not see the truth because he was too removed. In fact, I could not see it because I was too close.

Mag had not aged since long before we had met. And in all the battles we had fought in our youth, and then in Northwood, and on the long road since . . .

It was not that Mag could not be touched. It was that she always came back. And she hid it from me. From everyone.

"You kept it a secret," I said. "Every time I thought I saw you injured, and you turned out to be fine. I was right. You *were* wounded, many times. But you healed, and I ascribed it to the chaos of battle. I told myself I had seen something that had not happened."

"Yes," she said. "Yes, you have the right of it." Mag's body was mostly together now. She pushed herself up to sitting, dangling her arms over her knees. She was avoiding my gaze again. The rain had died out somewhat, and now it merely trickled onto us.

I could not help a snort of laughter. "No wonder you always hated my nickname. You were never the Uncut Lady at all."

She shook her head. "No. I was not. Just a lonely wanderer with a curse, and no memory of how it came to me."

"And you are *sure* it has nothing to do with the Lord?" I pressed. "I told you of Trisken in the mountains. And you have seen the brute woman here. The way their bodies heal themselves, no matter the wound . . ."

"It is *not* the same," said Mag, her voice low but fervent. "You said nothing of Trisken's pain when you told me of his power. And I have seen the brute woman suffer wounds. When she shrugs them off, her body is not wracked with agony. And then there is that tattoo they have—sky above, Albern, you have seen me naked often enough to know I do not have one, not on my neck or anywhere else. This enchantment their Lord has given them, and what happens to me . . . they may be similar in effect, but they are nothing alike in nature."

"Mayhap," I said thoughtfully. "And yet there may be a link. But that is a matter for another time, I suppose."

"If you say so," said Mag. She sounded as defeated as she had that morning, when we sat despondent by the fire together. Oku nuzzled her hands with his head, as he had when she lay broken in the mud. Mag scratched him halfheartedly behind the ears.

I reached out and put a hand on her shoulder, shaking my head. "So, this is why you ran off on your own," I said. "This is why you *always* go off on your own, no matter the danger. You know you will not die."

"Yes," whispered Mag. "And if I was injured, I did not want you to see it. I have worked hard to keep everyone from discovering what I am, because I do not understand it myself."

I leaned back, looking up into the greying sky. The sun was gone in the west, and its last light was quickly vanishing. "I suppose that makes sense."

Her gaze flitted to me, and then away again. "You are likely angry with me."

I thought about that. "Did Sten know?"

Mag nodded. "And one other. My old master, Duana, who taught me brewing in Shuiniu. I . . . I am sorry, Albern. I have known you longer than I knew either of them. It is no defense, but I promise I did not mean to tell them. They found out."

At that, I finally had to laugh out loud. The look of shock it put on her face was priceless. "Mag, stop it. Dark below, you do not have to apologize to me that your *husband* knew more about you than I did."

Her eyes were wide now, and she blinked twice at me. "I . . . I suppose I am surprised that you are not more upset with me."

"I . . ." My voice trailed off. To be honest, I did not entirely understand it myself. "Mag, it is your life. It is not mine. But I do wonder—and please believe that this is only curiosity—why did you *not* tell me? What were you afraid of?"

She shrugged. "I am not exactly sure. But it . . . when does one bring up something like this? Certainly not when we first met."

"And how about all the time after, when we were fighting together?" I smiled to reassure her I was not angry. "It would have been nice not to be terrified every time you ran off and did something foolish."

To my surprise, Mag shook her head sharply. "No. Never that. I never wanted it to be known to anyone I fought beside. Even you. I never wanted it to become an expectation in anyone else's mind. Would you put it past some of our commanders to fling me into the thickest fighting, if they did not have to worry about me dying? You have seen what coming back does to me. Every injury is twice as painful. I suffer all the agony of the wound itself, and then the pain of my body putting itself back together." A frown crossed her face. "I think . . . I am not certain, but I think that is why I learned to fight so well. So that I could protect myself from suffering in battle."

I frowned. "You *think* that is why you learned?"

Her expression grew bleak. "I do not remember learning it, Albern. I mean it when I say that I have always been this way. Everything before that forest in Shuiniu is . . . empty. There is nothing. I told you yesterday that I wanted an after. Mayhap that is because I have never had a before."

I leaned back on my hands, staring at her. "Mag. You damn fool. I am sorry I found out this way."

Mag's eyes locked on mine. "You what?"

"You never meant to tell me," I said. "You should not have had to tell me if you did not wish to. I should have found out on your terms, or not at all."

"*That* is what upsets you?" said Mag. "Albern, that would never have happened. I did not want you to know. And it was never something I had to worry about when I was in Northwood and you were in Strapa. But ever since we set out on this long road together, I have been terrified you would discover the secret and be hurt that I had not told you decades ago."

I waved a hand vaguely. "You are speaking to the wrong person for that, Mag. I had no *right* to any of your secrets, least of all this. But still—why come out here alone? Did you think you could succeed against Kaita by yourself when we have failed together every time?"

She sighed, licking her lips. "I had to try. I thought that, if I had only gone alone, when we went to that Shade encampment in the cave, I could have ended her. I could have plunged into the thick of them, and who cared if I raised the alarm? They could not have killed me. So that is what I was going to try to do. And that is what I must try to do again." She started to push herself up. "Now that I know of her hellskin form, I can act quickly enough to—"

"Whoa now," I said, pushing her back down. I

could never have done it if she were at full strength, but she was still weak from the healing. "You sit down, and you shush."

Mag's brows arched, and for a moment, she looked like her old self again. "Excuse me?"

"I will not." I thrust a finger at her. "You now find yourself in the same situation as everyone you have ever fought: you are facing a foe that you cannot hope to defeat in a fair fight. Instead you must be sneaky, as well as cunning. Now, to your detriment, you are terrible at both those things because they are skills you have never had to acquire. But fortunately for you, cunning is one thing I have in great abundance."

I looked off to the west, where Kaita and the brute woman had gone. Oku's ears perked up as he looked at me.

"Here is what we are going to do."

FORTY-FIVE

When Kaita and Tagata reached the Shade camp, Kaita returned to her tent. But it felt far too small to contain her. She emerged back into the open air and began to pace around a nearby campfire.

Her body felt weary, as if it had been somehow drained. She guessed it was from the effort of taking the hellskin form. She had never experienced this with any creature in her canon before, but of course, she had never commanded such immense power. Mayhap it taxed her body in some way with which she was not yet familiar.

But despite her underlying exhaustion, Kaita was also nearly bouncing with subdued energy. Her limbs would not stop moving, and any time she focused on her fingers, she found them drumming against her palms. Her eyes darted in all directions, seeking, searching, but she did not know for what.

Was this a heightened emotional state after finally killing Mag? It was possible. Or mayhap it was some aftereffect of the magestone. If so, it was far preferable to the weariness. But the two feelings combined made her feel an overwhelming desire to keep moving, while at the same time it seemed her body might give out at any moment.

Tagata had been watching her carefully ever since they had returned to the Shade camp. Kaita noticed it, and it did not entirely please her. But she tried to give a reassuring smile, and Tagata returned it.

"You did it," said Tagata quietly.

"I did," said Kaita. "I never need fear her again."

"Well done," said Tagata. "And now it would be good for you to rest. You are not used to the effects of the stones. You will feel better in the morning."

"I do not feel as if I *can* rest," said Kaita. She strode to Tagata, her gaze swinging back and forth, still seeking—seeking what? "I feel as though I can hardly stop moving. But that is fine. I can rest later, when we reach the Greatrocks." A smile twitched its way across her lips, and there it rested, quivering. She ran her fingers along the edges of Tagata's vest, tracing the lines of it. "Mayhap instead of resting, we should celebrate."

Tagata's smile dampened. "Not just now," she said. "But if you promise me you will sleep, I will happily accommodate you on the morrow."

Anger flared in Kaita's gut. She very nearly snarled before she could contain herself. Her hands leaped away from Tagata like she had been burned, and she turned to hide her ugly expression. Her sleeve rose to scrub at her forehead.

It was fine. Tagata did not understand what Kaita was feeling. How could she? And of course, if she did not wish to join Kaita in her bedroll, she did not have to.

And yet, why would she not want to? thought Kaita. *Why does she keep looking at me that way?*

She put a hand to her forehead. The weariness had begun to overpower the restlessness, weakening her limbs. It was a far cry from how she had felt when she ate the magestone.

The magestone. The rest of them were still in her cloak pocket. Mayhap another one would strengthen her. Before she could even decide to, her fingers began to steal towards them.

"Kaita."

She froze. Tagata was looking down at her, smile replaced with a stern scowl.

"What?" said Kaita, feeling her mood darken.

"You do not need another stone," said Tagata. "It will make things worse, not better."

Another flare of anger burned through Kaita's chest. "And what do you know about it?" she snapped. "You are no mage."

"Kaita," said Tagata again, and her voice was calm, "Rogan warned you of this, as he warned you not to go running after Mag on your own. The stones prey on your mind. You must remain aware of that, and you must resist them. Otherwise, you will be a danger to our kindred, not an asset."

A danger? Oh, yes, Kaita could be a danger. Her breath came faster, the fury rose in her mind until she could hear her heartbeat in her ears, and her hands clenched to—

No.

Kaita forced herself to be still. She took a long, slow breath, counting to ten, and then holding it for a moment before releasing it slowly.

Everything Tagata was saying was right. Kaita had known it since she was a child in the Academy, listening to fellow students whisper rumors. And Rogan *had* told her all this. And she had promised him, and through him, the Lord.

She would not prove too weak to keep her word. She could resist the stones.

"I am sorry," she said. She walked forwards and looked up into Tagata's face. When Tagata smiled at her, she laid her head against the woman's mighty chest. Tree-trunk arms enveloped her, and she lost herself in a deep sigh within them. "I have never felt this before. But the stones are not stronger than me. I will not succumb to their urges, and I will not disappoint you."

"I do not think you could ever do that," murmured Tagata. "Do you want me to hold them for you?"

Kaita's pulse quickened, and her breath came faster. "No," she said quickly. "At least . . . I do not want to give them to you. But when . . . when I fall asleep . . . would you take them from my pocket?"

"Of course, dear little one," said Tagata. "Now, let us get you in a bedroll. And no," she said with a smile, in response to Kaita's playfully raised eyebrow, "that does not mean anything more than it means."

"Fine," said Kaita with a snort. And for that brief moment, she felt almost like her old self again.

But then horns sounded at the camp's eastern end.

Both of them turned and froze, waiting for some further sign. But they could see nothing, and no sound came. The sun had long since vanished, and the moons were not quite high enough to illuminate anything.

"Come," rumbled Tagata. Together they ran for the eastern end of the camp.

They found a group of Shades already there, and more were gathering. But they were clustered behind tents, and they were all looking off to the east. Tagata and Kaita approached them at a low crouch, stooped to hide behind the tents.

"What is it?" said Tagata in a low voice. "The Mystics?"

"No redcloaks that I have seen," said a sergeant. "But mayhap one of their agents. Someone killed two of our sentries before he was spotted by a third. A man in a brown cloak."

Kaita's blood froze. She stood up in plain view, ignoring Tagata's panicked look.

There.

On a hill not far away, the twin moons silhouetted a figure. A bow was in his hand, and his brown cloak fluttered in the gentle night breeze. It was me, of course.

But the moment she saw me, I turned and vanished into the darkness.

"It is him!" she cried. She darted out from behind the tent, running east.

"Kaita!" cried Tagata. "Wait!"

"He is alone!" called Kaita over her shoulder. "I have kept my promise, Tagata. I will finish him off, and then I will return to you." She stopped for an instant, turning to meet Tagata's gaze. "I swear it, my love."

She turned and vanished into the same night that had taken me.

Tagata watched her go, feeling impotent and helpless despite all her vaunted strength. Almost she tried to run after Kaita, to keep her safe. But she looked around at her kindred, all of them looking confused, even frightened in the darkness. And she stayed put.

Mag was dead, after all. Any half-decent weremage

should be more than a match for a normal man like me. And Tagata knew that Kaita was far more than half-decent, even before she had the magestones in her blood.

She sighed and kept her gaze on the shadows where Kaita had vanished. *Sky watch you, my love. Until life ends.*

FORTY-SIX

THE MOMENT KAITA LEFT THE SHADE CAMP, SHE TOOK her hellskin form. Her body swelled into the enormous white creature, and every thundering step drove her spikes and blades into the dirt. It left a trail across the land like a great plow pulled by a Dragon.

But soon she realized that hers were the only tracks. She had run in the direction she had seen me flee, but soon she reached hard, rocky ground. She had no footprints to follow. And the hellskin form had poor senses compared to the lion, or even the bear, and so she had no scent to go by.

She paused, looking back over her shoulder. But Tagata had remained with the rest of the Shades.

That is fine, Kaita told herself. *I did not even need her help to kill Mag. I will not need her to end Albern.*

Her gaze drifted upwards into the sky, where the moons rose ever higher. It was a clear night, perfect for flying. From the air, she would be able to see me more easily.

She hesitated a long moment, looking around to make sure I was not lurking nearby. When she felt she was safe, her eyes glowed black, and her body shrank, resuming her human form. For a heart-stopping moment, she stood there in the night, feeling exposed, before her eyes flashed black again, and she took the raven form. In a few moments, she launched into the air.

Now he will be simple to find, she thought.

But to her surprise, she still had trouble. I had, after all, been trained as a ranger, even if I had never officially become one. And in the long years since we both lived in Tokana, I had kept my skills sharper than Kaita had kept hers. Only here and there could she glimpse a few shallow footprints in the moonslight. Beside the tracks of my boots, there were the clear tracks of a dog. She had seen Oku often enough to recognize the sign of him. But the trail always vanished into rocks again. Kaita was forced to circle and wheel aimlessly until she stumbled upon a fresh set of tracks. Always she had to be aware of her height and avoid swooping too low where I could get a good shot.

He thinks to lure me into a simpleton's trap, she thought savagely. *He must think me an even greater fool than Mag was.*

But Kaita was drawing closer to the Mystic camp now. That put a quiver of fear into her heart. Was I planning on retreating to them? She could not follow me there.

But she *could.* Who cared how many of them there were? In her hellskin form, no blade could—

No.

It took a monumental effort to marshal her thoughts, but she did it. She had promised Rogan. And she believed in the Lord. If he had not wanted Kaita to plunge into the midst of her foes, there was a reason. She had said she would never doubt him again, and she meant it.

And then she caught a flash of brown cloth. There I was, still several spans away from the Mystic camp. And I was not running east towards them, but south, towards a familiar cluster of boulders set against the base of a hill. It was the tunnel entrance. The Shades had come out this way when they attacked the Mystic camp. As Kaita flapped her wings hard, powering towards me, Oku and I descended into the shadows beneath the hill.

Kaita laughed in her mind as I clambered over the boulders and disappeared into the earth. *If he thinks a cave will save him, he is a fool,* she thought. Best of all, I was still alone, save for my hound. She could hunt me down without breaking her word.

She landed atop the hill and shifted into hellskin form as quickly as she could. With a few lumbering steps, she dropped into the darkness of the tunnel beneath the earth.

Immediately she was faced with a new problem. With the hellskin form's limited senses, she could neither see me nor follow my scent.

But she was invulnerable. Who cared about seeing? It mattered little if she stumbled into the walls—they could do nothing to her iron-hard skin.

So she stumbled blindly down the tunnel, lumbering into the stone walls every few steps. It was irritating, but hardly debilitating. Things became slightly worse as the tunnel began to swing more sharply left and right so that she sometimes crashed face-first into the stone. It did not exactly hurt, but it was disorienting, and she had to take a moment to get her bearings. She growled each time, and each time the sound grew a little deeper, a little crueler.

Albern must have brought a torch, she thought, wishing she had had the presence of mind to do the same.

Suddenly her foot came down on empty air. She was at the top of the stone wall she had climbed during her escape from the tunnels. For a heartbeat, she teetered, trying to recover. But in the end, she plummeted five paces and slammed into the stone floor. This time it *did* hurt, her weight sending a crushing lance of pain through her shoulder.

A frustrated, growling roar burst out of her. And to her surprise, there were words in the sound.

"Dark take you, Albern!" she thundered. "Stand and face me!"

For a moment she lay there, blinking. So, the hellskin form could speak. It was the only beast in her canon that could, other than the troll.

Slowly she clambered to her feet. "Where are you, little ranger?" she growled. "But then, I suppose you never really became a ranger. Not like Romil and me. Not like Ditra." She bared her fangs in the inky black and began to stalk forwards again. "Ah, Ditra. You know, do you not, that she is doomed? Now nothing can stop me from ending her. She will die screaming on my claws, and then I will have your niece as well."

Still the tunnel ahead remained silent. Kaita growled, and the sound of it shook the stone beneath her clawed feet.

"Come, Albern!" she roared. "Have we both not waited enough? Let the long road come to an end. Mag did. She was happy to see it done, finally."

No reply came floating out of the shadows.

Kaita considered her options. She *could* take the mountain lion form. It would let her see in the darkness far better than I could.

Of course, the lion was more vulnerable. But vulnerable to what? To me? Surely not. The hellskin form was for Mag. The lion would be more than enough to deal with me.

Again she felt a moment's trepidation as her form shifted to human, and she braced herself for an arrow to come flying from the dark. But nothing came. And as the lion form took her, the tunnel became visible—still dim, but at least she would not go running into walls. And she could smell. My scent was there, and so was Oku's. And there were lingering whiffs of others—all the Shades who had come this way during their escape, and then Kun's small army that had followed them. Kaita could even faintly detect Tagata's scent, and her stomach fluttered.

She forced herself to focus as she proceeded down the tunnel, moving at a quick trot now. This felt much more comfortable. As powerful as the hellskin form was, it was still too new for her to feel fully in command of it. And with the magestones in her blood, even the lion was stronger, faster, more deadly than it had been before.

My scent told her I was some way off. And as she had guessed, I had a torch. She could even see the faintest reflections of its light far down the tunnel. And yet there was something . . . strange about the torch. An acrid scent drifted towards her, borne by the faint breeze that seemed always to fill this space. Her nose twitched, and then she loosed a tremendous sneeze.

She recognized the smell at last. It was burning pycnandra from the Greenfrost. It stung the nose and eyes, and with the lion's sense of smell, Kaita was particularly sensitive to it. She sneezed again.

But in her mind, she laughed. *Is this the best he can do?* she thought. *What a fool. I shall rip him limb from limb, and I shall take my time with it.*

She pressed on a little faster now. Every so often, she had to sneeze again. The burning masked my scent, but that did not matter. The pycnandra torch was like a glowing beacon in the darkness, and it drew her straight towards me.

Finally, she reached the entrance to the vast cavern where the Shades had made their camp. She stopped. In the center of the cavern was a flame—but it was a little campfire, not a torch. And I was nowhere to be seen.

Kaita crouched low to the ground, baring her teeth in a silent snarl. *Clever,* she thought. *But not nearly clever enough.*

With a source of light in view, she could now see the entire cavern as if it were day. I was nowhere to be found, which meant I was hiding somewhere in the rocks. Yet Kaita would be able to see me at a much greater distance than I would be able to see her.

She hugged the cavern wall, circling to the right. But she did not get even halfway there before she spotted me. I was leaning forwards between two rocks, squinting heavily in the dim light. All my attention was focused on the southern tunnel through which she had emerged. I had a cloth tied over my nose and mouth to protect me from the pycnandra smoke.

He missed me in the dark. She chuckled in her mind. *But I will not miss him.* She could not see Oku, but who cared about that? I would be dead before the dog even knew what had happened.

Silently she stalked forwards on her padded feet. Soon she was within fifty paces of me. Then thirty. She edged slightly around so that she was directly behind me.

Only ten paces now. It was an easy leap for the lion form. She tensed, her body coiling. The tip of her tail swished back and forth.

I whirled to face her.

"Hello," I said. And I fired the arrow I had nocked.

Kaita was too surprised to dodge. The arrow sank into her shoulder. She snarled and darted aside before I could loose another shot. Twisting her neck, she seized the arrow in her teeth and ripped it out with a yowl. Her eyes glowed black, and the wound began to seal itself shut.

Steer, she spat in her mind. *One arrow? Your whole quiver would not be enough to stop me.* She readied herself to rush me.

And then, scentable beneath the pycnandra, something filled her nostrils.

Familiar. Dangerous.

Kaita panicked. She tried to turn and flee. But from nowhere, a spear butt crashed into her temple. Even as Kaita reeled back, the spear came around again to crash into the other side of her head.

She fell on her side. Her magic slipped from her, and the mountain lion form melted away.

Mag stepped into view, Oku at her side.

FORTY-SEVEN

While I had drawn Kaita to the western tunnel, Mag had brought the pycnandra sticks through the eastern tunnel. With them she had lit the campfire as soon as she had arrived. The acrid smoke had kept Kaita from scenting Mag, and focusing on me had kept her from noticing any other signs of Mag's approach.

Until it was too late.

Now, together, we loomed over Kaita. Mag had her spear, and my bow was in my hand with another arrow nocked. To my right, Oku growled and bristled at her, his teeth bared.

Kaita glared up at us with hatred, her eyes flitting back and forth. There was some strange frenetic energy in her, more than fear or rage. I guessed it was the effects of the magestones. But they would have no chance to do to her what I had seen them do to Xain.

Her eyes went black, and the blackness spilled out of her in a strange glow that further darkened the already dim cave. But before she could shift, Mag slammed her in the temples again. Kaita cried out in pain.

"This is impossible," she hissed, glaring up at Mag. "You died. I killed you."

"You did not do a good enough job, it seems," said Mag lightly. Her voice was muffled, for—like me—she was wearing a bandana against the pycnandra smoke.

"No!" snarled Kaita. "I *saw* the life leave your eyes. This is a gift of the Lord, and you are not his."

"You are right about that."

"We do not plan to toy with you long, Kaita," I said. "Not like you did with Mag. But we did have a few things to say before your tale ends."

Kaita snarled and looked ready to lunge. But then the tip of Mag's spear was at her throat. She went very still.

"I am certain you think this is all my fault," I went on, "because of what happened in Tokana in our youth. Or mayhap you think it is Mag's fault, for joining me in the Upangan Blades. Dark below, you might even blame your Shade friends. But I want you to know, from the bottom of my heart, that that is not true. This is your fault, and yours alone."

I knelt, elbows on my knees, and made sure her withering glare was on me as I continued.

"You are a spiteful, hateful person, Kaita. I suspect you always have been. Your own choices are what brought you to this cave. It is true that you fell under the influence of cruel people. But so did I." There was no hiding the note of bitterness that had crept into my voice. "And I did not turn into the sort of detestable scum that you are. It was your choice to turn that hatred outwards, to let it become violence."

Kaita looked ready to rip my skin from my body if Mag's spear had not been poised to strike. "You are a useless whelp," she spat, "and you always have been. You abandoned everyone who could have made you into something great. And you think you are better than *me?*"

I arched an eyebrow. "Which of us has the arrow ready, and which is on her back?"

"You would be nothing without the sow at your side!"

The dizziness from Mag's strikes had passed. Kaita slapped Mag's spear away and rolled aside, her eyes filling with the dark glow. But Mag swung the spear around with the momentum of Kaita's blow, slamming the flat of the blade into her head.

Kaita fell facedown on the ground, gasping. Mag stepped up and put her foot on the back of her neck.

"You are wrong," said Mag simply. She was not in her battle-trance. She did not need it. And I suspect that she wanted to feel every emotion and sensation of this moment. "You could not be more wrong. Albern *is* better than you, in the only way that matters." Her gaze met mine. "In many ways, he is better than me. And he always has been. But as for you . . . you and I have been enemies since before I knew who you were. You have been trying to hurt the ones I love since the first day I saw you. You could have turned back whenever you wanted, gone on to find another path. But you chose each step you took, and every one brought you closer to this place, and this time. And once you took Sten from me . . ."

Her voice shook. And I saw the trance start to come into her eyes, sliding across her face. But it stopped, and she pushed the mask away, letting the tears flow.

"You should have slit your own throat that day. It would have saved us all a great deal of time. You could *never* have escaped me once I decided to kill you. And you would have served your Lord better as a corpse than alive. Then, at least, he would not have lost everything we have taken from him already. And he would not now be destined to lose everything we will take in the future."

Kaita screeched, *"I will rip you apart in the dark below, you—"*

Mag drove the spear through her heart.

Kaita spasmed beneath her boot, her fingers clawing at Mag's ankle. But she could find no purchase. She tried desperately to reach the spear, but Mag twisted it, and Kaita's arms fell to the ground. Her eyes were wide as she kept gasping like a fish flung onto the shore. Her form started to shift, her eyes glowing black. But Mag had struck her too hard, too many times. Shock and the Mystics' trick kept her from sealing her wounds, or from taking another form. And yet still she tried.

Mag squatted beside her. Kaita tried to strike, but Mag caught the wrist—just to hold it, not even squeezing. A pace away, Oku stopped growling and sat back on his haunches. He cocked his head as he looked down at Kaita's jerking form.

"Fare well," said Mag. "Sten is avenged. You may see him briefly in the darkness below, while he is resting, and before the evil ones take you. I am sure it will put him at peace. That is the only service you have left to render."

And Kaita died.

I will not lie to you, Sun. It felt good. Oh, I know it did not solve anything. It did not bring Sten back, nor did it lessen the pain of his absence. I understand why people say that revenge is not the answer.

But neither should they say that it does not feel good in the moment. Because it does.

And some people just need to die.

Mag, Oku, and I turned and left the cave. We did not look back at her. Not even once.

FORTY-EIGHT

Captain Kun was in what remained of his camp, holding council.

It was dawn. In the day and a half that had passed since the Shade attack, his force had rested, recovered, and reclaimed as much of their supplies and possessions as they were going to. Now he was discussing his plans with Tou and the remaining lieutenants. He was listening to them as they spoke. But mostly, he was thinking of Zhen, of his sister's eyes in his nephew's face, staring at an empty, uncaring sky.

Kun was torn. He knew it was his duty to lead the

army to safety, to a place where they could resupply themselves and avoid starvation in the icy wilderness. But part of him wanted to go after Mag and I. He wanted to assemble a small group to hunt us down. And he wanted to lead the hunt himself, though that would endanger his forces.

It was not the right thing to do, but he wanted to do it all the same.

There came a hail from outside. One of Kun's guards had issued a challenge. The council all paused, looking towards the tent's large door. Tou glanced at Kun, and Kun met his gaze.

After a moment, the tent flap opened. In stepped Kun's guard, along with a tall archer of Feldemarian looks. Kun remembered his name as Chausiku. He had once been in my squadron.

Kun's jawline went rigid.

"Soldier," said Tou, frowning. "What is it?"

Chausiku lifted his hand. And now they could all see that it held an arrow, and to the arrow was tied a roll of parchment.

"This struck the ground near me, sir," said Chausiku. "It was only moments ago. The outside . . ."

"Let me see it, soldier," said Kun.

Chausiku swallowed hard. "Captain, mayhap I should give it to Lieutenant—"

"Yes, Captain, let me—" Tou began.

"Soldier," said Kun in a cold tone. "The arrow."

Chausiku hesitated a moment more, but finally, he

handed it over. And on the outside of the parchment scrawled in ink, Kun could see a few hastily written words:

Chausiku. Give this to the lieutenant for the captain.

Kun's grip on the parchment tightened.

"Do you see?" he said lightly. "It is even addressed to me."

He forced his fingers to loosen, seize the string, and untie it. The parchment unfurled in his hands, and he began to read silently.

Honorable Captain Zhou,

I, Sergeant Albern of the family Telfer, and Sergeant Mag, tender our resignations. Though she is not here to confirm this letter before it is sent, we feel qualified also to tender the resignation of Yue of the family Baolan. We regret the circumstances that necessitate we leave so abruptly. We regret, additionally and sincerely, the animosity between us at the parting.

We never intended you or your forces any harm. We love Underrealm. We hope that one day, with enough service on our part, you will see fit to approve a petition of clemency for us.

Speaking of service, we have spent the last day in pursuit of the enemy, and we have been successful. We have slain two sentries of the Shade army, and we can confirm that they are continuing their westward course towards the Greatrocks. We also have slain the weremage. You will find her corpse in the cave half a league to the northeast if you care to.

Captain, we are ashamed eternally for every detriment we were to your intention. We hope the squadrons we have trained are of great aid to you in the war. If you see fit to do so, give our love and our apologies to Tou and our units.

We hope to see you on the other side of the war, and we hope as well that you may think more kindly of us then.

Regretfully,
Albern of the family Telfer
Mag, the Wanderer

Kun read the letter. Then he read it again. Not once did he take his eyes from the parchment, but he curled the top and bottom ends of it, as though he was preparing to wrap it around the arrow again.

The letter solved nothing, of course. Mag and I had known what we were doing. We were criminals under the King's law, and Kun would punish us if he could.

Slaying the weremage was good for the cause, but it did not undo what else we had done. Not really.

But for the first time since we had left him, his smile returned to him. It was not as strong as it once had been. It might never be that strong again. But it was back.

Tou saw it. "Sir?" he said.

Kun handed him the letter. "Had I known of his penmanship, I would have retained him as a secretary instead of a sergeant. Remarkable to fit so much on a single sheet. Read this. Show no one else. Relay the sentiments or not, as you will. But burn the letter when you are done."

Tou looked confused, but he took the letter. He started to read, and almost at once, a look of fury began to build on his face. When he finished, he looked up at Kun.

"We must go after them, Captain."

"No," said Kun with a heavy sigh. "We must not. For one thing, I doubt we could catch them without . . . without a tracker of our own. For another, we simply do not have the supplies for it. We must find somewhere to procure more. Then we must proceed west to the Greatrocks with all possible speed, and find a way to send a message warning our comrades about the mountain passes."

"But Mag and Albern—"

Kun forestalled him with a raised hand. "My order is given, Lieutenant. Besides, while killing the weremage is far from deserving of a pardon, mayhap it has earned them a respite. Mayhap fate meant it to. Let them have a brief time, at least, where they need not fear us at their backs."

His eyes fell upon the empty tent door again. "It will not last forever. Their time will come, one day. I promise."

And then to himself, he thought, *I promise you, Zhen.*

FORTY-NINE

Some time later, we strode into the camp where Yue and Dryleaf were waiting. They were both awake, and they straightened when they heard us coming. Yue stood, and then she helped Dryleaf to his feet as well. Oku came running up to the old man, who reached down to scratch him behind the ears.

Mag gave me a look before we reached them. We had spoken already, and I knew she wanted me to say nothing of what I had learned. I gave her a quick, small nod to let her know I understood.

"Rest easy," Mag told them. "It is done."

"Truly?" said Dryleaf. He bowed his head. "After all this time."

"And all this long way," I agreed. "But yes. It is over."

"Well, I am glad," said Yue. "For the sake of avenging Lan Shui, if nothing else."

Mag went to Dryleaf and took his hand in hers, placing her other hand on his arm. "Come, my friend. Sit with me."

"Of course," said Dryleaf. He hobbled beside her and sat on the blankets when she helped him down, and then she took her place by his side. I was pleased to see that his head seemed to be getting better. Yue had changed the bandages, and the new ones hardly showed any blood at all. I walked up beside Yue and put my arm around her waist. She did the same to me.

"I am sorry," said Mag. "I know I have said it before, but I say it again now. By my actions, I placed you in danger, and that is nothing a friend should do."

Dryleaf straightened where he sat. His hands released his walking stick, and he placed them on his knees instead. Suddenly he looked quite regal.

"Mag," he pronounced, "my darling girl. You really must deflate your head, at least a little bit."

Mag's brows arched. "I . . . what?"

"You are a remarkable person," said Dryleaf. "You always have been. And because of it, others naturally look to you for guidance and leadership. That is a heavy burden. It gives you a mighty responsibility, and you must take that seriously—but you should not let it become too familiar. Sometimes it leads you to take choices away from others. You rob them of the power—and, yes, the pain—of making their own decisions." He gestured vaguely with his hand towards me. "I think Albern was reminded today that he is your partner, not your sidekick. Yue and I are the same way. We are not your followers, and it is not solely within your power to determine our fate. Mag, it was *my* advice that you and Albern join Kun's army. That is what led us all down this dark road. You are allowed to make mistakes and to feel the burden of them. But so am I. And you are *not* allowed to take that from me or from any of the rest of us."

I could see the chagrin in Mag's eyes. She, like me, could hear the truth in his words. With Mag around, it was easy to feel yourself starting to revolve around her, the way the moons spun around the world.

"You are wiser than I will ever be," she said. "And I will heed your wisdom. In that case, let me rescind my apology." She planted her hands on her hips like a scolding mother. "What were you thinking, you old fool, suggesting we join up with the Mystics? You sent us all headfirst and heedless into danger. I may never recover. Albern certainly will not."

Dryleaf's solemn countenance broke into a wrinkle-ridden grin. "There. You understand, now."

Yue rolled her eyes. "Such pleasantries aside," she said loudly, "what is your plan now? We cannot exactly return to Kun."

"We cannot," I said, smiling. "Though we sent word to him that we hope may alleviate at least a bit of his ire towards us. But as for us, now we mean to find the children."

Mag's expression dampened, though I did not know why. Yue only looked confused.

"The children?" she asked.

"Our friends from Northwood," I said. "Four of them, and then there is the wizard, though he is grown. They were my companions on a long road. Last we knew, they were making for a stronghold in Feldemar."

"Fortunately, that kingdom is not far from us now," said Dryleaf.

"Yet they could have gone anywhere since," said Mag. "We should listen for rumors as we go. If they have turned in another direction, we may hear of it. You remember how Gem was spreading legends of Loren. Mayhap they have spread far by now."

"Mayhap," I said with a nod. It seemed plausible, but I was still confused by Mag's strange behavior. I did not know where these words came from.

"In any case," said Yue gruffly, "if your road to this point has been any indication, I am certain something else will come up along the way. A village that needs saving from wurts, mayhap, or a farmhouse infested with imps."

"Why, that sounds like a pleasant respite after the trials we have endured," said Dryleaf with a broad smile. "I would be grateful to lend my advice in such an endeavor."

"But not today," said Mag. "Today, I would like to rest, and then to sleep for the first good night's sleep I have had in a long time."

"A long time," I agreed softly.

And so we did. The day passed without incident, and then we bedded down for the night. I was too weary even to make life interesting for Yue, though of course, it would not be my last chance to do so. And the next day, we readied ourselves for another journey. Not a hunt this time, but a search for friends.

Mag and I had one last conversation that is worth recounting now. As we were strapping our saddlebags to our horses, she glanced over at me.

"We are in the after."

For a moment I did not know what she was saying. Then I recalled the desperate words she had spoken the last time we rested in Kun's camp. "We are. How does it feel?"

"Unfamiliar," said Mag. "I never had a beginning in Shuiniu. Then it seemed I was in the middle for a very long time. And then, after Sten died, Kaita felt like the ending. But now that end has come and gone, and a new story has started. My first beginning. I hope we make it a good one."

"I am sure we shall," I told her. "As long as we take care of each other. And of Dryleaf." I chuckled. "Especially now that we do not have Nikau and Orla to help us. I will miss them more than most."

Mag blinked at me. "Who?"

"The lovers. From Kun's camp. You remember them."

Her lips parted, and I could see the lost look in her eyes.

I frowned at her, exasperated. "Sky above, Mag, we ate with them often enough. Do not tell me you—"

"I lost them," she said, cutting me off as if she had not heard me speaking. "I lost them when Kaita . . ." Her voice trailed off, and she looked over her shoulder to make sure Yue and Dryleaf were not within earshot. "When I died. I lost them."

She strapped her last saddlebag in place and went to help Dryleaf.

A chill crept down my spine.

FIFTY

It was late in the day now, and the sun had set. Albern had lit a fire in the hearth sometime during the tale, but Sun could not remember him doing so. She had gone through another mug of ale, and though the taste was no less sour, it was beginning to turn her head fuzzy. At first, she thought she had misheard him.

"What did she mean, she lost them?" said Sun.

"That answer is a complicated one," said Albern. "But to put it simply—whenever Mag was badly injured, or when she died, some part of her memory vanished, never to be recovered. The worse the harm, the more she lost."

Sun shook her head. "Why?"

He gave her a sad smile. "That, too, is an answer I am not willing to give. At least not yet."

"Why am I not surprised?" said Sun. Then she had a sudden thought. "Is . . . is that why she forgot everything before the forest? Before Shuiniu?"

Albern looked mildly surprised. "Yes. That was remarkably quick of you."

"She forgot *everything?*" Sun felt a sudden chill creeping down her back, just as Albern had described in the story. "What happened to her? It must have been bad to make her forget *everything.*"

"It was bad," said Albern softly. "But you shall learn. One day."

Sun took a deep breath. But she did not argue. She had learned her lesson by now, that Albern chose the order of his story carefully. And this one would not have been nearly as captivating if he had mixed it up in the telling.

"I am sorry for my anger earlier," she said. "You did not deserve that, and I was wrong. I thought you were lying to me. But everything you have told me so far . . . it was merely a beginning. The introduction to a larger tale."

Albern smiled, but it looked a little guarded. "You are not wrong."

Sun snorted. "I notice you do not say whether I am

right. Very well. Can you give me your best guess of when we will reach the end of the story?"

"End?" said Albern. "Who said the story has ended?"

"I mean the end of *Mag's* story, you twit," said Sun. Then her eyes went wide. "Albern . . . *has* she died? I mean in truth, not the way she 'died' when Kaita killed her. Is she still—"

A knock came at the front door. Sun jumped, but Albern's mouth twisted.

"There is my friend," he said.

"No, wait!" cried Sun. "Answer me. You *must* tell me before you open that door."

"It is too hard to answer," said Albern.

"Say yes or no!" cried Sun. "Why is that hard to answer?"

"I suppose we shall have to see."

He went to the door and peered through a viewing hole before turning and winking at Sun. "I am happy to report it is not your family's guards. This is the tavern's owner—or former owner, I should say. And, of course, our third partner in this venture."

Third partner? thought Sun.

Albern swung open the door. Two people entered. First was a large woman, with as much fat as muscle on her body. She had a thick jaw and a missing finger on her right hand. But the second woman caught all of Sun's attention. She was much slimmer, and the hood of her green cloak was cast back to reveal Dorsean features, hair cut a few fingers above the shoulders in a practical style.

Her skin was flawless, without a blemish or scar to be seen. She looked to be around twenty years old.

Sun froze.

Albern fixed her with a careful look. "Sun," he said, indicating the larger woman, "this is Zhaojia, the former owner of the tavern. And this here is Chao, a brewmaster who has graciously agreed to partner with me in purchasing and running this place."

Chao. Sun's wildly racing suspicions were confirmed in an instant. That was the false name Mag had used in the tales.

This was Mag. The Wanderer. The Uncut Lady . . . or at least, as far as anyone knew.

She could not speak. She could hardly breathe. This was not like meeting Albern in that tavern far away. This was like meeting an Elf, dangerous and extraordinary and entirely debilitating, for what could one do in the face of such incredible power?

Her mind began to work again, but slowly. If Mag was going by the name Chao, that meant she was pretending to be someone else. And she and Albern also seemed to be pretending not to know each other very well. Sun did not know why, but of course, she would not give away the scheme.

"I am very pleased to meet you, Chao," she said. "And you as well, Zhaojia."

"Pleased, I am sure," said Zhaojia with a nod. Then she turned to Albern. "You got my gift, I see."

Albern raised the mug of ale he had been in the middle of. "We did, and we thank you kindly for it. A fine concoction indeed."

Zhaojia scoffed. "You need not try to save my pride. I did not brew it, after all. It was what I could find that was fast and cheap, and that means it is not good, as a rule. We both know our mutual acquaintance here makes far better stuff than that swill. You have the rest of the money?"

"Of course." Albern reached to his belt and pulled out one of the thick purses he had received earlier. Then he paused and looked to Sun. "Sun, I mentioned before that you might find good use for your money by the end of the day. Would you like to join Chao and me in purchasing this tavern?"

An hour ago, this might have rendered Sun insensible, or mayhap caused her to faint straight away. But now, with Mag herself standing in the room, the absolute absurdity of the situation barely registered. "Why not?" she said. "I have no other plans."

"Wonderful," said Albern. "We shall sort out the details later, and I shall recover your portion of the payment."

Zhaojia and Mag both looked at Albern like he was sun-touched. But Zhaojia took the purse, opened it, counted the contents, and closed it up again.

"Very well," she said gruffly. "May you find better fortune here than I did. But then again, with her crafting your drink . . . ." She tossed her head at Mag. "Well, I wish you good fortune, in any case. And I am off."

She strode out the door, and Albern went to close it behind her. The whole time, Sun could not stop staring at Mag. Once the door was closed and they were alone again, she finally tore her gaze away to look at Albern.

"What in the *dark* below—"

"Now, calm down," said Albern.

Mag, meanwhile, stood with her arms folded. At Sun's outburst, she arched a brow. "And who exactly is this?" she asked Albern.

"Chao," said Albern, "this is Sun of the family Valgun."

"Valgun?" said Mag. "That is a name of Dulmish nobility. What are you doing purchasing a tavern halfway across the world?"

Sun barely glanced at her, but kept her gaze locked on Albern, awaiting his answer. Albern gave Mag a weak smile.

"Though both of your manners seem to have fled, let me assure each of you that the other is pleased to make your acquaintance."

"Albern, *what is going on?"* said Sun, very nearly in a shriek.

Mag frowned at Albern. "I thought your name was Kanohari."

Sun waved a hand. "Of course, you are using your fake names. *Kanohari,* I need answers."

Albern's expression grew troubled. "Sun—"

Now Mag was looking stern. "A fake name? Why would you give me a fake name? If you are not Kanohari, then who are you?"

That froze Sun in place. Albern shook his head slowly.

"Chao," he said, "if you would give me a moment to speak with our new partner?"

Mag folded her arms. "I suppose," she said. "But make it quick. And you had better have a good explanation when you return. I do not take well to being swindled."

"Well do I know it," muttered Albern as he came and gently took Sun's arm. "Out back, if you do not mind."

"What in the dark below is going on?" hissed Sun as she allowed him to pull her out into the alley behind the tavern.

"A great many things," said Albern. He made sure the door shut behind them, and then he listened at it as if making sure Mag had not followed them. "But here is what you must know. Her name is Chao, so far as she, or you, or anyone else is concerned. And she knows me as Kanohari. Though I suppose I shall have to tell her my true name is Albern, now that you have said it, and it has not seemed to harm her."

Sun glanced at the door. "She does not know your real name?"

"She does not," said Albern. The sadness in his eyes was one she had seen often, every time he had spoken of Mag's darkest moments in the story.

"But why?" said Sun, shaking her head.

"There is a long tale behind it—" Albern began.

"You cannot mean to make me wait—"

He held up a hand. "Stop, and listen to me. There is a *long* tale behind it, which I shall tell you in full. But I will give you a *short* answer now because you deserve it, and you will need it. And it will help you help me, in the way we must treat her now. You know something, at least, of the end of Mag's story."

"I thought I did," said Sun. "Though now it seems it was not the end at all."

"But it was," said Albern, and he had never sounded more earnest. "Something terrible happened, more terrible than any tale could convey, though I will try. And when it did . . . that *was* the end of Mag's story. She lost who she had been, the person I met in my youth, who I followed from mercenary company to mercenary company, and through the Necromancer's War. I was with her when it happened, and I have been with her ever since, helping her as much as I know how."

"So she forgot you," said Sun slowly, piecing it together. "Just as she forgot Nikau and Orla because Kaita killed her. She remembers nothing at all now, because when she died . . . really died . . . it was bad enough that she forgot everything. Like in the woods near Shuiniu."

"Yes," said Albern.

"And that is why you told me this tale," said Sun. "So I would understand when I met her."

"It is one reason."

A horrible thought struck Sun. When she voiced it, she could not speak above a whisper.

"Does she remember Sten?"

Albern did not answer, but his eyes filled with tears. And Sun's own tears fell freely down her cheeks, and she tried vigorously to scrub them away.

"We have to tell her," she said. "You should have told her already!"

"Do you think I did not try?" said Albern. "Please, Sun. I have been with her for a long while since . . . since it happened. I have thought of nearly everything you could think of, and I have tried it. You must trust me in this. If I say you must not speak of something, or you must treat her a certain way, I beg you to believe me. When I have tried to tell her of her past life, it has caused her great harm. She becomes a wreck for days, and when the spell passes, she forgets it all anyway. Please, Sun."

Sun could hardly understand him. All she wanted to do was run inside and tell Mag everything that had happened in Albern's stories. But she mastered herself. And finally, she nodded.

"Very well. I believe you."

"Thank you," said Albern gently. "Now, let us return inside before she takes it into her head to come out here and trounce us both."

"So she can still fight?" said Sun.

"Like you would not believe," grumbled Albern, and he led her back in.

Mag—Chao—was waiting for them in the tavern's common room, her arms still folded across her chest. She looked expectantly at Albern, and he gave her a disarming smile.

"Now then," he said. "I should tell you something I was planning to reveal at a more opportune time. As Sun here has already revealed, my real name is Albern. I am of the family Telfer."

Chao's eyebrows rose. "Telfer? A noble as well, but this time of Calentin. What in the dark below is going on here?"

"Nothing nefarious," said Albern. "We are both somewhat . . . out of favor with our families. In fact, that is how Sun came to my attention, for she faced similar troubles to the ones I experienced when I was her age. Those troubles are what led me to take the name Kanohari long ago. But Sun met me by my real name, and I never told her another one."

He looked to Sun. "From now on, when we are in front of others, I will request that you call me Kanohari," he said, and then turned back to Chao. "And when it is the three of us, it would please me if you called me Albern."

A shadow passed over her expression, but it was soon gone. "Albern," she said. "Like the tales from Calentin history."

"Just so," said Albern with a pleased smile. "I chose the name after my wending."

Again a shadow came over Chao's face, and this time it stayed there. She placed a hand to her forehead, and it was trembling.

"Chao?" said Albern, worry in his voice. "What is it?"

"Nothing," said Chao. She smiled weakly at him. "A dizzy spell. It is so damnably hot outside. But very well. If Albern is your wending name, then I vow never to use anything else unless you ask me to."

"Thank you," said Albern, bowing his head. Sun could hear the relief in his voice. Whatever had come over Chao briefly, it seemed to have passed. Was this what he meant when he said she would have spells when he tried to tell her of her old life?

"Now, as for you," said Chao, nodding to Sun. "Albern here says you are to be a partner, and I trust him. But you seem a bit young to me. What do you know of running a tavern?"

Sun looked to Albern for guidance, but he merely held out an encouraging hand, as if to coax her. "Nothing," she said simply.

Chao's mouth twisted. "Honesty is an admirable trait, but you may need better qualifications."

"She is young," said Albern. "But she is not much younger than you. And in our wanderings together, I have found her more than capable."

Sun had to duck her head to hide a sudden flush in her cheeks.

"Very well," said Chao with a sigh. "Tell me, girl. What did you think of the ale here?"

Sun's lip curled. "It was awful."

"I agree," said Chao. "Would you like some of mine? I brought a wagon of it when I transported Zhaojia here."

Suddenly Sun's mouth was watering. "I would like that very much," she squeaked. From the corner of her eye, she saw Albern's amusement at her wonderstruck expression.

Chao led her outside, where there was indeed a wagon of ale casks waiting. Together the three of them got all of them down to the cellar, except for one barrel, which Albern set up behind the bar. Chao tapped it, and they poured three mugs. Chao set to right away, and Albern joined her, but Sun took a moment. She sniffed it, and the bubbles seemed to break in the exact right way to fly up her nose, tickling her and making her giggle. Finally, she tipped the mug back, taking a sip.

It . . .

It . . .

Sky above. Sun wanted to weep. Never had she tasted anything like it.

It was like honeyed sunlight poured from bouncing clouds of gossamer. Like the clearest river water kissed by ocean breezes, and smoked in the cleansing glow of a good campfire. And yet it was heady and intense, with the barest hint of . . . was it brandy? Some sort of fine, sweet liquor, and the taste of it weakened her knees.

A sip turned into a swallow, and then into a long, long draught. Before Sun knew it, the mug was empty. She stayed there for a moment, eyes closed, feeling every drop of it sliding down her throat and into her gut.

When at last she opened her eyes, Chao was looking at her expectantly.

"That . . ." whimpered Sun. "That is the most wondrous thing I have ever tasted. By a wide, *wide* margin. I had heard from Albern that you made fine ale, but this . . . this is so far beyond anything I could ever have imagined."

Chao turned to Albern with a wide grin. "I suppose she might work out, after all."

They shared a laugh. And then their talk fell to the tavern and its construction, and where they could get tables, and what sort of chairs they all preferred. Then they went upstairs and claimed their rooms—Sun chose an excellent one on the front corner, with windows on two walls—and then back downstairs, where they talked of ale and wine and guests and ale and hiring help and ale again. Never did Albern or Chao talk over Sun, and they listened attentively whenever she gave ideas, even when she spoke hesitantly. And they argued for and against her ideas as vigorously as for their own plans.

Sun could not believe this was real. Here were two of the most significant figures of her favorite legends, and she was *working* with them. They were partners. No one could know how long it would last, of course, but Sun promised herself to cherish every moment of it.

At last, the night wound to a close. They had all had more than a few cups of ale, and their conversation had turned giddy and giggling. Finally, Chao rubbed at her eyes.

"I should sleep, or I will make even more of a fool of myself than I already have," she said.

"That is not possible," said Sun at once.

Chao arched an eyebrow. "Oh? Do you mean I could not appear more foolish?"

As Sun's cheeks flamed, Albern laughed aloud. "I think she meant you could not make a fool of yourself," he said. "This one's head is full of courtly graces, but she is new to tavern conversations. Forgive her."

Chao's mouth twisted in a wry smile. As she stepped around from behind the bar and towards the stairs, she paused. Slowly, she reached out a hand to Sun. Sun tentatively took it and found her wrist wrapped in a grip like iron.

"It is a pleasure to know you, Sun of the family Valgun," said Chao. "Forgive my doubtfulness before. I look forward to our partnership."

"As do I," said Sun, barely able to choke the words out.

Chao smiled, and then she gave Albern a nod. Finally, she turned and climbed the stairs towards her newly chosen room. Sun and Albern remained in the common room to clean up some of the mess they had all made. After a while, Sun looked over at him.

"Why all this, Albern? Why did you pick me? I thought it was for an adventure. Now you have me running a tavern. What is the purpose behind it all?"

Albern's lips puckered. He went behind the bar, took up a rag, and began to wipe off the small splashes of ale they had spilled.

"What I told you before is true," he said. "I saw a young child of nobility who seemed to hate her life, and I felt sympathy for your plight. But you are right. There is more behind it.

"I have told you that Mag was happiest in Northwood, with her inn, and with Sten. So many dark things happened after that. And I felt she deserved a return to that happiness. I thought this might be a way to give her such a gift."

He stopped wiping the bar and looked up at her. Sun met his gaze, but her breath caught in her throat.

"But that does not explain you, of course," said Albern. "I wanted to make sure you care about Chao. Because I wanted you to want to stay here with us and hear the rest of the story. I need someone else to know the whole truth of it. I cannot tell the whole world everything—that would be violating Mag's trust, and I vowed to her I would never do that. But one person should know everything, right down to the last. And I told you the story the way I did, jumping back and forth throughout Mag's life, so that when you met Chao, you would care enough about her to help me keep her secret."

Sun nodded. "I will," she said. "I swear it."

"Thank you," said Albern quietly. "At first, I thought the burden of this story was mine to bear alone. Then, when I learned the truth about Mag, I thought she would remember our deeds long after I had been laid beneath the dirt. But now . . ."

He gave a vague gesture towards the stairs. Sun nodded.

"Now, you are the only one," she said. "The only one who remembers everything."

"It is a heavier burden than I thought it would be," said Albern. "So I thank you, Sun, for the help you have been on the road so far, and for being willing to listen to an old man's story."

Sun lifted the broom and pointed it at him like a sword, frowning. "Willing? You would do better to call it *demanding*. I want you to resume the tale tomorrow, bright and early."

He eyed the stairs again. "I will not do so in Chao's presence. But whenever we have a moment alone, yes. I will continue the tale." He smiled at her. "And I will do so with pleasure."

Sun lowered the broom again and began to sweep. "You better had."

KEEP READING

You've finished the first three books of the Tales of the Wanderer. But there's more to the tale, in *Tales of the Wanderer Volume One.*

This compilation volume not only contains the first three novels of the trilogy, but also an additional 50 pages of historical essays and background information about the world of Underrealm.

Learn more about the story than you ever thought possible.

Underrealm.net/ToW1-3

ACKNOWLEDGEMENTS

As I write this, my country, and to a lesser degree the world, is in a bit of turmoil.

For four years, we have dealt with the temper of a man whose rhetoric and malfeasance have been the defining features of his time in office. Now my fellow citizens and I have rejected him—an outcome in which I had great hope, but little confidence—but he is still fighting to hold his place of power.

It occurred to me, as I was in the final stages of finishing this book, that I might be seen to be taking a stand against him in my work, and in this story. I want to reassure you, the reader, from the bottom of my heart, that this is not the case. Not because a stand should not be taken against him—it should—but because since the beginning of my career, I have aspired to Tolkien's cordial dislike of allegory. Yes, the real world has bled into this book and the two that came before it. I could not help that. But I wanted to keep the reality of today's horrors as far from these pages as I possibly could. Of all my wishes in life, few things could I have desired less than to validate that man's ego in even so mean a respect as to place him in this tale.

If any direct comparison must be drawn between my tale and reality, let it be that ordinary folk—not just the Mags of the world—will always unite to cast evildoers back into the obscurity to which they belong.

Real heroes are imperfect, they will never satisfy everyone, and on occasion they will fail—sometimes drastically—but that does not lessen their contribution to a better world.

This book took me so long because I, like Mag, had a hard time envisioning a future. Now I can. Now there is an "after," however murky, however tenuous.

To those who brought it about, and to you, dear reader, I hope this book is an acknowledgment.

That said, I have to give more direct thanks to a few people.

First and last: my wife, Meghan. It's been two years since I last completed a book. During that time, you've been even more exceptional than normal, and anyone who knows you knows what a compliment that is.

My parents still inspire everything I do. My dad passed away a few years ago now. My mom was gone before I put out my first book. But I think about them all the time, and whether they'd enjoy and be proud of the work I'm doing. They're still two of the top people I'm trying to impress.

My children continue to give me purpose. When I'm completely bogged down, I hang out with them, and they never fail to bring me out of it. Most of my favorite parts of this book were born of direct inspiration after hanging out with my kids. If you have a favorite part of this book, you can safely bet money that it's thanks to my children.

Karen Conlin is the editor every writer wants, but

few deserve—fortunately, I've managed to con her all this time into continuing to work with me.

My beta readers continue to provide superlative feedback that makes each book better than I could ever make it on my own. Dakota, Jess, Kristen, Lauren, and Robin, you've helped me see every word of this book in a new light. And considering they all came from my own fingers, that's quite an achievement.

I am supremely grateful for every one of my supporters on Patreon. All of you got to read the early stages of this book before anyone else. The fact that you're still around speaks more to your patience than my talent.

The Vloganovel crew continues to shine. Thank you for sticking around for two years (holy crap) of inconsistent streaming to get this book done.

And last, as she was first: Meghan. Every time I finish a book, I think I've run out of words to express how incredible you are. And then I finish the next one, and a whole new litany of your deeds continues to provide inspiration. I love you.

Garrett Robinson
November 2020

THANK YOU TO MY PATRONS

A number of you contribute to my Patreon. Your unswerving support means the world to me, and many times it's kept me going when I would otherwise have had to quit. Each and every one of you has my sincere gratitude.

If you'd like to become a supporter, you can find my Patreon at:

Patreon.com/GarrettBRobinson

(Patrons are listed in order of lifetime support).

STUDIO EXECUTIVES
Sybil R. Case, Hayley Marsden, Kris Nieder, A Howard, Mark Monroe, Dakota Heath, Sara Scimone, Mysery, Joshua Kluender

PRODUCERS
Erik Gross, Eric, Val Ritz, John Maryn

ABOVE THE LINE
Hank Green, Kai Chochinov, Kelsey Nolen, Eric Ugland, Felix, LupineKing, Jesse S, Sarah, Predawn, Dia Chappell, Renae Brown, Gin Hollan, Gerald Hornsby, Mike C, Lia Marie, Lauren Brender, Thoth Pro-

cess, Katy Schneider, Juniper, William Johnson, Meri, Dwight Kuhl, Dorothy Holzman, CherryFlight, Tim Beauchamp, Maeve Shea, Tammi Labrecque, Spinnerlynne, Aidn White

PATRONS

Michael O'Neal, Jack F Erikson, Kakirtog, the Charr in gold, Logan Rutherford, Rosie Reast, Brenna Gawain, Donovan Scherer, Mr. C, Kyle Hamman, Chad Kukahiko, Kj Caston, Nicholas Rem, Lady Bee Games, Amber Morant, Salgood Sam, Cathleen Mitchell, Alicia Garner, ExactoBeau, Melanie Shukost, Kimberly Grube, Wicketbird, Steven Geyer, Stephanie Glinski, Sean Cheasley, Peter Bromage, Paul Tressler, Nancy Pillot, Matthew McCray, Mary Paulk Powers, Jenny Kira Franke, Jeff Barrows, Game Programming Academy, Eric Cerini, Edwin Wallum, David Blaskovich, Ashton Sanders, Ailysha, Annalise Moore, Michael Bishop, Kris, Ian J Middleton, Brett Kane, CJ Edmunds, Summer Wilson

THE BOOKS OF UNDERREALM

THE NIGHTBLADE EPIC

NIGHTBLADE

MYSTIC

DARKFIRE

SHADEBORN

WEREMAGE

YERRIN

THE ACADEMY JOURNALS

THE ALCHEMIST'S TOUCH

THE MINDMAGE'S WRATH

THE FIREMAGE'S VENGEANCE

THE TALES OF THE WANDERER

BLOOD LUST

STONE HEART

HELL SKIN

THE TENTH KINGDOM

A CLOAK OF RED

RISE OF THE NECROMANCER

QUEST

THE CHRONICLES OF UNDERREALM
COLLECTION ONE

THE BOOKS OF UNDERREALM

CHRONOLOGICAL ORDER

NIGHTBLADE

MYSTIC

DARKFIRE

SHADEBORN

BLOOD LUST

THE ALCHEMIST'S TOUCH

WEREMAGE

THE MINDMAGE'S WRATH

STONE HEART

THE FIREMAGE'S VENGEANCE

HELL SKIN

YERRIN

QUEST

A CLOAK OF RED

THE CHRONICLES OF UNDERREALM

ABOUT THE AUTHOR

Garrett Robinson was born and raised in Los Angeles. The son of an author/painter father and a violinist/singer mother, no one was surprised when he grew up to be an artist.

After blooding himself in the independent film industry, he self-published his first book in 2012 and swiftly followed it with a stream of others, publishing more than two million words by 2014. Within months he topped numerous Amazon bestseller lists. Now he spends his time writing books and directing films.

A passionate fantasy author, his most popular books are the novels of Underrealm, including The Nightblade Epic, The Academy Journals, and The Tales of the Wanderer series.

However, he has delved into many other genres. Some works are for adult audiences only, such as *Non Zombie* and *Hit Girls,* but he has also published popular books for younger readers, including The Realm Keepers series and *The Ninjabread Man*, co-authored with Z.C. Bolger.

Garrett lives in Oregon with his wife Meghan, his children Dawn, Luke, and Desmond, and his dog Chewbacca.

Garrett can be found on:

EMAIL: garrett@garrettbrobinson.com
TWITTER: twitter.com/garrettauthor
FACEBOOK: facebook.com/garrettbrobinson

EPILOGUE

SUN HAD TROUBLE FALLING ASLEEP THAT NIGHT. HER mind was so full of thoughts from the day's incredible events that she could hardly close her eyes for a moment before opening them again, replaying the stories in her mind.

Eventually, she gave it up and went downstairs. She was not quite sure whether she wanted a drink or to walk around, but she certainly did not want to lie restless in bed, comfortable though it was.

She stood in the center of the common room and looked around. A tavern. And she was a one-third owner of it, along with Albern of the family Telfer, and Mag, the Wanderer. If she could have told herself even a month ago that all this would happen, she would have called herself a liar.

Footsteps sounded behind her. Sun turned to find Albern standing there, blinking at her in surprise.

"I cannot sleep," said Sun.

"Nor can I," said Albern.

"I keep thinking about the tavern, and about . . ." Sun glanced at the stairs. "About the story."

"Do not trouble yourself," said Albern. "She is asleep. I confess I do not face the same problem as you. My thoughts are still, but simple pain is what keeps me awake."

"I am sorry to hear that," said Sun. "Yet I suppose it is a good thing for me. I had a question. There is one answer you promised to give me earlier, but now I do not see how you can. You keep telling parts of the tale from Kaita's perspective. And you said you learned the details later. I thought you must have captured her, or interrogated her, or something. But Kaita died. So . . . how do you know what happened to her in such detail?"

Albern's expression grew dour. Instead of answering, he walked to the bar. Sun followed, plopping down on a stool. Albern pulled two large mugs of ale, and then he turned to hand one to Sun.

"Have a drink," he said solemnly.

Rogan approached the cave, the Lord at his side. Together they climbed over the boulders and stalked through the darkness of the tunnel. Though it was pitch-black, they walked unerringly, as though they knew exactly where they were going.

And in fact, they did. Rogan had already seen what he would find here, in this vast, empty cave. And he soon found it. Kaita's body lay facedown, twisted in pain. There was a hole through her back, and her blood covered the stone floor.

Weeping, Rogan fell to his knees beside her. He took up her hand, cradling it against his cheek, careless of the blood he spread on himself.

The Lord stepped up beside him, and then he felt his father's hand on his shoulder.

"Why?" said Rogan. "You said you knew why. I know our goals are worthy, more so than anyone else in the nine kingdoms. But this . . . this feels like too high a price."

The cave was silent for a long moment. When the Lord finally spoke, Rogan could hear the grief in his voice. "It *is* a high price. But no price would be too high to pay. The death of any one person—even Kaita, even Tagata, and yes, even you, my favored son—would be worth it in the end, if we achieve what we mean to. And yet now we may rejoice. Today, we need pay no price at all."

Rogan looked up at him in the darkness. "Father?"

"Lift her hair, my son."

As Rogan watched in wonder, the Lord pulled out a needle, ink, and a small hammer.

"Father," said Rogan. "I thought no wizard could receive your gift."

"So did I," said the Lord. "But now let us say, instead, that I never knew how to bestow it upon them. Not until I needed it most."

His hands were swift and deft as he tapped out a tattoo on the back of Kaita's neck. Rogan had seen it a dozen times before. But this tattoo was . . . different. It did not look like his own, like the design that all the shadeborn wore.

"Can you do this to anyone?" he asked in an awed voice. "Any other wizard, I mean?" His mind raced with the possibilities of what this could mean for the coming war.

"We shall see," said the Lord. "For now, put her on her back again."

Rogan did. The Lord placed his hand on Kaita's chest, where the spear had made its mark. And his eyes began to glow with a pure, unrelenting white light.

Her body began to convulse. She groaned, like a corpse expelling the last air from its lungs. Suddenly the groan erupted into a scream. Like Mag's when she had come back to life, Kaita's back arched, with only her head and pelvis still touching the ground. The scream bounced from the rocky walls and off itself again, becoming painful. Kaita's eyes were wide, and the blood vessels within them split, turning them red.

“Hold her, my son,” said the Lord, his voice halting with effort.

Rogan seized Kaita and held her down. He wished to comfort her, but he knew that was impossible. Not until the ritual was complete.

And then, finally, her screams subsided. Her body sank back onto the ground, plopping wetly in the blood pooled beneath her. Her blood-red eyes spun, and then finally they focused on Rogan, on the Lord. Her expression held only anguish.

“Rogan?” she croaked.

He scooped her up into his arms, holding her and weeping anew, but this time with joy. And the Lord, though weary from his exertions, stood and placed his hands on them both. Rogan’s heart filled with his warmth, with his love.

“My children,” said the Lord gently.

You see, Sun, you have already realized that this was not the end of Mag’s tale. It was merely the end of the beginning. What we did not know at the time was that another tale had begun as well.

www.ingramcontent.com/pod-product-compliance
Lightning Source LLC
Chambersburg PA
CBHW030809310726
48980CB00006B/435/J
* 9 7 8 1 9 4 1 0 7 6 7 7 4 *